The Pagan King

by Edison Marshall

Gothic Romance

The Pagan King (A tale of fifth-century England)
The Viking (A tale of the Sea Rovers of the ninth century)
Castle in the Swamp (A tale of the Carolina Low Country in the
   nineteenth century)

Biographical Novels

Great Smith (A tale of Captain John Smith)
Caravan to Xanadu (A tale of Marco Polo)
The Infinite Woman (A tale based on, or at least inspired by, the
   life of Lola Montez)

Regional Novels

Princess Sophia (A tale of Alaska in the period 1898–1918)
The Inevitable Hour (A tale of Martinique beginning in 1890 and
   terminating 7:39 A.M., May 8, 1902)

Historical Novels

Yankee Pasha (The adventures of a young American frontiersman
   from Salem to Tartary after the Revolutionary War)
The Gentleman (The adventures of a Charleston gambler at home,
   in the West Indies, and in South Africa, prior to the Civil War)
Benjamin Blake (A tale of the bastard son of an English squire at
   home and in the South Sea Islands in the period of our Revolutionary War)
American Captain (A tale of a young mariner in Maine, Malta,
   North Africa, East Africa, and England at the turn of the
   eighteenth century)
The Upstart (A tale of strolling players in England in the early
   years of the eighteenth century)
Gypsy Sixpence (A tale of a young Lancer on the Afghan frontier
   in India and of his long hunt in Africa in the middle years of
   the nineteenth century, his character and his story suggested by
   those of Richard Burton)

Books of Short Stories

Love Stories of India
The Heart of Little Shikara (Stories of animals of forest and jungle)
The Elephant Remembers (A jungle book)

Memoirs of Big-Game Hunting

The Heart of the Hunter (A looking-backward over hunting trails
   in Canada, Alaska, Africa, Indo-China, and India, and where
   they led at long last)
Shikar and Safari (A factual and objective account of various big-
   game hunts)

Doubleday & Company, Inc.
Garden City, New York, 1959

The Pagan King

by Edison Marshall

Library of Congress Catalog Card Number 59–9785
Copyright © 1959 by Edison Marshall
All Rights Reserved
Printed in the United States of America
First Edition

Chapter One
The Pagan King

In babyhood and boyhood I was called Ambrose. Why should I ever doubt it was my true name? It was our Cambrian way of cutting short the name Ambrosius, which I think is a Latin name, meaning immortal and perhaps divine. I was born in the great Land of Cambria, the western and better part of Britain, of which the Cambrian kings are the rightful kings. It is a great green land of wondrous waters and haunted hills and fearful forests, with droves of mast-fed swine, flocks of fat sheep, and wide-horned kine.

Do you know the year of the Wandering Star with the sky-wide tail? It came, and when its course was run and its signs were given plain to the eyes of our Wise Men, it went away, and on the night of its greatest glory, I, called Ambrose, was born. Remember this, ye who would doubt my story, set down in excellent Latin by a worshipper of Mithras. What was the year? It was according to whether you count by the Roman calendar—a number which I was once told but now forget—or by the calculations of the Wise Men of Old, or by the counting of a new sect called Christians, fools who deny our Gods, and who will soon be scattered and destroyed like the morning mists over the marshes of Severn.

By Christian counting I was born on All Hallows' Eve, in the year four hundred seventy-four. I would rather say that the year was the hundred and eighty-first after the main of the Second Legion, led by bronzed eagles on a stick, marched away with clanking shields from its vast metropolis called Isca, near the mouth of the River Usk. One of its ten cohorts remained, so legend tells, to garrison the fortress. Who had built its towers, walls, store-houses, assembly places, tanks, and temples that now rang so hallow? Some declare it was the work of unknown Gods, some say of human hands of magic skill.

Why need I deal in such brain-bursting sums? It is handier to remember I was born ninety years after Maximus, the last Roman Emperor of Britain—never King of Cambria, whose green hills would not nest his eagles—stripped Isca of its last cohort, then combed the Midland Plain of half of its stalwart sons. Where they were bound I know not, or whether they made port; but men yet alive when Merdin, whom I called Grandsire, was a man grown, remember their departure, although dimly, as in a dream. They saw with their own eyes the files moving down Watling Road, the soldiers keeping step, the rustics shambling. None saw their return, but tales are told in Cambria, and songs sung, of the maidens whom they loved weeping in vain.

The whitebeard gaffer, Merdin, had not told me of this exodus, and instead I had it from another of our household, Gerald, who called himself my cousin through his mother's line. He had had the story from his father, the son of Janus, a Centurion in the last cohort that marched from the Usk. Janus had a Roman name and pure Roman blood, but had taken a wife from the Mendip Hills. The noise of their short bright rivers chattered even in her ears. On May Eve before the cohort burned their barracks and set forth, she led her husband to a certain grove, and there a white-haired elder in a white robe slew with a bronze sword a slave of the value of two cows, and the elder read the auguries revealed in his guts bursting forth upon the ground. At first Janus would not heed those auguries. He had been born at the cantonment, and he had sworn before Mithras to live and die with his cohort. But what was the God Mithras compared to Lud, and what man of wit would go to Dalor, God of Death, when he had been called by Dagda, God of the Corn? So when the Legion made camp at sundown Janus had slipped away into the forest.

"Still, I am not sure that your grandsire should not have kept faith with Mithras and his comrades in life and in death," I said to Gerald when I was fifteen years old.

"His life was over," Gerald replied, his swarthy face flushing. "Our soldiers were leaving Britain, not to return in his lifetime. Death pays all debts, dissolves all bonds, and it be true, although I confess it sadly, he had not due reverence for his Roman heritage or he would not have married a hill-woman. She prevailed upon him to worship other gods than Mithras."

"It was he who taught you the craft of war?"

"He taught his son, my father, who schooled me."

"It hasn't done you much good, so far, that I know of."

"The time for that is not yet."

"When will the Roman soldiers return to Britain? They've been plagued long in coming."

"They may never come, but the Emperor may send ambassadors to set a crown upon the brow of a conqueror of all Britain. It may be

I shall be a general under that conqueror, and help lead his hosts to victory."

"I see no sign of it yet. So far you have led sheep to pasture and water. Such a conqueror must drive back the Painted Men of the North, and the Men of Eire from our coasts, and goad a score of little kings into pledging their troth. So far you have only driven cattle to the byres, and goaded plow-beasts."

"There are signs you do not see."

Again a spell had been on me which had been cast at certain times and weathers before now, during which I spoke with a bitter tongue. Truly, Gerald was no churl. He helped with the labor of our homestead on the uplands, but his main task, appointed by Merdin, that fierce old man with the burning eyes whom I called Grandfather, was to train me four hours every day in the art and craft of battle. He had inherited from his father a shield of iron, the like of which I had never seen, a thrusting-spear, a throwing-spear, and a short-sword. Somewhere he had got a sword of bronze, well-balanced and handy, and a shield of linden wood, iron-bound. Our daily game was a mock-fight, although more fray than frolic. His sword lowered, protected only by his shield, he would invite me to hack at him as hard as I could. Always he knocked aside my whizzing blade with his own, or caught it on his shield, or else he would leap back, then rush in when my hand was down and almost shave me with his sword edge. Sometimes I wet my breeches from the fright he gave me, and was ever reminded that were he my foeman he could have killed me like a helpless sheep. Striving with all my might, attempting many a feint, I was sixteen years old before I drew blood.

In the time that a viper could lash out, his left arm had remained unguarded and I peeled six inches of skin from his big muscle.

The red wine from his slit vein would have filled a flagon. This he called Merdin to see, and they gazed at each other in some kind of solemn joy that I shared but did not understand. Thereafter Gerald and I faced each other armed for battle, each with his shield and sword. Forgotten now are the myriad strokes I parried, took on my shield, or dodged by leaping sideways or back. Well-remembered are those few that bled me, as clear in my noddle as my urchin passages with a little milkmaid from the village, who used to come along the hillside when she fell to itching and follow me into the gorse. Shedding blood or riddance of another juice are alike good for shaking up a younker. At the first of these I panted and grunted from short wind, although never, in the hearing of the Gods, did I cry out at pain. At the second, I was as short of breath and came nigh to crying out from what was akin to pain.

Since I needed abundant red meat to restore the pith I lost, half of my waking hours I hunted in the forest, with throwing-spear and yew-bow. It is known that the roots of yew-trees seek a buried human body on which to feed, and that is why they grow tall and wax so green in burial grounds, and perhaps that was why a yew-bow cast a shaft so true at red deer, wild cattle, and wild boar; and even when launched at a shaggy bear or a devilish wolf, they hum like hornets in fury, the yew-wood being athirst for blood. So when I killed I gave my bow a crimson bath, scrubbing it well, whereby it remained agile and strong.

If I came upon my quarry close in the dim woods, I hurled my spear. While it did not sing like an arrow or find its aim so fiercely, it fetched a more grievous wound. Often a stag or a black bull would run off with my arrow thrust deep into his side and I would follow his track in vain. Sometimes he fell, only to rise and seek battle, and sometimes I finished him with my spear, and sometimes I fled in terror and shame, or perched like a scared housecat in a tree. But if my spearhead had plunged deep into his burly chest, almost always I found him stretched out, his horns low; and then we fed better than on mutton or pork, and a low fire burned far-down and deep in my grandsire's eyes.

Thus I became fit to play with Gerald a new heart-thrilling and heart-chilling game. It was to arm ourselves with spear and shield, and hunt each other in the gorse. Then I prized most highly my forest-lore, for each threw to kill his playmate if he were a heartbeat slow in dodging, or in fending with his shield. But on the eighteenth return of May Eve since the Gods gave me life, a grown man and of age to take a wife, Merdin stopped the game.

"You have both become too skilled to play any more," he said. "From thence on, it would be only a contest to see which one of you makes the first mistake, and that one might be Gerald, a grandson of Janus, or it might be Ambrose, grandson of—what does it matter? I decree ye both are swordsmen, spearmen, and wielders of the shield. Now there be better game afoot."

In these years I noticed two strange facts. Nay, I took them for granted, only now and then pondering them lightly, although for reasons I did not know they lay heavy on my heart.

One of them was, which any forest wanderer could see, that the woods spread wider than of old, and had swallowed the ruins of villages, fields that were once tilled, tumble-down walls, and roads of wondrous building. It must be, I thought, that Cambria lay under the displeasure of the Gods, with its beasts waxing and its men waning.

The other was that I had gained manhood without ever putting my hand to the common chores of the homestead. I had never plowed fields or planted seed, herded beasts, threshed grain, milked kine, or carried burdens except my quarry from the forest. This was by Merdin's tacit command. Did he think I was accursed, whereby the field would sour, the seed perish, the beasts sicken, the grain rot, the milk turn into poison, the burdens fall and break? Was I never to wed the smooth-skinned daughter of a villager, and lie with her in his household ring with our heads to the fire, to warm and be warmed when the winter winds blew cold off the Sea of Eire?

Instead I lay with my head to the fire, in a ring with Merdin, Gerald, two churls of the field, and a woman not young but beautiful who spoke only with her eyes and who cooked the wheat-cakes and our meat and looked up from her day-dreams when some one said "Anna!" sharply, and who shrunk from any touch. In our company lay our sheepdog, and Anna's only intimate, a white sow. So I had nothing to warm me but the low flickering fire and my robe of sheepskins. When the wind howled and sometimes screamed, I dreamed wildly.

2

Our homestead on the downs was not to be despised. Above us stretched pasturage for sheep, below were forty acres of good loam for growing corn, our cattle fattened on rich grass where the damming of the brook by a landslide had formed a marshy meadow where no trees took root, and in the oak-forest thick upon the clay our hogs fed greedily on mast. No dweller in the river village of Collen, two miles distant, had as fine a house, even the chief or the smith. Our house was twenty of my large feet long, about twelve wide. A tree cut down and delimbed except for a V-shaped top stood at each end and supported the ridgepole; other trees, each with one bough sloping upward, stood at the side, and these bough-ends, fastened to the ridgepole, provided the braces for the laying of the roof, of brush and thatch. The walls were of timber and wattle, the floor of rock-hard earth.

Inside were wooden benches, cunningly made, Merdin's iron-bound chest strongly locked, an ax with a leaden head that was holy in some way and never used, a fire-pit, a bronze caldron big enough to boil a whole lamb and said to be worth ten cattle, clay jugs for water, wooden mead-cups, and a spindle and loom. On a shelf stood our hour-glass, in which water dropped, beside a human head reposing unrotted in a precious oil from some Eastern land. These last two articles must never be touched by any hands but Merdin's own. I could see that the head was shaved except for forelocks hanging over the brow, and the face was that of a great warrior or perhaps a king. This was no stinking, smoke-dried head of kinfolk, such as were kept in some village houses. And of course only the house of a great chieftain, such as I had never seen, could boast an iron shield, two iron-tipped spears, and a Roman sword. The villagers' only weapons were axes with bronze or flint heads, ill-made bows and arrows, or stout cudgels with iron bands.

Even in our shed we had reaping hooks with bronze blades, flails, hoes, forks, and a precious plow with an iron share.

On the whole, my clothes were better than the smith's or the village chief's, second only to Merdin's. My woolen cloak was in handsome checks, my tunic of wool dyed green. One of my two pairs of breeches was likewise woolen, the other of deerskin. My hose had been fashioned of young goatskin by Anna's cunning hands. My shoes were well-made of alder wood, tough and light. Still, I longed for leather shoes such as Gerald had seen when an urchin. The art of making them had been well-known to the Romans, but had been lost, perhaps from the lack of metal pins to affix layers of leather at the bottoms. Some day, I thought, it would be regained. Wearing such shoes, with long, well-greased uppers and tight seams, I could wade the shallow pools in winter without the misery of chilled and aching feet.

The pride of our house was a wondrous thing, rarely seen except in the palace of a king. It was a Cambrian harp, and its fifteen strings of sheep gut were new, but its triangular frame unimaginably old, the wood silk-smooth from the touch of hands. So prized were such instruments that they were entailed by law to pass from father to son or to next of kin, and they could not be taken for debt. If a slave as much as touched the harp he was burned alive. It belonged to Merdin, and he could play it to cause the hearer's heart to leap, to exult, tremble, ache beyond telling, faint, or like to die. To its wild strains he sang wild melodies in his yet rich and manly voice. When once I made bold to ask how he had learned the art, he had made strange answer.

"By the Sun and the Moon, it was only in preparation for my great art."

I did not catch even a glimpse of his meaning, for the only other arts I had seen him practice, if arts they could be called, were the setting of the time for seed to be planted, beasts to be butchered, trees to be felled for fuel or timber, and such like chores. True, folk from the village visited him in the dark of night; and people from afar I had never seen, and once a kingly man on a fine horse with a necklace of amber and broaches of gold, wearing a cloth with eye-holes over his face. These spoke with him under an ancient oak, about which stood a circle of upright stones, and I never knew what business brought them here, or what counsel or aid he gave them.

Even so, it was hard for me to believe that his secret art could be greater than that of a master-harper. True, on every cloudless night he went forth to gaze into the heavens, sometimes staying only half an hour, on moonless nights much longer. On cold winter nights, when the stars blazed in myriad multitudes unguessed at other season, his bed would be hardly warmed. Too, he carried a thing that he kept in his chest, made of wood and metal, with an arm that could be raised and lowered. One night when I went out at Nature's bidding

I saw him holding it in front of his eyes, as though he were aiming at the North Star.

An equally puzzling incident seemed to show that he did not pay full heed to the old Cambrian Law of the Harp. It seemed to mean that something in his life mattered more than his music. A slave owned by the village smith, a rude, roistering fellow called Griffith, usually red in the face and reeling from double-brewed ale from his master's unguarded casks, wandered to our homestead, staggered through our door, and before any one could stop him, drew his hand across the strings of Merdin's harp, causing it to make harsh outcry. But the old man did not even mutter a curse, let alone have him hailed before the village chief and burned alive. Only his eyes glinted, then he looked thoughtful, and his long, thin lips curled in a faint smile.

It is hardly worth saying that I too could play the harp truly with great skill but without art. The instrument had fascinated me ever since I could walk, and because I had a good ear and deft fingers I learned to call forth every sound that it could make. An inexhaustible memory for tunes let me copy all that Merdin played. Yet when I practiced them Anna did not look up from her task, Gerald continued to polish or sharpen his weapons, Merdin made marks with a stick of chalk on his slate, and only the churls' eyes lighted, because even this poor showing was beyond their dreams.

"Never mind," Merdin told me quietly when I sighed. "You'll be a harper yet, if you live that long. Your knowledge of the instrument is excellent. But you have not lived enough, suffered enough, to make it sing."

"Could I ever be harper to a king? Then I would wear fur and wax fat."

"An equal chance of being king to a harper." Then Merdin uttered his harsh, rare bay of laughter.

3

At eighteen, I still had not looked into a mirror to find out what I was. There was a cracked looking-glass found in a Roman ruin hanging over the washstand under the eaves, and there I could see my face with a gash across it that moved a little as I raised or lowered my head, but from which I could never dodge in the small space. I could never help feeling it was a sign of some kind pertaining to me alone, although the same gash cleft Merdin's face when he stood there combing his white beard. I wanted to search a mirror that was wide, ocean-deep, and undimmed.

All that Merdin had ever told me of my beginnings was that he had sired a son out of wedlock, and the son, named March, had wandered away to North Cambria, and there had wedded a fishermaid, Igerna of Aberffraw. Both had been drowned in the same gale, while I lay warm and safe in her father's cot. On hearing of the loss, Merdin had set forth in a coracle, and fetched me home along with Anna, Igerna's cousin, whose husband had likewise perished. She gave me suck from her bounteous breast, and she had never spoken again. Aberffraw is the seat of the kingly house of Gwynedd on the great island that we call Mon Mam Cymru, which means the Nourisher of Cambria because of its corn traded at every fair. That Merdin had touched at Mon I could not doubt. The oaken handle of our leaden ax had carvings that Gerald had said were Monan, and I thought that the glass jar containing the pickled head had been worked by Monan glass-blowers famed in Roman times.

Often I had ached to ask more about my mother and father, and had sometimes ventured a questing remark, only to see Merdin's brow darken under his forelock, his fierce eyes redden, and a black web of blood-vessels show under the curve of his jaw.

Now what I saw in the cracked mirror emboldened me to speak of the matter again. Like Merdin, I had to stoop to look into it straight, while it was level with the eyes of Anna, a tall woman, and of Gerald, whose Roman forefathers had raised him to middle-height. The glass hung too high for our churls, which did not matter, since they never washed. There are two varieties of Cambrian folk, one very tall, who are fair-haired and blue-eyed, and the other short with white skins but with dark eyes and hair. Merdin and I belonged to the first sort. His eyes were iron-gray and sometimes they looked deep and wise, and sometimes they had surface-lights like a cat's in a torch-beam. My eyes were sky-blue and looked innocent. Still, the man they looked for was no reed. The bone of my face was bold, my nose large and humped, and my lips were thin and long. There was only silky down on my lips as yet, but I had not despaired of a noble mustache when the time was ripe. My body was unmarked except for trivial scars, and two well-healed holes, half an inch broad and deep, in front and back of my shoulder. I had been bitten in my infancy by a neighbor's sheepdog that had been fed mutton bones, or so Merdin told me.

"I wish I could thank Anna for the milk she gave me when I was a babe in arms," I said to Merdin on a mid-April night when wild geese honked overhead.

"Let that wait awhile," he answered, not looking up from his slate. Then, laying down his chalk, "It is a great debt, truly, but if she heard you and understood, which would be a wonder, it would only recall the loss of her own babe, and she would weep in silence, which I cannot bear to see."

"How was her babe lost?"

"How would I know? Perhaps it died of a fever, laid on it by a witch."

Witches could do worse than that, I knew full well. Our churls often spoke of them, and begged Merdin for charms to balk them, at which he smiled, and gave them scraps of cloth, or certain herbs, to put under their wooden pillows. No such stuff did he ever give me, although I ventured into the darkest forests, where dwelt old and scrawny witches of great power. Others, of dazzling beauty, lived in lakes and tarns, and were guardians of treasure. Perhaps the most bold, for I will not say wicked, lived on islands, as many as nine in a batch, practicing weird rites, and they were known to chase with great heat sailors and fishermen touching their shores, for these witches had not broken with warm humanity. But perhaps as protection against them, perhaps for some other reason, Merdin had given me a silver cross with arms of equal length, each of which bent back at a right angle, to wear on a cord around my neck.

"Have you any mementos in your chest of my father, March, and his wife, Igerna?" I asked.

"No."

"Was your paramour, the mother of March, of high descent, or was Igerna, my mother? I ask because if King Vortigern summons me before his throne I wish him to know of it."

"Both were free-folk, poor but comely. And why should the King summon you, one of a multitude? Every youth in the kingdom who has come to eighteen years since Beltane of last year will be assembled to pledge allegiance. Perhaps he has heard of Merdin, an old harpist whose lineage is lost, but what will he care for that?" And the old man gazed into the cooking-fire as he spoke, and his thoughts were busy as bees in a swarm, but I could not dream their pith.

Suddenly he turned to me and spoke in a low resonant voice, like that of his harp when he plucked its long strings. The hands of Gerald, which had slowed their task of carding wool, grew still.

"Ambrose, you were not born out of wedlock, but your father was. His name is unknown to the scribes, and so you are a nameless man. I concealed his birth, lest he be tested for bastardy, his infant body put on a shield in running water, and if it floated—and even a wooden shield with iron bands is not a good swimmer—he would be plucked out, but if he went down he was fish-food. Ambrose, there may be games held in the court of the palace, and you may play at them, but do not play too well! There is a time to stand back and a time to stand forth, and the last is not yet come. It might be because you are tall, mayhap the tallest of the striplings and still growing, that one of the King's sons, Modred the elder or Vortimer the younger, will challenge you to a game of some sort. If so, give him a good run, but do not win. The time to win has not yet come, but it may come, when the wild geese have winged northward for two, three Aprils hence. To win a little now might mean to lose all."

"Do you mean——?"

"Yes, by my Lord the Sun! Kings and the sons of kings are vastly proud. You know the tale of the king in Gaul who was asked by his son how he was able to reign so long in peace? To answer, he led his son to a wheat field, and plucked out every stalk that towered above the common. Rightful kings descend from the Gods, and often their smile is life and may be riches, and their frown is death. Will you heed me!"

"By my Lord the Sun"—and I had never before dared utter the oath—"I will."

"You will be told to raise your right hand and pledge your life and fortune to the King," Merdin went on. "When the time comes, touch the tip of your left thumb to the tip of the little finger, forming a circle. That is the Sign of the Sun. Thereby you pledge your troth. It is of greater pledging than you make to the King, and when you must choose between the command of the Gods and the command of the King, you will make the rightful choice."

"What if I am told to take oath over some holy relic, such as a bone of Lud?"

"The Sun is over all."

<h1 style="text-align:center">4</h1>

Merdin had told me that Woodwick, the King's palace, lay in the Valley of the Wye, in a region of Cambria called Radnor. It was three days' march with good luck, so Gerald and I set forth, with packs on our backs, four days before Beltane. After we had followed a wood-path for some distance, we struck an old Roman road running almost straight north, parts of which seemed good as ever, parts of it weathered or washed away or taken by forest. Still, I could hardly believe it was the work of frail human hands, although Gerald swore to it. And in two hours' march we came to the rubble of what was once a Roman town, with stone foundations of great buildings still visible among the thrusting trees, tumble-down walls that ran this way and that, and the headless image of a goddess, a stone spear in her hand, under an arch. The ruins lay under gray skies. There was no sound or far-off echo of marching feet. And as we gazed, with our brows furrowed and our backbones chilling, three wolves moved out from behind some thickets, and one turned to snarl at us as he trotted away.

"Wolves are bold beasts," I said casually to Gerald, to ease a catch in my heart.

"They were not so, always, and may not be always so."

"Rome perishes, and in a way I am sorry, and in another I am glad."

"Why should you be glad? If Rome ruled Britain, you might become a general under the Emperor, or perhaps even Count of the Saxon Shore."

"A new broom sweeps clean. I say to you, Rome is dead."

"But her ghost will walk many a year, perhaps many a century.

The Christian priests will chant, and their scribes will set down their jargon in the Roman tongue. You and I will trod old Roman roads when we can, rather than tracks through the forests. It may be we will do—other things in the Roman way, and as we tramp today I will tell you how Paulinus, a Roman general, defeated ten times his number under Boadicea at Deve."

"Gerald, why didn't Merdin come with us?"

"He told you. There is a time to stand back and a time to stand forth. He took a risk—you and I may be crows' meat seven days hence—but he will take greater ones before he's done. Merdin is a great gamester."

I thought to laugh at Gerald, although I did not. The idea of that old man, half past fifty, playing more than piddling games with slate and chalk, star-gazing with a trinket, giving forth charms and reading omens, was surely fit for laughter. Perhaps it was stuffed down my throat by Gerald's mention of the crows' dinner, and perhaps I did not feel like laughing anyway.

Just now we were entering a region where the road had been swallowed by forest. Its bed had been torn asunder by spreading roots. Tree-boughs meshed overhead, the light grew dim. A traveler longs to laugh, or whistle, or talk loudly with his companions in such deep woods, but his wits bid him walk in stillness, lest his noise attract attention of enemies, two-legged or four. Then we came into the uplands, where stood alder and ash instead of solemn oaks, and here lay farm-land aplenty were there enough men to till it, and now and then into sight of a lonesome-looking village. So we went on our journey, walking all day, sleeping by a watchfire on an open down. On its third day we began to see other younkers of my years, likewise bound for Woodwick, mostly poor freemen but a few in handsome dress with a churl or two in attendance. Some were escorted by their kinfolk, including buxom daughters hoping to catch husbands at the great assembly. I saw none as tall as I.

We came to the palace, and it was one of the wonders of Britain, I thought, if not of the wide world. It stood on a knoll, surrounded by a ditch which must be crossed on planks guarded by soldiers. I took it to be eighty feet long and thirty feet broad, its ridgepole fully twenty feet above ground. Holes had been cut in its wooden walls, covered by greased skins that admitted light. Instead of cut trees to support its beams, tall posts had been erected, with braced arms. Its thatch roof gave forth a great smoke, no doubt from a cooking-fire that would roast a whole sheep. The wattling between its planks was of twigs daubed with yellow clay, and no winter wind could crawl in to chill its princely inmates.

"How many live under that great roof?" I asked a soldier with a bronze shield, a two-edged short-sword, and an iron-tipped spear.

"Well, younker, there's first of all King Vortigern and Queen Enid. They sleep in a bed with legs, to hold it off the damp floor, and to keep out mice and cockroaches. They lie on a mattress stuffed with wool, under so many robes they do not need fire to keep them warm. When they go to bed a harper plays until they fall asleep, and he wakes them in the morning with sweet melody."

"I have never heard the like!"

"The next highest bed is Modred's, for he's heir to the King, and the next Vortimer's, who's the younger son. Around their walls are the cots of his officers, the Chief of the Household of equal richness to his bard's, his steward's in charge of meat and drink, the judge of his court, his chief falconer, his chief huntsman, his chief groom, and his page to run and carry. These are not all his attendants, or nearly all. In huts about, furnished from his stores, dwell his mead-brewer, cook, butcher, door-guard, candle-bearer, fuel-bringer, and smith. Long ago all the kings of Cambria had a magician-judge, who could see the right and wrong of every charge, but the Romans cut down their groves, and set the long-bearded men to herding pigs."

"The Romans are all gone," I said boldly.

The soldier looked troubled. "The Romans are like wolves. They go, but they return. The King's grandmother was the daughter of Maximus, last Emperor of Britain."

"What a household!" I said to change the subject.

"I've spoken only of the great ones who wear robes worth many cattle. Did you know that the King has a servant, and the Queen a maid, whose only task is to anoint the royal bodies and catch and comb out lice?"

Gerald, paying little attention, suddenly spoke. "How many men does the King keep under arms, subject to instant call?"

"More than a down-country shepherd can count," the officer answered. "Isn't it true that you number your flocks by counting the black sheep, judging there is one for every hundred white?"

"No, because our flocks are reduced, now that wolves are so thick. But you can count them, general, for I can see you are a man of learning."

"Why should I tell you?"

"Because we poor countrymen ache to know what force the King can put into the field when again the Scotti raid our coasts." Scotti are the Men of Eire, who cross in coracles, howl like wolves in battle, scorch the earth, and take no prisoners.

"You countrymen can sleep soundly in your beds of nights, because the King can rally a legion of five hundred, fully armed between sunrise and sundown."

Knowing Gerald's face well, I saw the scorn in it. He told me that a Roman legion had numbered from three to five thousand, although I choked on it from disbelief. Fearful that the soldier would discover Gerald's thought, I made haste to draw him away.

Gerald and I wandered away to look at the fair, being held to accommodate the crowd, and it was the greatest I had ever seen. All that made life good in Cambria was on sale—mead and sweet, sticky metheglin to warm the heart, honey, mashed beans, wheat- and oat-cakes, eels from the river, salt, flesh and fish, fat geese bringing a penny each, woolen and linen cloth, rusted iron found in a Roman ruins and of exceeding cost, hunting-dogs and falcons for the very rich, ingots of lead and tin for smiths, spices and herbs to hide the smell of meat hung too long, toys for children and ribbons for young maids. There were necklaces of shell, agates, and amber, and arm-bands which the huckster told us were solid gold, although truly of gilded lead. There were finger rings that might be silver, and I thought to buy one of them, since their price seemed fair, only to decide to wait until I could have a ring of gold, bearing a sparkling jewel.

At sundown the whole throng repaired to a big field, with clumps of trees, to celebrate Beltane. But ere we began the revels, what was like water from the snows of Mount Snowdon was poured on us by a sergeant, roaring through a birchbark horn. Only the children and the elders could drink themselves into bliss. If any man due to be sworn tomorrow at high sun failed in his duty from lying drunk, he would be fed to the King's wolfhounds. This was the King's word, which he never disavowed. However, to reduce the temptation, our sport would end at midnight, and thus the King tempered justice with mercy. Why, at midnight on May Eve the God who was the Sun was scarce two hours in bed!

Once I had watched Beltane revels at Caer Dyv, a big village at the mouth of the Taff River two leagues from our homestead, and where stands a stone wall ten feet high and a gate beyond all marvel. So there was nothing new to me in the young folk dancing and singing around the bonfires, or their jumping over the fires, the last to be eaten by the Black Sow, which I take it was only a name for the rushing shadows. Too, I had seen the wheels of fire rolled down the hill, these being limber canes with their ends tied together and festooned with bunches of dry grass which were set alight. But there would have been a new thing, and a sweet thing to my aching loins, except for a kind of accident. It was the Beltane custom for young men to snatch girls of fourteen and upward by the hand, and run with them into the groves where the grass spread green and soft. If during the run the maiden tugged backward hard enough to fall, her capturer must let her go and find another, but truly our flaxen-haired wenches were wondrous sure-footed on May Eve. The King smiled at the pleasant custom, and so did the old Cambrian Gods, and only the Christian priests muttered and clacked their tongues in disapproval. I had only intended to make about four forays, lest I be weakened in tomorrow's games and make not even the good showing that I proposed, but the Gods had decreed otherwise.

By one of the fires stood a tall, red-haired man in a once costly, now shabby cloak, and a fair-haired maiden. I gazed at her lightly for a second or two, then stared like the yokel I was. How could a face, having forehead, eyes, cheeks, brows, nose, mouth, and chin, flanked by ears, topped by hair, erected on a neck, be so different from other faces with the same fixtures? I had seen perhaps two thousand faces in my life. You would think their maker would take pains with half a dozen, or maybe a hundred, then build the rest alike from falling into habit, but of those I had seen no two had been identical. It was as though he had made this face for a special occasion, as a king's cook decorates a cake with topping of beaten egg. If I speak of it lightly, it is to keep from speaking with too great ardor, which now and then was my weakness which Merdin chided.

Nor can I tell you where the difference lay. Her forehead was curved and smooth, like most young foreheads, her eyes were big and gray-green, not rare in Cambria, her nose was typical of Cambrian maids, being short, narrow, and pointed, and her mouth . . . She ate and talked with it, and breathed through it, when she snored, and a bold jester might call it a hole in her face, but it had a rose-colored rim, and that rim was softer than silk, and warm and sweet. It might be I could kiss it. Kisses were given freely on May Eve, to conjure in a warm summer with abundant rain, good sense enough to any man of wit, for a pleasant kiss is never chill or dry. If I could do that, I would not run with any other maiden into a grove. Merely a taste from a king's plate is better than a churl's whole pot of gruel.

I knew she was at least fourteen, and nearer sixteen, because of her unusual height, for I could not rest my chin on the top of her head. She had on a linen shirt, frayed at the cuffs and open at the throat, and a close-fitting tunic of blue without sleeves, and on her feet she wore slippers of leather, not wooden clogs. Only a woman of fourteen or more filled a tunic in this fashion, high in front and low in the back. Her tunic was fastened over her breasts with a clasp that might be gold. It would be easy to undo by fingers as steady as mine at launching an arrow, and often at Beltane maidens who would not run to the groves permitted such unlatching. Gods of the Sky, the Air, and the Sea! If she would give as much, I would trade half an hour on earth for a hundred years in Elysium!

The maid did not look at me as I edged nearer, the back of my neck prickling, but I thought she knew of it. Then I bent my head to the gaffer of forty and spoke to him, as near as I could fetch it, in a courtly voice.

"My lord, may I address your daughter?"

"Are you a churl or earl?" he asked, looking at me straight.

"I am a freeman, and my grandsire is a land-holder."

"There is more hope in such than in earls who sell their birthright for the King's smiles," he told me strangely, and I knew he was a bold man—too bold for this dark age—to live long and protect his own. Well, I would protect her. I would build her a tower of stone, as strong as a Roman tower, for if they had done such wonders with their hands, the like could I.

"And this is Beltane," he went on. "It is the night that doves fly forth from their nests to try their wings. By my consent, you may take her to yonder bonfire, which the throng has deserted, and sit beside her on the grass until the drum beats the eleventh hour. But you must also ask her consent."

"Damosel," I said, "will you walk and talk with me?"

"Where did you learn that, younker?" the gentleman broke in quietly, such a quietness that sometimes marks an inward start.

"Sir, I don't know."

"It's an old form, in Mona. No matter."

Meanwhile the maiden was looking me over, head to heels. Her eyes were grave and wide open, and wide were her pretty nostrils, as though she were smelling hard. No trace of a smile curled her warm mouth. I would not have dared bet a farthing on the outcome, and had trouble drawing my breath.

"Why, yes, I will," she answered at last.

We walked side by side to the deserted fire, her hand lightly lain on my arm. As the light grew, I saw how white it was. We Cambrians are a white-skinned folk, but her hand was as white as a hawthorn blossom. Then I looked at her white neck and I thought of her white breast with its red buds. White as hawthorn, red as wild rose, pale-yellow as a delicate nameless flower in the deep forest on which I could never bring myself to step, eyes gray-green as mistletoe on ancient oaks that Merdin marked—these were her colors. Our Earth Goddess had painted her without dipping her brush in any other pot.

"What is your father's name?" I asked.

"Llewelan of the Lake."

"Is he a great earl?"

"He was, until he raised his voice against Vortigern. If he had not been great, his head would have rolled."

"What is your name?"

"Elain of the Lake." She gave me a few seconds to take it in, then asked, "What is your name?"

I had a habit of watching people's eyes instead of mouths or hands. No doubt I had picked it up in swordplay with Gerald, for although his eyes forecast his next stroke only a swallow's wing-beat before it was lashing at me, that warning had saved me many a painful jab and only the good Lud knew how much spilled blood. Likely I would have watched Elain's eyes in any case, because they were the kind that draws the sight—they were her jewels, better than jewels because they could speak. I had said they were gray-green. Just now they had darkened to hazel, and had grown somewhat larger. I reckoned that she was of quick, deep feelings, and my best hope was to touch her heart a little before I touched her body.

"I have no name but Ambrose."

"If you are bastard-born, it doesn't matter," she said. "Half the babies begotten tonight will never know their sires."

"I think that my only living forebear is high-born."

"Anyway, it's better to be the brat of a plowman and milkmaid who love each other than of a wedded pair who hate each other."

"Now that is true and wondrous wise," I said, wondering how soon our fire would burn out to shield us from Llewelan's eyes.

"You have scars on your face and hands."

"I got them a-hunting." For truly I had hunted for a break in Gerald's guard, bigger game in the long run than red deer, although I did not know why.

"Are you rich enough to own hawks and hounds?"

"I have arrows that fly faster than hawks, and a spear with a fang sharper than Ron."

"Where has a man without name heard of a spear named Ron?"

"Why, I don't remember. I think he was borne by some king of old, in a song my grandsire sung."

"He is the great spear of a king yet to be. It must be that your grandsire knows the Song of Camlon, that was the death-song of Cynfried, the last of the great Druids, and Great Gods spoke with his mouth."

"It may be so. Merdin knows many songs."

"Did he sing, too, of the sword named Caliburn?"

"I think now that he did."

"And of the wild boar, Droit?"

"Perhaps so."

"Ambrose, you must never repeat these names to any one. Forget that you ever heard them. Never let any one guess that your grandsire knows the Song of Camlon. It is a song forbidden in all Cambria. To sing it is a greater crime than to curse the King. The punishment is to be flayed alive, then gutted alive, and burned."

"I'll ask him to teach me the song and sing it under the King's eaves!" For it pleased me to see her eyes so wide and her face so lovely with alarm. I thought that she might put her arms around my neck to entreat me.

"Sing it like a blackbird in his willow cage," she answered, her eyes turning green. "But your cage will be made of dry thorn, to hang over a fire till you burn crow-black."

I could only gape at her.

"Be killed like a silly noddie, for all I care," she went on spitefully. "And Prince Modred will use your guts to bait eels."

Now a young maiden should be meek, low-voiced, modest, and timorous. That fact is well-known. Only when they grow old and scrawny may they turn shrew. Yet it must be I was bewitched, for I wanted to kiss her red wrathful mouth with a terrible wanting, and at the sight of her bosom like an angry swan's, almost bursting its confines, my head went aswim.

"I was only jesting," I said quickly.

"And I spoke too hotly, a great fault of mine," she answered, melting.

"Then shall we kiss and make up?"

"I will, if you swear by a holy token that you'll do what I asked."

She had not asked, she had commanded, and I could gain my ends and still be free.

"Truly."

She fished in the neck of her shirt, where I ached to lower a bait, and brought forth a silver cross with straight arms, not bent back in the middle like the cross I wore. I stared at it dumbfounded.

"By the Sun and the Moon, are you a Christian?"

"I fear not, Ambrose. My mother was, but my father worships the Old Gods, and I am a weather-cock, blowing this way and that. Still, this is a most potent charm. Take it in your hand and promise what I asked."

"All that you asked, I promise," I said, taking the trinket. But it jumped a little, and I came close to throwing it in the fire.

"If I had not been half-heathen, I wouldn't have come to celebrate Beltane," she went on, glancing down.

My blood spurted in my veins like the Dee in its gorge, and I caught her by the hand.

"If I should snatch you up and start running to the grove, as is the right of a lusty fellow with any maiden——"

"I'm a poor runner, Ambrose. My feet are big, and they trip me up." And true, they were somewhat big for so slender a girl, and it must be she often rode shanks' mare on our rough roads. Her white hands were quite large too, although smooth.

"At least you must honor your pledge, for it's dark now, the fire almost burned down, and your noble father won't see."

She gave me only a scant kiss, yet a thrill jumped downward through my body fast as along a bowstring when the shaft is loosed. And as I plotted and schemed how to get another, sweet as honey-dew that fairies eat, warm as summer rain on thirsty corn, a tall man walked out of the darkness into the dim glow of our fire.

I sprang to my feet. To my heart's deep sinking, Elain did the same. I never knew what made her do it, she an earl's daughter, but I knew too well the spring that had hurled me up like a jumping-jack at the fair, and that was the stranger's way of walking. He walked light-footed, like a red deer over turf. I saw it before I took note of his height, equal to my own, and his bright raiment. And all of these hurt my eyes as they leaped to his face, and his face I could not see, because over it he wore a cloth with eyeholes.

It is common at Beltane for young ladies of high birth to wear a face-cloth, and then if the fire-glow, and the mead-cups, and a harp's twanging and a horn-pipe's wail, and the spells cast by magicians and the seeded corn's ache to grow tall causes them to run into the groves with the sons of earls, no tales will be told of their merry-making. Only once before had I seen a man's face hidden, and it belonged to an older and stringier man. And suddenly it struck me that he might have been Elain's father, Llewelan.

"Young swain, I wish to pay court to this lady," the visitor told me in a merry voice, although with courteous manner. "So will you please retire?"

"My lord, I know of no reason why I should," I answered as well as I was able with my dry tongue.

"This is the reason."

He drew back the cloth and showed the face of a man of about my own age. It seemed that the dying fire leaped up to reveal it well, and truly a brand burst into flame with a humming sound. My first thought was, I had seen this face before. I groped deeply within myself, the remembrance hovering before it came to rest. No, I had not seen him but I had seen part of a broken image devilishly like him. It had lain in the ruins of Isca that we call Caerleon, where I had gone with Merdin. Once it had been a statue of a man on horseback, but only the head, the neck, and a piece of shoulder remained of the human image, and only the head and neck of the horse, the bigger fragments having been carted off for some mundane use. Then I could hardly quit looking at the remnants, and my neck had prickled. The face had been different from our Cambrian faces and was god-like and beautiful. There was no indentation at the top of the nose—seen in profile, the forehead and nose formed one bold and noble line. A peculiarity was the hair, standing up in a thick mat over the forehead, and another was the sideways tilt of the head on the neck, giving a boyish expectancy, a look of avid interest in everything the personage had heard or seen. He had been a great personage, at least a king, even greater than a king, if that could be. Nor was the head of the horse like that of our Cambrian nags! It was rather short and square, like an ox-head.

"The man's name was Alexander," Merdin had told me. "He lived on earth a long time ago, and he still lives in the minds of studious men. The horse's name was Bucephalus, which means ox-head."

This visitor's hair likewise grew in a thick mat in front, his head was likewise tilted on his neck, giving him an alert, eager, fun-loving expression. Later I had questioned Gerald about that Alexander, his strengths and his weaknesses. I looked for weaknesses in our visitor's face, and did not see any. All I saw was his smile, quietly gay. He was enjoying his visit here.

"My lord, I'm a stranger in these parts, and I don't recognize you."

"By good or ill fortune, I am Modred, older son of King Vortigern."

"Then if you command me to depart, I have no choice but to obey. But if you are as great a prince as you are tall a man, you wouldn't wield your princely power at Beltane."

"Well said, fellow," Elain broke in quietly. I noticed that she did not call my name.

Modred glanced at her and laughed quietly. "I will tell you both something about princely power. It is like that of the thunder, the wind, and the rain. Sometimes they rest, then they crash or blow or pelt down according to their whim, on Beltane or at any other time. Our house descends from Lear, King of Cambria before the Romans came. The bards relate the words of his daughter Gonaryl when her husband stormed at her for plotting his death. " 'I am the law, not you. Who can arraign me?' "

Another tall man, perhaps twice Modred's age, but looking strangely young, walked lightly to our gathering.

"Prince Modred, you have made one mistake," he said.

"Have I, indeed?"

"What you said is true of the King, not of his son, a prince. Lear's daughter was the Queen, her husband was not King. The power you speak of stems from him. Come with me, Elain. The drum sounds the eleventh hour."

"Good night, my lord," Elain said, touching her knee to the ground. Then looking me in the face, "Good night, fellow."

The two walked off together, a tall, proud two. Modred tossed his head and laughed.

"We are both balked. A bold man, Llewelan of the Lake, and Elain is his daughter."

I could not speak.

"You too are a bold man, I think," the Prince went on, "so I will see you at the games."

Smiling gayly, Modred vanished in the gloom of night.

Chapter Two
The Prophecy

In the wine-bright May Day sunlight, its like unknown in all Britain beyond our green Cambrian hills, the King's cryer smote ten times on his kettle-drum. The like of this drum I had never seen, and Gerald whispered to me it was no doubt Roman, and perhaps it had beaten for the legions of Claudius four centuries sped. At once our great crowd of unsworn men formed a long, straggly line which a soldier soon made straight and neat with the point of his spear. No attention was paid to our birthrights, young earls and freemen and churls standing shoulder to shoulder. For this I was happy enough, for otherwise my place would have been middling, a condition I had long ago resolved to change. Now, since the eleventh hour of May Eve and what had happened then, that resolve had become a fiery oath. I was not the man I was yesterday at noon, I would be no longer half-content to be lord over wild cattle, red deer, and boars in the dim and dismal woods. But what I should stop at, a logical limit to my dreams, I did not yet know.

There must have been two hundred younkers in our line, all born within twelve months. A like number of wenches had the same nativity! Setting the average age of my countrymen at forty, King Vortigern ruled over a host of sixteen thousand souls, which I reckoned raised Cambria among the most populous kingdoms of the civilized world. Fully two thousand old and young had gathered to celebrate Beltane and watch our pledging. But one of our appointed number was late in coming, and then I learned the awful might of a king.

Presently the King's trumpeter sounded a great blast, and out of his palace he strode, preceded by his harper, finely dressed, and three other musicians, less finely arrayed, playing a horn-pipe, a fiddle, and a jew's-harp. At once a huge cheer rose from the throng, and I fell to trembling. He was a tall man too, although not as tall as Modred, and he walked not as a stag on turf but as lord of all creation. He wore a splendid mustache of a color almost matching his golden crown, and his robe was said to be worth twenty cows. Around his shoulders hung a short garment of the fur of weasels from some cold northern realm, and snow-white except for their pitch-black tails. Well, one winter of severe cold, I myself had snared a white weasel, so soft and pretty that I had thought to wear the skin on the collar of my tunic until Merdin told me that in that case I would wear another collar, a hempen rope, for it was against the King's law for any one but himself and immediate family to wear royal ermine.

Behind the King walked Queen Enid, a fair woman but not as beautiful as our own mute Anna, with a band of gold about her flaxen hair. Her gown was not as rich as the King's, but worth fully ten cows, and her necklaces of amber and no doubt more precious stones, gold rings, bracelets, and broaches shone in the sunlight. Back of her came Modred, and at sight of him my heart stopped thrilling and went dead as a loose harp-string. He was the most graceful male-creature I had ever seen, barring not even the lynx of the mountains, and his hair was fluffed up and his head cocked and his mouth wanted to laugh. Vortimer, the younger son, came in sorry contrast; and behind their royalties, the officers of the court huffed and puffed.

The music stopped. The King raised his imperious voice.

"Officer, are all the candidates in line?"

"My liege, all are here but one. That one lies back of the throng, where Your Majesty's bailiffs have put him, lest the sight of him offend your royal eyes."

"Our royal eyes have seen worse sights, I doubt not. Have him fetched here."

And soon the crowd parted, staring, and there came into view the King's bailiffs, and a churl bearing on his shoulder a yokel with long straw-colored hair dangling from his low-hung head. In the great silence that set in, a woman uttered whimpering cries.

"Stand him up in the line," the King ordered.

The bailiffs raised the fellow on his feet, then stood back. He made a desperate effort to stand, for the warmth of the good ale had died in him, and a bitter chill was on him now, along with an awful realization. He swayed from side to side, and back and forth, and the throng did not breathe, and the King watched quietly, and the Queen peeped through her fingers raised to her face, and Modred looked alert as a terrier ere its master throws a stick. Then, as the countryman pitched forward on his face, all the people made a simultaneous sound, each utterance very soft, not to attract attention, only a low moan or a long sigh, yet their chorus filled all the air.

"Have him taken to the river and put him to bed with a rock on his back," the King commanded. "But see that you do it well down-stream from the holes where my churls fill their casks, for we don't wish to smell him in our broth."

"Sire, may I speak?" Modred asked in his merry voice.

"You may."

"Perhaps you should pardon him, seeing how lowly he has pros-trated himself before Your Majesty."

In the brief pause before the King replied, I wondered what had prompted Modred's remark. The people did not laugh, and only waited with open mouths. Perhaps he had meant to please them, for they too were mainly rustics, who sometimes drank too deep and slept too long. Would the heir to the throne of Cambria curry the favor of churls? Could it be his heart had been touched by a woman's whimper?

"Modred, our decree has been spoken and written down in Latin by the scribes, and it may not be set aside even for a jest," the King answered. "But we will extend this mercy. No doubt his bed in the woods was cold, and the bed of the river is colder still. Let him be hanged to yonder oak, so he may jump and cavort and warm himself. For that tree was once sacred to the Druids, and if any one here still longs for Druid law instead of ours, he may see what fruit it bears when our law is flouted."

It was a kingly speech. Vortigern delivered it in a voice that sounded larger than human. I thought of this, and not of a woman's whimpering, no louder than a little dog's, and thought not of a lout who lay like a stuck pig, although now and then he raised his head a little, only to let it fall. And I pondered in amazement the sight of a tall man, holding by the hand a tall, fair-haired girl breaking out of the throng and running like scared rabbits over the hill out of sight. Somehow I could not believe that they feared for their own skins, or they would not have come to Beltane. It seemed more likely that both had an aversion, caused by a weakness of the heart or liver, to watching a hanging. They had begun their flight before the King had finished his pronouncement, and he would not take kindly to that, or I missed my guess.

The bailiffs came and carried the young toper high in their arms, to a tree. A rope was handy, for it was often used; and a man of some substance and authority, in a rich robe, fixed a noose, tested its knot, and slipped it over the lout's head. A youth beside me whispered in awe that this was Gwyn, the King's hangman, and the best in all Britain. Lest I meet him again, I marked him well. He was tall and lank and lively, with a bald crown and a snag-tooth cropping out of his upper jaw. Agilely he climbed the tree and tied the rope-end to a bough, and his face was sharp as a fox as he descended.

"Leave him be, fellows," he ordered, standing back a distance—and that seemed all there was to a good hanging, an easy way to uproot a sapling eighteen years a-growing, to put out a very strange light mysteriously kindled. However, there occurred a minor accident, marring the orderliness of the procedure. The yokel wore no galluses and had held up his breeches by a cord around his lean waist. As he kicked and cavorted with great violence, this cord broke, and the garment tumbled down only a second before he voided his bladder with great force. Gwyn the Hangman, standing in front of him, had no time to dodge.

The throng gave a great cry, and perhaps it could be called a bay of laughter, although it sounded more like a yell of triumph, as if one of their own had scored over his enemies even in death. After the outcry, silence fell without even the rope creaking, and its depth called attention to another minor happening. The whimpering cries had ceased, and when the people gazed at the woman who had made them, they saw her lying huddled on the grass. Some one bent over her, shook her a little, then rose quickly to his feet. It was as though a mongrel bitch had whimpered for her puppy being taken away, and had broken her cord, and gone with him.

Then up spoke the King, causing all craning necks to stiffen, and gaping mouths to close.

"Now these subjects arrayed before us will pledge their fealty to our crown, our throne, our dynasty descended from the Gods, and our royal person."

The King's chief minister told us to raise our right hands as he declaimed the oath, first in what was no doubt choice Latin, then in the tongue of Cambria. With the tip of the little finger of my left hand I touched the thumb, forming a circle. That circle was symbol of the Sun that is over all. The air freshened in my nostrils. Every object of the scene, every hue of foliage and of sky, of royal splendor and of encircling hills, stood forth in magic sharpness. When again I gazed upon the King, I marked that except for his crown I stood the taller. With a crown on my own head, how tall would I stand?

2

To clear the ground for the games, two unsightly objects were taken away to be thrown in a shallow grave or to feed the King's dogs. The King waxed jovial as his new liegemen vied with another at weight-throwing, hurdling, the hop, skip, and jump, leapfrog, and run, sheep, run, the prize being quaffs of mead. I eschewed all these minor events, waiting for the contests that all comers could share. The first was a foot-race of a hundred paces, and I had no difficulty losing to a wiry fellow whose short legs scuttled like a wild pig's. The next was a free-for-all wrestling match, and I was about to take a place in the circle when, without quite knowing why, I stood back. But I stood forth for spear-throwing, making a good, but not winning, cast. The next game, if it could be called that, was announced as the main contest of the jubilee, a battle-royal with quarter-staffs to win a bronze cup from the King's hand. And when again I found myself reluctant to take part, I began to know why.

All the wrestlers and the winners of other games were sweating heavily and short of breath. I wanted neither condition, or the least fatigue or weakness; and when before had I spared my strong muscles and good wind? I remembered perfectly well. It was when I had followed the blood-trail of a wounded stag, or the tracks of wild black cattle, or of a bear or big boar. For sometimes the chase would end in a suddenly breaking storm, wild as lightning and thunder on our hills.

I could see no cloud in the sky, no sign of anything but royal jollity, but I smelled something, perhaps the miasma that Merdin had said lies thick about a throne. I went to speak to my sponsor, Gerald.

"Do you remember Merdin's parable of the king in the wheat field?"

"Yes, and you are a tall stalk."

"Can we slip away into the woods?"

"Not until the King and Queen return to the palace."

"Do you think——?"

"No, I think nothing. What I feel is moonshine. To Vortigern you are only a tall clodhopper. Even if he knows more about Merdin than either of us knows, a very king dares not shed innocent blood on May Day. Go back, and frolic with the others. No, wait a minute . . ."

The Master of the Revels, being a short, jolly fellow whose trumpet voice announced the contests and named their winners, was speaking again.

"Loyal subjects of the king! These games should not end without a passage of arms—two scratches out of three in sport. Prince Modred himself will wield one of the swords, and choose his own opponent. The prize is a silver cup, and even the loser wins a leaden cup set with agate. So stand forth, you lusty fellows! Who will be Modred's choice?"

"I will," I told myself, only half-believing it yet.

Modred began to pace with his springy step about the grounds, speaking briefly to likely-looking fellows, then moving on. I put myself in a position neither prominent nor obscure, for I felt that whatever happened had been decreed by the Gods, and I could not run from it if I tried. The Prince saw me at some distance and his head cocked a little more, and he came up to me, his eyes mirthful.

"You're the tallest man here save for myself," he remarked.

"My lord, I think I'm a shade taller," I answered. "My clogs haven't as thick soles as your fine boots from Gaul."

"I've heard your voice before, and seen your face. Now where the devil was it?"

"Last night, my lord. You came up to me when I sat by Beltane fire with Elain of the Lake."

"Blast me, but you're right. Now what was your name?"

"Ambrose."

"Short, and to the point. What need of more than one name when a man is tall and bold? Have you ever had truck with a sword?"

"Only in sport, my lord."

"I think it was good sport of no oafish sort. You've some scars on

your face and your wrists are overgrown. Well, I'll look no further if
you'll stand to me."

"Pray you, ask a young earl, a more fitting opposite."

"Bah, they are milksops who mouth Latin and play at quoits. And
you are not so meek as you make out, or your bold eyes lie. Let's have
it hot and heavy. We're both fresh, and need a good sweating, and
the yokels admire to hear a good clatter of iron. On a prince's oath,
you'll not be sorry."

My face was still, but my thoughts darted like falcons. I wondered
if a dead man could be sorry about anything, or even remember anything that had happened when he was quick. If not, it would be a
mercy, for even a downy-cheeked man of eighteen had a far greater
stock of things he would like to forget than to remember, and an
old man of forty must be weighed down with dismal memories, with
only a few shining things, like hard, bright, living kernels in a churl's
bag of rotted seed corn. Sometimes, late at night, I had talked to
Merdin about the Land of the Departed. He thought that they lived
on, their bodies somehow restored, in a place beyond the sea-mists,
but he said that one of the water-ways they must cross was named
Lethe, a word from some lost language meaning forgetfulness. So it
might be that Modred had been greatly amused when he gave me
that promise.

Why should he seek my life? Any common-sense answer was unthinkable. But if he did, here was a good chance to take it. He knew
the people's belief that sudden death, like lightning, strikes three times
in a row.

A lout had been hanged and a woman who had loved him had
followed him quickly away, and now if a tall yokel, unused to the
ways of court, happened to be cleft open, the watchers would shake
their heads, feel sorry for me, and murmur knowingly of the old
sayings being the true sayings, after all.

The fact remained I would like to have Modred try to kill me,
and fail. Of all the games I had ever played, it would be the best.
It would be against Merdin's stern admonition. There was no gain
that I knew of, and possibly great loss. But no man can feel himself a
man, escape the clinging web of the ordinary, live greatly, and

dream of crowns if he always takes good advice and follows that dull course, discretion.

"You are taking a long time to answer me," Modred said. "I am not usually this patient, and if I weren't persuaded you'd give me good sport, I'd slice off your ear with my sword and let you go." And his merry eyes gazed straight into mine.

"Pardon me, my lord. I can hardly bring myself to cross swords with an illustrious prince. Remember I have only one name, and that of no mark. Won't it shame you to joust with me?"

"You speak uncommonly well for a nameless man. No, nothing shames me that I enjoy; I am shamed only when I reject enjoyment for duty and the like. I live for pleasure."

"Then if this contest will pleasure you, I accept."

"Will long-swords suit you, and two good shields?"

"Yes, my lord." For I had been schooled on a long-sword.

"For the period of the bout we are equals, a nicety of Roman custom. Did not one of the emperors go in with the gladiators and take his raps in good grace? Scratch me if you can, my good foe. It will please the yokels if a little royal blood adorns the scene, and I can spare it well."

He turned to the Master of Revels and said I was his choice. The crowd cheered, for no reason I could guess except that we were the two tallest men there. That I was a common man would delight them if I won, but if I lost, what business had I anyway crossing swords with a prince? I quit thinking about losing.

Still, I did not believe that my prize of winning and penalty of losing could be as great as my wild imagination pictured. The sky was too blue, spring grass too green, the King looked contented as a drowsy duck from the cups he had emptied, and Modred's eyes sparkled with the joy of living. He and I took our places and crossed our swords. "Engage!" the Master shouted as though he were King.

The iron swords clashed and clattered with good din, and the crowd supposed we were thrusting with good vim. Truly each of us was asking the other if he knew the craft of the sword, and as truly we had guessed the answer aforetime. Then we began to question which of us was better, and likely we would not know for a long time yet, so fine shading it would be. If Fortune turned her wheel the least inch to favor either, the test would not be true. Our sweat starting, we began to hack, warding with our shields or twisting sideways or leaping every which way to dodge the down-strokes. I thought at first I might wear him down by endurance gained by Gerald's long assaults and my rough forest life. This notion I soon abandoned because he had the strength of oak and the suppleness of yew. Only better swordsmanship could win for me, and I never knew before what a swordsman Gerald was, to have fittened me to stand against this swordsman.

Thoughts stay cool in such high contest, at least at this stage. If they warm overly, they fuse, and defeat follows fast. As action by one of us caused an equally vigorous reaction by the other, I began to love the game, partly for its danger even though we sought to graze and skin, not to cleave open. Now in the fencing-play with long-swords that I had seen at a fair, practiced by two gypsies of some sort, their blades became strangely wedded, in an embrace not unlike the embrace of love, thrusting, retreating, warding, kissing lightly, clutching, closely binding. It was a pretty thing to see, but I reckoned it not half as hazardous as our good, old-fashioned hacking, perhaps learned from the Romans, or more likely taught them by the doughty swordsmen of Cambria. And it could well be that Gerald, Modred, and I had no peers from Severn to Deemouth.

Would I had been born a prince, to fight in fine vestments, and overthrow the mighty and the proud!

Then I took thought of two little things that at first I had merely noted. Modred's footwork appeared faster than mine; and if barely perceptible, it might loom large in the outcome. If I too had worn soft leather boots with stout soling instead of wooden clogs, I could have matched him. Aye, if—and if the dog had not stopped to squirt a tree, we Cambrians say, he would have caught the rabbit.

The other thing was more troublesome. At first I had taken pleasure or at least I had found no fault in Modred's gayety, taking it as the nature of the man, evinced by his mirthful eyes and the gay cock of his head. Now I perceived that while it was his nature, it might also be his tool.

He larked more and more, skipping when he dodged my stroke, pretending almost to swoon with fright, and making me out an oaf. It came to me that he was seeking to rile me, to win an easy victory.

There was no danger of his succeeding, for Gerald had taught me never to lose my head lest some one roll it. My own victory would be the sweeter because of his antics. If I had stopped at that shallow and consoling thinking—and I came too near it—I might have reeled back into quicksand. Instead I forced myself to think harder, casting out comfortable thoughts as a good farmer casts out and kills sick hogs from his drove.

I would keep my head, but would the crowd know it? And then the truth came to me, cold and quiet in the deep of my brain, that Modred had thought a great span further than I, that his brain was more subtle than mine, that my flight of fancy had fetched me to the truth, and he had laid a plot to kill me.

I did not question it now. The questioning was all done. I did not ask why, the rhyme and reason of it all; I accepted it like an icy wind blowing over the moors, unseen, but biting to the bone. My backbone chilled, then began to tingle. I loved life and I hated death more than ever before, and my soul changed in my body in one surge, and my youth died with one gasp, and I was a man of war.

Yet even if I passed his ward, I could not strike to kill, or the oak tree would bear new fruit until I had kicked awhile, and then I would be cut down, and flayed and gutted alive, and God knew what else to feed Vortigern's revenge. So I tried to slash Modred's right arm, allowing for his sideways leap, and the blow promised well. Instead his plan advanced an immeasurable distance, perhaps too far for me to overtake. His spring was a little slower than before, although it would not look so to the crowd, and surely he gambled with dire death, and that was what he loved if the prize was bright enough to his fox-bright eyes.

It must be a mighty prize, and I did not know what it was or seek to dream.

My blade missed cutting off his arm by half a foot and by an instant too brief to measure. And then the King's voice rolled forth.

"Stop the fray! The yokel is incensed and struck to kill."

"I did not, my liege," I answered, lowering my blade, as did Modred. "I pray you, look into my face to see if I am furied." And it was a little but a strange thing that I said "my liege" instead of "Your Majesty," as though I were high-born.

"Why, it's red as fire. But, Modred, you are well-served for choosing a churl for your opponent. Don't you know that a cur dog will bite when cornered? Smite him with the flat and send him howling home."

Modred cocked his head, smiled with what came close to beauty, and spoke in a merry tone.

"Royal Father, I beg to appeal your decree. This good fellow is not wrathful; or so I believe; and even a high-bred hound sometimes breaks from the leash from too great ardor. We're a good match, and it would shame me not to settle it with victory or defeat."

"You're too trustful, my son. You may go on with the contest, but keep close guard. If you see murder in his eyes, I command that you slay without mercy."

"Then, Ambrose, my good companion, will you re-engage?"

I thought to tell him I would yield, but my tongue stuck. Much stood to be lost, and yet, as in a dream, I saw a whole world to win.

"If it's your princely wish."

It must be that fright filled every inch of my body, so that no sense remained to observe the condition, for I moved nimbly, and vision did not forsake my eyes. I remembered one great truth. With good enough swordsmanship I could still win.

We crossed our swords. To keep Modred off-balance, I hacked lustily, caring no longer if the crowd thought rage was on me, and what the King saw made no difference, he being party to the plot. The worst he could do if I won was to kill me by naked power, and I would be no deader if cleft to the breast-bone by Modred's sword. Truly, though, I was not enraged. It seemed I had no heat to spare from the heat of the fray, and I moved as coldly and as rhythmically as a water-wheel perfectly balanced. When Modred hacked, I sprang away, buoyant as a cock in a barnyard fight. And soon I did not know the King, or the crowd either, they having turned to wraiths, and all that was left solid and alive under the sweet May sky was my enemy and me.

He stopped his larking and began to lay on his strokes in a certain pattern, as a good chess-player moves his pawns, and at its end he meant to give me his last stroke. There was no mirth in his eyes now, and no ferocity either; there was only implacable intent.

I began what looked like a mighty hack at the side of his left arm. He leaped to the right, even as his arm flexed to strike when my point lowered. But I changed the direction of my swipe with my sword mid-air. It took great strength of wrist, but had not Modred told me, to butter me into acceptance of his challenge, that my wrists were overgrown? Whizzing over his head, my blade chopped down at an angle, and it did not miss, the Gods did not let it miss, for if they loved me not at all, they loved good strife; it made them goggle in their high seats, and they wanted more of it in due course between Modred and me, and why spoil their own sport?

I could have cut off Modred's right arm easier than nick it, but he would have died from gushing blood. Still, it was a good nick, indeed a chunk of the large muscle big enough to bait a fox-trap flew off like a chip under the ax. His red blood quickly followed, a fine flow, and his arm fell to his side, and it was all he could do to hold on to his sword and ground its point.

Busy-bodies rushed forward, and stuffed the hole with moss, and tied on a cloth. They made very little sound, and Modred himself made none, and I saw from the corner of my eye that the King was pale and tongue-tied. So it came to pass that I was the first to speak.

"My lord, the rules specified two hits out of three to decide the winner. Are you ready to fall to again?"

"Wielding the sword with my left arm?" the Prince answered with a smile. "I would make a fine fool of myself, if I haven't already. No, good swain and excellent swordsman, I yield to you."

I touched my knee to the ground, and then the King made haste to recover himself.

"Hear ye all! Our subject Ambrose has won the match, and we hereby award the prize, this cup of silver worth ten cows, which we will fill with mead, and pass to him with our own hands."

The Master of Ceremonies nudged me forward. As the filled cup passed close to Queen Enid she spit in it like a viper, but what was a little royal spit to a hardened man of battle? I drained it without compunction and in hearty gulps. When I had knelt and drawn back, the King waved to his musicians; they began to play with great vim, and he turned to enter his doorway. As soon as he had disappeared, with some of his lesser attendants still in sight, I made as fast as I dared to join Gerald. I thought some of the crowd might delay me to pat my back or praise my prowess, but all got out of the way and hardly glanced in my direction.

No, I had not caught the plague. I had only bested and drawn blood from the Crown Prince. To show favor to such a one could be worse luck than failing to leave out milk for household elves. I was being tutored swiftly in the might and majesty of kings.

3

When Gerald and I were trudging the road alone, he spoke in riddles not overly hard to read.

"Ambrose, it is a common thing for thieves to lurk about on the night of May Day, to rob celebrants faring homeward."

"I have nothing worth stealing but a silver cup."

"The Queen spit in it, and that makes it a great prize, even though it is not silver but some base metal painted with quicksilver in the Roman practice."

"In that case, it would be no great loss."

"Some thieves take more than a traveler's belongings, so if he sees their faces, he will not bear witness against them."

"If they cut out his tongue he can not talk, but it would be easier and safer to slit his throat."

"Thank the Gods that the cup of mead from the King's hand didn't addle your head. You will need all its wits before this night is over. And I will be little help to you, my cousin Ambrose. I am not a frequenter of the forest, only a pig-drover, as you once called me, with some little skill at arms. Playing as though we were the hunted, not the hunter, the stag and not the hound, how would you go about it to see the Sun rise?"

"If I were a stag, I would only run. But if I were a wolf, I would maze my trail—drown it in water—perhaps double back, and if the chance came, leap from ambush."

"Gods, but your blood is up! Quiet it a little, and think only of our safety. I have much to teach you yet—thrice you missed chances to break your foeman's skin, and he missed five chances to pierce yours. We Romans do not grow to manhood in one day, as do you Cambrian savages, yet Rome conquered the world."

"You are only a mongrel Roman. Your grandam was a hill-woman. And Alexander, who taught Rome the phalanx, commanded Macedonia at sixteen, and conquered at Chaeronea at seventeen, or so Merdin told me."

"You have a good memory. But you'll lose it if thieves come in the night and mash your head like a ripe pumpkin. It's cheaper to use a cudgel than a blade, because sometimes a blade sticks in the bone."

"A thief with a golden crown?"

"Don't be a fool! A king need not leave his warm bed to get trivial matters done. He speaks, or only nods or jerks his thumb, and his minions move. Modred might leave his bed, for he is a night-creature who loves prowling in the dark. He is no more wicked than a wolf, who kills for food, for pride, and sometimes for sport. Did you ever look into the eyes of a wolf? They dance with merriment. We in Cambria will all turn into wolves unless the Romans return with Roman law, Roman roads, Roman arms. Modred has made the change already. And he will soon be King."

"Rome is dead. Some Cambrian youth will rise and slay the wolves. The forest will return to its old boundaries. The Scotti will fear to come in their coracles and the Picts on their stealing feet, and the Horned Hats in their ships. The Gods have already told it in the Song of Camlon."

Gerald walked a distance in silence, then spoke softly from the side of his mouth.

"You have never heard the Song of Camlon?"

"Not all of it, only snatches of it. Sometimes when Merdin thinks he is only thinking, he mumbles to himself."

"Bah! It is only the ravings of some long-dead rhymester that the people swallowed, lacking good ale. Only the Sibylline Books foretell the truth—that Rome will yet conquer the whole earth within the encircling seas. Now I'll give you a piece of Roman wisdom. It is what the Centurions tell their men when, ringed about with danger, they pitch camp in enemy domain. Live tonight! If you live to see the Sun rise, you may see it set."

"Did Varus tell his legions this in the Dörn pass? If so, they didn't heed him!"

Gerald gave me a wide-eyed glance.

"Before the Gods, I've never told you of that slaughter! It rolled us back from our farthest reach; it was the beginning of—I'll never say the end—of the great storm that Rome will weather. Do I also mumble secrets?"

"Coming home from market, your belly full of double-brewed ale, you chatter like a blackbird."

"It's the hill-blood cropping out. I forget I'm a Roman, and turn into a Welshman—for that is the name the Cambrians bear in Kent—strangers and thieves! Well, I shall make it do as long as Merdin lives or, perhaps, you live. Will you live tonight?"

He spoke this last with such quiet tension that my belly clutched itself with cramp and I glanced over my shoulder at the stragglers on the road.

"We'll begin to maze our trail like hunted wolves, but speak truly once again. Did Vortigern descend from King Lear, as he claims, or from some flatterer whom Maximus raised to power?"

"By the Earth and the Sky, Ambrose, he descended from great Lear, through his daughter Cordell, wedded to a Frankish chieftain. What does it matter to a swain of the Taff?"

"King Lear had no issue through his sons?"

"He had no sons."

"I wish to have many, so we must live through the night."

4

Powerless to probe the danger, I was able to believe in it mainly because of the long-proven hardness of Gerald's head and of something I had seen in Modred's face when I had drained the mead-cup which the Queen had kissed. And since I could not flee from what lurked anywhere, I thought to give it a rough welcome. Mark that a Cambrian man of eighteen is not like your dull-eyed swains of the Midland Plain. The air we breathe is different air, it is always fresh and thrills our backbones, our eagles scream in our ears, the wind strums our tree-tops like harp-strings, the brooks out of our hills chatter in the day, sing full-throated in the night. Life is so good in Cambria, and hazard is its best part, and I craved to make Gerald proud of me—the old man too when he heard the tale—and perhaps I would catch the eye of Tyr, God of War.

So when we had rounded a bend in the road we turned off into the woods. Flanking the road a short distance, we crossed it again where our footprints would not show on a rock upcropping and again dipped into the ancient wold, deep-rooted in clay, with trunks greater than the span of two men's arms. The big boughs spread wide and intertwined, and although the flush of May was on the leaves the light was more like early dusk than mid-afternoon. This was the home of the sleek red deer, the black elk, wild bulls of huge horn and scrotum, savage-tempered boars with little hateful eyes and ready tushes, shaggy bears, and the lean, terrible wolves. Some of the wolves were common flesh and blood, but until his blood ran from arrow or spear-point, you could not tell one of them from a were-wolf, housing the ghost of the unblessed dead.

Witches of great age dwelt here, abominably ugly, and very rarely a young and beautiful witch would come and lie down by a forester beside his watchfire. Sometimes his wits were turned, but if he had served well a young witch's itch, in the morning he might find a trail of aspen-leaves, gold-tinted by frost, that led to a pot of gold. Sometimes, amid the ruins of a stone tower, dwelt creatures who looked like little men save for their misshapen and foul-colored faces. These gnomes were guardians of treasure, and if he could catch one, Merdin knew exactly how to force him to yield his hoard, the business requiring thongs from the hide of a spotted bull, mistletoe, and a thorn cudgel.

The treasure on which I doted, and Gerald the like, was our own lives, which we had somehow got in the bellies of our dams, by law worth twenty cows each, and which our poor ghosts could not redeem with two hundred cows, if tonight we lost them. And the chance was all too likely, if we were resolutely chased, for this stretch of forest did not grow to our advantage. Our feet could not keep from leaving tracks in its mossy floor. Brooks were few, shallow, easily muddied to give sign; and the King kept a stable of ten horses on which he and his court chased deer.

I wondered if a stag, hotly pursued by hounds running ahead of royal horsemen, thought how sweet was his life now in jeopardy, whereby his gait quickened, and new strength surged to his tiring heart. Did he think of the woodland pools where he richly fed? Did he remember his great battles with rival stags, their horns clattering, their bounding mighty and light, their slashing hooves drawing blood with its rich smell, and the pride and the glory of victory? Did he think of a sleek doe he had seen on the last Moon, not in season yet, for the leaves were not yet colored by frost, and the fever of the rut not yet waked; yet in October she would fly from him even as she called him, and he would die rather than let her go.

So I took thought upon the supper-table at our homestead, the good meat that greased the chins and kindled the eyes of our two churls, and the barley-cakes that Anna baked and that we dunked in milk. Long after supper the light held, and I was loath to go to sleep, while Gerald dressed his weapons, and Anna span, her spindle making a soft sound as she turned it against her thigh but herself no whisper of sound, and sometimes Merdin strummed his wondrous harp.

And I thought of a maid whose presence on earth I had not dreamed until last night, white as a white rose except for her gray-green eyes, hair of paler gold than the golden clasp of her tunic, and the red-rose buds of her breast. Would I see her again? For that, I would enter woods so black that a black wolf could walk unseen; and for that, a two-legged stag would be a little harder to catch and kill.

The sound of a hunting horn stole through the still woods. It had carried, I thought, about a mile. That is a short distance for men on horses to overtake lubbers on shanks' mare. But the Sun served us prettily by his swift pitch over the hill. If Gerald and I could live another hour, we would likely live tonight.

"We'll drown our tracks in the brook and find a hiding-place," I told Gerald.

"Before the Gods, Ambrose, if I pass the night in the forest I'll die with chills and fever," he answered. "Then who will teach you to cover the loop in your guard over your left belly? Can't we find a clearing?"

I started to say that neither of our guts would be worth guarding when the King's men were done, only to remember the way of a fox when chased by our old sheepdog. He would circle to the naked crest of a hill, sit down at his ease, and no doubt laugh. The small brook we were approaching chattered as it ran. I felt its water still warm from sunlight. We took up it, wading, and in a hundred paces it rushed from a ravine; and in five minutes' climb we were gaining the top of a big mound; and by what whim of the Gods it had been raised in that flat forest only the Gods knew. Then a chill ran through me, because the failing light revealed what looked like a ring of men standing guard on its summit. In an instant they were revealed as upright stones, forming such a circle as I had seen before, far-scattered on our hills, made by giants in bygone ages, and this ground we were about to tread was holy ground.

But I climbed staunchly and Gerald did so without a tremor, because he worshipped Mithras, the bull-god of the Roman soldiery, and did not give a snap of his finger for our Halls of Sacrifice. And I took comfort in thinking that if one of the stones did not heave itself out of the ground and leap through the air and mash us flat, here was the safest retreat we could hit upon. Even if they found the mound in the falling night, our foemen would not look for us atop it, persuading themselves that no country bumpkins would dare set foot there, putting us in the same boat with themselves. Then my thoughts ran deeper as my fears slacked off, and it seemed to me that the great victors among men must be those who knew about such boats, knew how many fellows would climb into them, but stayed out of them themselves.

King Vortigern was such a victor, and Modred was his heir. The Prince harbored no hate of me, if his eyes told truth. He would not likely seek revenge for a sore arm got in swordplay with a yokel from the Taff, but he might love hunting with surpassing love. If that yokel was bigger game than he himself could believe, might not Modred lead the pack while the King took his ease in bed? The notion dizzied my head while it somehow thrilled my heart. Still, it would be no greater wonder than some I had lately met.

The hunters crossed the brook, and Gerald and I knew the instant that they lost our trail. The hillward breeze brought up a surprised exclamation, then a confused shouting, and then a yell of pain from the first speaker: no doubt he had been struck with a club or the flat of a sword. There followed much questing about and around, and some hearty cursing from some one of high standing in the company. This voice was not Modred's, I thought; and it came to me he would never curse in loud tones, only very softly if at all, and more likely when others cursed he would only laugh.

"Those two foxes have holed, and the hunt's done till daylight," came a high, clear-carrying voice.

"I fear as much," a minion answered.

"We're ordered not to cross the Usk into the old man's country. That means 'twill be touch-and-go."

"Why didn't we take the King's hounds? We'd had 'em treed by now."

"You fool, they'd heard their baying from here to the Dee. Our best stratagem was surprise, and Owain blasted it when he blew his cursed horn. But we're not beaten yet. All of ye take posts a hundred paces apart up and down the brook, and listen with all your ears. They can't leave their holes without making racket on a night dark as this, and if you hear 'em start, sound the alarm."

This command was carried out with a deal of calling back and forth, for the night was dark and silent save for a slight rustling of leaves, and a man's solitude bit deep. Some of the band moved closer to our hiding-place, others further off. One man who walked lightly gained the ravine, and I heard him scrambling up the bank to an easy resting place. He must be a bold fellow, I thought, to take the lonely end of the line. I kept thinking of him while the night, which had seemed black and full some moments ago, continued to press down.

He might be a fellow who kept to himself a good deal and who kept a closed mouth during trivial parley, only saying at last what was to be done. And now, although the forest looked like a pitch-black sea ringing our eminence under the whole sky, our hilltop appeared bathed in mist too dark to be cold luminance, and yet which showed me the black shape of Gerald distinct on naked clay. A multitude of tiny stars had lighted their minute lamps, and the big stars blazed. It might be that the Gods had thinned the dark a little for their own better watch, and it might be that my eyes were gaining night-sight, like those of a prowling lynx.

I waited another hour, and then spoke in low tones to Gerald.

"Take off your clogs and tie them with mine to wear around your neck."

"A Roman is shamed to walk barefooted," he complained.

"Tonight you are not even half a Roman, but half of a pair of wolves."

"Wolf I will be, then, for you know these cursed woods, and I do not."

"Now lend me the knife you wear under your tunic."

"What's in your mind, Ambrose?" he asked in an anxious whisper. "Remember Merdin put you in my care, not t'other way round."

"At sixteen Alexander ruled Macedonia. I could have done the like, with a little more counsel from Merdin, and schooling in war from you. At nineteen did he kill his father the King? That was a monstrous crime before the Gods, and wouldn't have happened if some one had killed Alexander before then. A stitch in time saves nine."

"The moon isn't shining on your head, to cause lunacy. Is it the smell of the forest? It's a devilish smell that causes fever."

"I'm touched with a little fever, I confess." And truly the smell of the forest at this time of year was fever-waking as the smell of a fair-haired girl when heated from dalliance.

"I'll lend you the knife, for it may have been foretold that I did so, although I've not heard of it."

I had no notion what he meant, and paid little heed, from admiring the heft of the knife in my hand and running my finger along its double blade. It was sharp enough to shave with.

"In the name of the Gods, take care," Gerald muttered as I went out of the ring of stones.

It was no trouble to steal down the hill as softly as the breese climbing the hill, and where the brook had been fed by springs I walked in its bed, trusting to its chatter to hide the crunch of pebbles and little splashings impossible to prevent. At the summit of the ravine the stalk became more rigorous, for a real wolf would be hard put to it to penetrate the brushwood in silence. I wormed through it, on strict guard against a misstep or a branch scraping my clothes, and an hour-glass was half-emptied before I came to an open space. Nothing had been lost by my patience, except sweat and heat, leaving me cold as a viper. That creature carried a short fang in his mouth, I

172618

a long fang in my hand. My quarry would be sleeping more deeply because of the wait.

I made out his dim shape in his grassy bed, not as long as I expected, then remembered that even tall men look shortened when lying down. As I crawled nearer, I still could not see his face except as a wan blur, because tree-limbs shaded it from starlight. He might easily be only a hanger-on of the court, or even a thrall. Even so, I wanted to leave my mark on some one in the hunting party.

I crept to his side and spoke in low tones.

"Modred? This is Ambrose."

As he waked, I struck, and it came about he only half-waked before he went back to sleep, and that sleep would be plagued long, I thought, before he waked for a long waking in some land beyond the sea-mists. His flesh would melt and his bones crumble before they could be restored by the sorceries of Lud. Were these the sinewy flesh and supple bones of Modred? My hopes were falling fast, and when I felt along the crown for a mat of upright hair, I found it almost bald. But he was not a thrall: his clothes were too fine.

I studied his face in the gloom and something waked in my mind. Sticking my finger in his open mouth, I drew it along his upper jaw. Midway in the arch, with gaps on both sides, grew a snag-tooth.

He was only Gwyn, the King's hangman. Even so, when could Vortigern find another who could stretch a neck as handy and as well? He could well fly into a royal rage when he heard the news, and two spirits, those of a farm-boy and his mother not long in the land of shades, still not at home there, wandering drearily about, might wax merry.

I was far from merry but not cast down when I returned to the mound-top, gave Gerald his well-wiped knife, and we started together down the opposite slope on our journey homeward.

5

As we came in sight of our homestead, the scene was peaceful. One of our churls was leading to the fold our flock of sheep, many of the ewes with lambs not yet accustomed to their legs, let alone this world so enormous and different from the cozy small world of the womb they had lately left. They had dreamed no more what it would be like than I could dream of a new world to which I might have flitted if my passage-of-arms with Modred, and my dealings with the hunters, had had a different end. For at this moment, my fancy was roving free mainly to escape from dwelling on what had happened, almost unthinkable now that I saw the quietly wreathing smoke from the chinnies in our roof. Truly it made me sick in the belly to think of it because I could not for a moment credit that I was done with it.

I could wish it had been no more than a fantastic dream in the night, from which the sleeper wakes up panting, thanking the Gods for the quietude and his returning sense. But if wishes were oxen I would drive me a span—so goes an old peasant saying—and if willows were swords I'd become a king's man.

Gerald and I entered our doorway, and I looked about as if expecting to see great changes, only to find none. Anna looked up from her bread making, then glanced quickly away; Merdin gave me a little nod, then went on casting sums on his slate. We two travelers sat down to supper and ate heartily, then Merdin wiped his beard. It meant he was ready for me to speak.

"Grandsire, will you walk with me along the hillside? It's a fine, fair evening."

"Why, yes. I wish to behold the Evening Star when she tops the hills."

"Gerald, will you come with us?"

"Pray you, excuse me while I look to my weapons. They have gone untended a full week in damp weather."

"You've never said 'pray you' to me before. What ails you?"

"Nothing that a good night's sleep won't cure, if the household elves will let me have it and not tug at my toes. They're already sore from running barefoot in that cursed woods."

"A Roman go barefoot?" Merdin asked quietly. "And at the season when the bitch-viper has newly spawned?"

"Old man, do you think I did it for sport, as might an urchin? Ask my captain, who a week ago was my apprentice. For when a Roman or even half a Roman runs at all, let alone barefoot, there is much else afoot."

"I can see that much without looking in my book. Perhaps I should have—but come, Ambrose. It's a fine, fair night, as you said."

We two went forth into the calm and spacious evening. As soon as we gained the hillside we tramped side by side, he a little above me but his head level with mine. All today's march I had dreaded telling him of the trouble I had not invited but might have avoided somehow, whereby both of our heads would sit more securely on our necks. Now the dread was gone, for the stars shone with solemn splendor, and they knew I had not opposed them, and indeed had pursued their great design. A nightingale in a nearby copse uttered song as pure and liquid as sometimes Merdin summoned from his harp. It was an evening great in my fate.

So I told him in a rush of words all that was momentous in my journey—meeting and kissing Elain, fighting and besting Modred, stalking and killing the King's hangman. He showed no great surprise and not the least anger. Often, as I spoke, he glanced at the heavens, and once he stopped and listened to a far-off sound that could be the scream of a banshee but that seemed more likely the wild outcry of a loon in our meadow-pool. Before he gathered his thoughts to reply he made one quiet comment.

"Well, since you were fated to go hunting in the dark, I'm glad that your quarry was Gwyn. If I am to be hanged—and a cruel end awaits me when my work is done—I am glad that it won't be he who fixes the noose. He always draws back his lips and shows his snag-tooth. I have seen it in evil dreams."

"Merdin, have I hastened that end by my rashness?"

"It may be so. Both remain the will of the Gods. Only the time of these happenings is not in accord with my calculations. Could I have made a mistake? I'll get my stellarscope and see."

We had tramped a distance and turned back, so we were not far from our door. He left me in quick strides and presently returned with the thing with the movable arm with which he looked at the stars. He leveled it at a red star and worked the movable part, meanwhile mumbling to himself. Then with his toe in the dirt he drew a series of figures that resembled Roman numerals I had seen on blocks of stone.

"Your Sign is the Scorpion," he told me. "Three nights ago there blazed forth within that Sign the red star Tyr, our God of War, whom the Romans called Mars. But the year—how could I have confused the year? Maximus departed Britain ninety years before the Year of the Comet. Your age, eighteen, added to ninety, makes the sum of one hundred and eight, and as written down in the Cambrian numerals it gives one, zero, and eight, and their sum gives the number nine! By the Earth and the Sky! Ninety years before the Comet, or nine as the Pythagoreans counted, added to the nine obtained by adding one and eight, the numerals of your years, come to—eighteen! According to the Song of Camlon, a hundred and ten years must pass, but that was a rounding out, and it was the ninth day of the Moon that you were born, and I am in my fifty-fourth year, which numbers add up to nine. Blind fool that I am! The great storm breaking without my seeing its first cloud sweep across my Lord the Sun! Yet we have a year—perhaps two—to make ready for its full onslaught. Wait here!"

Again he entered the house, and now when he emerged I trembled, for he wore a white robe and carried his harp close against his breast.

Beckoning for me to follow, he led the way to what he called the Dolmen Ground, nearly a mile from our homestead, which some one—I supposed it was Merdin, long ago,—had warned me to avoid. It happened that in following a wounded deer, I had seen what was there, little enough to interest an urchin hot on the chase, and plain-looking in broad daylight. Nothing remained of an ancient working but a large, flat stone across the tops of two upright stones, which Gerald called a cromlech, and about forty other stones of about the same size strewn on the ground. A single oak tree stood nearby, not nearly as massive as the giants of the wold, and perhaps no older than forty years.

All was changed tonight by the common magic of the horned Moon, only three days old, hanging in the open western sky bright as a silver jewel. Now the oak tree appeared kingly. The gray slabs lying about told of ancient, immemorial things, great affairs begun in hope, blessed by the Gods, conducted for a thousand years, and at last ending in impotence and ruin. The cromlech was a crude monument compared to many raised by the Romans, yet it seemed a symbol of the world itself, this world where men were born, lived, toiled, teemed, and died, world without end, massive and immutable. Ghosts of a thousand dead men thronged this spot, returning to the place of their assembly when they were warm and quick; they were thicker than the blades of grass, I thought, and they had come to hear Merdin and to look at me.

"There was once a ring of cromlechs here," Merdin told me, his voice changed in his throat until it was like a trumpet heard far-off, "and their tops fitted on another in a solid circle of which a knife-blade could not probe the joinings. Then Agricola, greatest of the Roman governors, sent his Ninth Legion here, and with machines big as catapults, they tore apart the temple and scattered its stones. All save one. They were about to raze this one too, when a black cloud spread, and a whirlwind raved, and lightning flashed and thunder roared and such rain fell as no living man had ever seen."

"Did Tor send the whirlwind?" I asked when Merdin paused, and my voice also was like a muted trumpet in my throat.

"I think that he did. The God that they called Jupiter turning upon them in his awful wrath."

"I will offer to him two snow-white bulls. If then he isn't content, I'll give him my first-born."

"It may be that you will. It may be the ancient due unto the Gods will be once more given, and their anger against the people will be assuaged. Mark you, now, the fate of the Ninth Legion, five thousand soldiers of the best in the Empire. The Gods let them eat, sleep, drill, fight, woo fair-haired girls—all this they were let do, and no shadow of their marching doom stifled their laughter. The Wise Ones waited in patience—the Druids, as they were called—for they had read the prophecies in the spilled guts of a Centurion of the Ninth who had wandered away from the camp, alone except for a single tracker, to hunt deer. The tracker was one of ours. He led the officer with his burnished weapons not to the wood-ponds but to an oaken grove so deep in the forest that Agricola's woodsmen had not yet found it and hacked it down."

"What did the spilled guts tell the Wise Men and when did it come true?" I was having trouble drawing a deep and even breath.

"The Ninth Legion was sent into the North, into the Vale of York, and there, in battle with the Brigantes, whose name means

Mountain Men, the Romans were cut down to the last man, and their banners were trampled in the dust."

"Now that is good. Did Agricola, spoiler of our temples and ax-man of the Sacred Groves, die in the fullness of years, surrounded by his grandchildren, and in peace?"

"No, Ambrose, he did not. Within seven years after his return to Rome he was stricken in the night with a bloody sweat and died in agony the next day. Perhaps one of our own had followed him there as a trusted servant. Perhaps Dalor, the God of Death, had come to his bedside and blew his cold breath into Agricola's mouth as he lay snoring. In either case, the Gods had moved, and the prophecy was fulfilled."

In the tree-top roosting ravens croaked and clamored, and I would have thought they were only quarreling over the best perches if it were not the way of ravens to cry out when some one speaks of death. They are the watchers of the dying, the eaters of the dead, and some say they guide ghosts of men to the land of shades.

"Now the Roman soldiers have all gone," I said, trembling so I could scarcely speak.

"They are gone ninety years plus eighteen years, making one hundred and eight, which is again nine. Would you be afraid to sit under the roof-stone of the cromlech?"

I glanced at its shape in the moonlight, pale-colored as our brooks after light rain, and it was of awesome shape, and I feared it to the marrow of my bones, but my breath caught at last and I gave forth an answer from my spirit, not from my jellied flesh.

"Not if it is your command."

"I may command you no more. As your heart beckons, follow."

I climbed under the slab of rock, the upright rocks at my left and right, and became one with the darkness there, although I could still see Merdin standing unearthly tall, his white forelocks silvery-looking.

"Draw your knees up to your chin, if you will, in a position of a babe in the womb, for the song I am about to sing was sung a thousand years ago to the unborn."

I did so, and a feeling of warmth and safety fought against a great dread of changes soon to come, a different life and a different world.

"I will sing you only the first part of the Song of Camlon," Merdin told me, striking a chord on his harp. "The rest you will hear later— if you live."

He began to pluck the strings. His harp sang alone for a space, a melody I had never heard before, wild and strange as the trumpet of the wind blowing through the defiles of the mountains. No human brain, I thought, could have conceived those half-notes and quarter-notes of fairy beauty in juxtaposition with harsh outcries, as of a buck wolf howling while his bitch suckled her cubs. Then Merdin sang with his harp, sometimes above and sometimes below the melody, and he and the harp became man and wife in strange way. And this was his song:

The Eagles will fly southward, and the long years will pass with no sound of their screaming,

They will go to their nests in the distant Seven Hills, and their shapes will be seen no more in our sweet Cambrian sky.

There will be a sound of clanking shields and marching feet but it will die away in the distance,

And the years will pass, and the sound will not return,

A hundred and ten long years will pass, with the flocks and the herds less, and the beasts of the forest more.

While the Picts raid unbalked, and the Scotti ravish, and the Saxons scourge the coasts,

And the long years will pass as though Cambria were forgotten of our Gods,

As though they slept in their golden beds and did not hear our prayers.

The deep voice fell quiet while the long fingers continued to pluck the harp-strings, although in a lower key. What the music suggested to the heart was power: a great God was speaking his intent, not boastfully, because boasting is for beings of doubted power, and instead with quietness, as though he himself could not stop the works of his great hands, and with immeasurable beauty. I thought that the ravens listened with their heads bent, and a fox that had wandered onto the holy ground stood with her head up and one foot raised, still as the stone itself, and the young Moon bent down and was thinking that in all her waxings and wanings she had not heard music so like that which Gwydion played when the Sea, her mother, brought her forth, sired by the Sun.

Then Merdin sang softly and in great wonder:

Who is this who walks in the forest when the leaves are painted with frost?

When the leaves are gay in their autumn dress a little ere they fall and flutter down?

He wears a white gown, and his hair touched with gray grows in a forelock.

Last night he gazed at the stars and their grouping in the heavens and a voice in the wind told him to walk forth.

What is this he finds in an ancient ring of stones—a common thing that scarce need summon him from thought?

It is only the burrow of a wild boar, smelling of old bones and blood.

But what is this he hears as he starts to pass on?

It is the wail of a male-child.

He stops and tears at the ground in great haste and brings him forth.

Some one had left him in the woods to die, and the boar had closed his teeth on his shoulder and brought him to his burrow,

And there he would eat him when hunger ached again.

In the rear and the front of his right shoulder there are bleeding holes, but the child yet lives.

And what is this vision that the old man beholds?

It is of a child that grows to manhood carefully guarded from the King,

It is the Son of Battle with great prowess with sword and shield,

And in the same vision men make war, arms clash, and the roots of the grass drink blood.

And by that drinking, is the land of Cambria refreshed?

Do the oak trees in the holy groves again stand tall, crowned with mistletoe gray-green?

And who shall wear the crown of Cambria and sit her ancient throne?

And this is the first canto of the Song of Camlon,

And my fingers ache, and my throat wearies.

The listening fox crept away. The Moon sailed through a little wisp of cloud. Merdin beckoned me from my house of stone, and in weariness led the way homeward. I was in sight of our household, smoke making a little smudge between us and the stars when I dared speak.

"Merdin, what you told me of being son to your bastard son was not true."

"No, it wasn't. I had no sons, by law or lust, and no wife. I am wedded to the mistletoe."

"It was not a sheepdog that bit me, but a wild boar."

"The name of the boar is Droit, and he still lives."

"You told me there could be a year to make ready? Shouldn't we begin when my Lord the Sun tops the hills?"

"We will make a beginning before he sets. Now we will eat of the broken meats and sleep, for the way on is long."

With the passing days, there was very little sign of a great storm brewing. Indeed, you would have thought that the events of Beltane and May Day and after-dark had been a passing squall. On the first day of our return Merdin paid a visit to an old friend, or so he explained his absence from the homestead of about ten hours. Unless it was the start he had promised to make of our great emprise, as misty in my head as a half-remembered dream, I knew not what it was.

He had left orders that we should half-starve our old sheepdog, Evan, on the baked guts of mast-fed hogs today and every day until further notice, and turn him out at night. Now a hungry dog is a watchful dog, sleeping lightly, and hogs raised in the forest are as wary as red deer in scenting an enemy, and being strong-gutted beasts, they are wondrous brave, so I felt sure Merdin was trying to guard our house against surprise attack. On the following night, and four nights in succession, Merdin had visitors from nearby hamlets, including the blacksmith of Collen, the master of the fishing fleet on the Caer Dyv coast, and an old man, the grandson of long-dead Bedwyr of Glamorgan, one of the last of the great earls.

Thereafter Merdin and I made the short journey to Caerleon, near the mouth of the Usk, its great fort forsaken by its last, lingering garrison ninety years before I was born. Nine and ought are nine, and one and eight are nine, and two nines make eighteen. All of the Ninth Legion except that garrison, a single cohort, had marched away a hundred and ninety-nine years ago, and the sum of one and nine and nine are nineteen. Thinking of happy future things, not of sad things long ago, I thought to be a king at nineteen, with Elain for my beauteous queen.

"Look," Merdin directed with a great sweep of his arm toward the crumbling, empty, silent city. And look I must.

At every view of it heretofore I had mazed with wonder. Today it was deeper than before, although why I did not know unless, suddenly pitched into manhood, wanting to live up to it, I started to dwell on the greatness of which men were capable, and on the smallness into which they could fall. The citadel of the Legion was fully fifty acres, enclosed by a deep ditch, an earthworks with a steep, stone-faced bank, and what remained of a twelve-foot wall of stone with turrets every fifty paces. There were four gates, each with its bridge now in ruin, and stone roads ran between the gates. Within stood the remains of buildings, mainly of stone, one of the villa of the General, which in its day must have made the King's palace look like a cow-barn, others being barracks for five thousand men and officers, and perhaps granaries and armories. Outside of the ditch were the relics of many houses of wood or stone, and what Merdin said were baths with heated water, although this I could not believe, and a temple to our Goddess Belisame, whom the Romans call Minerva. Also there was an assembly place where six thousand people might sit to watch some kind of show, a world removed and yet perhaps akin to the shows a score or so of yokels might view at a fair, displaying a bear that did tricks, a clown who told jokes, and a man who could throw, catch, and keep throwing six wooden balls without dropping one, meanwhile balancing a stick on the end of his nose. Could six thousand folk be assembled in one evening anywhere on earth except Imperial Rome? Now there were hardly that many in all South Cambria.

Of all the buildings, the temple was the worst ruined and still the most beautiful. I could not get enough of looking at the few remaining upright pillars of carved stone, and it seemed then that I could truly believe all the rest that Gerald had told me about the Romans, in which case they were not men but half-gods.

"I came here to look again at yonder wall," Merdin told me. "I had wondered if it could be rebuilt as a great fort against which the King's soldiers would hurl themselves, and be slain by arrows and spears and burning pitch thrown from the top. But more than I thought has been undermined by seepage, and the rents are greater than I thought, and the art of cutting and fitting stones has been lost. Bah, I was a fool to dream of it! As Gerald has told me twenty times, victory must be won in the field."

"Merdin, were the Romans men like us Cambrians? Did they even look like us?"

"Very much like us. I have seen many images of their governors and generals carved in stone. They were shorter, I think, and legend tells that their skins were darker, but their parts were the same."

"I can hardly believe it."

"I had another reason for coming here—so that indeed you could hardly believe that the Romans were men like us. They are gone from

Britain, their great empire has decayed into warring provinces; the Goth Alaric has breached the walls of Rome itself and taken a great tribute. Still, in all our reckoning we must not omit the Romans. They have the only language in the wide world that can be transmitted, by little marks, to leather scrolls, and these may be read and understood by any one knowing Latin five hundred years later or five thousand miles away. Think of a piece of leather speaking to you like a man at your side! Rome is still a name to conjure with in all Britain. Our people will more willingly follow a king allied somehow with Rome. And according to the Song of Camlon, the great king to come will help to strengthen his throne by taking a white damosel of Roman blood for his queen."

"I don't like the sound of it," I said after a long, troubled silence.

"Did you like that part of the Song that asked, but did not tell, who would wear the crown of Cambria and sit her throne? I believe, as you do, that the Singer referred to the one who, as a babe, had been saved from the den of Droit, and whose shoulders bear the marks of his teeth, but belief is not assurance, and likelihood is not proof. It may be that he who bears those marks, and has become schooled in the use of weapons, will not be worthy of the hinted promise, will not wield the sword with enough valor and perseverance, or in some other way slack his duty and turn from the hard path. In the Second Canto of the Song of Camlon, the Singer tells of the King's choice— called the White Maiden of the Green Shore, beautiful beyond all maidens in all Britain, with the blood of the wall-guarder, the balker of the Painted Men, flowing in her blue veins."

"Why, that could be Elain of the Lake," I said with a dry mouth when Merdin had waited silent, his burning eyes fixed on mine. "She's white as a white swan."

"Elain is the daughter of a great earl, not of the Caesars."

"Hadrian built the great wall. She could easily be his descendant."

"But the guarder of the Wall was Maximus. And in Cornwall dwells his great-granddaughter, Wander, whose name in the ancient tongue means white. Ambrose, the meaning of the passage is beyond question. And if one prophecy in the Song of Camlon is not fulfilled, none will be fulfilled."

From where we stood, we could look across the wide blue estuary of the Usk, now at full tide. Its waters had flowed in this same majesty a thousand years before the first stone of Caerleon was laid, rising and falling at the beckonings of the Moon. Deep in its flood dwelt water-witches, with pearls fixed in their tresses, and a shaggy bear with webbed feet, and these remembered the first outpouring of the Song of Camlon.

Then in my mind I gazed upon Elain as she had stood tall and proud by the fire of Beltane, and her hair was the color of its palest flame, and her eyes were gray-green, and all the rest of her that I had seen was white as water-lilies in the lake of Llewelan's palace, where, perhaps, she laved. I wished I had laved beside her, and we had rested on a bed of moss, and a yearning in her eyes had reflected mine. Then when we had matched and inter-twined as the necks of mating swans, the witches had gazed at us from their crypts panting with passion, and I had got me a son before I had ever heard of Wander with the blood of Maximus in her veins. And now, most likely, I would never see Elain again. Modred could have her for his toy until I put out his mirthful eyes that had danced at the sight of her white limbs, and until I drained his veins of the red wine that had dizzied his brain.

So I turned and spoke to Merdin, in mingled sorrow and glory.

"I will wed Wander of Cornwall, so that all the prophecies will come true."

2

When we had returned to our homestead, and Merdin and Gerald and I sat on the grass out of hearing of Anna and the thralls, I asked them what four hundred yokels rising against Vortigern would do for weapons. As far as I knew, there were not twenty iron swords and iron-bound shields in all South Cambria.

They sat and looked at me with furrowed brows, unable to reply. We would get the arms somehow, I thought, for no one could brook the will of the Gods, yet the way of it was a hard riddle.

"There are many axes with leaden heads and some with bronze," Merdin replied at last with a nervous rasp in his voice. "They are a good match for long-swords."

"No, Merdin, they are not, for their cutting edge is too short," Gerald answered. "Also, our ax-heads are too small to balance well on a long shaft. Our farmers could make shields of beechwood, but they won't stand a hard blow unless iron-bound. Vortigern's front rank will have Roman shields of solid iron."

"Our farmers are expert with reaping hooks," Merdin offered feebly. "Couldn't some strategy of surprise . . . ?" And his voice died away.

"Merdin, our forces must be as well-armed as the King's, or they won't stand fast. No Roman general would have wasted his breath to speak a fact so well-known. Soldiers are only soldiers, rejoicing in battle only when they have the advantage or at least an equal chance. Also they rejoice in rich meat, good wine, and pretty girls, none of any use to dead soldiers. And there is a saying older than the wisest words in the Song of Camlon. The Gods help only those who help themselves."

"Gerald, we will help ourselves," I said. "Merdin, if by your art you could find a treasure of some great king, couldn't we take ship and buy weapons in Spain? You told me there was an armorer in every Spanish village."

"We would not have to go that far," he answered. "Enough gold will buy figs in a desert of thorn. I know of a Roman general in Brittany who will sell Roman shields for five silver pieces each, swords for twenty pieces—and ask no questions. But my art is weak when it comes to finding treasure. Treasure lies in the care of gnomes who worship fiends, not the true Gods."

We ate our supper with nothing settled but our stomachs. Yet on the following morning at least one weapon, of a queer sort, came queerly into our hands.

On the north down a brisk walker appeared, leading what at first I thought was a colt, or a well-grown calf. Still, the animal looked exactly like neither one, and I could almost be persuaded it was a lioness, a decrepit specimen of which I had once seen, brought into Ludton by mountebanks who had got her from a Roman circus, and later led about through Britain to be viewed at fairs. Then the light cleared, or else my eyes made a harder try, and I saw it was some manner of dog.

Our sheepdog, Evan, made the same discovery, and his hackles rose. But he did not bark as the pair drew nigh, and through some understanding the two brutes had reached by means no man could guess, he decided to show his best manners. On the other hand, the visiting dog scarcely deigned him a glance, and as his leader spoke to Merdin, Gerald, and me, he regarded us gravely out of large, dark eyes, and quietly waited.

He was the biggest dog I had ever seen. Some sort of mastiff, he was likely of a species bred in Ludton for sale across the channel, and used in hunting heavy game; or perhaps he was an Irish dog of war, leading the charge of the fierce Scotti in olden times. He was pitch-black except for the brown in his eyes and for reddish ankles and his dark red tongue. Although he weighed more than the heaviest jack-wolf, fully ten stone, he appeared too peaceful to be of much use either in battle or the chase.

"Her is a watchdog, and her name Cavell," the small, dark man told us in pleasant voice and tones. His use of "her" for a male dog, and his look and manner were not Cambrian and could easily be from the Avon Valley or beyond the Cotswold. But I stopped dwelling on the matter to marvel at Merdin.

"Did you say—Cavell?" he muttered. And the first sign of Merdin's great amazement was always a muttering of speech.

" 'Tis a silly name, I grant 'ee. But ol' master name her and wouldn't hear o' my calling her Big Boy, or Lubber, or any name to fit her. But her a mighty good dog right on."

"Your master must be a man of learning."

"Her can read Latin like one of 'em Christian priests from over the water. 'Ee know her well, 'ee honor. Her Llewelan of the Lake."

"He sent the great hound for me to keep?"

"That her did. He say to tell 'ee 'twould be best that the swain hide out awhile, till the wind blow strong in her favor, and 'ee need a good watchdog to warn 'ee of strangers coming nigh at night, and to tear 'em down if they be only two or three, seeking to kill 'ee and get blood-money. If they be a big passel, Cavell will hold 'em off until 'ee can slip away."

"Why doesn't Llewelan keep him? He's in danger too."

" 'Cause her and the wench take off from home, to 'scape the King's men."

"Is the dog well-trained?"

"Her's like 'ee never see! Her can smell a stranger like a Greek sutler can smell siller. Mind you, I don't say her can smell good up the wind, but her peepers is amazing sharp, and she can listen out like a red deer hind wi' fawn. Her run all night around 'ee homestead, a mile or more out, and if her discover a stranger her bay to wake old Bran in her mossy grave. And if 'ee say 'Go get him'—down, Cavell!"

For the dog's whole demeanor had instantly changed. His magnificent muscles flexed, a look of wild alertness came into his countenance, and his gentle brown eyes had a deadly glare as he confronted us new acquaintances. Just as quickly the ferocious spell passed off, and he lay down at the countryman's feet.

" 'Ee see what I mean. When her master say 'em words, her's off like an arry from a bow, and then her don't stop to worry, but kills straight off. No use of the wretch throwing her spear or crouching down behind it. Cavell, her watches it, and swerves a little, or runs in under the point. Mostly her kills by tearing out the big vein in the neck, one leap and bite so fast 'ee can hardly see it, or if the scoundrel be a-running, her bites her in the neck behind and breaks it. Now pray one of 'ee go into the house and get three bones. No matter if they sheep bones—Cavar won't sink to killing no sheep. I need the bones to learn her 'ee are her new masters."

"There is a woman who lives with us, and two churls," I said. "Will he bother them?"

"No, for the smell of one of 'ee will be on all of 'ee a-living in the house. To tell truth, I need only one bone to learn her to 'bey all three of 'ee, but I'll do it hansome."

Gerald hurried off and returned with three beef bones, well-gnawed but not quite bare. The yokel took them, showed them to Cavell, then handed one of them to Merdin. "Come up and hold it out to her," he instructed. "She'll take it from 'ee hand as gentle as a wench takes a flower."

It happened so, and twice again when Gerald and I made our offerings.

"Is Cavell good for hunting?" I asked.

"Not p'ticlar. Her a king among dogs, and likes two-legged quarry. She'll help 'ee kill wolves, or a big boar wi' tushes. Her won't fool with no sow or shoats, no yet with no deer. But her will catch hares and such like for 'ee supper."

"He'll be very useful," Merdin said. "I want you to thank your master in our behalf as soon as you see him."

"I don't know when 'twill be."

"Then I can't write an epistle to him, because he'd not get it." There might be even a better reason, I was thinking—there was no quill or inkpot in our house, or any sign that Merdin could read and write Latin.

"Oh, 'ee'll be seeing her, and the wench too, before many days. I half forgot to tell 'ee."

"You don't mean it." And I thought that event was moving faster than the old man had foreseen.

"That is, 'ee honor, if they're not catched by the King's men. I don't reckon they'll be catched, 'cause Old Earl scraped up all her gold and siller and fixed for a journey, and hired boatmen to meet her at the mouth of Aeron first thing after coming home from seeing the look o' things at court. Besides, her had a full day's warning. Her told me to tell 'ee there was much to talk o'er together, and much to do. They'll be in the mouth of Taff on the night of the full Moon, and pray 'ee build a little fire on the bank so her can find 'ee."

"So we will, and I thank you too for the safe delivery of Cavell and the messages."

"'Twas by the old earl's bidding, and her told me if I bitched it her'd flay me alive, and I reckon her'd do it if the wench, too tender o' heart in these bad times, didn't bid her hold."

"Will you eat before you start back? We've good mutton broth and wheat-cakes."

"Nay, 'ee honor, I've a hare in my pouch what Cavell catched for me, and I'll roast and eat her whole. Cavell, 'ee stay here. 'Ee hear me, Cavell? And good day to 'ee all."

Cavell gazed mournfully after him as long as he remained in sight, then came and licked my hand.

3

The full Moon topped the hills in broad daylight. She was enormous past belief, persuading me that her bed was not nearly as far distant as the dome of the sky where she reigned; yet away in Kent, a good hundred and fifty miles, she was also said to come up in the east, so I took it she must sleep at night in the Strait of Dover, and how she returned there after her western setting addled my head. Perhaps she put out her light and returned in the dark unseen, after only a cat-nap. In any case, she must be bigger than all Radnor Forest to loom so large at two hundred miles away, and fly faster than a pochard duck to go and get back, rising high in the air to boot, from sundown to sundown.

Musing over this, while Merdin, Gerald, and I sat a little way back from the reeds of Taff, helped to pass the time until Llewelan's boat should come in sight. I was glad to be alive in a world of such wonders as the Moon. Yet hardly a lesser wonder, or so it seemed to my young heart, was a maiden as white as she, who, if the countryman spoke truth, might be making a little journey up our channel, drawing nearer to me at every stroke of the oars. The Moon was a Goddess, while Elain was as mortal as myself. I had taken the hand of Elain, and heard her laugh and scold, and caressed her soft skin, and touched my lips to hers, whereby I had felt tall and proud, while I could only gaze upon the Moon and gape like a witless fool.

Tonight I might get no more than a glimpse of Elain, then the oars would dip again and she would fade from my sight. So I reflected, mumbling it under my breath, to ward off fiends. Plenty of them dwelt along this lonely estuary, and a mortal's least expectation of good fortune brought on their fiendish tricks. Truly, though, in my closed throbbing heart lay hope for much more.

Why had Merdin ordered Gerald and me to bring bow-and-arrows and our swords and shields? Also he had had us fix a big sheepskin bag of provisions—dried meat and beans, wheat-cakes, salt and fat for frying—along with fish-hooks and lines, cord for setting snares, a cooking pot, and an ax with a bronze head. Perhaps he had intended them for the two fugitives if they were in need, but he had been mumbling in his beard off and on since hearing from Llewelan's messenger of the price on my head. So the long wait did not irk me, and only gave scope to my dreams.

Our Lady the Moon was up the breadth of my two hands before a bonfire would attract the attention of boatmen in mid-river. So when I struck sparks with flint on a bit of dried moss, blew it to burning, and set it under a pile of dry reeds and driftwood, I recited an old charm:

> *Leap, flame,*
> *Remember my name.*
> *For this wood,*
> *Bring good.*
> *Keep me warm,*
> *Save me harm,*
> *Blaze bright,*
> *All night,*
> *Death's dire,*
> *Life's fire*
> *Darkness lighten,*
> *Fortune brighten.*

I had scarcely returned to my seat when I made out a minute dark spot on the sheen of moonlit waters far down the estuary. I made sure that it moved before I called Gerald's attention to it. He found it at once, but Gerald and I must give patient directions to Merdin's fading eyes before they could pick it up. With the rising tide under and behind it, it made good way, and before long it showed unquestionably a boat, manned by four oarsmen and carrying two passengers. They were being guided by our bonfire.

In a little while more I could not have taken oath before Lud that the tall passenger was Llewelan, although being sure of it as of my own hand, but I would have pledged my soul that the less tall, more slender shape beside him was Elain's. I had seen her in far-away Radnor at the King's court, and now I saw her in a stone's throw, and only a few hours' pace of my long legs from our homestead. I would never again doubt the glory of my fortune, as long as it would last. I took my eyes off her yellow hair to glance with gratitude at the yellow fire, smacking its lips and reveling in its brief life, that came out of my Lord the Sun.

Gerald and I waded knee-deep into the flood to help the oarsmen beach the boat. Still she grounded too far out for Elain to step dry-shod on shore, so when she stood up, I encircled her legs with my arm just below her buttocks, and as she stood upright, her feet in my left hand, I wafted her to the land. Her father did not gaze in our direction. Merdin looked down.

There followed instantly a little parley between Merdin and Llewelan, in hearing of all of us, in which I stood ready to put an oar at the first opening. It was brief and to the point, and the truth came plain that the time was short, and the pass serious.

"To put it bluntly, Merdin," Llewelan said, "There's a price on my head, not as high as the price on Ambrose's, but still a rich prize for its taker."

"On what grounds are you proclaimed?"

"Vortigern needs no grounds, except that on which he stands as King. He gave some excuses that the yokels won't swallow, but that will be good enough for some loyal subject to glean fifty pieces of silver, all in good conscience."

"Still, I'd like to hear 'em."

"I'm proclaimed as a traitor to his realm, seeking the return of Druid laws to mock and defy the King's law. Well, if that is treason, I've a hanging due. The Druid judges had to answer to the Gods, while the King's judges only to the King, and all Britain was a fitter place to live. Also he knows I am in Ambrose's party, win or lose, and the King must make an example of me, one of the last of the great earls. I intend to seek refuge in the Mendip Hills, once part of my domain, and where my name is not forgot and carries some small weight. And while there, I mean to recruit two or three score of their archers, the best in Britain and most likely in all Europe, to serve in the coming war."

"I wish you could get two hundred," Gerald said quickly.

"My friend, I'll do well to muster two score. Men are less and beasts more in the Mendip, as elsewhere on our God-forsaken island. Besides, the hillmen have suffered greatly from wandering bands of robbers, who covet their cloth and lead and iron."

My heart had tumbled and spilled part of its hope, but some of this remained, because of something I had once heard regarding the folk of the Mendip.

"You propose to take with you your daughter Elain?" I asked.

"No, I cannot, and that is why I journey this round-about way to speak to great Merdin. Ambrose, I cannot take Elain into the Mendip because of a barrier intangible as air, but as strong as Hadrian's Wall in the days of its glory. Those hillmen trace their descent through their mothers, not their sires. It is a custom almost as old as their own hills, and as solid. They are a small, dark people of lost and ancient origin, with a ridge of bone under their eyebrows, and their law decrees that while men of other stocks may come among them, to sell salt, to buy cloth, or sometimes a visitor may even become one of the husbands of their daughters, no woman of our tall, fair race may come through their passes. Every clan traces through the female line to some daughter of their Gods. To tell you the strange truth, I doubt if they know that the men have anything to do with the generations, and instead they believe their women become pregnant by basking in moonlight, or laving in certain pools, or walking in mist and rain. They make offerings to a round stone, with a hole in it, not to the pillars of Hercules. Call them fools if you will, this is the way they preserve their tribal entity. And as a little consequence, Elain has no safe refuge from the King's fury against me—unless Merdin can offer her one."

A spark of hot desire flew into my brain and set it smoldering as though it were dry moss. I spoke quickly, while Merdin was sucking his breath.

"The King's fury is as hot against Merdin as against you, Llewelan. His beard is white from many winters, and the most he can do is safeguard himself until the battle you spoke of can be won. Now I, Ambrose, must also safeguard myself, for we are not nearly ready to do battle, and the King's murderers will range far and wide."

"That is full true, Ambrose," Merdin broke in, "as my aging mind has been slow to accept, and did not wholly accept until Llewelan sent the giant hound. But I meant that your flight should begin tonight, in that we were journeying this far eastward, and that was why I had you bring your weapons and provisions."

"Fear not, Llewelan, that I shall survive this period of waiting," I went on. "I am at home in the darkest forest, along with the gray wolf. And by your leave, I will take Elain with me, and keep her safe until you can return from the Mendip Hills."

Llewelan looked me long in the face, then turned to the old seer.

"Merdin, have you no better plan?" he asked. "If Elain is captured, I will have no choice but surrender, but Ambrose is but one sword——"

"I am not even that, old friend," Merdin replied. "If enough of the King's men come for me, I must fly, and I am too old and lame to have care for any skin but my own wrinkled skin. Let her go with Ambrose. No doubt remains that he too must play the fox and hole in a dark den until the word and the faith are carried throughout Cambria. But mayhap I may think of a better hiding-place than the deep wood."

"My daughter is a maiden——" Llewelan paused, glanced at Elain, then at me.

"And my ward is the rightful King of Britain," Merdin answered quietly.

It was the first time he had said so in plain words. I was glad that the Sun had set, with the waters and the sky no longer blue, and instead the land and river lay dim and obscure under the Moon. I could believe it now. A song as true as the Song of Camlon came softly to my ears, and if its notes were the lap of water in the reeds, the rustle of a breese, and the cries of waking waterfowl, still its burden was the same, and the healed holes in my shoulders front and back itched fiercely. The seal was put on it by the action of Llewelan, a great earl.

Looking at me, he touched his knee to the ground.

I believed all this in intense belief and in no great astonishment, only a quiet wonder. What I could not quite believe was Elain, standing a little back, her eyes raised and fixed on some star potent in her fate, and saying not a word. But as I looked at her she took a long step forward and spoke.

"My lord," she said to Llewelan, "will the King-to-be swear by the Circle of the Sun that he'll return me to your care with my virgin knot still fast? If he won't, we'll run the roads together, come what may."

"Will you, Ambrose?" Merdin asked.

I reflected quickly. The set of her beautiful face told me that she meant what she said. My sudden kingliness ran out of me, and besides, I remember an old rustic saying of Cornishmen. "Iffen 'ee can't catch a salmon in 'ee net, make do wi' a char."

"Yes, Merdin, I will."

"Then bring forth the Sign of the Sun you wear around your neck, and hold it in your right hand, and make your pledge."

I did so, and at the same time crossed the index and middle finger of my left hand. Now that is the sign foul Christians make when they vow to renounce their false Gods and worship the true Gods; still, it was not meant to nullify my vow. Surely I intended to keep it in letter and spirit, not beat the fiend Obidicut around the gooseberry bush! All I knew was, Elain looked beautiful as a wood-nymph. Also I remembered what old wives warn their daughters—that a part of a man is too far below his chin to hear him plighting troth.

"Well, if it's settled, where will you go?" Llewelan asked me solemnly.

"Perhaps the Exmoor Forest. When the rains have washed out our tracks——"

"Not the forest, the moor itself," Merdin broke in. "Not far from Porlock Bay, where the boat can put you, and close by the remnant of a lost road, stands Pillicock Hill. The name appears in the Song of Camlon——"

"Does it?" Llewelan asked quickly. "I don't remember it——"

"I'm sure of it. And on the crest of the hill is a stone tower, built by Romans or by our forefathers before the Romans came. It affords a good lookout, and since it's believed to be guarded by gnomes, hunters would not look for you there. The streams abound in fish. You can set snares for hares and heath-hens. Deer come out of the woods to graze. You could live well."

I was pleased with the prospect, and perhaps Elain the like, for she stood a little different than before, with a different cock of her head. Then the chance came for Merdin to tell me something in private.

"That tower has always quickened my curiosity," he said. "There is nothing to indicate it could have any military use. Some one built it for some good purpose—but what? And you know, Ambrose, that the main business of gnomes is to guard treasure."

"So I've always heard."

"Could King Lear himself have had the tower raised, that year he was known to wander, half-mad, on the Cornish moors? In those days, the Cornishmen knew the arts of cutting and fitting stones; and they were loyal to Lear in his war with the Prince of Cornwall. I had intended to see if that tower was the depository for his treasure, for this was known to disappear from his vaults when his daughter Regan and her husband drove him forth. Now you can attend to the matter for me."

"That I will. Was it a great treasure?"

"So our books say, amassed in war with the Scotti. Perhaps enough to buy four hundred swords and shields. But there will be another treasure in that tower as entrancing to a lusty fellow as gold and jewels; and there will pass long days in which it steals into the mind, and long nights to lie wakeful. Abjure it if you can."

"Merdin, I've taken a solemn pledge——"

"So did Tristan, when he went forth to bring beauteous Isolde of the White Hands to his uncle, King Mark, her betrothed. Much can be forgiven the King-to-be, but Llewelan knows you are betrothed to Wander by the Song of Camlon, and he would take it amiss if you put the Light of His Eyes with child."

"You speak of the King-to-be. Merdin, we will be parting soon, and the time has come to tell me the name and the lineage of the infant you found in the boar's burrow, and how he came there."

"Aye, it is time. The truth can not be proven before the people except by the sword, but there's no doubt of it, as I knew when I saw your face. Vortigern's first wife was Ina of the Wood, daughter of King Rische of North Wales, and through him descended from the God Artay, whom the Romans called Mercury. But Vortigern hated her, and his true love was Enid, sister of the Queen of Cornwall. It chanced that Ina and Enid were with child in the same year, and teemed in the same week. In her favored place, Enid prevailed upon the King to have Ina's babe cast forth into the forest for wolves or boars to eat, so that her own babe, Modred, could be King of Cambria.

Not long after this Ina died in the night, with a scullion's knife through her breast."

"Which of the two babes was born first?" I asked, leaning forward, "Modred or the other?"

"The other, Ina's babe, came forth and uttered its first wail at sundown of All Hallows' Eve, Modred not until after midnight."

"That is good. I have only one more question, then I'll start forth for Pillicock Hill as soon as the gear is ready. It is the custom of courts to give a name to a king's son the instant that he breathes, usually the name of the god from whom he descends, although later a more handy name is given. Was I honored with a name of such sort before I was cast out to die?"

"An old woman, in waiting to Queen Ina, said that she kissed you and called you Artay."

Deep in my heart it seemed I could almost remember the kiss of greeting. Surely I must have known soft arms and a sweet teat or I would not be so conjured by these on young and pretty maidens.

"Artay is an ugly name, and I'll stick to Ambrose for a while longer," I told Merdin. "But when you had dug me out of the bear's den, who gave me suck until I was weaned?"

"The woman Anna, who had lately lost her own babe. She did not speak in words, but as she looked down at you, sucking noisily like a pig, her face spoke."

"Well, I'm glad that she did." And some of my gladness was caused by a slight thing—that part of the story Merdin had told me in my boyhood had been true. Perhaps the story he had told me tonight was completely true, since it hung together well; still, I could not swear to it, because Merdin was a great gamester, as Gerald had told me, and he would not let the telling of lies interfere with his winning. Perhaps almost no one did so, how great or how small the prize, Gods and men alike, and particularly women, and perhaps I had inherited from him a great facility in the art. Then I remembered, with a start, that as far as I knew, I had none of Merdin's blood.

"It must be that Vortigern guessed that I was his son Artay, saved from the beasts, as soon as he looked at me."

"Ambrose, I think now that he guessed it, and well nigh knew it, long before then; and fool that I am, I couldn't credit him with the cunning, and sent you defenseless against Modred's sword."

"I was not altogether defenseless," I said with the demon Pride fastening on my heart. "This time I cut only a hunk from his big muscle. Next time——" But a big star winked at our Lady the Moon and I bit my tongue. "Merdin, I would like to start across the channel with Elain as soon as possible, so not to shorten the distance between us and the hunters. Is it needful that we return to the homestead before putting forth? Llewelan has an extra robe of sheepskins."

"I thought you would see that. Keep your mind off beds, Ambrose my son, and apply it more to battle and the kingship of all Britain. No, there is no need of a trip home. You are well-supplied for the journey."

"I wish I had thongs made from the hide of a spotted bull, for tying up any gnomes I might catch, but perhaps ordinary leather will do as well."

"It happens that I have such thongs, in the rucksack."

I wondered if Merdin had been told the need of them in a dream. Surely his head was not long enough to have foreseen tonight's twists and turns of Fortune, the will of the Gods.

4

I had thought that so young a maiden might bemoan her starting off with a swain on a perilous adventure, parting with her sire for how long only the Gods knew, but she kissed him tenderly, wished him the blessings of Lud and of the Christian God, and with eyes dry and very bright climbed into the boat. It was the best lesson I had had so far in the urgency of her own and Llewelan's flight. Evidently their race this far had been nip and tuck.

I had loaded in the gear, and presently the oars dipped, the dark water rippled on our bow and streamed bubbling from our aft, and the yellow flame of our watchfire slowly dimmed. Elain looked back from time to time. I could not begrudge her this, despite the joy I took in looking ahead. Before long the only light was of twinkling stars in the heavens and drowned stars in the sea, for the Moon was hidden by bands of cloud, and the blaze I had kindled burned itself out.

"There is a little space aft where I can spread the sheepskin robe," I told her. "It is dry, and by lying cramped, you may go to sleep."

"I thank Your Highness." And whether she paid me this address on her own behalf or because she had seen Llewelan kneel to me I did not know.

The voyage was about thirty miles from Taffmouth to Porlock Bay, where we would disembark to proceed to Pillicock Hill. I had never visited that part of the great land south of the channel, itself large enough to comprise the kingdom of a not too vaunting king, now under the nominal sway of King Cador of Cornwall. But Merdin had given me good directions, describing landmarks such as streams and Tors, and I had little fear of losing our way. Elain slept until daylight, and I the like, sitting on a thwart. When she waked, she asked me how long before we would set foot on dry land. Three hours or more, I told her. Then she bade me turn my back, the oarsmen to do the same, while she attended to her person. I had never beheld such delicacy of feeling except, strangely enough, in Anna; and my heart warmed to the wench, and I resolved not to be hasty with her, or in the least harsh, at least as long as she was agreeable to my wishes.

On all the seven-league breadth of the channel we saw only one boat, she a trawler of some sort, almost out of sight in the distance. Yet Merdin had told me that in Roman times these waters had been so stirred by passing craft that the herring shotted before their season and the fat ducks wasted to flesh and bone from everlasting flushing.

When we had made our landing I spoke to the chief of the boatmen.

"I've no money with me, but I'll give you some of our provision."

" 'Ee'll need it all on those cursed moors, unless 'ee can live on wind and fog," the man answered with spirit. "Besides, our lord, he gave us siller, for all we'd made the trip for naught but his bare word, and kept a closed mouth besides."

They made off, and a little way above the beach Elain and I found rain-washed ruts worn by heavy carts in the long-ago. These led us to the remains of a Roman road, although not in the least like Watling Street, and which had never been more than an earthen causeway prevented from washing clean away by heather and deep-rooted grass. As it was, runnels broke through it, and often I had to carry Elain, a pleasant enough chore, for at every ride I clasped her tighter. Some of the waters were so deep and wide that I feared I must swim for it, Elain on my back, returning for my heavy pack. Still she showed no alarm and Fortune had it that I never waded above my waist.

By now we knew what the boatmen meant by "cursed moors." Before now I had trod moorland in holes and corners of Cambria, but never before had seen it wide as a sea. It was a wilderness of wild heath, gray rock, and black water as far as sight could cast, with now and then patches of low forest growing on the flanks of huge masses of granite, streaked with green where moss grew in their seams, and of strange and forbidding shape. These Merdin called Tors, and no doubt they were named for one of our mightiest Gods, Tor of the Thunder. If he had raised them, only he and the other Gods knew why.

The only mists we saw lay over the big pools, this being a day of ardent sunshine; and the air felt soft and warm, although it was in motion swifter than I could hardly realize, and made a lonesome sound in the vast loneliness. Not one work of human hands broke the spell of infinite solitude—no field was in corn, no shepherd tended his flocks. Yet Merdin had told me that long ago flint workers had dwelt here, and some had buried their dead in long burrows, and some had set big stones in circles. The world had been young then, I supposed; Lud had been pleased with it and set himself in the sky to watch over it. Now the Romans had come and gone and the world was old, and I deemed it might not last much longer, with the beasts increasing and men decreasing; and I had better be about my chores, before Lud sickened of its sight and broke it in little pieces.

"How are we going to live?" Elain asked. "The food you brought won't last long."

"Wait and see."

"I guess that even a little chance is better than none at all, which we'd had if we'd stayed in Cambria."

"How much do you weigh, Elain?"

"Eight stone."

"'Twill be more when you leave here."

If I had thought twice, I would not have said this. There is more than one way for a pretty wench to gain weight. Still, I reckoned I could fatten her a little off the country, bleak, empty, and forbidding though it seemed. I had noticed swirls in the ponds and creeks made by fishes of varied sorts, wild ducks winged back and forth and basked on the sunlight waters, and presently I saw tracks of red deer crossing the road. Maybe I could find some bee-trees, and wild berries would be ripening soon.

We had walked, I reckoned, for two hours, when the road came to an abrupt end, as though its builders had suddenly forsaken the undertaking. I had a picture in my head of a man in a toga, an important fellow, on a horse or hurrying on shanks' mare, perhaps with a small following, bringing a parchment to the chief roadmaker, and the latter looking at it, or asking the bringer to read it aloud, and then he crying out on Jove, either in anger or relief; and if it were a true picture it had rehearsed a scene of a century and more ago. And here, according to Merdin's directions, we should find an old cart-road straggling off toward a big Tor about a mile away. I got down and searched for it in the rank grass, and before long I found it—a pair of deep-cut ruts. The same road-builders, whether soldiers or pressed men from the town, must have been made to lay it, cursing their luck, and to build a tower too if the tower was a fact and not an old man's dream. But they had finished whatever the job was— its purpose had failed or succeeded—and then they had left the country to eagles that could fly instead of being carried on a stick, fowls of many sorts, furred and finny folk, and some old marsh-donkeys, one of which brayed at us from a patch of thickets.

I gazed at the only Tor toward which the road wended, and could see no tower to show this was Pillicock Hill. Yet when the view shifted a little more, an abrupt cliff shunted silently aside, I made out an edifice about thirty feet high, commanding the only slope that could be easily climbed. Its top projected a little from its base with what looked like a small balcony from which defenders could hurl arrows and pitch. It seemed built of well-fitted stones, and between the stones the moss of the ages had grown and greened.

We had drawn within a quarter of mile when some sort of a creature ran from the door and vanished in some thickets. It ran on two legs in a curious motion, and it was not tall enough to be a man, and yet the body and head resembled one. I had heard of gnomes all my days, and many folk had seen them, but this was my first glimpse of one of the eerie creatures. My neck prickled fiercely, and I considered it almost certain he was guarding the treasure of King Lear, and I meant to get my hands on it before I left the trove. Still, I said nothing of the matter to Elain, lest she be afraid.

We climbed to the tower and had no trouble entering the ground floor. Oddly enough, this ground was pure chalk, carved out of what must be a chalk outcropping adjacent to the granite cliffs. From this led a ladder, once of hewn lumber but repaired so often that it was more wild vine than wood, and I was glad of the sword at my side when I climbed up, Elain staunch behind me.

We came to the main room of a tower with a dry floor of planks very little rotted, and plainly this was the living-quarters of the guardian gnomes. In one corner was a bed of deerskins, and scattered about lay some clay utensils, of a shape and design I had never seen, and one of them held the remains of a meat stew and another a handful of heath-blossoms set in water. I stared like a witless man, for it had never occurred to me that supernatural beings such as gnomes must eat like mortals, let alone like the sight and smell of flowers. But when I came to think of it our household elves drank the milk we set out for them, chasing off the cat that one of our churls loved, and sometimes they left bright pieces of quartz, once a very beautiful agate, to show they were pleased with us.

In one corner was a pile of rubbish that I had not looked at yet, being eager to climb to the balcony and see what I could see. Indeed, I saw nothing but the lonesome moor, and when I returned to the main room Elain held something in her hand.

"Do you know what this is?"

"It's a musical instrument of some kind."

"It's a Roman lyre. I saw one once before. I found it among the old things in the corner."

And that played hob with my hopes that this tower had been built by King Lear, as a depository for his treasure. No lyre had ever been seen in Britain since before the Romans came.

"Do you think you could put in new strings?" she asked.

82

"I don't see why not. We have no sheep to take their guts and make strings, but swans have stout guts, and they ought to be better than sheep guts, because swans sing so sweetly."

"Now, that stands to reason," Elain told me.

"I saw a good many, and I can spear them in the shallow pools, or kill some with arrows, and if this fails I know how to make a bird-lime out of ground chalk and a kind of sticky clay found in cat-tail beds."

"Still—you wouldn't know how to play it, would you?"

"I think I could pluck some music of it, with a little practice."

"I hope so. It will be so long between sundown and dark."

I climbed again to the balcony, and this time I made out a rustling in the thickets where the gnome had disappeared. With a little catch in my heart—for it is either good luck or very bad to address supernatural beings—I called to him.

"Ho, there! Who are you?"

I must say I did not expect an answer, for I had never heard that gnomes could understand or reply to human speech.

"I am Pillicock," came a full-ringing, manly voice.

"Nonsense. Pillicock is the name of a hill, not a gnome."

"'Pillicock sat on Pillicock Hill.' Have you ne'er heard the song? Hey, ho, nonny!"

This was not a stranger thing than much else that had happened, still I felt creepy, and Elain at the foot of the stairs gazed with wide eyes.

"We mean you no harm," I called, "if you will give us the treasure you are guarding."

"Unless you go the way you came, I'll give you aching bones, and spider-bite, and chilblain, and the itch. All that I can do with the charms I know. Go away, soldier, with the angel-girl. There have been no soldiers here this hundred years."

"I'm not a soldier. I am a king."

"I, Pillicock, am King of Pillicock Hill, and you have usurped my tower."

"You can have it back when I'm done."

I left him to think it over and went down to eat a midday meal with Elain. We ate from our supplies, after which she rested a little while in the day's heat, I surrendering to day-dreams as now and then I glanced at her calm brow, closed eyes, and listened in this deep silence to her quiet breathing. In the afternoon I wanted to venture with her onto the moors and shoot something succulent for our supper, and was hard put to it what to do with our gear and supplies in our absence. I had thought to hang them out of Pillicock's reach on nails, a few of which I carried in my kit, when Elain made the discovery that the door of the lower floor of the tower had a big bronze key, which we need only turn behind us and carry with us.

"It seems a pity to lock the King of the Gnomes out of his own tower," she told me, her eyes wide.

"Gnomes are known to be evil," I answered, "and in the service of demons."

We went forth, and I stalked a wild mallard on a pool and killed it cleanly with an arrow at thirty paces. While it did not seem likely we would bag any more game on this short trip, I felt the presence of good fortune, which might have taken the lovely shape of this tall girl at my side; and when we had gone a little further, the Gods sent a swan to a shallow mere, and there she sat pruning her feathers, paying no more heed to us than though we were marsh-donkeys. Plainly it was their design that I repair the old lyre and see what music I could pluck from it, to pass the long evenings.

When we returned I cleaned both fowls, saving the guts of the mallard for fish-bait and those of the swan to clean, treat, and dry as Merdin had taught me. Pillicock did his cooking in a brush shelter behind the tower, and here we made a fire, spitting the mallard, proposing to hang the plucked swan for another day. As Elain was preparing the meal and I sat at ease save for fuel cutting, we heard sounds in the brushwood all about us, and what could we believe other than they were Pillicock's footsteps, as he watched us from his covert? I thought that even Merdin, who had had many dealings with fairies, witches, and the like, had never sat with a kind of equanimity in twenty paces of a goblin spy.

I split the roast duck with the knife Gerald had furnished me. When we each ate half, she gnawed so daintily that I, soon to be King, was half-abashed, and wished for a rag to wipe my chin. Then when we went back to our quarters, we walked hand in hand a distance, both of us busy with our thoughts. I wished I could look into her head. It might be that she had caught a little of the fever that consumed me, although truly she showed no sign of it, her face being tranquil and her gray-green eyes grave.

I spread our sheepskin robe for her bed and was preparing to lie down on Pillicock's mangy deerskins when she looked at me, swallowed painfully, and spoke.

"Don't you think, my lord, that you should carry the gnome's skins up to the balcony and drop them down for his use? Maybe if we treat him kindly he won't lay on the plagues he threatened us with."

"Why, it's a good notion. At least it would be well to get him in the habit of trusting us, so when I bait a trap for him I can catch him."

"I feel sorry for him, somehow—living all alone in this lonely place —maybe guarding a treasure—perhaps for a thousand years. Ambrose, won't the bare floor be hard to your bones?"

"I can stand it."

"My sire told me an old tale of a princess and a king's son who slept in the same bed with a naked sword between them."

"I've not heard the story, but it could well be true."

"If you wish for us to do it, I'd have no objection."

So that was the way we made our bed, lying down half-dressed, and the cold iron assuaged my heat a little, for it came to me if I were false to him tonight, he might be false to me in battle. Elain was sound asleep, sometimes humming snatches of songs, long before my eyes would close. About two hours before sunrise the night turned chill, perhaps from a sea-breese waking. I came wide awake as Elain stirred, and then she did something that she did not know, and I know not why it gave me such pleasure, out of all proportion to its little cause. Half-asleep, she took hold of the sword and laid him on the far side of our bed, then squirmed close to me and fitted her warm, sweet body against my back.

By the Gods, instead of being possessed by lust, I felt tenderly toward her, and rejoiced to give of her of my body's natural heat; and although I could hardly believe it, I felt no shame over not taking advantage of her trust in me, or any less the man! What did I do, but go back to sleep myself! It must be that some good fairy who had blessed her at her borning had touched my eyelids with her charmed fingers. When again I awakened, the Sun shone through the barred window, my sword once more lay between Elain and me, and her face was ruddy as a child's, perhaps from blushing in her slumber.

Chapter Four
The Visitors

On our rising we ate only enough wheat-cakes to stay our stomachs, and at once spitted the swan over a slow fire. As heavy as a lamb, she took a deal of baking before she browned, and her fat dripping and sizzing was a pleasant sight and sound. Then she gave forth a delectable smell, so when at last Elain and I fell to, we ate like harvest hands. Still a great part of her carcass was left, and instead of saving it for our supper, Elain made shift to leave it for Pillicock. Remembering that the more he was tamed, the easier he would be to catch and bind, whereupon a sound enough thrashing with a willow would make him disclose his hoard.

I caught a fleet, good glimpse of him that afternoon at no more than twenty paces. Plainly gnomes varied in feature and form from the common description, because his face looked human enough except for a certain coarseness, and if his powerful body had been perched on full-length legs, he could have passed for a human being.

"Pillicock, we are leaving this carcass for your dinner," Elain said, knowing he would hear her in his covert.

"And for that, my lady, the plagues I will put on you will not be quite so heavy," he answered in a manly voice. And suddenly it had dawned on me that he spoke our good Cambrian speech, not some outlandish tongue. Perhaps he had guarded some Cambrian treasure before he had been forced to yield it up and had been appointed by the King of Gnomes to a new watch.

Such was our lives for a matter of a fortnight. The gnome grew tamer every day, and when Elain walked about alone, he often came shyly up to her, always with some little offering, such as a water-lily, or a bouquet of heath-flowers, and once a wooden horn filled with wild honey. Meanwhile he kept a sharp eye out for me, and at first sight would dash on his short legs into the thickets. I wondered where he slept, now that we had deposed him of his tower I could see no sign of his making a bed of leaves and grass in the open; and after a night of heavy rain his garments of deerskin looked bone-dry.

I was half-afeared to eat the honey, lest it contain poison or some evil charm, but when Elain ate greedily, I was ashamed not to partake, and truly it was delicious, and caused not even cramps. One night I got out linen line to prepare a snare, to be baited with a wheat-cake of which he was passing fond. When, at her question, I told Elain of my plan, I had half-expected her to protest, she having such queer notions of what should or should not be done. What I did not expect from an earl's daughter to a prince of Cambria was an outburst of anger. You would have thought my own royal blood would enforce some due punishment. Instead I did not raise my voice in reply, the same as when she had railed at me on Beltane Eve, before I had heard Merdin sing of Camlon. Why I remained so meek, at first my soul did not confide.

"Is that the way you treat people who are kind to you?" she demanded harshly. "Returning evil for good!"

"Gnomes can't be called people," I answered. "They are devil-spawn. And when he brings you gifts, he's up to some devilish trick."

"Don't judge others by yourself. You've a base heart, while Pillicock is a harmless child of nature. I pity the poor people if you ever become King."

"We won't punish you for your offense to our place and person," I said loftily.

"Try to punish me if you dare! And what do you mean by 'we'? Do you think you are King already? What are you but a rustic from the wilds of Taff, in terror of Modred's sword?"

"Elain——"

"And tonight I'll sleep on the floor! I don't want to touch you or smell you."

"What ails you? Has Pillicock bewitched you? You know how I've saved the wheat-cakes to bait him with, giving you your share but eating none myself. The Gods meant me to become King. I can't do it without the treasure that Pillicock guards."

The green sheen on her eyes dimmed a little.

"I admit you were generous with the cakes. I take back what I said about you being afraid of Modred, for I've heard that you fought him bravely, as a true prince. Yes, and I honor you for your gentleness with me, although it may be a vile trick to take my maidenhead. Will you believe me, Ambrose, that all the whippings and scourgings you could give Pillicock would never make him reveal the treasure? You should see his back, not an inch of it unseamed by lashes——"

"How do you know?"

"Because he showed it to me, and told me how he stood fast. He had been caught by Gwyn, the King's hangman, when he went to hang some rebels in the Black Mountains. Pillicock was only a young gnome then, and couldn't run very fast, and Gwyn's horsemen rode him down. Gwyn brought him to King Vortigern, who wanted to make him do tricks to make the court laugh—the only gnome owned by any king in Britain. But Pillicock is proud in some way I don't understand, and he refused. Vortigern had him whipped terribly— at least the lash made him jump about, the King said—sometimes he wielded the whip himself—but Pillicock would die rather than yield. And, Ambrose, don't get that shine in your eyes when I speak the King's name. What he did to Pillicock was only a little worse than you proposed to do."

"That's not true. I was going to whip him to make him surrender the treasure, to use for buying weapons so I can take my rightful place. I was going to tie him with thongs cut from a spotted cow-hide, as the Gods provide. King Vortigern wanted only to make sport."

"Well, he didn't make it. Queen Ina fooled him, by the Gods' consent, and helped Pillicock escape. He came to this hill, and named it after himself, and made his abode in the old tower."

I was suddenly weak in the belly. "But Merdin said that Pillicock Hill was in the Song of Camlon."

"I think Merdin made that up. My father, Llewelan, didn't re- member hearing of it. Merdin thought this tower was a good place to look for treasure, and wanted us to come here, since we had to go somewhere to hide. He shouldn't lie about the Song of the Gods, but maybe he does—a little."

"He'd not dare tamper with it very much. Too many people know it. But think of this, Elain. If Pillicock came here in Queen Ina's time, running away from the court, how can we be sure there's a treasure here? It's the business of gnomes to guard treasure—everyone knows that. Do you suppose the Gods sent him some sort of a guide— maybe one of their servants disguised as an old marsh-donkey— because the treasure here needed guarding?" And I looked hopefully into her face, forgetting all about her spiteful speech of a few minutes ago.

"It's possible," she answered. "And somehow I do believe he's guarding something. And the way to get it is to be kind to him, not trap and whip him. I've already told him that you drove a knife into Gwyn's heart—and you should have seen him jump up and down with joy. Just be patient, Ambrose. This is a haunted tower—I dream of many men going in and out—and we'll see what happens."

I had had no such dream as yet, but from other dreams about my bedmate I had waked up aching. On our fourth night in the tower, something with more substance than a dream had summoned me from sleep. The hour had been close to midnight, and the waning Moon had looked in the barred window that faced the east. She had been seeking something beautiful to gaze upon, and she had found it where Elain's shirt had slipped down a little and one of her breasts had escaped its confines and burst forth. Although the light had been dim, I had seen its perfect roundness and whiteness and could almost see the blood-color of its bud. My hand had moved of itself, escaping from my command, and then the sword that had lain between us had moved of himself, and almost cut me. That fairies were guarding her and reminding me of my oath, I could have no doubt.

Still I had hopes that the Gods would move in some fashion, setting me free, and perhaps that prospect had been in the back of my mind when I had borne so tamely her shrewish speech. Whatever the Great Gods did in my behalf, still I best keep on the good side of a small mortal maiden.

Now that we were friends again, one evening after supper I brought forth a surprise for her—the Roman lyre stringed with swan gut. This last had been provided by four of the huge fowls, more than I had expected to bag this soon, and in fact I had shot only one more, the other two coming to hand in ways that puzzled me. One was found hanging on the door-latch, where doubtless the gnome had left it, to please Elain. He must have snared it in some fashion the evening before, for it had no arrow wound or any sign it had been struck by a stone, a sling being the only weapon he appeared to possess. Elain herself had obtained the other, bringing it to me with wide, limpid eyes, explaining that she had seen it on the moors, unable to fly, and in chasing it she had tripped on the bank of a puddle and wetted her hair. Finally she had overtaken it and wrung its neck, yet I could not see where either wing had been broken, and she appeared not to have been bitten or beaten by its wings. To compound the mystery, when

I cleaned it I found its lungs were water-soaked. So I did not believe her story, suspecting that the gnome had got it by means of some charm.

Cleaned of fat, soaked in chalk-water, smoked, their strands twisted and dried in the sun, the guts had made stout strings that would do in a pass. The instrument itself was easy to play compared to a Cambrian harp. In half an hour's practice I could pluck forth the tunes of some of our country songs. No doubt Merdin would have plugged his ears from the sound; happily, Elain was more amiable. When I played for her on a balmy evening, her eyes had a soft brilliance a world removed from the wildcat sheen I had seen lately. In the nearby gorse I could make out Pillicock's form stretched on the ground, trustful that I would not run and pinion him, and since he stayed so still it might be that he too was taken by the melodies.

"Do you know this song?" Elain asked, humming snatches from it.

"I know the tune. I've never heard the words."

"Play it, and I'll try to sing it."

I played it only passably, even considering the strangeness of the instrument and its rough-and-ready stringing, but Elain sang it with strange beauty. I should have known she could sing well, from the richness of her voice and the purity of its tone even when she scolded, and perhaps the truest clew was her humming snatches of tunes in her sleep, proof that they wove through her dreams. Even so, there had been nothing to show the feeling she put into the song, the notes finding their way straight to the heart. Those notes appeared to glimmer in the twilight, and suddenly I remembered that her name, Elain, derived from an ancient Cambrian word meaning bright.

This was the song:

> Still through the hawthorn blows the cold wind,
> And the lowering clouds are gray.
> I will search the lorn moor, but who will I find
> To take my forlornness away?
> Wild are the winds that blow through a life,
> Until heart, hope, and happiness chill;
> But the wind through the hawthorn cuts like a knife,
> And gone are white blossoms and little bird's fife,

And in death and decay lies all that was blithe,
And the deep frost violets kill,
Once the hawthorn and I, our hearts could meet,
White was my blossom, my perfume sweet,
He gave me his shadow, I slept at his feet,
And I would that I slept there still.

Still through the hawthorn blows the cold wind,
Now I pass him unknown, he is deaf, he is blind.
Bed, I will come to thee, sleep I shall find.
Blow rain, blow snow, blow soft, blow shrill,
While I drift with the mist where I will.

The pure outpouring ceased. The gorse rustled, and out of it rose the gnome, and then he came walking toward us, his head bowed. I could hardly believe my eyes to see tears pouring from his eyes, down his coarse but not inhuman face. He did not look at me. He came without a sound, and dropped on both knees before Elain, and his big chest heaved in a great tempest of feeling.

"There, there, poor Gnome," she told him, stroking his wild, rough hair. "It was only a song, and I'll not leave you now. And when I go, you can come with me, and stay always. I love you, Gnome."

But suddenly a great doubt had struck my mind that Pillicock was truly a gnome, instead of a man like me on whom the Gods had laid affliction.

2

"Will you come into the tower?" I asked Elain when Pillicock had dashed away, fast as he could run on his short legs.

"Why, Ambrose? The wind's not cold and the evening's warm and soft."

"You told me I was not yet a king, and I'm not, but I want to pretend that I am, and give you the prize that a king gives to a beautiful maiden when she pleases him."

"I think I know what it is, yet I'll come."

When we had climbed to our lodging, I held her arms lightly in both hands and looked into her face.

"I'm half-afraid to give it to you," I said in a sudden need of being honest in her limpid eyes.

"You needn't be. But give it to me not from a pretended king to a maiden of his court but from you yourself."

So I kissed her beautiful soft mouth, the second time I had done so. All the wonder of that night returned to me then, and I hardly knew where I was, or who Ambrose was, and least of all who this maiden was, that by the pressing of my mouth to hers I should come upon such bliss. We stood in a haunted tower gazing at each other. The moor stretched wide and far, with the twilight softening the harsh shape of the Tors, waterfowl babbled in the reeds before they slept, red deer fed quietly, and perhaps only the shaggy marsh-donkeys who might have dwelt in its beautiful desolation for a hundred years knew why the Gods had made it, and what was its meaning. It had some wondrous meaning, if I could only grasp it. And the sad song that Elain had sung was bound up with it, and I thought our kiss was also, although this made no sense.

Suddenly the vision faded, and the sense of here and now returned to me with the fresh smell of the moor blowing in the window. Perhaps I had left Elain for not more than half a minute, so swiftly visions glide, and I could not spare even that much time away, so wildly beat my heart and so deep were my yearnings. I felt my strong life asurge in my veins, and I wanted to share it with this maiden, so strangely cast away with me, and surely the Gods would be angry if I abstained, for it was by their doing that we were here.

But I addressed her humbly, which I somehow knew would be to my gain.

"Will you give me back what I gave you?"

Her eyes lighted and she made sweet reply.

"Why, yes, if you wish. But then if you give me any more, I might contract a bigger debt than I can pay."

So it happened that our arms went about each other, and before many minutes I was seated on our sheepskin bed, with her breast against mine. Our debts to each other were soon beyond all count, and we could only lay claim to more and more of each other's belongings. I levied on her round firm tongue, as sweet to touch as its notes of song were to hear, only to have her seize on mine; and in such defense of her rights she was a true Cambrian maid, fiery and quick, and needing no spur but the first aggression. When my hand stole inside her collar she spread my shirt and bit, as though to take a pound of flesh nearest the heart, as is told in a tale as old as Ludton. And so blissful was the pinch of her little teeth that I bared more of my chest to her pillage.

Thereby I made a mistake that cost me dear. My thoughts had leaped far and beyond my actions, yet I had hardly dared dream the outcome of the contest, when suddenly she fairly leaped out of my arms, and sat up straight with her eyes burning mine.

"You've abjured your vow and mean to dishonor me," she said. Yet her voice was not sharp, as when she had berated me before.

"No, but I thought you might release me from it, from warmth of heart."

"Heat of blood, you mean. I can't condemn you, for when you lighted the fires, I helped feed 'em. Perhaps I would have released you if I had let myself forget that you are betrothed. But now I've seen the proof."

"I've never plighted my troth to any maiden," I said, speaking with great earnestness, as men are prone to do when they employ true words carrying a false meaning.

"I don't reckon you have. But you plighted it to Merdin to marry Wander of Cornwall. He would have asked for it because it's in the Song of Camlon, and you would have given it in order to be King, and he knew you'd keep it, or he would have never let us go off together into the moors. Yet my itching was so great I could give mind to nothing else—until I saw the deep hole in your shoulder." She stretched her arm around me and found the opposite mark, and when she put her finger in it, my whole skin prickled.

"There they both are," she said, a still beauty on her face I had not yet seen. "The tooth-marks of Droit the Boar."

"I can't escape my fate."

"You'll not try, and I don't blame you, and instead you'll run to meet it, as a man must. As the song tells, so it will be."

"Does it mean you and I can never have each other?"

"I won't say that in the hearing of the Gods. No one knows what they intend beyond what is told—what they will do for pity's sake, or for laughter. But tonight you, Prince, will sleep on the sheepskin robe, and I'll ask Pillicock to pluck up grass, and I'll make my bed on the floor. For no sword between us could protect me now, now that we've both lighted the fires of passion. And so it will be as long as we remain on the moors and until you are King of Cambria."

Tears rolled out of her gray-green eyes, but these were no sign of weakness, and, as often with womankind, a declaration of her intent. As for me, I would sleep alone on the skeepskin robe. It might be a succuba or a witch of the moors would visit me in the night, for no locked door would balk the creature if she wished to come and warm herself in the fires that a mortal maid had kindled; and by relieving her own itching she would remove the aching strain from my sinews. In the morning I would give my whole bent of mind to obtaining the treasure which Elain believed that Pillicock guarded, her maiden insight the best sign yet, and which I believed with all my heart and soul.

"Pillicock sat on Pillicock Hill," the gnome had shouted at us—if he were a gnome. There was something inside the hill that had made him sit there, and had had to do with a Roman road stopping short on the moors, and a cart-road straggling off to the nearest Tor, and still caused the ghosts of long-dead men to throng our bed-chamber, and sometimes reveal their shapes on the cart-road as dark blotches moving in file, in the evening mists. I must have the hoard with which to buy weapons for the fighting men of Cambria, whereby I could seize Vortigern's throne instead of Elain's own treasure. Before the Gods, I would stop at no half-measures to get hand on it.

3

The wind blew when it had a mind, day or night, and when it rested the moor-mists lay close, and when it waked again, the ghostly stuff was torn into shreds and skeins, which streamed willy-nilly over the wastes. On the fourth morning following my blissful contest with Elain, the stars burned long in the dawn, so clear was the sky, and a hot, bold Sun rolled up, sucking off even the little, ragged mists that even on breesy days formed, floated away, and formed again on the deep pools. Almost no breese stirred this morning. I kept wondering what was so queer about the moor, until I discovered its enormous silence. Also, its most delicate as well as boldest hues, the pond's perfect imagery of the serene sky, greens of all shades, and patches of color of wild-flower beds unseen by mortal eye were unveiled by the searching Sun. Gazing from the balcony, I picked out features of the landscape I had never noticed or at least recognized before. It was as though an old man, with dim and watery eyes, had suddenly regained the brilliant vision of his youth.

After going out to give her breakfast leavings to Pillicock, Elain came to me with roundness of eyes and less palpable signs in her face and carriage of some fresh and perhaps alarming news.

"Will you go to the door, Ambrose?" she asked. "The gnome wants to speak to you."

"I hope he's going to tell me about the treasure, to bear out your faith in him," I answered. Truly, though, I held no such hope, and was only trying to make light of her concern and perhaps my own.

"It's not that. He'll tell you what it is. Please speak to him respectfully and make no sudden movements."

Waiting outside the door, I saw the two making toward me from behind a rocky outcropping. Pillicock walked a little back of her, she holding his big strong hand in hers. They approached me within ten steps, a look of trouble and of some deep and abiding shame, a cruel affliction, patent in his heavy man-like face. This last might arise because I stood so tall.

"Speak to the Prince," Elain urged, "and tell him what you told me."

"I am Pillicock, of Pillicock Hill," he said, trying to raise the full gaze of his eyes to mine.

"Good morning to you."

"Prince, my nose itches, and that is a sign that there's some one coming."

I looked at his coarse nose, bold of nostril, and it was more red than usual. The sign was well-known to the folk of Cambria and I was inclined to believe it. Anyway, if some people had been waiting for a day of brilliant light to do some hunting, they might well start forth today.

"Is it only one person, or many?" I asked.

"That, I can't tell, but I can find out. The Tor of the Eagles is the highest on this moor, and is only an hour's journey by the paths I know. If you bid me to do so, I'll climb it and search the waters for a boat, and the land for what seems tall sticks moving slowly."

The thought came to me to catch him now and confine him, before he told the enemy our hiding-place. But there were two things wrong with the notion, neither of which was Elain's opposition, which would be violent. In the first place, if the King's men visited this lonely region in our pursuit, it would be because they too knew of the tower and suspected that it was our retreat. In the second place, if Pillicock had desired to inform on us he would have slipped away like a cloud shadow on the moor.

"It might be that if you parleyed with the people, you could delay them long enough for us to find a new hiding-place," I said boldly, at which the Sun appeared to glance in Elain's eyes, they appeared so bright.

"I could show you a hiding-place that a fox, born on these moors, could not find. You could stay there, and I would get food for you, until they sickened of the search, and of lying in the rain. For I wouldn't give them shelter in the tower, as I gave ye twain. There would be thorns in their beds, spiders in their broth, vipers in the corners. I would not have given shelter to you, except that I knew you were fugitives from some evil court, the same as I, and Elain was an angel-child. But it may be I could do better than that."

Elain and I stared at him, and the coarseness of his face seemed gone, and it was the face of a true man, and a wise man.

"My lord, I know this weather. I have seen its like, and the curlew's cry tells me what's coming. The day will be bright only until mid-morning. The wind is down, and when again it stirs to a breese, it will come off the sea, bringing the fog. It will blow across the moor, giving only brief glimpses of the land, then it will settle in so thick that you hardly see the end of a pair of wading stilts you're carrying on your shoulder. A bush looks like a tree. A tree looks like a Tor. A little pool where mallards nest looks like a lake. If the King's men are lost on the moor they'll need a guide full sore. They won't think I'm a gnome; I won't get close enough for them to see my short legs.

You'd have never thought I was one if you hadn't found me in a tower where you expected one."

"Where would you lead the party, Pillicock? Into quicksand?"

"There's no quicksand on this moor; there's chalk underneath. But I could lead their captain to you, and I've heard of princes taking hostages for their own victory or protection."

"Before the Gods, I leave it all to you," I cried out.

"I thank you, Prince. When you hear a big stone rolling down the Tor, be ready."

In five minutes he had gone. Within two hours tatters of mist were streaming across the sky from the north, and when one passed under my Lord the Sun, he showed like a silver coin. Soon after midday the fog came and went in cool, damp, nebulous clouds, and it was a strange thing to see the moor alternately brighten and fade from sight as the Sun peered down between them and when his great golden eyes went blind. In another hour the wind stopped his blowing as though out of breath, and panted softly. The fog packed in and filled all the space between Earth and the lowering clouds of Heaven. Peering from the barred window, Elain and I could see only the near edge of the granite cliff and hardly enough of the hillside to throw out slop. The thick folds seemed to smother all sound; we heard no bird cry out, no murmur of waters, no rattle of shifting pebbles; and the tower was as hushed and lost as though it had been raised by shadowy ghosts who never spoke.

To breach that silence, and to pass the time, I got out the lyre and played it for Elain to sing. She knew countless songs and I knew innumerable tunes, no great wonder since we Cambrians are a music-loving people, for music eases the ache that the Gods saw fit to lodge in our hearts. Still the hours dragged. There was no danger, I thought, of our enemies finding our hiding-place in the blind fog, or of them stirring from some hastily pitched camp—unless, of course, both of us had been cozened by Pillicock's protestations. Perhaps he was not of woman born after all but the spawn of a witch of the moors. There was no use of wishing he had shown us a new hiding-place before he had departed, for if the one had been cozenage, the other would be also. Somehow I was readier to believe that he had over-

estimated his own capacities, had been caught, scourged, and, defending us still, had been killed.

At about the ninth hour past noon, with the ghostly light still holding, we heard a rattle and a roar a little way below the tower, signs
that a big boulder had been dislodged and was rolling downhill.
Elain and I glanced once into each other's eyes, then I quickly buckled
on my sword and put my shield on my arm. I was waiting behind the
edge of the crag when a ghostly figure took shape in the mist—not
a man's height but climbing steadily. In a matter of seconds a second
form appeared and for some seconds more I did not know who it was.
The tall man bore no arms. His garments were drenched with water,
his face and lower legs and forearms plastered with mud; he had lost
one boot and the bare foot streamed blood, and he moved in circling
arcs, reeling from side to side. Although his head now hung on his
neck, his eyes half-closed, and was not now carried at one side, in
amused alertness, his muddied red-gold hair grew in a fluff above his
forehead. I stood forth to meet him. He stared, and I thought he
laughed softly.

"Prince Modred, welcome here," I said.

He collected himself to answer.

"Not well come, but most evilly come, if I guess aright. But give
me food, drink too if you have it other than the cursed water of the
moor, and let me rest awhile before you kill me. I'm not fit to go to
the Gods in this beastly guise."

"Why, Modred, you doubt my brotherly reception. You'll have the
best that the house affords, and can rest on my own bed." Then I
turned to Pillicock, whose face looked white in the mist. "Our royal
guest doesn't relish our moor-water; and looking upon him, I can't
say that I blame him. Have you any liquor in your cell, such as the wine
of dewberries, that will quench his thirst?"

"No, my lord, but I have mead made with wild honey."

"Get a horn of it, in honor of this visit of my brother. Have no
fear that he'll attack me in your absence, unless he's lost his wits on
the moor."

Pillicock moved on his brisk short legs and the fog instantly hid
him. Modred reeled to the wall of the tower and leaned against it.

"A sturdy fellow, Rufus," Modred remarked in a feeble voice, the voice of a spent man, yet with a suggestion of his old sociability.

"Do you mean the gnome?"

"He's no more of a gnome than you or I, as you know full well. I feel sure now that he is Rufus the Monster, whom my royal father had at court awhile in the days of Queen Ina and who had no cause to love him. The hangman described him to me once—Gwyn, the first chessman you took, and now you've got one who stands next to the King. Alas, the remembrance didn't strike me until I was too deep in the fog to find my way back to our bivouac, and I had to go on trusting him. You see, he didn't come close during the negotiations— he stayed blurred by the mist and he looked taller than he was—everything does in that cursed smother."

"You were speaking of him being sturdy," I reminded him politely.

"Your pardon, Prince Artay. I'm weak as a reed—he's still fresh. In half an hour more I'd have lain down to die. Part of it was his knowing how to wade through mire. Also he chose the least deep— he could tell by the look—but the holes he made filled up before I could get there, and I bogged up to my knees. Still, short-legged animals are almost always strong—for instance, a bear or a boar. Maybe it's a matter of leverage."

Pillicock loomed out of the mist with a wooden horn. I wondered what else he kept in his underground lair, and how large it might be. I thanked the Gods that had bade Elain keep me from whipping him.

"If you pardon me, Prince Modred, I'll climb up first. Then my follower will boost you up, and I'll give you a hand. You must expect rough quarters, nothing like the palace of the King."

"I'll be grateful for the shed where King Lear took shelter from the storm. The fog is soft, only a little chill, but it's clammy, and has some rank poison that curdles the blood in the brain. Now shut me away from the sight of it—the little while longer I have to live."

So I climbed the ladder, to find Elain waiting in our lodging, very white in the face. Pillicock boosted the exhausted Prince, and I hauled him the rest of the way. Elain descended half-way to get the horn of mead, which she handed him, touching her knee to the floor. He drank deeply, and slowly a faint color returned to his gray face.

"By your leave, my lady, I'll take off these muddied clothes before I lie down on the clean skins."

"I thank you for your care, and my modesty will take no harm."

"If I had a cloth, I'd wipe the mire from my face and hands and feet."

"I've a cloth that will take no harm, and I'll wipe 'em."

She did so, kneeling at his feet. Cambrians go naked at certain ceremonies of seeding and harvest, so she thought nothing of his unclothed body except perhaps to admire it. He had long, smooth muscles such as I had seen in the remains of Roman statuary, not bunchy like mine.

"Naked I was born," he remarked, "and naked I'll die."

"I have no doubt you will," I answered.

"I hope you'll feel the same regret I would have felt if 'twere t'other way round."

"Better say, I'll take the same pleasure."

"Artay, you comprehend me less than you do the wench. But before I go into that—and the strengths and weaknesses of the conquered should interest the conqueror—let me tell a brief tale of your fellow Rufus. He managed the whole affair remarkably well. What a figure I cut, following him like a lost sheep across those cursed moors! Artay, I think you have a gift for putting me in ridiculous positions—as when you hacked a piece from my muscle after I had conspired with my royal father, Vortigern, to cleave you to your gullet!"

"I marvel that you speak of that just now."

"Why not? You know it, you have it on your mind, and to speak of it will neither hasten nor delay your revenge. Let me speak further of Rufus, whom you call Pillicock. He stood half-concealed in the fog near our bivouac, and shouted that a tall stranger with a fair-haired wench had stolen his lodging and provision. If he led our captain to the lair, would he hide in the brushwood and shoot the thief with an arrow? If so, he could take the maiden for his sport, and Rufus would give his benefactor a haunch of venison to boot. It sounds fishy as I repeat it, but I swear to you that the fellow put such conviction in his voice, such real fury, that none of us doubted him, and thought that our excursion, the outcome of which we had begun to doubt, would end in immediate triumph."

"And it was an enterprise just to your taste," I remarked calmly.

"There you're wrong. I told you, Artay—for I knew who you were at first sight of you and had trouble remembering to call you Ambrose —that I live for pleasure. To kill you from ambush would provide none at all. However, there were other inducements. In the first place, King Vortigern was greatly upset by the failure of the hunt in the forest, along with the loss of a hangman that he prized more than his golden cup. He insisted that I could have led the party to success, and he would take umbrage—let me say he would fly into a rage—if on this journey I returned without your head. An even greater inducement would be the capture of Elain of the Lake. Tired as I am, I can barely keep from making a show of myself when I look at her. Maidens of such quiet beauty, with high tempers, provide excellent sport—as no doubt you know. Pardon me, my lady, for my frank speech—remember that though I am a captive, I am yet a prince, who by Cambric law may take any liberty with an unwedded maiden. Now I'll continue the tale of my misfortunes. I rather enjoy telling it, being a sociable fellow, and it takes my mind off what is to come."

"We are enchanted by it," Elain said gravely, touching her knee to the floor.

"Rufus led me to a Tor, then gave the finest imitation of a befuddled man that you could imagine. He stammered apologies—it was the wrong Tor—he had missed his turn only a hundred paces back. We started on again, and he made a sharp turn—and after a half hour's tramp we fetched up at another Tor, again the wrong one. By now I was suspicious and resolved to kill the fellow and wait till the fog lifted to find my way back to our bivouac. But when I started to aim an arrow at his back he melted away into mist. When he appeared, he was behind me, with a sling loaded with a stone, and he could have killed me with the greatest ease. This happened several times. Then he began to lead me through bogs and into water-holes, where soon I fell and wetted my bowstring. The hours passed, my strength was giving out, my mind became clouded, and I could think of nothing to do but follow that terrible, short-legged little man who held my life in his hand. Think of Prince Modred being slain by a stone hurled by a dwarf! Well, I've stretched the tale as far as it will go. Here I am. What death are you going to give me? If you'll use your sword in one clean hack, I'll consider it a favor and sing your praises to the Gods. I have reasons to think they love me—at least my quest of pleasure has met with success until very lately."

I hardly heard his last words, my brain was so busy. I was thinking that taking Modred's life would give me only momentary satisfaction, for the fog would lift tomorrow, and his armed followers would find the way to the tower. Elain and I would be well-hidden, but they must either have vengeance or their own heads rolled, and their search would not be brief but plagued long and, only too likely, successful. In the other hand, Modred was a strange man to be born in these gross times.

I decided to take a great risk perhaps to avoid a greater.

"Modred, what would you do for me if I let you live?"

"Gods! Are you as long-headed as that? I thought I'd not propose what you are thinking, because I hadn't the least hope you'd act on it. The Song of Camlon tells you'll be King. Could it be you'll make a great king?"

"You haven't answered my question."

"Why, I'd bathe, and ask Elain to clean my clothes, and return to the bivouac, and tell my followers I'd been on a goose-chase, that this tower is ruined and forsaken, that you both had fled Cambria, and that Rufus had meant to murder me and take my sword and shield, and I'd given him my sword in another fashion. Then I'd order immediate departure from this coast."

"Would you take oath on a holy relic?"

"I never take oath. To do so is a slight to the name of prince. But I'll give my word."

"He'll keep it, Ambrose, believe me," Elain said.

"But understand, please, Artay, that the truce ends as soon as you return to Cambria," Modred told me earnestly. "I think the Gods will give royal sport to both of us in days to come."

Chapter Five
The Roman

Time had advanced a week, and my affair with Elain had not in the least advanced, when Pillicock's nose itched again, on the other side this time, meaning that the people who were coming were friends, not enemies. Again he climbed to the top of the Tor of the Eagles, and soon returned with word that a boat was in sight, about to land at Porlock Bay, and that her square sail and other marks identified her as a fisherman he had seen before in these waters. Her captain had a white beard and a tailed cap, and one of her occupants, who took no part in sailing her, was a middle-sized sturdy fellow, with black hair and a clean-shaven face, rare among Cambrians.

Well, in that case the boat was the *Curlew*, which docked at the river town of Collen, and her captain and crew were Merdin's trusted friends. The sturdy fellow was probably Gerald, I thought, who shaved cleanly in the Roman style and had black hair.

If this was Gerald, within an hour he was heading up the remains of the Roman road, accompanied by one of the boatmen. Not long after that I had identified him beyond doubt, by a soldierly movement of his arms as he tramped. I went down to meet him on the cart-road, and knew in one glance into his face that his news was good.

"I've come to take you home," he began.

"Where's Merdin?" I asked. "Are he and Llewelan still in hiding? What danger to Elain?"

"Ambrose, much has happened in your absence. The word has got around among the countryfolk that you are Vortigern's son; also their hopes are aroused that the Song of Camlon may soon come true—although some other prophecies must be fulfilled before they'll feel certain. Anyway, the King's hands are tied as far as sending swordsmen into our region to murder you, Merdin, and Llewelan, or to take Elain captive. If he tried it, rebellion would break out, and there's unrest all over Cambria because of rumors flying. At present he's putting his trust in the excitement dying down long before you can arm a large enough band to make open war."

"It's a stout prospect to put faith on," I said harshly, "unless——"

"Unless what?" Gerald's face looked deeply lined.

"Unless something I hope, and what Elain believes, happens in the next few hours."

"I take it you've not found treasure."

"Not of any sort."

"At least, Ambrose, you've more time to work in, and far less danger of being cut down except from ambush. You can live at home, with Cavell on guard. Llewelan and Elain and an old serving-wench will stay in the old lodge on the island in Swan Lake, only three miles from us. The will of the Gods will be fulfilled."

With hardly another word Gerald and I made our way up the cart-road and climbed Pillicock Hill. At his first sight of Pillicock, who stood boldly forth beside Elain, Gerald gave a great start.

"By the Great God Jove, that's Rufus, who was at the King's court in Queen Ina's time!"

"It never crossed your mind he might be a gnome?"

"How could it, when I'd seen him with my own eyes? Anyway, we Romans don't believe in gnomes—only the Britains and other barbarians can see them."

I colored slightly, half-ashamed that I had been such a fool.

"I'm going to take him with me, if he still wants to go."

"As a servant? I think it would be a good notion. He'd arouse awe among the bumpkins."

"I'm going to take him as a follower, and make use of his great strength and his wits."

Pillicock's intent I meant to know at once. I asked Elain and him to walk with me a little way around the hillside and sit down on a flat rock that overlooked the moor, leaving Gerald to study the tower, the exact like of which he had never seen, and which puzzled him deeply. I put the matter in plain words.

"Elain and I must leave this place today and go back across the channel," I told Pillicock. "If you would like to come with me, to help me all you can in my coming war with King Vortigern, I would welcome your service."

His short legs threshed a little, like those of a dreaming dog, and a look of dignity, as I might expect to see in a great earl, came into his face.

"Would I be parted from the angel-child, Elain?"

"In times of war you would be parted from her. At other times you could stay with her and her noble father, Llewelan. But if you stay here you'd be parted from her forever."

"Would I ever see again this moor that to some seems a foe, but has always been friend to me?" And he looked out over its wild expanse.

"I think you will see it again. I know of nothing to stop you."

"Then, Prince, I'll go."

"There is one thing more. I ask it as your prince and protector. Elain thinks there is treasure hereabouts of which you know, and which you have guarded the best you could. If so, I need it in my great emprise to be King of all Britain, and to fulfill the will of the Gods. Will you answer yes or no, whether it exists, and if it does, take Elain and me to the hiding-place, and put it to my use?"

"Yes, Prince, there is something hidden not far from under our feet, and it would be for you to say whether it is treasure. But I cannot show it to you unless its guardian consents. He too must say whether you may have it in your charge. I will call him up and ask him to tell how it came here, for he has often told me. That much I can surely do. As for the rest, we can only wait and see."

"Pillicock, I don't understand what you mean by the guardian of the treasure or any of the last part you said."

"He is one who visits me in dreams. His soul is greatly troubled to find rest. Often I have wakened to hear him speaking through my mouth, employing the Cambrian speech, yet in a tone that is not mine, and sometimes using words I do not know. Long ago I ate a plant that grows in damp places where wood and greenery have rotted away. It put me in a spell so that I drifted on the soft wind, needing not my malformed legs to bear me far, and I was no longer ashamed of them, and my spirit exulted. Then, when I returned to the tower, this man came, and spoke with my tongue of matters long ago. Sometimes still I eat this plant, for my soul's peace, and always he comes up, and stays and talks awhile, and if I have eaten a good quantity he stays long, and tells the whole tale. It is a sad tale and I think it has great meaning, if I could understand. It is not a dream. Often I waken from a half-dream to hear his voice ringing in the room."

"Do you think the plant is poison and causes madness?"

"It may be poison, if enough is eaten, but if I eat only one or two I have no ache or pain or sickness, and in an hour I waken with my wits about me. Wait here, Prince, and my lady. I'll show you the plant.

Then I will eat of it, and I will go with you into the tower, where I will go to sleep and he will come. And by your leave, ask the chief who is half-Roman to listen also, for I think he may understand better than any of us."

Pillicock scrambled up and hurried away. Within five minutes he returned with two of what we call toadstools, not very large, and with yellow tops. "They are common on this hill, but I've never seen them growing on the moor," he told me.

"Will you go into the tower to eat them?" I asked as respectfully as though I were speaking to Merdin.

"No, my lord, I will eat them now, then go into the tower. Some minutes pass before they work."

He ate them slowly, chewing them well. I could not tell if their taste was pleasing or displeasing; his face that looked so big on so short a man told me nothing.

"By your leave, we will go up now," he said when he had finished the strange repast.

We did so, and found Gerald looking at the pile of rubbish in the corner of the tower-room. I asked him to take a seat against the wall, Elain and I doing the like, and he threw me an astonished glance when Pillicock lay down on the sheepskin robe, one of the pillows of grass under his head. Already the pupils of his dark eyes filled the iris.

As we waited in silence, he began to fall asleep, peacefully enough except for an occasional twitch of his legs. Presently he began to tremble violently, a spell that lasted perhaps a minute. Then he quieted, a quiet almost as deep as death's, breathing very slowly, and his very identity seemed wiped from his face as from the face of a dead man.

And then Gerald gave a violent start, and my skin prickled throughout and Elain's eyes were big and wild, because we could have all sworn that a newcomer had entered the room. A voice filled it, and although Pillicock's lips moved, the voice was not at all like his, and seemed the voice of a younger, more affable, and whole man.

"My salutations, Pillicock!" he burst out. "I am glad you sent for me, for when you don't, I have a devilish time getting in. Have you kept the watch well? Is everything well with the Emperor's belongings?"

A slight pause ensued, then the visitor spoke on.

"Yes, I can tell that others are here—a maiden, a tall Cambrian, and a man whom I would think was one of ours, by his coloring and the black bar of his eyebrows. I take it he is of mixed blood. But all are so dim I must strain my eyes to see them . . . Yes, if you wish I will tell of the coming, and the departure. Why not, since it will pass the time, of which I have too much on my hands? If they are your friends, it will do no harm.

"Shall I tell all? Very well. My name is Marcus Cassius; I was a Centurion of the Fourth Cohort of the Second Legion. I was born at Isca that you call Caerleon—our cohort was garrisoned there—but my parents were not long from Rome itself. Until that summer that rumors began to fly, I hardly dreamed that our long banishment would ever end. We called our cohort the Forgotten Fourth, and the term was only too true. While the rest of the Legion saw service from Vectis to Dubrae, we had remained to guard a crumbling fortress and the placid waters of the estuary. Still, it was not unpleasant duty for easy-going fellows. Deer were fat, salmon rose to a bit of bucktail on a barb flicked out with a limber cane, and the Cambrian maidens were pretty and warm of heart.

"According to these rumors, Maximus had conquered and killed Gratian, and was now Emperor of both Gaul and Britain. Then we heard of threatened war between him and Theodosius, Emperor of Rome itself; and some had it that Maximus would conquer, and then all the legions that had left Britain would return, and some believed that Theodosius, a greater general than his father, would surely prevail. Then came that strange letter from Maximus to Lucillius Claudius, commander of our cohort. We were to cross Sabrina with a thousand laborers, slaves and churls, and build a road from the bay that the Dumnonii called Porlock, to intercept and follow down their River Exe clear to their capital, Isca, at Exmouth. Roma Dea! What sense did it make?"

The speaker paused, and Gerald whispered quickly in my ear:

"Dumnonii was the Roman name for Cornish folk! May the Gods defend us!"

"Lucillius Claudius had a lame leg," the visitor went on in an ironic tone. "He chose to remain in his snug quarters at the fort. The rest of us set forth, under the command of our First Centurion, a prim fellow named Cinna. The men thought it a great lark, glad of a change of scene, and only we officers had misgivings. You understand, Pillicock, the Exe River country was *terra incognita*. However, Porlock Bay had a better harbor than in your time. There was a long spit that served as a break-water which has since disappeared, and the bay itself has accumulated silt. Yes, and we were to build forts both on Sabrina Coast and east and west of Isca—to fight off Scotti and Saxons. So there was no real reason to believe that Maximus had lost his keen Iberian mind.

"The workmen began to build the road—and the soldiers to grumble. It was a rainy summer and we fell into more bogs than we could count. And when we had run it two of your hellish long Cambrian leagues, there arrived the second letter. It was from Lucillius Claudius, still cozy in Caerleon, but now, thank the Gods, he must bestir himself, lame leg or no. The meat of it was, Maximus had ordered the Fourth Cohort to Gaul! We were to abandon the road-building, erect one tower 'to command the upper waters of the Exe,' store what impedimenta we could not take, and leave it in the care of Marcus Cassius and twenty auxiliaries until relieved. Before great Jove, I had never guessed before that Lucillius hated me. Obviously he had found out that I was the one who had lured away his pretty Cambrian sweetheart. I thought that relief might be fairly long in coming." And the visitor laughed bitterly in Pillicock's mouth.

"The place Cinna chose to erect the tower was defensible against any small force, but I don't know of any other military merit it possessed," the visitor went on. "All hands took part in the labor, and in excavating the chalk underneath for a large store-room. The weather continued unspeakable. I suppose you've heard that old West Country song:

"'*The rain, it raineth every day,*
Hey, ho, the wind and the rain!'"

The visitor did not speak the words, he sang them in a rich baritone, and Elain slipped her hand into mine, and it was icy cold.

"That was the way it was with us. Long before the excavations were finished the Cambrian churls and the German slaves began to desert. They left first in two and threes, then in batches, then in droves. The whole enterprise had been cursed by their Gods, they thought—Lud, Woden, the usual heathen pantheon. The soldiers were well-disciplined in the Roman fashion and they stuck, working like beavers; and happily the chalk was easy to excavate. They finished the job, stored all the road-building equipment, everything else they could spare in the way of supplies, and started southward across the moor. Our remainder stood on the hillside and watched them go. A few turned and waved their hands, but very few. Their minds were fixed on getting out of there in a hurry. I didn't blame them.

"Cinna had been ordered to take the cohort by way of Moridunum to Aquae Sulis, where Lucillius would resume active command. In ten days they were back, minus Cinna and about fifty others. They hadn't been able to descend the Exe because of floods—the whole country was a morass. When they had tried to keep to high ground they had been picked off by hidden archers—Scotti, some of them thought, others said Picts, although as far as I knew, the Painted Men had never come south of Coccium, and a few thought the deviltry was done by flint workers, such as still lived in huts and holes north of Eburacum. Their arrows had flint heads, but they cut through leather and human skin as well as iron, and made uglier wounds. The bows had long range and must have been good. It became pretty plain that no one had bothered to bury Cinna with military honors, and worse yet, our wounded had been left to die.

"While the cohort milled about the tower, there arrived the third letter—and the last. It was brought by a civilian official, who called himself Dunmvir of Silures. The writing was the shortest yet—that Maximus had fought Theodosius near Aquileia, and had been defeated and beheaded. But the official had come in a boat; we could use it to collect other boats, and the soldiers could get to Vectis by sea, from where they could surely reach Gaul. The only trouble with that was, the wretch slipped away in the night, and was not seen again.

"Well, we were Romans and re-established some kind of order. The cohort replenished its provision from the store-room—there was plenty for all—and took off again northward, looking for any kind of boat that would take them to a Roman settlement. On this trip they were absent twenty-one days. They had gone forth in fairly good marching-order—they came back in a straggling file. They had combed the South Sabrina coast and there were no boats. The fishing villages were deserted. The cultivators had fled from their fields. They had lost fifty men by desertion, twenty by drownings, quicksand, and such like. It seemed to me a picture, on a small scale, of what was happening to the whole Roman Empire."

"Spirit," Gerald cried with an anguished face. "It was only a minor incident that cannot weigh against the great conquests. If your wenching commander had properly disciplined the men it wouldn't have happened. Rome will yet rule the whole world, and Artay will be her vassal King of Britain."

"Pillicock, I thought I heard something then," the visitor went on. "It was like a human voice a long way off. I'll go on with the tale—what little remains. The men encamped beside the tower—using equipment and provision from the store-rooms. They didn't relish the stay, surrounded by the flooded moor, but their officers could not agree on which way to turn. And while they were here about a half-dozen Dumnonii—wild-looking fellows—came up under a flag of truce. They offered for a certain sum in gold to lead what remained of the cohort over secret paths to Aquae Sulis. However, they imposed certain conditions for their own safety—you, Pillicock, knew what these were. The officers had to agree, and once more the men set out, and I've always wondered whether they arrived safely or were slain from ambush. None of them ever told me. They don't come to the places I frequent.

"My detachment of twenty remained to watch over Imperial property until relieved. We had provision which we could supplement with fresh fish. We kept military order, including calling the roll at sunrise. But in about a week, the line looked a little short. There were only eighteen.

"The number melted away after that. I had fifteen, and then ten, and when five disappeared in one night, I had five left. They were sturdy fellows, and a month or more passed, until one morning there were three. One of these hanged himself on the rope-ladder. A second went out on the hill and fell on his sword. The last stayed with me half a year; it was summer again, and we both believed relief would come at last, or so we swore to each other by Mars, the god of soldiers, whom you call Tyr. One day in trying to climb the rock wall, God knew why, he lost his footing and fell. I buried him with military honors and took up the watch alone.

"I had plenty to eat. The waters had receded, and I learned to snare fowls of various sorts, and could still catch fish. Then a hill-viper bit me, a rather small specimen, but I couldn't get rid of the poison. The time came that I could go down for my needs only once a day, and only once every hour of daylight rise and go to the window to see if relief was in sight. But no soldiers came marching over the moor. I saw only the endless green, the waters, the rocks, the Tors, and the beasts and birds in their habitat. One morning, to my amazement, I went to the window without effort. I turned and looked back, and how well I remember my disgust of the wasted remnant of me lying on my bed.

"Still I kept the watch, and a long watch it was, until you, Pillicock, came to relieve me. You were not a Roman soldier, you were a monster, yet you were staunch, and with you here, I felt free to come and go with the wind. That is all the tale, and why have you asked me to tell it again, when you know it so well?"

There fell a short silence, and then the visitor asked in a tone of amazement, "What did you say?"

After another silence, somewhat longer, the Roman Marcus Cassius spoke in a low voice charged with excitement.

"The rightful King of Cambria! I suppose the Cambrians have the right to say who will be King, since our soldiers have not returned; and, after all, I am in command of the stores, and may do with them what seems best. Why, yes! To tell you the truth, their care still weighs heavily on my mind. Will you take him down and make him their custodian, to use as he sees fit? Then it may be I can go to the Hesperides. I've carried out my orders as well as I can, and I believe admittance will not be denied me. Farewell!"

Then suddenly there was no one in the room but us three witnesses, and Pillicock asleep in the bed. We did not say a word, only watched him, as little by little, the trance in which he lay passed off. After awhile he stirred a little, sighed, drowsed, then stirred again. Rather abruptly he opened his eyes and sat up.

"Are you all right, dear Gnome?" Elain asked in her sweet voice, coming to his side and stroking his rough hair.

"I am well." He stood up on his short legs, and his face became animated. "We will go down now."

We followed him out of the tower, to a flat rock about four feet square that I had noticed and took to be immovable.

"It is shallowly cut," Pillicock told us, "still somewhat heavy. I can move it with pries, but if the Prince and the Roman will lend a hand, it will save time."

We three men moved it without great difficulty, for Pillicock, as Modred had told me, was strong as a bear. We gazed down into darkness until Pillicock prepared and lighted a torch, then he led the way to easy footholds cut in the chalk wall. From thence we came into a passage where the chalk walls glimmered in the torchlight and followed it to an immense chamber.

He did not throw his beam on what I thought was a great heap of tools of all sorts, wooden boxes rotting away and spilling their contents, and what might be the rotted fabric of tents and blankets. Instead he brought us to an immense stack of round things that had a metal shimmer, and to a big uneven pile of short and long objects of peculiar and unmistakable shape.

The latter were short Roman swords, each with its belt and scabbard, thrown down with Roman javelins with wooden shafts and iron heads. The orderly stack was of iron shields. There were fully five hundred of these and as many of each of the two weapons.

Gerald was first to speak.

"I know now what the deal was that the Cornish guides made for their own safety," he said in low, quiet tones. "Still, I would have never believed that Roman soldiers would have agreed to it."

"They did so because our Gods were greater than the Roman Gods," I answered. "And now their will be done!"

Chapter Six

Auguries Unfolding

The change of feeling toward me by the people in our part of Cambria did not become manifest to my sight until about a week after my return from across the channel. Elain and Llewelan, and their stout henchman Pillicock, had taken abode in the best house in these parts, built of stone quite well preserved on an island in Swan Lake, once the fishing and fowling resort of that same Lucillius, commander of the garrison at Caerleon, who had banished Marcus Cassius to the tower. The occasion of my discovery was the Fish Fair at the river village of Collen, held every year on the night of June twenty-first, the shortest night in the year. In this season fish were in great supply, a-run in the rivers, teeming in the sea, more being caught than the fisherfolk could well salt down or dry, and hence they were sold cheap. Poor folk could stuff their bellies, and those with jingling pockets could lay in a great store, preserving them in various ways for future needs.

Fully five hundred folk attended the fair, since Collen was the largest fish-market north of the channel between Seal's Eye at the mouth of the Taw and far and away up the Severn; for the River Usk, emptying below Caerleon, had no such run as our Taff. Our salmon were fatter and finer, and the mullets of the estuary, and the herring of the coastal waters, being not only more numerous but of better flavor. With a fine aroma of fish getting ever stronger in our nostrils, Merdin, Gerald, and I, with Cavell quiet at my heel, approached the stalls. And we were almost on the flank of the great throng when Merdin stopped briefly in the road and gave me some last-minute coaching.

"Frolic none and slap no backs," he said. "Return all greetings in pleasant voice, engage no man in private conversation, and if some person kneels to you, give him your hand but take it as your due."

"I will."

"Go into no holes and corners. Keep your wits about you. The King has many men who are not known as kingsmen, and some may be in the assembly. Avoid any sort of quarrel. Look out for yourself."

"I will, and Cavell will help me. Have no fear."

We four—for Cavell seemed more like a person than a dog—entered the throng, and it stirred in response to a swift-running wave of excitement. Only from a distance did people gape at us; when we came nigh, they looked a little sideways for politeness's sake, I supposed, perhaps from faint embarrassment, but certainly not from wanting detachment from us, as the yokels had looked and stood aside when I had bested Modred in the sword-fight. I, not Merdin, was the main subject of their thoughts. Only a few bold fellows kneeled to me, but for a good while I failed to see one face that was not friendly and animated, and I was treated with great courtesy by everyone. In some eyes, I saw something very like triumph, and, in almost all, fierce hope. And a great many eyes became wide and questioning when they looked at the great black shape of Cavell.

Merdin bought some smoked salmon, marvelous marching fodder, and delicious to my taste, although our churls sniffed and rejected it. Then we strolled over to the amusement booths, where a clown stuck his head through a curtain, to be pitched at with balls of pressed manure at a farthing for three throws; and yokels could lift heavy stones free of charge if they heaved them off the ground; and where a wrestler took all comers on a penny wager, losing frequently enough to attract the burly fellows in the throng, but generally winning. The most popular booth offered ax-throwing at a barrelhead of soft pine, a farthing to heave, two farthings back if the blade stuck. The axes were short-handled, with bronze blades, in the Cambrian style, and since ax-throwing was an old pastime hereabouts, a noisy crowd of men were taking turns.

"Let me show you bumpkins how to heave an ax," cried a meanly dressed fellow whose heavy face suggested strength and whose close-lidded three-cornered eyes had an intent gaze. Although I could not remember ever having seen him before tonight, I felt a haunting sense of the familiar, and I wished my brain would bestir itself and tell me what it was.

He gave the impression of having done himself too well at the ale-booth. His stand was unsteady, he talked loudly, and he brandished the ax around his head in a wild fashion before he wildly threw. Afeared they would be struck by the recklessly whirled weapon, the rustics stood back, laughing at him. Not looking at him, watching his shadow cast by the big bonfire built just beyond the booth, I did not laugh and instead became passing thoughtful. Something like a little snake of memory uncoiled in my head, then there was a great light within, and the man was no longer quite so much the stranger.

It was not his face and lean, agile form that had signaled my mind, but his somewhat high voice. I had heard it before, in the darkness of Radnor Forest. It was the voice that had posted the hunting party along the brook, on Beltane night.

I moved closer to him and a little back, so I could watch him out of the corner of my eye. He continued his larking for awhile, and I knew the fraction of a second that it ceased. He turned a little toward me, and the ax was swinging into position over his right shoulder. Just as it left his hand, I sprang aside and spoke.

"Take him, Cavell!"

The great beast leaped almost as swiftly at the ax in the hunter's hand. They met and passed each other about half-way the distance between us, and the ax whizzed by where my head had loomed only an instant before, missing it by five feet. Cavell did not miss by an inch. He reared up and his teeth closed dead on the target, and the curious proof was a jet of bright-red blood that arched up and out and spattered on the ground. At the same instant its late owner toppled. There were a few more jets, not as strong, and in only a few seconds, while the crowd gaped, the crimson fountain flowed tamely and scant, soon dying away.

"Down, Cavell," I ordered. He came to my heel as I walked to the crumbled man and unbuttoned the collar of his tunic. From a fine silver chain around his neck hung a Roman coin of copper, the stamped head on which, representing one of the Caesars, had been scratched so that it appeared to wear a crown and the shaven upper lip a mustache in the style of Cambria, all in all a crude representation of King Vortigern.

I showed the ornament to a few of the older, bolder men who had pressed close to me. They nodded to each other and to me, and one after another touched his knee to the ground. Then I walked away, Cavell composed and quiet at my heels, to a booth selling shredded fish-cakes. As I sat eating, all the noise of the fair died quickly away.

2

No great to-do was made over the death of the King's man, although the yokels' faces remained a little flushed for an hour or more, as though from draining big horns of ale; and Cavell, dogging my heels, received many furtive glances and some admiring ones. In a press of people, one farm-woman held up her tots, one after another, for a good look at him. A brewer who was also a magistrate, appointed by the King, with the common Cambrian name of Morgan, did not seem to know what should be done with the fellow's body, he having consulted the blacksmith, the captain of the *Curlew*, and some other worthies, all of whom shook their heads. Busy and bustling, he finally came to me.

"My lord, Riis that the dog tore down was in good esteem with the King, as the badge on his neck shows plainly. I fear he'd take it amiss if his body is left to lie on the fairground, like a beggar killed in a knifing," he said. "Will Your Highness say what's best to be done?"

"Why, that's easy," I answered. "Yonder stands an ox, used to haul fuel for the bonfires. I doubt not that her owner would lend her to you, long enough to drag the corpse to the top of the hill. The ravens will come at sunrise, there's a good hole in his neck for them to start on, and they'll be finished with the feast in three days. Then they'll fly to King Vortigern's palace and caw the news."

"By your leave, I'll order it so." And Morgan touched his knee to the ground in the sight of whole assembly.

It turned out that Morgan did not order the work done, but did it himself, for the simple reason that no one would help with it. A fellow who had been with Riis, a charcoal burner who a few minutes ago had seemed as flushed with ale as his fellow-roisterer, remained out of sight. I kept a lookout for him, wondering what had happened to him, and saw not his hide or hair. Meanwhile I could not refrain from wondering what Morgan would have said and done, and what effect it would have had upon our yokels, if Riis's ax had found its target.

Merdin, Gerald, and I tramped homeward, neither of my two companions speaking of the incident. Of course I did not mention it, despite my pleasure in it, and Cavell heeled me with great sedateness; and to look at him no one would guess he had tasted any richer dish than beef bones. We followed the cart-road without scanning the shadows, and made nothing of entering black spinneys into whose depths the Moon did not peer. When our house-door was shut and bolted, and Cavell roamed far and wide on his night-watch, Gerald started snoring within ten minutes after lying down, Merdin puttered awhile, mumbling, and as soon as he was quiet I slept and dreamed of Elain.

Nearly two weeks passed without Gerald mentioning the sudden death of Riis, even when his tongue was loosed by dipping it in ale. Merdin spoke of it finally only when he and I were angling in a big pool, into which our big brook tumbled, and above which stood some ruins, with a great stone cut in the circle, which even Merdin could not explain.

"Riis was the best ax-thrower in all Cambria," he remarked when he had hauled in and strung a fat fish.

"Then the King may take it amiss that his throwing's done."

"I think he will. I think he has begun to lay wakeful of nights, which should give you satisfaction and worry too. Vortigern has a lively mind, and he's a pains-taking man. I hear that he's trying to recruit more men-at-arms—without great success—and to buy iron shields for all his soldiers who haven't 'em."

"Still, he must feel that the crown rests firmly on his head, because as far as he knows, we have access to naught but a few bronze swords and wooden shields. If it weren't for the Song of Camlon he'd sleep in Enid's arms without ever a cold sweat."

"I will speak presently of the Song. Artay, you took note of the charcoal burner who larked with Riis just before they—stopped larking. His name was Ian. He had ambitions beyond his station—and now they'll never be fulfilled."

"Merdin, why do you say 'was' and not 'is'? Why 'had' and not 'has'? He looked healthy enough, the last glimpse I had of him."

"He's not so healthy now, or at least on our side of the sea-mists. While he was cutting wood to make charcoal, his guts were ripped out by the tush of a gigantic boar."

"Why, I'm glad to hear it. Was the boar named Droit?"

"Artay, I think that is his name. I haven't seen him lately, you mind, to make out the scar on his neck that Droit bears, and the woodsmen who have caught glimpses of him took no time to look for scars, being too busy with their own legs. Certainly he wandered here from the Black Forest. That is in accord with the prophecy—'out of the forest into whose depths the Sun looks not'—and the time of his coming was only six days later than my calculations warned me, and quite possibly he had remained unseen by any wood-cutter for that long."

"Since he killed Ian for me, I should feed him corn, not give him battle," I proposed.

Merdin shook his head, and his big, open, big-veined hands slowly closed.

"You forget the holes front and back in your right shoulder," he told me solemnly. "They were marks that must be avenged. It was no other boar than Droit who carried you to his burrow, intending to eat you, and he was larger than any boar in the Forest of Radnor, where he lived—I caught a glimpse of him in the thickets and saw the brand on his neck. Artay, he came to our forest to meet you. It was an appointment neither of you could fail, because it was decreed by the Gods—Droit's mouth still watering and his little eyes still blazing over the meal that he missed, Artay bearing two wounds made by his tushes. According to my calculations, you must meet—three days from now, when the God Artay, your ancestor, is in the Sign of the Lion, which means that some beast of great fierceness is seeking battle with you."

"How can we find each other in all these woods?"

"You will find each other without fail."

"Perhaps if Cavell would trail him——"

"No, you must go alone. That is the way it was written. You may take your sword and spear, but not your shield, for the Gods gave no shield to Droit other than his hair and hide. You will go up the Ravine of Dhu, where at present he has his lair."

"The Ravine of Dhu climbs to a narrow gorge, filled with a waterfall, and having steep cliffs. It's a dead end for any creature that can't fly."

"All the better for you and Droit. Each of you will block the other's passage. There will be no choice but battle."

"It's strange that I feel no hate for him. Sometimes the holes in my shoulder itch and burn—but not now. Still, if he slaughters men—next time some wood-cutter loyal to me—the sooner I kill him, the better."

"Far and beyond that, it is sung in the Song of Camlon. If one prophecy is not fulfilled, by your sloth or for any reason, none will be fulfilled."

"Then I'll go to fight Droit three days from now."

"Enter the gorge at sunrise. That is the best time, when the God Artay, whom the Romans called Mercury, is full in the Sign of the Lion. I will go with you to the mouth of the Ravine of Dhu, and I'll be waiting there for your return."

"Old man, what if I don't return? Old boars are tough of hide, tough of life, still fast as deer, and terrible in rage."

"Artay, for the love of the Gods, for your hate of Vortigern, who cast you in the woods to die, even for such little love your heart may bear for an old harpist—come back with blood on your hands and the ear of Droit pinned over your heart. Then only one great prophecy will remain to be fulfilled—and a few minor things to be done—before you will arm the host that will overwhelm the King. The forest will return to its old bounds. Men will be more, and beasts less."

Merdin and I left our door in the cool dark just before dawn. Gerald had risen to see us off and to give me some last-minute coaching; Cavell ached to come with me, but was too proud to beg, and when I gave him his orders he jumped up to lick my face, nearly knocking me down with his weight, then ran gallantly away on his night-watch. In an hour the light was clearing fast, and we were almost to the ravine, for it was not far from our homestead, and here, sprawled on an old cart-track that wood-cutters used, lay the form of a man.

"More of Droit's work," Merdin said quietly.

I went ahead of Merdin and looked at it. The wound in his side was deep and gaping, and since it was not from an upward slash, instead a straight plunge inward, I caught myself wondering how the great boar had swung his head in order to strike. Then I looked closely into the dead man's face, and my heart missed a beat.

"Why, it's Griffith, the blacksmith's drunken slave," I said.

"Is it, indeed? He's drained his last cup."

"Do you remember when he came in our door, reeling, and drew his fingers across the strings of your harp? You didn't have him burned alive, as he deserved by law, and didn't even admonish him, and I think you smiled at him. It must be that the Gods wait a long time, sometimes, to move."

"No, it was only the work of Droit, who encountered him on the road. His skin is cold, his limbs stiffening. They met before sundown last night, or so I would judge."

"A boar who kills men is as wicked as a wolf. No doubt Griffith deserved death, but I'll not count that when Droit and I meet. My hands feel cold, still I think I'm in better fettle for the meeting."

"The Sun will look down and watch that meeting, his golden fingers probing between the walls of the ravine, and will rejoice you're in good fettle."

We walked on, and at the mouth of the ravine waited a few minutes for the Sun to rise. I was sure that I smelled the rank smell of an old boar. My Lord topped the hills, monarch of all. I seemed to feel a chillness in his rays. But Merdin and I shook hands, he dropping on one knee, and I went on alone.

The canyon walls closed in, higher, and steeper. More and more often I had to wade the shallows of the brook, often now a little cataract leaping from shelf to shelf, swirling around boulders, and making a singing, swishing noise that underlay its occasional heavy splashings. Merdin had spoken true that the Sun would watch the meeting between Droit and me. The canyon ran generally from east to west, without many curves or sharp turns, and the dimness of those stretches into which the Sun did not gaze emphasized the brilliance of its main reaches, wet rocks glistening, sand and the gravel of the bed gleaming like gold, foam-white as any snow. What little bank remained on each side bore the tracks of Droit, new tracks and old, and some barely showed on the hard-packed gravel, and some were deep holes in wet sand, and they were the largest tracks of a boar I had ever seen. My feet and lower legs felt numb from the chill of the waters, and cold chills I could neither deny nor hold in check ran up and down my back, and sometimes they spread across my shoulders, but turned into a burning sensation when they ran into the two holes made by Droit's tushes. And then came a great bounding of my heart that kept up a good two minutes, because I perceived that his very freshest tracks, not more than an hour old, followed steadily up the ravine and did not return.

"And, Droit, they never will return, if the Song of Camlon was truly sung," I thought.

Soon I came to a region where the brook pressed closely against one abrupt wall of the canyon, leaving a dry passage-way, not more than four feet broad, on the other side. Here Droit's tracks were so numerous that they could not be traced, indeed the ground had a harrowed look, and here and there were scattered what looked like barley-corns. My scalp tightened on my head and perhaps my hair rustled up, because if this was barley it must be it had been scattered by one of the Gods, perhaps no other than the God of Battles, worshipped in Cambria since the days of the flint workers, whom they had called Tyr and who was still called so by our country-people, and whom the Romans worshipped as Mars. If this was so, he must have done it in order to attract Droit to this very place, where the fight would be more even than in the forest, my sword and spear against his two long white tushes; and where the Sun could watch it well and with delight; and where if the heart of one of the contestants failed, still he could not flinch.

But as Droit's tracks continued on up the bank, ever nearer to the waterfall that would block his passage, the thought came to me that the corns might not be barley after all, but of some plant with seeds very like barley growing on the crest of the ravine, and washed down by the rains. Still, it would be by the will of the Gods, even if they had not been cast here by the Gods' own hands.

Now I began to hear the noise of the waterfall, a low-pitched steady roar over or under splashings that varied somewhat and rose and fell, and I knew my appointment with Droit was near. The ravine veered a little, and I walked into dimness, the cliffs dark gray, the brook running darkly. Then it resumed its true course, and the Sun blazed again. And more vivid than any colored thing in his pitch blackness, near the foot of the waterfall stood Droit, the boar.

He must have smelled me, for he could not have heard my light step above the roar of the falls. Or perhaps the Gods told him it was time for me to come, for our predestined battle to begin, because he turned full toward me, looking into my face. So I called to him and the rock walls re-echoed my shout and he heard me plain.

"Are you Droit?"

He lowered his head in assent, and the sunlight gleamed on his tushes long as a man's hand.

"I am Artay, unloved son of the King, who cast me forth into the woods to be eaten. You had fed well before you found me, and could not eat me then, but you carried me to your burrow, intending to eat me as soon as you hungered again. In my shoulder, fore and back, I bear the marks of your teeth. And for that we are fated to fight to the death."

He drew back his lips and the hair stood stiff all along his back, but not yet did he attack.

"If you kill me, you may eat me now," I shouted. "Your meal has been delayed, but it would still be sweet. If I kill you, I won't eat of your flesh that grew from your eating people, but I'll cut off your ear and wear it over my heart. Come, Droit! Why do you delay? The way is open to your return to the forest if you can pass me. Think of the good eating to come, the wallowing in the mire, the sleep at midday, while you squeal and grunt with pleasure. Think of the wild sows you may cover and kindle, and no beast loves it as dearly as a boar. What ails you, Droit? Must I come and kill you as you lie cowering?"

Meanwhile I was moving toward him, my spear ready. But my last taunt stung him deeply, and he gave voice to his wrath. It would be called a squeal, this being the sound that the Gods gave to swine to utter, but it was of frightful force, ringing from the cliffs and more savage than the roar of a raging bear. Terrible and swift was his run, his head low, ready to sweep sideways and up, to bathe his tushes in blood. And when I could see his little eyes red with hate and fury, I hurled my javelin.

The Gods had not intended that our long war should be decided at a distance from each other, nor that I should close with an adversary weakened by a wound. Either he saw the iron spearhead glisten in the sunlight as it darted toward him and swerved with wondrous agility, or else the Gods had so laid the ground that he must turn a little to reach me sooner. The spear only slit his hide a little at one side, enough to draw blood and to enrage him all the more, bringing no thought of death and heightening his scorn of defeat equal to a God's. My heart leaped in joy that the stroke had missed. I was waiting with my long-sword, and it too flashed in the sun, and Droit saw it well with his red eyes, and onward rushed.

So we met, my enemy and I, and I sprang sideways from his first slash, meanwhile striking at his neck. My blade struck the shoulder bone and glanced a little, and though I dealt him a bloody wound, he whirled and slashed again, and I all but toppled in the brook to avoid the sweeping tush. He could have swept by me now, and a lesser boar might have done so. Not Droit, for he remembered the theft of his waiting dinner nigh twenty years ago, and had brooded over it as he roamed the forests. He could have it now, if he could rip my belly open. Again he struck, and I felt his tush burn my side, the third wound he had given me, and this not even as deep as the others, although my tunic hung in rags. Then he reversed his sweep, to slash with his other tush, as I leaped sideways.

For him to get in range of me again took the sliced edge of an instant. Meanwhile my sword was swinging, and I put all my strength into what would be the death-blow or else my own death beside the rushing waters, for if I missed or did not cut deep enough, I would have no time or room to dodge his next attack. It was launched, he squealed in fury and what he deemed was triumph, and his right tush was in a handsbreadth of my naked side when my steel smote. Downward it drove, clefting his backbone, and his blood leaped in a fountain as fine as that which had played from Riis's throat when the fangs of Cavell had closed.

Droit dropped down, hacked almost in twain, and gave up his yearning ghost, and his red eyes slowly dimmed in the mists of death.

Except for one great wave of rapture that quickly passed, I remained quiet. I did not exult over my fallen foe, perhaps from thinking of infinitely greater forces who stood between me and the victory my soul demanded. Also he had fought well for his great life that the Gods had given the King of the Boars, at the same time decreeing when it would end.

Asking Droit's pardon for the disfiguration of his noble-looking corpse, I cut off his right ear and fastened it on my torn tunic with a bent nail. Since he would look better with no ears than with one, I removed his left as well, pocketing it for some future use. I thought too of cutting out his fine tushes, beautifully chiseled by a weapon-maker employed by the Gods, the same that fashions the falcon's beak and the eight barbs of his feet, the dog-fangs of Cavell, and the slashing front feet of a buck. The tushes were white and all the finer-looking for being fastened to that ugly swinish head. Still, I thought to let him wear them wherever he was going, perhaps to a kind of Elysium for swine, rich with ever-ripe corn, warm sunshine in which to sleep, and other great boars to do him battle, and squealing, biting, pinching, lascivious sows.

So I started back, and had not gone far when I saw Merdin coming, he having been unable to wait in patience at the mouth of the ravine. I spread my bloody hands for him to see, and he saw well enough the trophy I wore over my heart.

Before Merdin spoke to me, he raised both hands to the Sun, mumbling in his beard. Then he asked:

"Did Droit give you a good fight?"

"A noble fight," I said. "I've a mind to name this sword after him, Droit, and every time I hew down a foeman his spirit can be proud."

"Do so, Artay, but that is not the sword that you will carry in battle against the King. The sword to come has another name, given him by the Gods."

3

It was my fortune to lay eyes on Elain within five days after Droit and I had done battle. Merdin had told me that he had business of great weight to discuss with Llewelan of the Lake, who now dwelt far from the lake of his ancestral cognomen. Swan Lake, an island of which was his present abode, was one of a chain of lakes formed by land-slides damming a big brook. To wait on Elain was an old serving-wench, and Pillicock stood stout guard.

I doubted if Merdin's business here was as weighty as he maintained. More likely he wanted to rejoice with the once great earl over my battle with Droit, the news of which had carried like the ring of bells through the countryside.

We hallooed from the shore; and none other than Pillicock brought the craft across the weedy waters, rowing powerfully and swiftly, for I knew no man with stronger arms. He had little to say, but his face told me something as he touched his knee to the ground, and perhaps it said that the shame of short legs was a little less, now that he lived with people of flesh and blood, rather than with troubled ghosts in a haunted tower. The thought struck me that Llewelan's bearing and countenance were far more kingly—at least as I imaged these in the great kings of old—than King Vortigern's. And I would wager that Elain was more princess-like in beauty and probably in pride than Wander of Cornwall.

"Merdin, does royal blood flow in Llewelan's veins?" I asked, out of simple curiosity, as he disembarked.

"He descends from Hugh the Mighty," Merdin answered. "But Hugh was poisoned by an evil witch, and the crown passed to the father of Lear, from whom Vortigern descends. Still, if you had been slain by Droit, I would have lent Llewelan what strength I have, to make him King of Cambria."

We came to the island, and the tall nobleman and the tall maiden came down to the landing to greet us. The two old men immediately entered the house, whose stones were mossy with age, although still standing firm, so well had the Romans built it as a pleasure-palace for their commander, Lucillius. At my invitation, Elain entered the boat, and I rowed a little way to pluck water-lilies to match her whiteness. Pillicock had dashed off.

"It pleasured all the people that you killed Droit the Boar," Elain remarked.

"Did it pleasure you?"

"Yes, because he ate men, or at least killed them, and I didn't want him to kill you. Still, how could you help but win when it was decreed by the Gods? They wouldn't go back on their word."

"Droit didn't seem to know it when he came at me, and in truth I wasn't at all sure. Those words were sung in the days of Bran. It must be that even the Gods have lapses of memory."

"And now you're that much nearer your marriage with Wander of Cornwall." Her face changed expression slightly although she still smiled.

"Now that may be true."

"And, Ambrose—I will call you Artay—I never thanked you for

your keeping your vow when we were in the tower, although it was more from fear of the Gods—and perhaps a secret lack of inclination—than from honor."

"By the ancient law of Cambria, a king or the son of a king may honorably untie the virgin knot of any maiden other than the daughter of a king."

"It's a wicked law. I won't obey it. When you are King—if it ever happens—you can have me hanged. You spoke of forgetfulness by the very Gods. I wish I could forget what I did in the tower after you had weakened my will with sweet music."

"Why should you have trouble forgetting? It was only a few kisses and a little biting."

"So it seemed to you, because you make as free with every maiden in your reach. Besides, you did more than that."

"Yes, I did, and speaking of it makes me ache to do it again."

Her face flushed, and she did not answer me as soon or as fiercely as I expected, and seemed tongue-tied. Her hand stole to her nipple as though it itched.

"It's a good thing we are in open sunlight and in full view of my lord Llewelan, or you would overturn the boat in your fierce passions, and drown us both. Speak no more of it. I can scarcely control my anger, even though you are a prince."

"I'd rather you be hot, even with anger, than cold." And I had started to say, with great magnanimity, that with her I would forget I was a prince and become her subject, only to think better of it. And before we could continue our quarrel, which had heated me more than mead and was somehow sweeter to my taste, out from the house came Merdin and Llewelan, and we must put into shore.

That very night, Merdin invited me to come with him as he went forth with what he called his stellarscope to look at the signs of Heaven. He had made only a casual search when he saw something that made him start and grunt, and then he was silent a long minute, and I knew that great tidings were on the wing.

"Could it be this soon?" he asked himself as he lowered the thing.

"I don't know what you mean."

"The star Artay, whom the Romans called Mercury, is entering the Sign of the Fishes. What is pending has to do with bodies of water, where fishes dwell, and those stars burn steadily and do not twinkle, showing it is a body of still water, not the sea. You were out on such waters today, but you saw no swan?"

"No!"

"So the body of water is not Swan Lake. What sign was given you, if any?"

Many signs were given me, of my own desires, not the will of the Gods.

"I saw Max's bull that came to drink——"

"Ah! The Sign of the Bull. And Tyr, sometimes called Mars, is entering into that Sign, and his symbol is the sword! And there I behold Tor, who is Jupiter, full in the Sign of the Water-Carrier, and the Goddess Brigit, who is called Venus, in the Sign of the Ram. The Bull—the Water-Carrier—the Ram! Artay, is there a lake nearby where shepherds water their flocks as well as fill their jars?"

"Merdin, you know well that Witch Lake, the largest of the chain of lakes that numbers Swan Lake, is a great watering place, and the shepherds swear that its many weeds purify it, and they drink of it rather than any other."

"All that is true. I fear I am getting old and my mind fails me. But the riddle is now read. Tomorrow night, ere the Moon climbs to her high throne, we will go to Witch Lake. And what befalls there —will befall!"

He would tell me no more. That night I dreamed wildly of witches who sometimes took the form and face of Elain in order to cast a spell upon me. The next day dragged, although I practiced swordsmanship with Gerald for a good four hours, learning how to ward a stroke to my right belly, which warding might save my life on some day of savage fray. Merdin, Gerald, and I set forth not long after the Moon rose in her silvery glory, leaving Cavell howling, for he too wanted to go, and I could not guess Merdin's reason for not letting him.

We took our stand beside a skiff pulled upon the shore of Witch Lake. It lay strange-looking in the radiance of my Lady the Moon, partly because of its pale sheen, broken here and there by patches of dark weed, and the silver track she made across it by her image. No breath of wind ruffled its calm, or breath of sound disturbed its silence, and I could well believe how the lake had got its name—that at certain times Morgan the Fairy came here in mortal guise to visit her lover, who guarded a treasure-trove in its depths, and who sometimes showed himself in the shape of a great fish.

Before long Llewelan came to join us—his house was hardly a mile distant—and, saying very little, took his watch beside us. A few more dwellers in the neighborhood took form in the dimness, not joining us, but posting themselves where they could watch the whole expanse of the lake. Since they knew nothing of fortune-telling, it must be that Merdin had told them that some great wonder had been foretold by the stars.

As the Moon drew near her zenith, a light wind rustled the tree-leaves, as almost always occurred this time of night, and her bright path shimmered a little. And shortly after this, I noticed a slight commotion in the water, no more than would be made by a trout playing or feeding, perhaps two hundred yards from our post. Watching it closely, I saw something long and narrow, somewhat brighter than the moonlight, surface and move rapidly and disappear.

"What did you see, Artay?" Merdin asked in his deep voice.

"I do not know, old man."

"What did it look like?"

"Like nothing I can think of, unless it were a naked sword brandished by a mermaid, and that makes no sense."

"Take the boat, Artay my son, and row to the place, and explore this mystery. It is the time of year that Morgan the Fairy visits her lover."

So I got into the skiff, with moss growing in its seams, and in long and quiet strokes made for the scene of the happening, which I could easily identify because it was only forty feet or so from a heavy bed of floating moss, such as often hid a wounded mallard. Half-way there, I was thinking that I had come on a fool's errand, and only a long, slim, silvery fish had danced on his tail, as fish sometimes do on summer nights. Then the water broke again, and again the object showed shimmering-white in the moonlight, then quickly disappeared. So I kept on, rowing backwards, looking over my shoulder, and shortly had drawn within my boat's length of the place.

I rested on my oars and spoke, not loudly enough to be heard on shore, but easy hearing to a water-witch floating just below the faintly ruffled surface.

"Morgan the Fairy! If you are in hearing, and have a message or a token for me, give it to me now. I am Artay, son of Vortigern the King."

I waited and watched, my pulse throbbing in my finger-tips, my skin atingle. And then there came a swirl in the waters, and the naked beautiful arm of a maiden rose out of the deeps, and in her hand was a wondrous sword.

Three times she brandished his shimmering blade, perhaps in some awful warning, but if so I heeded it not, and at his first emergence drove my boat with a great pull of the oars to get in reach of him. I thought I glimpsed a dim, naked form, slender as any dryad's, a few inches below the surface, and this too I did not heed, and instead I reached my hand to the fairy's hand, and strongly seized the hilt. The arm disappeared. Faded also the wan, lovely form. Firm in my hand reposed the Sword.

Laying him carefully in the bottom, my knee across him lest he attempt to leap out of the boat, I rowed back to shore. At the landing waited, wonder-struck, not only Merdin, Gerald, and Llewelan, but the rustics who had come to watch, and although they stood a little back, their eyes were full as wide. I stopped the boat one length from the shore. Then I picked up the Sword, and he made no effort to escape my hand, and truly his hilt seemed to nestle in my palm. Carefully I looked at him, hilt to point, before speaking or looking up.

He was a long-sword, and of wonderfully hardened iron to keep such a sharp edge in the Gods knew how many centuries under water. His heavy blade bore no grain of rust, he balanced well against my strong right arm, and his hilt sparkled in the moonlight because of what might be precious jewels set in the wood in fantastic design.

Holding him in my free hand, I waded to shore, dragging the boat with the other. Merdin addressed me first.

"What do you have there, Artay?"

"The Sword."

"How did you come by him, if you'll tell us? We could not see clearly from here."

"The naked arm of a water-witch, perhaps Morgan, perhaps some other, rose with him out of the deep, and brandished him, and I took him from her hand."

"Before my Lord the Sun now resting in his palace, and before my Lady the Moon, Great Lud, and by the Land and the Water and the Air, by the Hills and the Plains, by the Wind that blows and the Rain that falls, by the good wheat and the good grass, by all the works of the Gods, and men, I declare to you that this Sword was wielded by Bran of Old and was part of his hoard guarded by some being of the deep, and that his name is Caliburn, as written in the Song of Camlon, and by his swift bite and stab and slash, you will overwhelm your enemies and come into your kingdom."

"Artay the King!" one of the rustics shouted, his voice shaking.

All of these men as well as Merdin and Llewelan, and with a certain awkwardness Gerald too, touched their knees to the ground.

By a silver cord looped about the hilt, I secured the Sword to my belt in easy reach of my right hand.

Merdin, Gerald, and I plotted together. There was no doubt, now, that five hundred of our South Cambrian swains would follow me in making war against the King, and to help lead them would come all the men of ancient name in these parts, provided, of course, that all were well-armed, as I intended they would be. I believe we could have rallied something like a thousand. Our present danger lay in Vortigern marching southward and striking our army before it was practiced in arms.

To guard against this, Merdin proposed that we send half a dozen of our worthiest and most cunning fellows into the Land of Cheshire and the Midland Plain, lying eastward of the Cambrian Mountains, whose people the Romans called Cornovii, and send another batch into the mountainous kingdom north of the plain, whose hardy folk the Romans had called Brigantes, and whom they had fought to their sore cost. Their purpose was to start rumors that Vortigern was arming against these kingdoms, whereby their kings would themselves arm, whereupon Vortigern would fear attack and make no long marches against a mob of rebellious yokels with wooden arms.

Merdin had me order that every man who would follow my banner make himself a short wooden sword and a wooden shield. With these they could drill, and have the promise of the Gods, seen by Merdin in the stars, that on a certain day after harvest-home the crude weapons would miraculously change to swords and shields of the finest Roman iron. Gerald and a few others who had skill at arms set to training the recruits in various gathering places throughout South Cambria. With the help of the *Curlew* and several other fisher craft of known loyalty to our party I undertook the task of freighting five hundred iron swords and shields from Pillicock Hill across Sabrina. After counsel with Gerald, I decided against bringing the iron-headed javelins at this time. Even the rudiments of sword-and-shield craft would be all that our yokels' heads could hold until schooled in war; and they would still be better armed than Vortigern's troops, who did not carry spears.

I was hard put to it what to use for an armory until our men would be ready to receive the metal weapons and march. Happily Merdin told me of a long burrow, used by our forefathers for burial of their dead, only two miles from the sea on the southern moors, and never entered by shepherds for fear of being cursed by the spirits of the dead. It proved to be a well-nigh perfect depository. My stout mariners, each loaded with five swords and five shields, could not take a step in the dim chamber, covered by a turf-green roof, without kicking bones and setting skulls to rolling, but I reckoned that the perils of the sea which they met with almost every day had steadied their nerves.

In just under two weeks, the weapons were stored away, waiting for the day that we would march. Before the end of September, with the crops in, all our supplies were assembled, dried beans, corn, and salted meat for rations, and sheepskin robes to erect as pavilions against heavy rain. Also I had my banner of silk cloth brought from Gaul, which bore a fine painting of my Lord the Sun in bright yellow, and a star meant to be Artay basking in his loving rays. My whole army of five hundred stalwarts assembled on the first day of October. I marched in front with a fine-looking tunic with which Llewelan had provided me, a bronze helmet boasting a horse-tail on my head, Caliburn at my side, Pillicock a little behind me and to one side, ready to run messages, Merdin walking opposite and in a white robe and carrying a staff somewhat like a reaping hook with a high-polished bronze blade, and Gerald and Llewelan on either side of the great host. On my left arm was my shield. On my right hand was the glass jar containing the human head that had long reposed on our shelf.

We had assembled about two miles from the Long Burrow, more so that the men could see the magnitude of our army on the march and thus work up their ardor for the miracle that Merdin had promised them before midday. When we came to the burrow, he stood before a single cromlech erected near its entrance, and spoke in his deep, rolling voice.

"This is the day chosen by the Gods," he told the assembly. "First, the dwarf Pillicock will build a fire, for he is beloved of my Lord the Sun, and you will march to it in file and throw on it your wooden shields and swords. When these are consumed, it may be that Tyr, God of War, and Artay, God of Soothsayers, and very Lud will demand a test of bravery of every one of you, such as entering yon burrow erected by our forefathers, and there receiving your weapons in the sight of the dead, weapons with which to destroy Vortigern's army, so that your true King may take his throne, and the happy days return."

The men shouted. Pillicock built a fire of dried moss and brushwood, and as it was swiftly fed by the wooden swords and shields of one soldier after another, its flame began to leap high and crackle in triumph. By the time its food was half-consumed, it stood as high as a house, golden as the Sun, and green as the Land of Cambria and blue as our deep rivers amid the heap of unburned stuff, giving forth a wondrous roar, and no doubt seen by fisherfolk many miles at sea.

"Artay, it is such a fire as used to be kindled in the holy groves," Merdin told me, "in thankfulness to the Gods. Often the Wise Ones gave it, besides its common food, a wicker cage in which five, seven, sometimes as many as ten slaves were confined, and their yelling could scarcely be heard above the roar of the great fire. It was pleasing to our Gods to receive this sacrifice, and the slaves chosen were almost always unruly fellows, who had broached their masters' casks or committed other offenses deserving death. Perhaps the Gods will take it amiss that we did not do the same today, for this is the great day, the day that the tide of ill flowing over Cambria at last turns back. But Llewelan told me he would withhold his power from us, including fifty archers from the Mendip Hills, if a single human soul were sacrificed to the Gods."

"Elain put him up to it," I said bitterly. "She cares nothing for the triumph of our cause, or even the Song of Camlon. If you ask me what I think, she is half-persuaded to become a foul Christian."

"No, Artay, she cares more than you know. I have had proof of that. And to speak truth, I too was reluctant to burn slaves alive, because of some frailty within my heart come upon me with my white hairs, although I would have gladly given two or three an easy passing to Elysium. Well, we will sacrifice the spotted bull, and read the auguries of his spilled guts, then throw his carcass on the coals to make a good smell for the Gods above, and surely obtain good fortune in the coming war."

"Since Elain loves slaves so much, I will make her one, or at least a man-child without a name, little better than a slave. And that I'll do whether she says yea or nay."

"Not until you are King of Cambria. She is beloved of the Gods— I have seen that also—and Pillicock would turn against you, and your followers would think that a sign of evil fortune. After you are King, any child she bears you would have an honored name."

So I let the matter go, and Merdin borrowed Caliburn and slaughtered the spotted ox. It went against my gorge to have the first blood that it spilled the blood of a beast. Then I bethought myself quickly, remembering that the beast was in sacrifice to the High Gods who had willed me the sword. To ward off their anger, I gave to the fire a thing I deeply prized, being the left ear of Droit. I had intended to present it to Wander on our bridal night, for making a little purse to be worn on her neck, containing a lock of my hair.

Merdin looked at the ox's guts, poked at them with a stick, then again spoke to the wide-eyed assembly.

"Once more the Gods have spoken! First, the big gut bulged forth before the little gut, showing that the great one here—you know his name—has been confined too long in South Cambria, and is bursting forth to encompass first all of Cambria, then all of Britain. Mark you how the small gut twists and turns, while the big gut follows a straight path. That means that his enemies will twist and turn, seeking escape from their just doom, but it will avail them not, and at last they must yield their strength to the big gut. Mark you this small dark part of the liver, and the large red part. The dark part quivers like jelly, and that stands for Vortigern the Pretender, and the red part sits firmly on the throne of the backbone, and that stands for Artay the King. No wonder that Vortigern quivers, seeing in his dreams this host marching against him! And see the heart, the surest sign of all. This piece of membrane that lies upon its strong shoulder stands for the right ear of Droit, which the King wears over his heart. And what is this I see? The big gut, which the Latins called Arto, winds clear around this organ known to the Romans as the Vort. That I have never seen before, and what can it mean except that King Artay will completely encircle and confine the pretender Vortigern?" And at that point in Merdin's solemn discourse, I could not understand the lively glint like mirth in Llewelan's eyes.

Merdin raised both hands to the Sun.

"Hear me, my lord. By my long learning I have read the signs you
have given. This host will march northward with its trust in your
majesty and power, and the majesty and power of the other Gods,
knowing that with Artay to lead them, and I to counsel him, and
Gerald the Roman and other chiefs to array them for battle, they
will be victorious. Vortigern and his slavish followers will become
crows' meat, and the ancient glories of Cambria will come again. Now
I stir the fire for the last time, ere we take up our weapons and depart.
Aye, and I will throw into it this packet of cloth, containing hair
cut from the head of Vortigern by one who hated him and held by
the faith of the Druids. And it may be, ere it is consumed, that the
Gods will give us one more sign——"

He stopped, as though too astonished for utterance. I felt my eyes
growing round and my jaw dropping, for surely all of us here were
beholding a miracle. The big bonfire had been burning with a fine
column of pure yellow flame. Suddenly the sheets were shot through
with green, blue, purple, red, and orange sparks. The wonder lasted
only a second or so, in which the men held their breaths, then let
them go in one great heave. With his fingers Merdin combed his
long white beard.

"Now, if it be Artay's will, you may enter the Long Burrow and
see if it be true that the God Tyr has provided iron weapons in place
of the wooden toys. Fear not the bones that rattle under your feet!
Ye be soldiers of the King."

As the host pressed about the entrance, a long, lank countryman
born east of the Usk spoke to his comrade.

"Seeing is believing, and until I see wi' mine own peepers, I'll
not believe. 'Tis well enough for yon ol' gaffer to mumble over bull
guts. And I've seen a fire sparkle nigh as pretty when fed wi' salty
wood from the beach. But for shields and swords o' iron in the dead
men's house—one each for us all—I'll bet 'ee a lump o' my cheese
agin 'ee salt-mutton her signs won't work today, nor yet tomorrow,
nor yet the day after . . ."

The twain passed out of hearing. A confused shouting began to
rise from the men who had already entered the burrow. Then some
of them wormed out through the press in great quiet, each with a

shield at his arm and a short-sword at his side. Their dazed expressions would have made me laugh, had I not borne the honors of a king.

"A little healthy doubt is not a bad thing," Merdin remarked to me, his keen ears having overheard the countryman's carping. "Then when the truth is rammed down the doubter's neck, it's good belly-timber. Even so, Artay, if you hear of an impious yokel raising too many questions, have him straightway hanged."

"So I will," I answered, for such was the business of a king.

Gerald had divided our force into ten cohorts, each of fifty men under a captain. No doubt fifty was a small number to bear the name, but only a few of our force had heard that a Roman cohort numbered five hundred men, and I myself dismissed the figure from my mind as one of the marvels of old, beyond man's wit to understand, such as the wall of Caer Dyv, and the rings of giant stones. And truly when my army had formed in two lines, each thrice as long as an arrow could cast from a strong bow, no Roman emperor reviewing his legions could have stood more proud. True, the dress of the men was of all sorts. Their shields and swords did not glitter in the Sun, because bronze had been mixed with the iron, or so Gerald told me; but by the same token, they had not rusted. Polishing with wet sand would brighten them, and files of flint would make the swords sharp as Gerald's knife. Both of these jobs I meant to have done before we stood trial of battle.

"Shout to your followers, and tell them that the Archdruid Merdin will speak to them before we set out," Merdin said in low tones.

But I had thought of something to say of good meat. In my place as the King, I shouted it forth before I spoke of Merdin, startling the old man somewhat.

"General of the King's Army!"

"Aye, my liege!"

"As a younker, I bore the name Ambrosius, before I knew my rightful name. Since it is a Roman name and half your blood is Roman and in Roman ways of war you are second to none, you may take it if you choose for your own. When your victories under my banner are inscribed in Latin and dispatched to the Emperor of Rome, doubtless he will be gratified that they were won by a soldier of Roman descent and cognomen."

"My liege, I have never seen the wondrous city and doubt if I ever will. My grandmother was a hill-woman, and I have breathed naught but Cambrian air, drunk Cambrian water, eaten Cambrian corn, so by your leave, I'll stick to the common Cambrian name of Gerald."

The men cheered in one voice; and for an instant I was jealous because he, not I, had scored, then I thought upon what he had said, and it came so near my heart that I was overjoyed.

When the uproar ceased, I called out that the Archdruid Merdin would now speak; and that he had tidings of great moment, I did not doubt.

"Soldiers of King Artay! You are now armed better than the slavish followers of the pretender Vortigern. Also you have the favor of the Gods, as you have seen. But you have a great defender born of woman like yourselves, yet with the might of a God, and he will go before us on the march, and you may see him with your own eyes. You have heard his name from your grandsires, and they from their grandsires, and so it lives on, since the stones of Stonehenge were first raised by his own hand. And in the Song of Camlon it is told that when he, this mighty man of old, rises from his mossy grave and leads the host of the men of Cambria, no mortal power may turn them back, and the good days will return, and the dark forest will retreat to its old boundaries, and the wolves will flee your folds, and no alien ax will cut down the Sacred Groves, and the laws will be the Ancient Law under the King, and belike he will hold sway over all Britain and the lands beyond the seas, and the Emperor of very Rome will walk in his chains. Your Majesty Artay, will you take the cover from the great jar you bear in your left arm?"

I did so, my hands shaking. Merdin reached into it with both hands, and brought forth the head that it contained, and held it aloft.

"Bran!" Merdin roared like thunder. "The father of Druids and King of the Bards. March with Bran!"

The men stood pale and very still. And then one of them blew a Roman trumpet, called a lituus, that we had found in the vaults under Pillicock Tower, a long blast that re-echoed between the waters and the sky, and thrilled every heart. In a moment more the lines

wheeled, and King Artay, his magician, his liegemen, and his mighty
army, guarded by the ghost of great Bran, moved on the march to
war. What force under Heaven could turn us back, or balk my great
designs?

2

For the time being, I must forgo the counsel and the aid of one of
my most prized liegemen. When we halted for the men to eat a late
midday meal, Llewelan asked my leave to return to his house at Swan
Lake, where he had left Elain unguarded except by a serving-wench.
"Your Majesty, I am not now, and I never was, fashioned by the
Gods for war. The smell of human blood sickens me. I cannot endure
the groaning of men when they lie wounded. My heart, which is like
the heart of a tender woman when prisoners are to be slaughtered or
cowards hanged, causes me to beg mercy for them, and in these dark
times a king's heart must be like stone. But I will rule in your name
all our part of South Cambria, keep the peace there, be ready to
furnish you men and provision at your call, and serve you well."

"You have my leave to go, and take good care of Elain," I told
him when he had knelt and laid both his hands on mine. Perhaps I
should not have given a thought to any maiden, let alone one who
had disobeyed and mocked me, at this hour when the Great Gods
were moving to make me King, but I could not help myself.

We had struck the cart-road that ran up the Taff from Caer Dyv;
and on the second day's march we entered the Forest of Fawr. In the
afternoon Gerald sent forth scouts to advance in our fore and at our
flanks, to protect us against surprise attack and to capture or kill the
King's spies. Truly neither he nor I expected any trouble this early
in our advance, but the precaution was according to Roman practice,
and he stuck to it. Of course Vortigern had been informed of our
rustics' drilling with wooden weapons, and perhaps some one in his
train, and I thought I knew the one, might have divined that it was
not all fiddle-faddle, and our other actions had been watched. Still,
if a warning of our array had somehow been signaled to Woodwick
by fires on the hilltops, the King's army could hardly have set forth
in time to lay an ambush.

We pitched camp on a furze-grown hillside, and a specious pavilion, made of oiled linen, with a sheepskin floor, was erected for me, the King. The long day had not yet died, the western sky still glimmered, and only a scattering of large, pale stars had lighted their lamps when Gerald entreated admittance.

"My liege, the scouts saw no hide or hair of spies," he told me. "One ancient woodsman was seen carrying faggots, and a maiden, who gave her name as Vivain, was found trying to make her way, weeping, down the old track from the Valley of the Wye to Your Highness' forces."

"How did she know we were here?"

"She saw it in a dream. You Cambrians are great dreamers; we Romans depend on our five wits. She had spent the night in hiding with an old woodsman, perhaps the very one our scouts encountered, but she knew he couldn't guard her much longer. I thought you might like to question her before you slept. She was at Woodwick only a fortnight gone. Also she is good to look upon, despite the thorn-scratches on her face and arms and the rags that serve her for clothes."

"Is she white or brown?" I asked, my pulse leaping at thought of her rags.

"Truly she is brown. I should guess there is flint-worker blood in her, from the Northern Mountains. You can judge for yourself, if you like."

"Yes, we will judge for ourselves," I answered with royal usage, to reprove him mildly for his blunt address. "You may send the wench here."

In a moment she entered through the vent of my tent and dropped on both knees at my feet. I took one good look at her in the light of four candles burning in wooden bowls, then could no longer refrain from bidding her rise. I had been half-tempted to give her my hand. A maiden so woebegone and yet so pleasant to my sight I had never seen.

She wore no tunic, and her shirt and skirt had been flimsy to start with and now hung in tatters. Ugly scratches were to be seen wherever the rents revealed her ale-brown skin; her long hair was restrained from wildly flowing by a piece of vine fastened about it at the back of her neck; and her face and neck were far from clean.

"I pray Your Majesty's pardon for my rags and dirt," she said in an oddly deep and pleasing voice as she stood with her head hung.

"Raise your face, so I may see it better," I ordered. "For how do I know you're not Vortigern's spy?"

"Your Highness cannot tell by looking at my face. Faces and mouths may lie; only actions do not lie. If you give me shelter—and a few scraps of food—behind the shield of your meanest churl, my actions will prove my troth."

Yet she had raised her face full in the candlelight, as I had bade her, and there was something unearthly about it, although I did not know what. It was small, dark, and exquisitely refined, like a golden neckchain I had once seen, found in a long burrow old when the Romans came. The little ridge of bone under the eyebrows I had seen in many faces was slightly more prominent in this face, curving down to form the eyesockets, so that her cheekbones stood high and bold. The eyes themselves were narrow and long, and so black throughout that they seemed to have no pupils, and were set at a slight slant. Her eyebrows were likewise black, narrow, and clean-looking, but they did not arch over her eyes and instead flared up a little at the outer ends.

Her nose was wonderfully delicate, narrow and short, and her mouth of brighter red than any I could remember, wide, full-lipped, and higher on one side than the other, giving it a beautiful oddness, and her small ears seemed to have pointed tops. And even now, before I looked carefully at her body, small, shaped to befuddle a man's thinking, the thought struck me with great force that she might be a witch of these very woods. It was well-known that such beings often approach kings in various raiment and mien, to do them evil or good, according to the command of some witch-master. But if so, surely she was a very wistful witch.

"What is your name?" I asked, although I had been told.

"Vivain of the Hill."

"Are you of ancient lineage?"

"More ancient than Wander of Cornwall—on my mother's side. How it came about, I pray not to tell you yet, for you wouldn't believe me. My father was a woodsman whose name was Powys, or so he told my mother, Calypso of the Hill, when they lay under the linden tree, where she had enticed him."

"Is he alive now?"

"No, we heard how he was killed and eaten by the boar Droit."

"Droit is through with eating people." I did not point to the trophy pinned on my tunic for she saw it plain enough.

A sheen came upon her black eyes, and what could it mean but unspeakable joy at Droit's destruction?

"Your speech is that of the high-born," I said. "That is a strange thing if your mother was a wanton."

"My mother could speak in all the tongues of Britain, and in many more tongues. She came to the Forest of Fawr a long time ago, from some island in a distant sea."

"She was very poor?"

"In all that the forest did not provide, she was very poor. But I had enough to eat, and clothes made of deerskin."

"How did you happen to go to Vortigern's court?"

"Because the King asked my mother's help in a great war presently to be waged. I went there at her command."

"King Vortigern asked the help of an old woman of the forest?"

"Yes, but she was very old and lame, and her powers have faded because she angered the God Tyr, and she sent me in her place."

"I see it now," I said, my scalp tight on my pate. "Not you, but she, is a witch."

"That is true, my liege. I am of flesh and blood, the same as Elain."

"Why do you speak of her, witch-spawn?"

"Her too I saw in a dream. She is beautiful and tender, and your true love."

"No, she didn't love me enough to give me her flower before I set forth to perilous war."

"Forgive her, my liege. She loves you truly, but is jealous of your betrothed, Wander of Cornwall."

"You too are of gentle heart, and it's not your fault you were conceived in the womb of a witch. Why did you flee from Vortigern's court, and if you won his favor, why are you dressed in rags?"

"My lord, I did not win his favor, nor did I seek it. I won his hate."

"I bid you tell me how."

"By not obeying his princely wishes. Well I know that the wishes of the King are the law of the land, second only to the will of the Gods, and I would have obeyed them if he had been still the King, even though—but that too you would not believe. He still wore the crown and sat on the throne of Cambria, but the true king had been long known to the Gods, and known to all men when Morgan the Fairy brought up from the waters the Sword Caliburn, and you took it in your hand to wear at your side. The Gods had decreed Vortigern's fall when he committed a monstrous crime against his own blood, but they are patient, and their mills grind slowly. So when the news came to me of the new, the true king, I was no longer bound to obey him, and I left the robe he had given me, along with a necklace of amber with a golden clasp, in the place he had given me to sleep, and I put on my own poor raiment and fled his court."

"What were his wishes that you disobeyed?"

"My lord, you probe deep. You force me to tell what a beggar-maid should not, at least until by your own searching you had found proof of its truth. I was got by my father, the woodsman Powys, under a linden tree when the full Moon was atop the sky. It is the whim of the Gods—or some intent that I know not—that I yield my flower likewise under a linden tree when the full Moon sits her throne, and if I do otherwise I will be accursed, and the child I bear will be created of spleen. My mother, Calypso, saw the vision in her boiling cauldron, and told me of it, and so despite what I fear is a certain wildness, even a wantonness in my nature which I sucked in from her milk, I have until now——"

"You've spoken truth so far, Vivain of the Hill, as far as I can tell. Too, I can believe in the wildness and the wantonness, unseen in your sweet face, and which sets my blood on fire. But that ardor, and your sleeping in the same palace with Modred, will not let me believe what you were about to say; and so that you may retain my trust, do not say it, and that is my royal command."

"My liege, I obey your command. But if I am not a maiden, will you grant me a boon?"

"Ask it."

"It is not your favor or your gold. Only feed me to your dog of war, Cavell."

"Maiden, you may tell my quartermaster to give you food and a secure place to sleep. Now you have my leave to go."

She knelt, and slipped away in the thickening dark. Once I had mistaken a mortal man, with malformed legs, for a gnome; so it was no wonder I had mistaken a demi-witch for a common damosel. Yet I marveled over her presence in our camp, about which sentries walked, and where rustics ate, drank, grumbled, snored, and did all common things. I would have never laid eyes on her if I had not been King. More clearly than before I glimpsed the vast void that lies between kings and all other folk that walk the earth. I began to see how they were the deputies of the High Gods, and how the Law was theirs, as Regan had said, and who on earth could arraign them for its breach? Why, a king's whim had more weight than the clamor of a whole people, or why had the Gods let this whim drift into his heart?

I opened the vent of my pavilion, and looked up at my Lady the Moon. She rode high in the sky at a darting pace through patches of cloud, and tomorrow night her rising would be a splendid thing in the glory of her fullness and in the fullness of her glory. I lay down and dropped off to sleep, in love with being a king.

3

Late in the following afternoon, as our long file wove in and out of the southern fringes of Radnor Forest, a runner came up to me, panting, bringing word that the damosel Vivain would speak to me on an urgent matter.

My first thought was that the day's tramp through rough country had overtaxed her and she wanted some kind of a litter. If so, I had no intention of providing it, thinking that if an unburdened demi-witch could not keep pace with chawbacons each with shield, sword, and heavy rucksack, she could lag behind. I was about to dismiss the messenger when I perceived that he was frightened.

"Did she say what the matter was?" I asked.

"Nay, lord, but she'd seen some kind of vision, and its spell was on her, 'cause she could hardly speak, and her eyes be wild as a lynx-cat's. 'Blood, blood,' she kept muttering. 'Blood spilled on the ground.' "

It was time for the men to fall out a little while, to ease their various members, so I had Gerald order a halt, and in a moment or two Vivain was speaking to me out of hearing of my followers. She was over the worst of her fright, but a wildness still glimmered in her long black eyes.

"My liege, sometimes I see visions," she told me. "Usually they come to me in my dreams, but sometimes when I am wide awake, and sometimes they are true, and sometimes false. I implore you to remember that I am not as other maidens, but the daughter of Calypso of the Hill, and I cannot draw out the witchery she gave me in her blood and milk."

"Speak freely, daughter of Calypso."

"There is an ambush laid within a mile. There is a spinny of trees that I think are thorn, on the left and close to the road. In it a band of men, more than twenty and less than forty, lie concealed, and all have axes with bronze heads, of the sort that men throw at marks. It comes to me that they mean to throw and flee, and they won't waste their weapons on your common followers, and all will let fly at you, the old magician, and Gerald, your General. And I saw blood spilled on the ground, but whether it was the blood of my great protector, or of one of his chiefs, or of the lyers-in-wait, balked in their design, I could not tell."

"If your vision is true, the blood will be spilled by the lyers-in-wait, and I will know that you were sent to me by the Gods."

As I thought of measures to turn the tables on the foe, I wondered if our scouts, about a mile ahead of our main body, would discover their ambush. It seemed to me unlikely if the band comprised only one or two score, who would be able to lie low amid down-timber or in a steep-banked water-course, and anyway, our spies would be fanned out, and hardly be expecting attack from a spinny in ax-throw of the road.

So I bade Gerald have nine of our ten cohorts advance at a slow pace, with their usual noise of clanking shields, shouted commands, and murmur of talk, while one cohort moved swiftly and silently to flank the road at about two hundred paces, keeping the best cover the men could find. Of course I would go with this detachment, for Gerald had told me never to withhold my presence from the thick of any fight, and to let my bronze helmet shine before all, or the Gods would withhold victory. And truly I had not needed this sage advice, because of my heart's surgings.

Merdin was too old and stiff in the joints to advantage our enterprise, and I would leave him mumbling in his beard. Just now the mumble had increased to a mutter because he had surmised that Vivain had stolen his thunder and had been given signs which his aging eyes had missed. But there was another with our band, young and with nimble joints, who might serve us well.

"Vivain, will you go with us?" I asked when Gerald and I had completed our brief parley and the men were taking off their helmets. "If you do, the blood on the ground may be your own witchy blood, spilled by a well-aimed ax."

"How could you find the place of ambush without my help?" was her blunt response. "There are scores of spinnys, and only I can recognize the one shown me in my day-dream. I fear no ax that your enemy can throw."

So began our hunt, and the very spies Gerald had sent out, whose watch over us I had lately doubted, might have spoiled it for us. Truly they were questing closer than I had realized, combing the woods, and surely one would have found the ambush and doubled back to warn us, or at least shouted a warning before felled with an ax. Truly, too, Gerald was a greater general than I had yet perceived. But he was able to signal in the leader of the scouts, and bid him have his men avoid the region Vivain had described, so as not to flush the enemy band.

As we advanced, she proved the nimblest hunter in our party, slithering, it seemed, through thickets where my tall yokels were half-stuck, leaping logs like a fox, easily keeping pace a little at my rear. I could not help but turn and glance at her sometimes, for her small body being so lively caused pleasant glowings in my blood, and her face, sharp now with her intent, was more captivating than in candlelight. It would be a joy to see, I thought, in a full flood of moonlight.

We had gone short of a mile when she ran forward and made bold to touch my arm.

"There it is," she told me, her eyes gleaming. And she pointed to a dark spinny of thorn close to the road and about two hundred paces on my right hand.

I showed it to Gerald. His quick eyes studied the terrain, then he had our men form a line of attack, to advance about six feet apart, hidden from the foe by a thinly wooded hilltop. They moved forward in good order, red of face and bright of eye, their bare feet made no sound on the turf, and it seemed to me that all went wondrous well. Near the crest of the hill, he signaled them to halt, while he and I crept forward to peer over. Then we glanced at each other in dismay. We could see the soldiers plainly at about a hundred paces, hidden by tall thickets from a column advancing up the road, waiting with axes ready to hurl through an open place, taking its unwary leaders from the rear. But between us and them, the downslope of the hill lay completely naked, to expose us instantly if we launched a charge.

There were thirty of them, fifty of us. Again Gerald and I glanced at each other, for we were thinking the same thing, and his eyes asked a question. If the foe stood, we could overwhelm them, but they would not stand; they would wait till we came in easy ax-range, throw, and run. We would lose a good twenty of our men, and the rest could overtake and kill only a handful. So I answered Gerald with a shake of my head.

There was nothing for us then but to turn back, cross the slope, descend into the woods, and approach their ambush on far less favorable ground. Still, the movement was progressing well. I dreamed again we might take the whole band by surprise when at a stone's throw from our goal we came on a naked gully which we must cross unseen. We had begun to worm our way down when one of the enemy band shouted the alarm. Their plan foiled, they did not linger to do battle but took to their heels.

All but one! As we surged across the gully toward the spinny, an officer who had caught his foot between two fallen logs tugged in vain to free himself, then turned and faced us with his ax raised.

"By the Great Gods, one of you will die if I can't buy my life," he shouted. Because all too likely he spoke the truth, and his fellows had made good their escape into thick woods, I yelled for the men to halt.

"What price will you pay for your life?" I asked. And if it was not enough, I knew ways to make his tongue wag freely.

"Your Highness, I'll pay not with gold or silver, but with a fact it will profit you to know."

"What is it?"

"If I tell you, and if you see the profit in it, will you pledge yourself to spare me, and put me not to torture, and when your war with Vortigern is over set me free?"

"Why, I see no harm in that."

Meanwhile there was a little stir in the woods behind him. I thought some one of the enemy band might have hidden there, until I looked closer, and perceived vaguely that the person was very small, child-like in appearance, and the truth did not break upon me until too late. Quick as a fox Vivain sprang out of the thickets. Her hand was out and black, holding something that glittered in the sunlight, then its glitter died as it passed into shadow. The prisoner raised a great cry, dropped to his knees, then pitched to the ground. On that ground blood was spilled, as Vivain had foretold.

He would tell no secrets now, with a handslength of iron blade in his back. Then Vivain ran to me wailing, and dropped on her knees at my feet.

"Whip me," she begged. "Make my back bleed with the lash, for I obeyed my evil heart instead of my King's command."

"What did you have against him, Vivain, that you should kill him when he and I were in parley?"

"Nothing. Nothing more than his leading the band that set forth to kill the King. The rest was wickedness."

"I wouldn't call that wickedness, my liege," rose a voice from our band, a big voice with bumpkin accents, and I thought it the voice of the lank man who had questioned Merdin's auguries. "Whatever the knave had told you, it would have been a cheat."

"That may be true," I said without looking at the speaker. "Again, he might have told us free for what now we must pay dearly. Vivain, come to my tent tonight when my Lady the Moon is well-sped on her journey. I mean that you too shall suffer pain."

"Aye, my liege," she answered, woebegone.

"Now all of you make your way to the road, rest your legs till the others come up, and fall in."

4

The Moon rose in splendor in the seventh hour after noon. Not until nearly midnight would she gain her throne, mistress of all the hosts of Heaven, and when I had supped well I slept until the eleventh hour. All the camp lay hushed except for the march of sentries when I rose, summoned Pillicock, and bade him carry my sheepskin robe, along with its grass-filled pillow to the nearest linden tree adjacent to my bivouac. His countenance looked troubled under the searching gaze of the round and beauteous Moon, and he had guessed what was afoot, and his thoughts dwelt upon Elain, alone with her father in their island stronghold. My thoughts too lighted on her briefly, I felt one sharp qualm of regret, then remembered the promise she had had me make, and also that I was the King.

He was gone a third part of an hour, returning empty-handed and with face longer than before. Still I could not bring myself to chide him, let alone deal him a blow, for it was his love of Elain, more than duty to me, that had caused him to reveal the hoard of weapons with which I could wage war.

"Why were you gone so long?"

"My liege, there is only one linden tree in our environs, and it was hard to find."

"Does it stand in our guarded ground?"

"No, a little way beyond it, on the hillside in heavy woods. One who sleeps beneath it would be easy to surprise, but hard to chance upon, by roaming spies."

"That is good enough. The Great Gods will defend me against evil chance. They too relish good sport, and will not blame me for seeking it, and my Lady the Moon will smile down."

He took me a little way and pointed out the tree. Even by moonlight I could see its big heart-shaped leaves, which were no doubt the cause of Vivain's mother, Calypso, choosing this kind of tree to shield her bed when she enticed Powys the woodsman. Probably she had seen him at work in the forest, and had doted upon him, and surely the heart-shaped leaves rustling above the lovers would benefit their love. "Don't be alarmed if you see no more of me until sunrise," I told Gerald as I stopped by his supper-fire.

"It may be that tomorrow our army will fall foul of Vortigern's army," he answered, "and a great battle will ensue. I pray you not weaken yourself by venery."

"We wish to give our favors to one who has served us well," I answered royally. "Besides, what we do tonight will strengthen our thews."

"It may be so, my liege. But kings are men first of all."

"In any case, do not come near the linden tree on the slope of the hill eastward, and let none of our followers blunder by."

"My liege, none will pass beyond our lines into a forest deep and thick as you will enter."

In my tent I found Vivain waiting, her eyes cast down. How could I have lusted for Elain's hawthorn-blossom whiteness and her tall queenly form when the forest had held secret, waiting for me to come, a small brown demi-witch whose upward-stealing glance of jet-black eyes dizzied my brain? The side of one breast showed through a rent in her shirt. Her ripped skirt revealed a reach of a slim brown thigh, and I could not stay my hand from the entrance-way torn by a friendly thorn. I would love Elain always, I told myself, and bring her to great honor, and perhaps give her in marriage to one of my earls. By Wander I would beget sons, to reign after me and defend the dynasty that I would found. Vivain I would keep in my palace, for her witchy wisdom that would warn me of plots against my throne, and for my delicious plaything.

"This is our appointed hour, Vivain of the Hill," I told her, "and I will take you to the appointed place."

"My liege, I entreat that you take thought on the rashness of it. There is no proof that the lyers-in-wait you foiled today have fled far. They might still be lingering in the woods, waiting their chance."

I laughed to see the maiden's eyes grow big. "Folly is on your tongue," I told her, "and I would rather have its honey. Never before have those ax-bearing oafs seen a real king. They have seen only Vortigern, a mock-king. They will beat hares a-running, and little pigs a-squealing, until they can smell their own dung-heaps."

"I pray you, my liege, not to dismiss lightly your father, Vortigern, for he is a man of might and wondrous cunning that long years have taught him. Wait till this Moon wanes and again waxes full. That will be only eight-and-twenty nights, and by then you'll have won the great war, and he will lie in chains, or in ground as cold."

"Kings cannot wait their heart's desire. It is more fierce and commanding than that of common hearts. A king's will is mightier than common wills, and it must not be balked." And as always, when I spoke of kingliness, I found myself employing more stately language than was my wont, and not the slurred speech of the people. Strangely enough, Vivain used such language always. It had to do with her being a demi-witch, I thought, but I did not know in what connection, and my thoughts were too tangled to seek it.

"Still, I implore you to wait till the next full Moon."

"Vivain, have you not felt the fever that consumes me?"

"A touch of it, I confess."

"Then how can you brook delay?"

"For your safety's sake, I can, even though I toss all night in my cold bed, and burn as with fire."

"I bid you take my hand and come with me."

"Is that your royal command? If so, I may not disobey it. But I beg you——"

"It is my royal command."

"Then I can say no more."

At once I unharnessed Caliburn, and hung him on my tent-pole, and I need not have decreed death to any of my followers that lay hand on him, for they would have rather touched a viper than his jeweled hilt. In his place, for I had sworn to the Gods never to bear him on any enterprise other than war, I buckled on the sword that I called Droit, good enough for striking with its flat any yokel who blundered near our tryst. Then I held out my big hand. Into it slipped a small brown hand, hard but silky-smooth. Then we stole out into wondrous silver-gray that my Lady the Moon pours down in enormous flood, and walking wide of the watchfires, we made for the hill.

We came under the linden tree, and a little brush of breeze struck it the second of our arrival, so that its big heart-shaped leaves rustled together as though to tell us something. We sat down on the white sheepskin robe, and I thought to make no haste, lest I frighten the witch-child. Already she was struggling against alarm, or so I judged from the chill of her small hand and the alert look on her face revealed by moonlight which sifted in silver flakes through the foliage above us. Midnight had not quite set in and the Moon had a step or two to climb before she gained her utmost throne and three hours would pass before the mists of dawn would sift and settle on the hillside.

"You know now what I meant when I said I'd give you pain?"

"I knew it before you said it, for I had been told of it in dreams."

"Are you afraid?"

"Of pain? No, my liege. My mother, Calypso, taught me pain before I could walk, with a whip with the barb of a sting-ray at its tip. She loved me, but knew that unless I could bear pain I could never be witch or woman."

"I am told it is not too great, and I'll be gentle."

"Do not be gentle, my lord. Be the man who is chosen King. But since you ask of my fears, I will speak of one."

"What is it?"

"At the instant I was conceived, Powys, my sire, uttered a great cry. Such is not uncommon among men, Calypso told me, when they make a life great in their fates, and you know how the mandrake screams when its roots are torn out. I fear that you too may make outcry, and some enemy may hear you, and be led to our hiding-place and strike you off guard."

I did not know why her telling me this excited me beyond bounds. I took hold of her, and tore her raiment worse than had the thorns, until she lay, pale-brown, of fairy forming, drawing deep breaths in my arms. Then I began to woo her in a score of ways in which youth need not be taught by an itching widow. The lore is implanted in him before he can talk quite plain by the goddess we call Sul, whom the Romans sometimes called Venus, sometimes Persephone, and sometimes Diana, who may be our Lady the Moon. At least this holds true of our hot-blooded Cambrian youth. Whether it applies to oafs of the Midland Plain I cannot swear.

"Will my Lord take off his clothes, to make me his good match?" she asked. And before I could answer she did the service for me, her hands wondrously quick at my buckles and latchings, although prone to linger now and then, while she nearly wept from inward conflict between duty and temptation. Heat rose within her, delicious in my nostrils, when my whole body, smooth as any king's reared in a palace, was free for her wanton play. But when I thought to mellow her still more, to save her pain, she pressed me down upon her, whispering in my ear even as she snapped at it with her small, fox-sharp teeth.

"Now, my liege, my lover. See, the Moon has almost gained her throne, and you will be too late." But I deemed it not the Moon's swift climb that stirred her to such haste but the upsurge of her own humors, and she had seized upon a ladylike excuse. Other seizures followed, I too could no longer wait, and small though she was, looking even smaller in the clutch of my big arms, I did not spare her travail that maids are born to bear to make them more grateful to the Gods for what might follow.

She bore it with no sound but a little whimpering. But only a moment later, when the pain was drowned in rapture, she could well remember the warning she had given me, for it was she, not I, who had needed it. As the Moon reached the apex of her ascent, and we too had soared so high that in a moment we must fall, Vivain uttered a yell such as our farm-wenches give forth in a hay-cock, scaring their own sheep. Truly, though, I heard it only dimly, for the whole wide world had climbed inside of me somehow, and lost itself, and nothing mattered or could scarcely exist but the riveted bond between our bodies.

A huge running, climbing sea broke against rock. Then, before I could find myself, or know where I was, there was a great confusion in the dark woods, close and thick about me, and human shapes in swift movement in and out of moonlit patches, and then a brain-rocking blow on the back of my head that stunned me into helplessness. I could not cry out. I heard some one running down the hill, and dimly knew he sought to help me, and since the footfalls were too fast for a man of full-length legs, it was surely Pillicock who in vain had tried to guard me. Suddenly the sound ceased and I knew he had fallen into an ambush and I had little hope that he still lived.

Men bent over me with ropes in their hands, and one had a club raised to dash out my brains if I found breath to shout. I did not have it, I could only lie like a poled ox. Not so, Vivain. I caught a glimpse of her with her knife bared, fighting with three soldiers, and one of them she slashed in the side, and when another seized her wrist, she scratched and bit like a cornered wildcat. But she was soon trussed, with a rag stuck in her mouth.

Some one picked up her clothes and mine. My ropes were fast by now; and she on the back of a soldier, and I over the shoulder of a huge fair-haired slave, we were lugged along the hillside in the fore of a band of about ten. Two or three of them conferred together, then climbed the hill a distance to look at something, and I took it that the object of their gaze would be Pillicock, since he had run from that direction, and if he were dead they would let him lie, and if wounded finish him off. We had not gone far when we found other men, waiting with two horses. I was laid on the back of one, my long legs lashed together under his belly. Vivain was allowed to sit her horse, with her hands bound, and a man to lead him. And before we had well started on our way the men who had left the band rejoined it, with Pillicock, his wrists bound, his mouth gagged, and with a kind of hobble about his ankles to shorten his step still more, tramping stolidly and strongly in their fore. His head was bloodied from a blow, as mine was, and his strength was returning swiftly, and mine the like.

But what good could it do me now? My head swam no more, or was it any longer dizzied by lust, and all I could think of was that my kingliness had ended before it had well begun.

5

I noticed that our captors did not wheel back to the cart-road, and instead kept to the thick woods. It could only mean that they feared the alarm of my disappearance would soon be raised, and they would be chased and perhaps overtaken before they could carry out the orders they were under. They did not know that I had told Gerald I might be absent, making sport with Vivain, until sunrise, and to let no yokel blunder near our tryst.

But I had as well rejoice in the sport already made, seeing that its like and all forms of merry-making, and everything else I was used to doing, were no doubt drawing to a sudden close. Would the Great Gods, who can move mountains, and who had dwelt with me so handsomely until now, stoop down, cut my small ropes, and set me free? When I tried to believe they would do me this slight favor, my brain balked. Instead I wondered if the Song of Camlon had been one of their monstrous jests.

Yet presently the Gods did move, and in a sudden and surprising way, whether to help or harm I could not tell. The breese that usually sprung up shortly after midnight kept rising above its common level, swaying the tree-tops, shaking the leaves, and clouds began to thrust their strange shapes up from the eastern horizon, blotting out stars. Our guards gazed skyward with strain in their faces, talking in undertones. Again and again I thought the outward thrust of the dark pall had stopped or begun to retreat, only to see that more of the lights of Heaven had gone out, and the Moon turned pale in her high place. In a moment or two more there were no more rents through which she could gaze, and the darkness thickened as the sky filled, and when the last lone star to the westward gave up the ghost, the breese smelled wet, and suddenly it was blowing a misty rain.

In no time it wet my mouth cloth, so I could breathe better. It was cool but not cold, and it quickened my skin and bestirred my brain and somehow revived a little hope in my sick heart. Our captors tried to keep their course, only to lose it in a few paces and to stumble and curse amid thickets and fallen logs. Presently they halted and gathered to confer. I could not make out their shapes ten steps away, and if my knot-tyer had not rivaled the hangman Gwyn in skill, I would have loosed myself and vanished in the darkness. Because they could not see me, they seemed to reckon I could not hear their talk, or else they thought that the light wind and the rattled rain were making enough noise to blanket their voices. I did not know one speaker from another for all spoke with a kind of sameness, since all were too discomfited and at a loss to put on tricks of speech.

"Max, what made this storm come up so quick?"

"Why, the cursed weather."

"No, I think it was the Gods. They favor Artay over Vortigern, as they've shown full well by his five hundred followers obtaining arms overnight."

"Perhaps it's so, but for me, I'll 'bey the King's command, lest I wear a hempen collar."

"If you ask me, I think it's an enchantment worked by the witch-girl he was so snug with. What happened to Cadwallader? Is he here?"

"No, he stopped to fix the bandage where the witch slashed him. 'Twas half an hour ago, and I reckon he's bled to death."

" 'Twas not her who brought this weather; or so I figure. 'Twas that monster, Rufus. Those freaks of nature have wondrous power over weather and such like. I wish when O'Neill bashed him, he'd spilled his brains."

"The King said to bring him back alive. He's never got over the smart of Rufus escaping him, with Queen Ina helping. But you can spill 'em now, if you like. There's naught to stop you."

"Not me. If the King said bring him alive, 'tis what I'll do."

"Short of 'em getting away?" asked a deep-voiced fellow. " 'Tis his very words. Why not give each a good clout, and say they tried to break, and 'twas either lop 'em down or lose 'em?"

" 'Ee can do it if 'ee's a mind," said a rustic from the Wilts Country. "But 'twill be on 'ee hands. Who are 'ee, anyhow? I've never seen 'ee before today."

"I serve the King. And 'twould be good service to him, even if he don't know it, to bring him only heads on this black night, not whole men who might've broke and run. I'll spare the wench. The King might fancy her. But here's a stone that my toe bumped—just the thing . . ."

He fell silent, because he was picking up the stone. It was the moment of greatest danger since our capture. A chill that must be the augury of swift death coursed through my blood.

" 'Ee had best take thought before 'ee goes too far," the Wilts countryman warned. "The King's word be, her wants 'em alive."

"Why do you reckon?" broke in another voice, and it might be the voice of a God speaking with the mouth of a common man, to divert the stranger from his murderous intent. My tiny flickering flame of hope, fighting my chill, burned steadier.

"I take it, he means to burn the Prince in a wooden cage," some one answered. "No old man ever hated a younger with more vim, let alone a father unto his son."

"Before that, he'd hold him hostage against those crazed South Cambrians who'd follow the old magician, or even the Roman general, to take such a blood-price as never was. But by dangling him in the smoke and flame one minute the first day, two the second, three the third, and so on, the King could soon make them lay down their arms. But I'd not 'spect you, Price, to think of that. 'Tis the business of courts, and beyond your cowherd wit."

"It may be so," resounded the deep voice, no longer resolute. "But I know one who'd not let the business of courts stay him from a little head-knocking, if 'twould save trouble, and there's a man as well as a prince. I wish he was here to tell us what to do. He said he would be." And a dropped stone thudded on the ground.

"We've lost him in the dark."

"Stop your cawing, you crows, for I hear something."

They listened with all their ears and I with mine. All I could hear was the ripple of water.

"That's Barney Brook," the same voice said. " 'Tis not an arrow-cast in our van. If we follow up two arrow-casts, we'll come on what's left of Barney Village. Four or five of the houses still have roofs. At least we can build fire, and dry ourselves, till the light begins to clear and we can find our way."

"Why, 'tis a good notion," said some one who had appointed himself a kind of leader of the band, or at least an arbiter of its disputes.

So at once we were on the move, with no trouble to find the brook, and an old village path gave good walking up its bank. Then I made out the ghosts of roof-trees in the black dark, and presently was being hauled off the horse's back. I had awaited this moment in great coldness of bosom, hoping that when my feet were freed from each other I could break and run, only to have the bad luck of some little fellow, with his head well-screwed on his shoulders, take charge of my unhorsing, and with it, take great pains. When one of my feet was freed he kept a strong grip on the rope, and he gave it a yank as I hit ground, upsetting me. While another held his knife point on my throat, he latched both feet again, and I was helpless as a trussed hen at market. Once more the brawny fair-haired slave heaved me on his back and carried me into a dank-smelling hut, and rolled me on the earthen floor against the wall.

No other prisoner was put with me, perhaps an honor paid my princehood for the last time. Or more likely one of the band had his attention fixed on Vivain, she having troubled his mind and disturbed his members ever since the rude interruption of our sport, and he had put her in another hut for his own use. Still, it would take a bold man, I thought, to woo an unwilling witch. Pillicock I had lost track of before we had gained the brook, and I could not help but hope he had crept away.

"Will those ropes hold?" asked the self-appointed leader.

"If they don't, you can fix me a noose, and I'll stick my head in it," the head ropeman answered.

"Then you can come to the fire that O'Neill's building in the old smithery. We've some chestnuts to put in it, and some gullet-wash to ward off fever."

I was left in the dark alone. I could not even rub off the wet rag stopping my mouth. If I were able to do this, could I not get my hands up in reach of my teeth to bite the rope in two. Two pennies' worth of flaxen cord between me and a kingdom! Still I did not go mad, as did King Lear in no better hut than this and as naked as I. I lay listening.

In only a few minutes I had the sense of some one in the room with me. I could not see him, the Gods knew, and any noise he had made was drowned by the rattle of rain, so it must be I smelled him. I sniffed deeply, and detected a medley of smells, as pleasant as the wild smell of otter fur. He was moving quietly toward me. It might be he meant to kill me, but what other purpose his visit might have I did not dare hope.

Long before he reached me I knew it was not Pillicock. The step was too light. I felt the rag give way at my mouth as a keen knife cut the knot.

"Friend or foe?" I whispered.

"Your foe, but friend of myself, the only friend I have."

My hair raised up for the low, amused tone could issue from only one mouth.

"What do you want here?" I whispered. "My life?"

"Not tonight. I'll seek it later. Tonight I want to pay a debt, for its weight displeasures me, and ties my hands. You spared me in the tower because I gave you a promise. Give me one, and I'll spare you, at least till we meet again."

"What is it?"

"You bargain like a Greek pedlar instead of jumping at the chance. My brother Artay, if you knew your predicament—but I'll get on. I promised to tell my followers that you'd fled Cambria. You must promise to tell no one of my visit here, as long as I live. Let the people believe that Vivain or Rufus the Monster loosed your ropes by enchantment."

"I ask that you free them too, or at least keep them alive until I can rescue them by force of arms, and that trial should give you good sport."

"I'll loose them too." Meanwhile he slid his knife through the ropes at my feet. "Rufus outwitted me, Modred, in the fog, and so deserves a better end than my royal father would provide. Vivain is in love with you, it seems, and the love of even a half-witch will raise the devil in your life, and no doubt get you into other fixes such as you got in tonight. I'll give all three of you the fourth part of an hour, then I'll interrupt the roisterers in the smithery, ask about the prisoners, and Tor in his wrath won't hold a candle to me when they gape at the empty cages. My trouble will be to save 'em a hanging when we return to Woodwick."

Meanwhile he had freed my wrists, and I stretched and flexed my arms to drive off numbness.

"Modred, I know not what to say."

"Try saying nothing. You South Cambrians are a windy lot; restrain yourself. And for love of the Gods, don't thank me. I'll be well-rewarded by your survival for awhile yet, never fear. Also, I

165

would almost give my right hand to see you return to camp, naked as a new-hatched daw. A fine predicament for a would-be king!" And I could well imagine the mirth in his eyes.

"I'll shake hands with you if you will, in token that we're even up to this moment."

"Up to fifteen minutes from now, then we'll start our hunt." But he groped in the dark for my hand.

"Farewell for now, brother Modred."

"Tell Vivain she can wear a leaf from a linden tree—if it doesn't wither in the heat. Farewell for now—fare ill in the future—at my hands, no other's. No kingly hate will spoil my sport, if I can help it."

I slipped out the broken door into the close dark. Laughing and loud talk poured from the smithery, and I saw the black shapes of the guards against firelight. I returned to the brook, waded it a distance, then struck off through the forest toward our bivouacs. Somehow I could not doubt that Vivain and Pillicock were likewise on the move. The clouds were lightening a little, I observed; now and then my Lady the Moon showed her wan shape.

The High Gods had moved in my behalf, that I would never doubt, and belike they had taught me a lesson fit for a king. It was not to mix fighting a war with frolicking with wenches, especially witches.

Chapter Eight
The Great Battle

Just short of our bivouacs, I saw two figures, one very short of stature, the other far from tall, walking the cart-road. One I made out to be Pillicock, taking his usual sturdy stride, and the other was Vivain, with a vine bearing thick foliage looped about her waist. I thought to fasten a similar vine about my waist, only to conclude it would heighten the ridiculous of my appearance. So I walked on in the same raiment in which I was born.

The hour was approaching the sixth after midnight, and although my Lord the Sun still lingered behind the eastern hills, reluctant to get up, his face was shining into the mirror of the sky, and the forest shadows had fled. And immediately I learned that Gerald had not waited until sunrise for my return from the tryst, but somehow had found out I had disappeared, for I heard the bugle stridently blowing to assemble our whole force. We hastened on, to find the men fully armed, their lines almost formed, their faces long, Merdin's and Gerald's faces ghostly-white. They saw me a few seconds later, and the change sent a great glow to my heart, and I no longer thought about my unkingly appearance; and if Modred had been watching, the big laugh that he would have expected would have choked him.

While the men yelled their joy, I sent Vivain to her lodging, then, with Pillicock staunch behind me, I approached their lines. Bidding Malcolm order that these be dressed, every man having his sword and shield in place, chin up, back straight, eyes front, standing motionless as Romans before Caesar, stark-naked I reviewed my whole force, front and rear, stopping now and then to run my finger along the edge of a sword, and praised or chided according to its merits, and sometimes pushed in a belly with my fist, or squared a man's shoulders with my hands.

"General, you may dismiss them now, to eat a hearty breakfast," I said when I had completed the inspection, "for in half an hour we will march."

All the eyes that I could see were bright and beady.

At the start of the march Merdin veered close to me, with deep trouble in his face.

"Your Majesty, if you'll kindly tell me, how did you lose your garments and your sword?"

"Vivain and I were surprised as we were pleasuring each other, and taken captive. Pillicock, running to my help, was knocked down and likewise taken."

"You left word with Gerald, when you and the damosel set forth, not to be alarmed if you did not return until sunrise. Sometimes even kings, especially young kings, do rashly. You had told me no such thing, and at four hours past midnight, when I inquired for you, I lost no time in seeking you. I found your bed well beyond our guarded ground, and in the thick woods of the hillside. It was stained with blood, and a great deal of blood was seen where some one had been knived. Plainly the Gods freed you from captivity, but they are not always so forgiving of those who have been careless of their great gifts, and have behaved like fools."

"Merdin, I am the King. Guard your tongue well."

"That I'll not do, were you ten times the King. I believe Vivain to be a witch, or part-witch. It is the nature of witches to delight in brabble. They love it more than they can ever love a man, even a king. There was once a King of the Picts who dealt with witches, and they persuaded him to undertake ventures against which his good sense warned him, and one of these brought about his death. According to the tale, they favored neither him nor his opponent, and sometimes they took one side and sometimes the other, for all they wanted was the sight of men fighting and killing each other. I think that witches hate all men. Even when they itch and seek pleasure from them, they hate them still."

"Vivain is half-woman. And she fought for me like a bitch-wolf, killing one of the hiders-out and another of the same band that took us prisoner."

"Such is not strange in a witch, especially if she be half-woman. I grant that her vision of men in wait came true."

"Also she warned me against lying with her last night, with enemies about."

"That too would not be strange conduct in a witch. At war with all men, they know the nature of man. So I come to you with my counsel, to which I add my heart-felt petition. First, I urge that you tell her none of our plan of battle or any secret which can be used against us. Second, that starting tonight you post a guard over her, on the excuse of protecting her, but with orders to see that she doesn't fade away into the forest or pass signals to any one. Third, that you never go with her into unguarded places, and if you wish to enjoy her, do so in your tent like a king, not like a scullion with a churl's wife in a hay-mow."

I looked upon the old man, and although his mistrust of Vivain could easily rise from jealousy, I remembered too well his good care and guidance to answer harshly. Anyway, I had been closely shaved and I did not want Vortigern's razor nigh my throat again.

"Merdin, I will do all that you ask, and thank you for your counsel."

He went and talked to Gerald and they both looked relieved. We continued our march, guarded closely against ambush, and that night we camped at the farther edge of Radnor Forest, within a day's march of Woodwick. Somewhere between, Vortigern's great army was encamped and waiting for us, the field where he meant to engage us all to his advantage. But this choice we did not intend for him to have.

In the twilight, when I had finished supper, Pillicock brought word that Vivain sought audience with me. I had her come into my tent, better-dressed than I had seen her yet, she having bought some secondhand garments at a fair we had passed, of a size to fit a twelve-year-old girl of the kind we raised in Cambria. I wondered where she had garnered the copper coins to pay for them, and decided she had some little hoard that she had hidden away before the night of our capture, quite possibly tossed to her when she had stayed at Woodwick. A daughter of a churl could have hardly showed more modest as she knelt before me, and I had trouble believing in the lecherous witch-spawn trying to consume me under the linden tree; but I did believe it when I had looked her over, head to heel, and the bright remembrance caused stirrings and glowings and quiverings throughout my body. She showed no visible sign of the rough treatment by our captors except a chaffing at her wrists caused by her rope.

She kept her black eyes on the floor, and I expected them to fill with tears. They did not, and then I remembered that witches never wept, one way of telling them from mortal maidens.

"My liege, I have come to ask a boon," she said.

"You may."

"I have already brought you near to death, because when you

tempted me, I only warned you of the danger, and did not somehow find a way to resist your royal will."

"That I grant."

"Yet how could I believe that the King could be attacked under a tree the like of which had shaded Calypso and my woodsman sire the instant I was made? Its big leaves, shaped like the human heart, promised safety for lovers."

"Perhaps the spirit of the tree was out visiting. Such is well-known to happen."

"It could be so. And, my liege, the boon I seek is to sit all night at your bedside, with a fan made of oak-twigs, and keep flies from molesting you, and air stirring to keep you cool. All too likely tomorrow's Sun will see the great battle, and even a king needs a good night's rest, ere he stands trial."

"Vivain, your presence in my pavilion would heat me more than your fan could cool me."

"What about flies?"

"Let them wander at their pleasure, for they are beloved of the Gods, or they could not walk upside down on a wall without falling, that being against nature."

"Then you refuse my plea?"

"With great sorrow."

"One thing more. I think I am with child. The cry I uttered, which was nearly our undoing, would declare so. It was his own cry, rising from my womb, to announce to the world his coming nine months hence. If so, will you cherish him? Take thought that he will be only one-fourth wizard, not enough that the evil humors of his body can triumph over the good."

"If he is loyal to me, and you the like, he shall be made an earl."

"Then in due course he will wed a damosel all flesh and blood, and the blood of his son will be only an eighth witch, and his son a sixteenth, and so on, diminishing with every generation, until only a drop remains, like one black snowflake in a winter fall. And then the evil spawning of my mother by a goblin a thousand years ago will be expatiated, and he can take her by the throat and kill her, for it is well-known that only the blood-descendant of a witch, five or more times removed, can put an end to her wicked life."

171

"Half a witch came close to death last night. How did you escape?"

"I called upon Calypso, and she came, although in a form I did not recognize in the darkness of my prison. She had already seen my trouble in her boiling cauldron, and was on her way on the wings of the wind to set me free, but she serves King Vortigern, and she would not set you also free, and the monster Rufus, until I swore by the Gods I would either live with you or die. She was forced to agree, because she loves me. In what form did she appear to you?"

"I saw nothing of her. I was asleep."

"My liege, in some form she will be at Vortigern's side in tomorrow's battle. And I am the best one to know what tricks she will employ, and what charms she will cast, to help him win, and these I will know how to combat, if I be at your side."

"No, I will rely on the Great Gods to confound her, and on Merdin, and on my General Gerald, and my stout-hearted followers." And I hoped that the Gods heard me say so.

"Now that is kingly wisdom. If some of his chiefs come up to parley, very likely I would steal behind them and stab them in the back, for such is my wickedness. I wish I had been born of the humblest dairy-maid rather than a witch."

She looked so wistful that my arm jumped to reach for her, and then my resolution not to toy with her until the battle was won came nigh to being broken, but I rebuked my rebellious heart, and resisted. In a moment she left, disappointed and ashamed, and only when sleep overcame me, quenching my appetite, did I get shed of remorse.

About midnight I wakened, and stood a few moments at the door of my tent. The night was wondrous clear, my Lady the Moon riding high and only a little lop-sided, and the great stars were doing their best to shine, while the little ones did not bring fire to their cold lanterns. I kept close watch for a sign from the Gods. Surely they would give me one, on this night of nights, the eve of one of the greatest battles ever fought in the memory of man, such a sign as a great tailed star that had shown on the night of my birth, or of one of the common stars shooting from its sphere and igniting all the heavens. It did not come to pass. No thunder dunted on the right or left, or any sign came from the earth such as ghosts rising from their graves.

No owl hooted in the woods, no bat flitted over the watchfires. It seemed that the Gods had forgotten their own foretelling.

If so, I thought, I would conquer anyway by the might of arms. Resolving on this, I went back to my bed and almost instantly fell asleep.

2

About the fourth hour after noon our scouts returned with word that they had sighted Vortigern's army, fully mustered, stoutly armed, and set for battle. And his own scouts had been seen running to their King to bring word of our approach.

Soon we too were viewing the handsome sight. Vortigern had thrown his men across a bench of a ravine, between two steep hills. Behind them the ravine itself rose steeply to a mountainside, all but unclimbable, which meant that we could not outflank his force in strength, or attack from the rear. By the same token, it could not retreat in good order if at all, hence it must conquer or be cut down. And that, Gerald told me, was a sign of his lack of confidence in his fellows, and a good sign.

The fact remained that he had over six hundred to our five hundred. Also, the King and his two sons straddled horses, so they could move quickly up and down the lines, encourage the dastards, and throw spare men into gaps or where they were most needed.

"We've got to dislodge them from their roost, or lose the battle," Gerald told me.

"I don't see how."

"I think I know the way."

But before he could tell me, the two princes, followed by ten men on foot, rode forward carrying a white flag. Now this was an invitation to parley, to which the display of a white flag meant acceptance, and a red flag refusal.

"I urge you, my liege, to show a white flag," Gerald said. "Parley can do no harm, the men can rest a bit without strain, and you can judge the fighting spirit of the foe. But I pray you, accept no terms that might be trickery."

"I'll accept none but surrender."

"That is what great Caesar would have done. And now I'll have Llewelan's archers lie down in the grass, where our visitors won't see their weapons."

I displayed a white flag, and the princes and their attendants approached within fifty paces.

"Hail, my brother Artay," Modred shouted, stopping his horse.

"Hail, Prince Modred."

"My father, Vortigern, is a man of tender heart, loath to shed needless blood—so he bade me say. Also, he will weep to see Cambrians fighting Cambrians, children of the same earth, worshippers of the same Gods, instead of them fighting foul Christians and outlanders from beyond our hills. Hence, if you will join forces with him, you and he will march together into the Midland Plain, and he will make you Prince of all the lands conquered, owing allegiance to none but him."

" 'Tis a handsome offer," I replied, "but tell my father, Vortigern, that today he shall journey further than the Midland Plain, and I shall sit his throne."

"I have made you his first offer. Now I will tell you his last. If you join forces with him, you may be King of all the lands the two of you may conquer, and be not his liegeman but his brother. Or, if you will return in peace, you may be King of all Cambrian land south of the River Aeron across to the River Lugg, with neither of you kneeling to the other, and reign over your separate kingdoms in brotherly peace."

"Now that I have known Vortigern's fatherly care, I would rather be brother to Droit the Boar. And that is my final word."

"I, for one, am glad to hear it. You have a stout army, as do we, and we will see whom the Gods favor, and pass the time pleasantly, as long as it lasts. And the crows will be happier than either of us, Artay. Their victory is certain. Farewell."

The party rode back. Our army moved forward a distance, until the hill would screen our maneuvering, and then Gerald sent Llewelan's fifty archers to climb it, with orders to fetch up within fifty paces of the enemy line, somewhat above it, and with open vision. All these men had come down from the Mendip Hills. They could scramble up heights that would frighten a goat. They had no arms but their yew-bows and a quiver holding fifty flint or metal-headed arrows. These could cast a hundred paces and cut through the toughest leather.

"Start shooting when you are in good position," Gerald had ordered the hillman leader.

They had their own way of doing battle, which they had adopted only the Gods knew how long ago, and which no doubt had worked well in a hundred nameless fights between them and valley people who had coveted their little pastures, or perhaps their mines of lead and tin. Three archers stepped forth from their line, drew their bows in unison, and let fly. The three shafts arched out and down, vivid in the sunlight as falcons with burnished wings, all taking off at the same instant although one flew highest of the three, one a little lower, and one the lowest. The first did not keep up with the second or the second with the third, for the steeper their climb, the slower their forward advance. But the wonder of it to our sight was the ending of the flights of each of the three arrows, as though taking ordered turns, one, two, three. The one that flew the lowest reached its target first, and a fellow less than midway down Vortigern's battle line, perhaps sixty yards from its sender, uttered a great yell and toppled.

The second-lowest flyer dived at a man fully twenty places down the line, at least a hundred yards' cast, and narrowly missed the mark. The highest flyer was still in flight for another second, then it arched down at a man still further off, and he clutched at his throat, from which the shaft protruded, uttering strangled sounds, and dancing about. I could not have believed that it had flown and killed a good hundred and fifty paces had my own eyes not borne witness.

"Beautiful, beautiful," Gerald cried. "You would think that only Romans could work so well together. Those goat-herders of the hills are stingy fellows, not wanting to waste shafts. They must be fashioned with great care to fly so straight. Why risk two of 'em at the same target? And think of it—two hits out of three!"

"I wish I had two hundred of their like. I could conquer all Britain in half a year."

"Be glad of fifty, for you'll not get any more. It takes half a lifetime to master bow-and-arrow. Look, they're not younkers, like most of your fellows. Note their black beards and quietness and steadiness. They're like legionnaires of ten years' service. And now——"

Three other archers had taken the places of the first batch, and already their arrows were in flight. Again they had aimed at widely spread targets, again the shafts flew at different heights, and dove one, two, three in turn. Only the middle arrow hit home, but when the skewered man dropped without a sound the whole enemy line was watching.

"They must have marvelous bows," Gerald went on with his quiet discourse. "It takes months of cunning craft to make 'em. Now three more of the bearded devils are stepping forward. Watch them draw—every movement steady and sure. There the shafts take off and—Great Jupiter Olympus! One of Vortigern's captains down and spouting blood, and a soldier running, howling. I tell you there are no such archers left on earth, lest it be the Scythians."

All three of the next set missed, which might have cheered Vortigern somewhat, and steadied the men, but if so, the satisfaction was short-lived. Of the next flight, every arrow found its mark, and our lines gave forth a great cheer to see one of the enemy lying still, a second rolling about in agony, and a third tugging desperately at a shaft that had pierced his shoulder.

"At this rate, we'll win without losing a man," I said.

"Don't fool yourself, my liege. It's a matter of minutes now till we face a desperate charge. And remember Vortigern set up those targets like tethered cattle. The Sun is full in their eyes—they can't see the shafts in flight. The archers have him at their backs, and it's bloody murder."

The next set of bowmen made only one hit, but that was enough to shake still more the already tremulous line of foemen. No doubt they had been told that we would attack uphill, in smaller numbers than they, and no better armed, and they had only to stand fast to butcher our panting army, yet no drop of our blood had been shed and they themselves were being tracked down and slain by a darting invisible death out of the sky. Every man was wondering if his turn were next. They stared at the fallen, and gazed at one another, and more and more turned their heads to watch their chiefs in council, royal Vortigern and his two sons. Anxious, angry talk it was, sharp of tone. Now the horses smelled blood and became hard to handle.

Still Vortigern could hardly bear to forsake his strong position.

Three times more the sets of three hillmen loosed their shafts, nine little sticks with flint or metal heads and feathered feet that laid low four of his soldiery. Then Modred's taunts and Prince Vortimer's cursings and his own desperation drove him to act. He gave an order. All three horsemen rode swiftly up and down the line. Swifter still was the flight of three arrows, and then another flight of three, with four more men picked off, before the enemy captains could shout the royal orders, and the line moved.

"It's the moment I've been waiting for more than eighteen years," Gerald told me, his voice low and calm. Then, shouting, "Men, make ready, and take 'em in the teeth!"

3

Unlike Vortigern, Gerald had spread our forces in two lines, one fifty yards in advance of the other. Instead of the men standing shoulder to shoulder, there was a four-foot gap between each, and no doubt this was a great comfort to the advancing foe, for they stood close and thick, outnumbering our front line two to one, and surely they could slaughter half my army without great loss; and seeing the carnage, the other half would fly. I would have been of the same mind if one of the attacking force, and truly I had been hard put to it to believe in Gerald's tactics, for they seemed against common sense. I agreed to them at last only as an act of faith in him, remembering what a swordsman he was, and his great knowledge of bygone wars. Especially I remembered his study of Roman tactics when they had beaten forces of ten times their sum.

The men in the front line had been warned that they would be greatly outnumbered at the first clash of battle, but to keep their heads, jab right and left, and make good use of their shields. Truly they stood staunch, grim and silent, as the foe drew nigh. Vortigern rode in advance of the center of his line, his two sons a good distance on either side, and as Modred caught sight of my glimmering helmet he raised his sword in salute. Pillicock stood at my left, with a sling in his hand and a bag of stones slung on his shoulder. Gerald was at my right.

Between our two lines stood Merdin, with the head of Bran raised high over his head, and only at my harsh command had he taken this stand instead of in the van of our whole force. I turned my head and waved at him, rejoicing at his stalwartness and the glitter in his eyes. And now, when only fifty paces separated the two armies, Vortigern and his sons flung off their rearing horses, and three fellows who had run forward caught their bridles. Their line broke into two halves to pass the beasts, but closed again, and at that instant our main force struck its first blow, which was a stone hurled from Pillicock's sling. It struck a fellow in the shoulder, perhaps the one at whom he had aimed, perhaps some other. It knocked him down and he disappeared from view.

I had hardly time to draw another breath before the battle was joined. I caught sight of Modred trying to get at me, his eyes brighter than his polished blade, but he could not, because of the press of his own men. And then my heart gave a great leap, because of the dawning of a great truth. What Gerald said would happen was happening before my eyes. The line of foemen stood so close to each other that they got in one another's way, whereby they could hardly employ their weapons. No few of our fellows fell, gaps appearing here and there all down the line, but almost always with bloody swords, for hardly anyone had missed making up for his loss by at least one deadly stroke, and the best of those that died, the liveliest and the most skilled, took off for Elysium with contented bellies, having downed two, three, sometimes four of the foemen before they had cast their own souls with a yell, a grunt, a last taunt, or in deep quiet.

I stayed in the hot heart of the fight, where I loved being. There I could prove my prowess with my sword and especially my shield. Often by the favor of the Gods I thrust home a death-stroke in reply to a mere cut, when an opponent had overstretched himself. True, I did not have to contend with Modred at this moment, and for that I thanked the Great God Tyr of Battles, Modred being as tall as I, as agile, and as patient to await an opening for his swift sword. I divined that he was too crafty to impede himself in the thick of the howling line, and too pleasure-loving to seek settlement with me until we were off to ourselves. So he had whacked some of his own soldiers to one side and was engaging Gerald.

Pillicock ran back and forth on his short legs just behind our front line, slinging stones through its gaps, and rarely did the missile fail to whack a foeman's head, and that head to crack open like a dropped melon, for he threw with terrific force. It came to me if the tally of the battle were ever known, his count of dead would be higher than any king's or prince's, or full-statured soldier's. And now Vortigern's line was desperately bedeviled from behind. As they had been told, the Mendip archers had descended from their roost, formed a hundred paces at its rear, and were calmly and methodically shooting arrows into his soldiers' backs.

More than six score of Vortigern's followers had fallen dead or maimed while I lost less than forty. He and his son Vortimer had remained surrounded by brave defenders and had not been hit by sword, arrow, or stone. Modred had exposed himself to all three, but good fortune and his own great prowess had saved him from deep hurt, although his clothes were slashed and his hands and feet bloody. How much time had passed since the lines had first closed, I had no notion, for it sped as in a dream. But it was not long, for my Lord the Sun seemed to stand in the same place. The number of fallen gave no hint, for killing is quick work. On both sides the men engaged had no other thought or bent but to live and kill. Howbeit, the moment had come for Gerald to deal the last great blow, which he had held back like a hunting-hound in leash.

Our bugler blew a shrill blast, rising like an eagle's scream above the clash of arms, savage yells, shrieks, and groans; and our second line, which he called his reserves, moved forward in a dog-trot. Suddenly every space he had left vacant in our line of battle was filled by a fresh soldier, his blood unblanched, his heart burning, and his sword athirst. Truly it was a dreadful moment for our brave foemen, as when an evil dream does not pale and pass at waking, but turns into ghastly fact. They could not endure the new onslaught, and their spirits quailed, and they began to give ground.

All too plainly the hated shape of defeat rose before Vortigern's eyes. He gave some signal I did not see or hear, and behind the wavering line the three grooms ran forward, leading the royal horses. Young Vortimer, being nimble, was the first up, while Vortigern scrambled and scrabbled in frantic haste, and through a gap in the line I saw his golden crown fall off his head and tumble on the ground.

He glanced over his shoulder, as though of a mind to pick it up, then his next glance took in our force in irresistible advance.

And what is this we see? King Vortigern, lately lord of all Cambria, heaving himself upon his horse with no thought of his woeful loss. Not one of his men stop, stoop, and hand him up the regal headgear, and it must be that some mighty matter of state calls him from the bloody field, for he does not look back again, and instead spurs his plunging beast and departs in great haste. Of the royal three, only Modred seems loath to leave, and there is no mirth in his eyes now, and where his face is not bloody it is red with shame. And although he does not refuse the proffered bridle, yet his farewell to me is somehow an act of faith.

With all his strength he hurled his sword, hoping to impale me, only to see it stab the ground at my feet. "I'll be back, my brother Artay," he yelled in great voice as he sprang up lightly. "Be patient, Your Majesty King of Cambria," streamed back his shout as he rode off, waving his bloody hand. "We shall meet again."

Then the enemy line broke, in dire disorder, and our foemen took to their heels. Still our fellows kept rank against all temptation to chase and butcher, for so they had been rigorously taught. Not one dared step over the crown lying on the ground, let alone touch it, and all swung a little wide of it until I could reach it, cast off my helmet, and clap the golden diadem on my head. Our archers had scampered on ahead of the beaten foe, for their numbers were too few to make a stand, and presently we saw them scrambling up the hill they had lately left. The runaways yearned to follow them up the only way out of the valley but they dared not, lest the archers turn and let fly their humming hornets. A few struggled up the ravine, or the opposite steeper hill, but the main dropped their weapons and held up their hands.

"Cry havoc?" a captain called to Gerald. And that meant to slaughter all prisoners, in revenge for the hurts they had given us and to teach other opposers a lesson.

"Not unless the King orders it," Gerald answered sternly.

I decided not to give the dread cry and instead to let the beaten men pledge allegiance to my crown, if they were of that mind. I reached the decision partly from thinking of other kings whom I must conquer, ere I could rule Britain, and partly because that would be what Modred would do in my place. I knew it as well as though he had told me, his eyes bright with mirth. I took no pleasure of mind in emulating my great foe, but could not help myself. Perhaps a wise king will glean wisdom where he finds it, even from a lover in his wife's bed.

We marched in good order to the throng of white-faced soldiery at the foot of the hill. Gerald had our lines halt, and I stood forth, the glory and power of kingliness full upon me, and the men did not even shout scurrilous jests to the beaten.

"All who wish to serve under my banner, line up, and put their hands in mine," I ordered.

Their brightening faces were a wonderful thing to see. I need speak no threat to those who might refuse, for every mother's son of them save one, plainly a great earl, indeed Garth of the Usk, ran to get a place near the head of the line. Soon they were filing past me, and I marveled at their likeness to my own yokels, most of them blond-headed and blue-eyed, and with the same way of walking, taught by our Cambrian hills, and the same bashfulness. Each knelt to me and put both hands in mine.

When all had passed, I bade them pick up their dropped arms, and somehow I knew that these would be as stout in my support as their stoutness in the battle, and perhaps the shields would clatter and the blades dart with even greater vim, for these knew by the staunch grasp of their wielders and a stir in their iron hearts that I was the rightful king, chosen by the Gods.

Lastly I turned to Garth, lord of the Usk, who touched his knee to the ground but did not put his hands in mine.

"You do not desire to pledge me your allegiance?"

"Your Majesty, I am not a Cambrian," he answered. "My lands lie eastward of your hills, and I am properly subject to the Prince of Monmouth. And I know such a great king as yourself would not ask me to break faith."

"My Lord the Sun was only a little higher in his sky when I saw you in attendance upon Vortigern, lately the King of Cambria."

"Your Majesty, he is a kinsman of my Prince, who bade me serve him in this war, and now that service is done, I entreat to return to his palace."

"You did not come without power. Where are the men who followed you here?"

"Your Majesty, they have all pledged allegiance to you."

"Truly, I have no fault to find with your return to your Prince, and I'll provide you a garment that does you honor."

It had happened that on yesterday's noon-day halt my men had found an old marsh-donkey with his leg broken in a fall. I had had them brain him and skin him according to my careful directions. The skin we had brought with us, and now it lay with the men's baggage, where they had arrayed for battle. In low tones I told Pillicock to walk and fetch it.

The distance was not far; his legs were long enough to serve such haste as I was under, which was almost none. Indeed, I was pleased enough to stand about before my greatly strengthened army, jest with Merdin and Gerald, look at and order bandaging of the men's cuts, and watch Garth sweat.

Pillicock brought the donkey's skin and I bade him present it, with my compliments, to our noble prisoner.

"You are to put it on and wear it on your homeward journey and when you report to your master, Prince of Monmouth," I told him. "If one of my subjects sees you pass unmantled in it, thus scorning my royal gift, I will not wait, as I now intend, to march to the Usk. Since your master is only a petty prince, I am willing that he grease his knees a few months more before he drops on them before me, but if you fail the present duty, you may expect me before the New Moon, and in that case, he shall swim naked in the river, and you'll dance on air."

Garth had no choice but to don the mangy skin, and I showed him how its head could be prettily draped over his own, with the tail dangling from the place it would properly grow. For a little while longer the men restrained their mirth due to my royal presence, but they were choking on it, red in the face. Whereupon Gerald could no longer withhold his own, Merdin lost his dignity and cackled, and Pillicock laughed aloud for the first time in my hearing. Then they let it come forth in a great roar re-echoing from the hills.

We returned to the battlefield and made litters for the badly wounded who yet breathed. Then we set out for Woodwick, only an hour's march, which we could easily make before dark, and my promise of a feast from Vortigern's pantries and a horn of ale from his casks for every dusty throat caused every man in my host to step forth with vim. And now, to judge by their jollity, you could not tell the conquerors from the conquered. Truly it seemed that a new day had dawned in Cambria.

The land lay fairly open in this part of the Wye Valley, and we caught no glimpse of three horsemen. I had thought that Vortigern might risk a brief visit to his palace to garner his hoard of gold, silver, and jewels, and to bid some of his train follow him with his robes of state and his ermine cloak, and perhaps he would let Enid, his well-loved Queen, straddle his horse behind him, ere he set forth to seek sanctuary and to league with some king of the Midland Plain. But to do so would take him a long way from a straight course, and no doubt he was in great haste.

The openness of the country would permit hangers-on of his court, posting themselves on the rooftops of Woodwick and in handy trees, to vie with one another in being the first to spy Vortigern's army, returning victorious with spoil of battle, and the head of Artay stuck on a pole. But they carried no such news to the waiting Queen, and when we came in sight of the palace all its armed sentries had left their posts, and only a handful of his ministers clustered about the entrance. I did not glance at them, except with the corner of my eye, as they kneeled and hailed me King. Bidding my soldiers wait at ease, which they did in great cheer, I entered unattended except by Merdin, Gerald, and Pillicock. The expression on the monster's face appalled me a little, because it hinted at much feeling not clearly revealed. I could guess some of it though, for this was his return after many years of absence and too well he remembered when Vortigern had used his whip in vain to make him play the clown.

I found Enid waiting in the throne-room, the first I had ever seen. A platform twelve feet long and nearly as broad had been built in the center of the spacious chamber, and on it stood two chairs that must have been brought from Rome in olden days, for I had never seen their like for splendor. The larger had been gilded, and contained a tasseled cushion of finest silk. The smaller provided no softness for Enid's hams, but was ornamented with copper nails. She rose as I entered, and stepped down from the platform and bowed low. I think too that she tried to smile, but her ashen-colored, frozen-looking face would not follow her intent.

"Is the King dead?" she asked from a tight throat.

"No, the King is alive and well, and stands before you wearing his crown."

"I meant to ask of my Lord Vortigern, and of my sons, Modred and Vortimer."

"All have gone visiting, and I do not know when they will return."

"Then I take it they've lost the battle."

"You take it rightly, Enid. But my men are wearied from fighting and marching, so bid your ministers serve them meat and ale in great abundance, and first of all bring here the oldest and best cask of mead, that the King and his liegemen may enjoy the old King's bounty, and you may toast the new King."

"Will you promise me safety from outrage by some ruffian in your train?"

"Enid, you would be safe from such alone in the Black Forest."

The cask was brought immediately and broached by the head of Vortigern's household. Gilt and silver cups were quickly provided for us, but I needs must remind the white-faced, quivering crew to bring Vortigern's golden cup. This I set aside for my own use, but I bade the head minister fill one of the silver cups for the Queen, which I would pass to her with my own hand.

Before I did so, I spat in it copiously. "See, the King has kissed the cup," I told her.

"To your good health, Artay, King of Cambria," she replied, her eyes glittering with hate. Then she emptied the cup in hearty gulps.

I mounted the platform, took my seat on the throne, and bade her sit on the floor so I could put my bare feet in her lap in an ancient Cambrian custom of taking one's ease. And so I took my ease as the men feasted.

I deemed that Enid had never expected such doings when she had persuaded my father to cast me into the forest to be eaten by wolves or wild swine. Still, I had come only one great stride of my long way.

On the morrow I intended to begin the business of being King. It would include the dispatch of messengers to the chief men of my realm, such as earls, mayors, and bailiffs. I must bid them come and be judged whether they were my true liegemen or still pined and plotted for the return of Vortigern. No mere protestations and pliant knees would prove their faith. I meant to have Merdin employ sorcery to discover their true bents, and, because of her weird powers, post the demi-witch Vivain behind a curtain to signal thumbs-up or thumbs-down, as did the crowds at the gladiatorial circuses in Rome. Those who harbored treachery would be straightway hanged. Weather-cocks would be stripped of their offices and their goods and sent into exile. Those who were worthy could kiss my hand and obtain preferment.

Seated tonight on my throne, sipping mead from a golden cup, I dwelt with greater pleasure on my own duty to the Gods who had set me here. Also tomorrow would go forth keen-eyed fellows, used to hunting, to find the tracks of three horsemen fleeing eastward. These they would follow until enemy country blocked their way, and they would make inquiries of travelers they might meet. Thus I might surmise to which one of the twenty and more kingdoms and principalities in vast Britain the runaways were bound, to bargain for their return to royal power.

No such shelter would serve them long, I vowed. As soon as my own realm was secure, I meant for my great army to begin its eastward march, led by the King of Cambria and his General Gerald, while Merdin remained at Woodwick to enforce the King's law. We would conquer every kingdom in our path. Every king who did not pay me willing tribute in followers and goods would straightway find his neck without a noddle, and I meant to weaken those whom I let live, so they could not rise behind me. When I thought of Vortigern begging mercy, the holes in my shoulder smarted, and my hand went of itself to the jeweled hilt of Caliburn. For Vortigern alone, of all the kings whose heads would roll in solemn execution, would be put to my own great Sword, so wondrously given me, because he was the King's father. My brother Vortimer I might spare with only the loss of his right hand, since I bore him no hot hate. What my heart felt toward Modred I could not unentangle in my mind. I knew only I meant to slay him in fair and open combat.

Enraptured by these prospects, and warmed with mead, I became so eager to begin that I gave thought to Enid, seated on the floor before my throne, holding my unshod feet. She might quite likely know or at least have a good notion where Vortigern was bound, having heard with which king he had close ties. I knew ways of causing her hard-pressed lips to tell such matters. Since she had plotted my cruel murder when I was a helpless infant, I would rejoice to see her hanging from the palace ridgepole, her toes scrabbling on the earthen floor. The reason I did not order it so was really naught but warmth of the cordial drink that sent my thoughts at first stealing, and then swarming, upon Vivain. Did these collide with her thoughts swarming hotly toward me? Since our meeting under the linden tree my spies had seen her give no sideways glance at one of my tall captains. Surely this was proof of love in a creature of such wild heart, over and above any care of her own neck. Just now she was waiting by one of the watchfires that ringed the palace. Since the great battle had been won, and my vow of continence was no longer in force, did she not cock her pointed ears and watch with glistening black eyes at every opening of the door?

I glanced at Vortigern's and Enid's magnificent bed. It had fine linen curtains that could be lowered by ropes attached to cross-bars fastened to the ridgepole. Still, if Merdin and Gerald slept against the wall in official beds, they might be kept awake, so I decided that the whole vast chamber would stand empty tonight except for the King and his handmaiden, with stout guards at every door and window. At once I sent Enid, under guard, to sleep in the hut of Vortigern's scullion, then bade Gerald attend me.

"My liege, I hope the half-witch won't take her knife to bed with her," he said when he had heard my command.

"What harm might she do with it against our person?" I asked harshly.

"Why, none, according to her thinking. But if Your Majesty were called forth on some great affair of state at a moment when she most wished you to remain, she might in pure vexation stick six inches of its blade into your royal back."

"Since you speak in jest, I'll take no offense, and since there is some point to it, bid her leave the trinket in your care."

Gerald took pleasure in my answer, as I could see from his sparkling eyes, and if I were not King he would have slapped my back. He went away cheerfully, whereupon I resolved always to humor my under-chiefs as far as possible, for I doubted not that great Caesar had done the same. Besides, they might be right.

The chamber was vacated, the bed-curtains lowered, and the guards took their posts. Countless candles were left burning, casting only a dim and reflected light on the bed itself, where I repaired. Still, when little hard brown hands thrust the cloth aside, I saw well as in bright moonlight the elfin face with its narrow, upward-flaring eyebrows, the pitch-black eyes narrow and slanted and having a soft sheen that must have risen from their depths, and best of all, the tilt of her wide mouth. She kicked off her leathern shoes and placed them neatly beside my own rude footgear, then sat with her legs crossed on the great bed.

"Is my King well-rested from the battle and the long march?" she asked, her eyes cast down.

"I was never tired," I replied.

"The Gods have given you the strength of a giant. And today they have kept their promise made in the Song of Camlon, and you wear the crown of Cambria."

I was still wearing it, in fact, not from forgetting to take it off, rather from loathness to do so, it being such new gear to my head, and perhaps because of a feeling that when my brows were bare, I would hardly be able to believe that I was King. Still, I could not sleep in it, let alone make love in hearty fashion. So I took it off and solemnly set it aside.

"May I touch it with my little finger?" Vivain asked timidly.

"No human hand may touch it except my own. I was the first to touch it when it fell from Vortigern's head, as he fled in terror from my Sword, and that is a sign I may wear it all my days. Also that the will of the Gods will be done whereby it shall become the crown of Britain that no man since Maximus has worn, and my oldest son whom Wander shall bear me shall wear it after me."

"It is a good sign, my liege."

Still my head felt light, and I must glance at it again to see it was within my reach. Then I glanced at Caliburn, thinking how I took him off or buckled him on at my need and comfort, although his coming to me was a greater miracle than the crown's tumbling from the head of a vanquished king. I had laid him at the far edge of the bed, in easy reach of my hand. And seeing the gleam of his long blade bestirred my mind into playing a trick on me, a scurvy trick in a way, considering my eyes were wandering as far as they would go up Vivain's crossed legs, and my hand ached to follow. It sped an errant memory to the tower on Pillicock Hill, to a lowly bed of sheepskins a kingdom removed from this high and royal bed, and to a common sword, later winning the name of Droit, that lay naked between Elain and me. Once he had tried to cut me when I had reached across him to her beauteous breast, but once she herself had put him aside in the cool of early morning. The lecherous ache went out of my hand with some of the fire in my blood, and neither would return until the vision faded, which I reckoned would be soon.

So to fill the space of silence I said what I had started to say after her first mention of the Song of Camlon, and which had somehow stuck on the back of my tongue while it uttered other words.

"Aye, the Gods have awarded me the crown of Cambria. But Vortigern is not yet crows' meat, made so by my Sword, as the Song likewise foretells."

"Why should you bother your head with that on the night of your great victory?" she said after a brief pause, and a small, upright line came into sight between her brows. "He will be soon, I have little doubt."

"You say 'little doubt.' Why should you have any doubt at all, when so many of the prophecies have come true?"

"Do not be vexed with me, my King, for my faulty speech. How could I have the slightest doubt?"

"You ask a question and do not make a statement. Also I saw a sign of worry in your face."

"It was only that your thoughts were wholly upon Vortigern and your revenge, instead of one little thought wandering to me. Unfit to be your bedfellow though I am, the daughter of a wicked witch, still I have woman's longings, and I thought that your summoning me here was a sign of your favor."

"Those longings and mine can wait a moment more. Did not the Song of Camlon prophesy that I would be King of Britain?"

"Truly that was its meaning."

"And did it not prophesy also that Vortigern would be cut into crows' meat by my Sword?"

"My liege, did Merdin, the great Druid, tell you it did? If so, why need you speak of it?"

"Again you ask questions instead of making answers. Take thought of your pretty throat, lest it be cut."

"My liege, I am not well-versed in the Song of Camlon. I have heard it only once and that against Calypso's command, for she fell into disfavor with the God Lud a thousand years ago, when she cast a spell of icy coldness on a maid he coveted, and she angered Tyr when she took the side of the Romans at their great battle with Queen Boadicea. But doubtless Merdin has sung it to you till you know it by heart."

"He sang part of it to me, and that much of it I know well. He did not sing it all."

"My liege, after it speaks of your marriage to Wander, the words are no longer plain. It is as though the Singer, who was Gwydion, had thickened his tongue with too many cups of mead. Or perhaps some other singer took his place, to whom the prophecies of the Gods did not come so clear. But your servant begs you to give no more thought to it tonight. Rejoice in your great victory. If I may have some small part in your rejoicings——"

"Does it say that Vortigern outlives Artay?"

"By the God of Witches and the God of Love, I do not know."

"Rejoice, you say? How can I rejoice? How can I sleep and peacefully dream until I know whether the Gods have not given me their favor only to snatch it away? Vivain, I take back my threat against your small and pretty throat. Out of it came truth, or at least words that will make me seek truth which even Merdin has not dared unfold. From henceforth my trust in you is greater than ever. But tonight I have no heart for sweet passages of love. You have our leave to go."

"Great King, I have cheated myself of a rich feast, such as no other in the wide world may spread for me. Yet if I have put you on guard against evil fortune—which may seek to strike you down but which you may buffet with the help of a half-witch—I go from you gladly, my heart taking comfort to atone for my other members left cold and hungry. May the God Modo, little known in Cambria but worshipped widely in other courts, be in ever attendance upon you."

She was there beside me, speaking in her soft, deep voice, and her eyes were shining in the dimness, perhaps from unshed tears; and then she had gone. I put on such raiment as I had taken off, buckled on Caliburn, and put the crown of Cambria on my head. Then I summoned a guard, gave him a message to convey to Merdin asleep or awake, and again mounted my throne.

In a moment Merdin entered the great chamber, and the candles showed his face troubled and pale. He knelt before me.

"You may rise, old man," I told him. "And I would have saved you some steps of your tired feet, had I bade you bring your harp. Get it now, and you shall play and sing."

"Some song of rejoicing? I will, if you command it, but my hands also are weary at this late hour, and my voice weak, so the music my harp could make will hardly give you pleasure."

"I do not seek pleasure. I seek knowledge. I call upon you to finish singing the Song of Camlon."

"That I'll not do tonight, even if you weave a rope out of my snowy beard, and throttle me with it."

What could I say to that? I loved the gaffer more than any one on earth, partly for the very power of will, his great pride and his fearless heart, by which he would not yield. Also I knew that an Archdruid had never been subject to the King's law in matters that concerned Druidic law, wizardry, and worship of the Gods.

"When will you sing it?"

"I had hoped never to sing it until all its prophecies had come true. But I can see now that you are truly the King, no longer the younker who yearned for a bedmate beside the cottage fire, and I will sing it, at the suitable place and time. That place will be Stonehenge, that the Gods of Heaven and the ghosts of Earth frequent, the Master Circle of all the Circles on the Earth, and it may come to pass that vision will come into my eyes and voices in my ears so

I may know the meaning of some of its more cryptic passages, whether for good or evil. The time will be when we have marched, crossed Avon, and descended into Wilts along our course to Cornwall. You know of the vast marshes that stretch almost from Gloster along the Sabrina, and spread eastward from Brigwater Bay to Avalon. By following the Roman road from Gloster via the Baths of Sul to Ilchester, we avoid those impenetrable marshes, and Stonehenge lies only a long day's march eastward of Fosse Way."

"I would go ten days' march to know the Song's ending. Will you tell me, old man, what is its next foretelling after I wed Wander?"

"You will hear. You will be one of the few, other than Druids living and dead, who have ever heard, because it is not well to sing that part of the song to yokels. They do not know that a great king must look his fate in the face, whether it be glorious or black as night. Meanwhile be of stout heart. Tomorrow the loyal and the lickspittles will begin kneeling at your throne. Sit before them and judge them like the great King that I pray to my Lord the Sun you may become. Now lie down and sleep."

2

For forty days, ever more brief and chill as though in ominous forecast, I labored from the fifth hour after midnight to the fifth before midnight to make strong my throne and firm my crown, then reeled brain-weary to bed without thought of wench or wassail. A cluster of claimants hung ever about the palace door. As it opened to let out one petitioner, it admitted another. Mostly they were Vortigern's administrators and holders of preferment, and the least that any of them wanted was his old privilege, and most asked for more. Tax-gatherers pleaded that the Crown levy two additional farthings in every pence, of which they would keep but one to pay them for their added labor of flattening poor folks' purses, or of hanging them by the heels to shake out their hidden hoards, or by the necks if their evasion was judged treason. The royal treasury would fatten on the other farthing. Rich merchants wished sole right to buy and sell fish, fur, timber, wheat, and the Gods only knew what all. Neighbors offered to inform on neighbors, certain proof of plotting against me, and they would be satisfied with my royal thanks and perhaps a quarter of the plotter's goods, the rest to come to the Crown when the knave had been duly hanged.

The most insistent clamorers, and the most frightened, were Vortigern's judges. If they dared not plead to retain their exclusive power, they asked to sit side by side with the Druids, each authorized to collect fines and impose punishments, for if one judge was of benefit to the Crown, two would be better. Since they were a fat and greasy lot, I took a certain pleasure in throwing them out of their chairs, to be supplanted by Merdin's men, but thereby I made implacable and powerful foes.

Without Merdin seated below the dais on my right hand, now and then rising to whisper in my ear, I would not have known how to answer the petitions and complaints half as well as I did. Gerald, on my left hand, when a matter concerning the King's forces was being broached, was also a stout counselor. Too, in respect to her occult powers, I had kept to my plan of posting Vivain behind the curtains of Modred's bed, a little shake of the cloth meaning the petitioner was loyal and I should grant his plea, and a tug on the ropes an appropriate signal that he should be hanged. Howbeit, when her verdict was opposite from Merdin's, I was prone to follow him as a greater wizard than she a witch, or at least with an older head.

Perhaps I did wrong in many instances, for she had proven her second-sight in Radnor Forest. Even so, it had failed her sadly on the second day of the hearings, when a burly fellow pled to be made Captain of the Palace Guard to fill the place of the officer in command of the lyers-in-wait, he who had caught his foot between two logs, and then caught his back on an iron thorn.

He gave the name of Morys of the Glen, and said that his grandsire had been an earl. I had never heard of him, to my knowledge, and was certain I had never seen his face. Thus I could not understand, as he spoke volubly, my feeling of having had business of some kind with him, less than a week before. Merdin sat with his head bowed, paying little attention; Vivain gave her curtain a big shake, to advise me to grant the fellow's plea.

Suddenly I perceived something familiar in his voice. Then with a great heaving of my brain I recognized it beyond doubt. It was not the first time that sound had served me as faithfully as sight, almost in its place, no great wonder in a man trained in music.

The greater wonder was that I called back an event of the recent past which had escaped the witchy visions of Vivain. I saw only darkness and the dimness of men's shapes, and heard the rustle of leaves in the wind and the patter of rain, and truly I could almost feel rain's wetness on my face. I was lashed on a horse's back, the like of my beautiful companion. Our capturers stood in parley as to what to do with us, in the blind night, and one of them, a deep-voiced fellow, made a sound suggestion.

"So you wish to be Captain of the Palace Guard," I said to Morys as solemnly as a Christian Bishop.

"Yes, my liege, I aspire to that office, for I have long waited the day that Your Majesty should come to your rightful place, and I wish to be foremost in your protection against wicked enemies."

"The badge of your captaincy would be a necklace of amber, from which dangles the likeness of the King stamped on a silver coin."

" 'Tis true, my liege."

"You will pursue and catch rebels, and when they are a bother on a black night, you will favor knocking them on the head, and telling your master that you did so to prevent their escape."

His eyes popped and his face paled, then he squared himself and said quietly:

"Your Majesty has a good memory."

"I remember too that you spoke in rustic dialect, not the good speech you now employ."

"I had newly come from Mona, and King Vortigern sent me to spy on the other rebel-catchers, fearing treachery from some one in the band, which fear was well-founded, as was shown when some one, not an enchantress, cut your bonds. And if the oafs had taken my hint, or better yet if my King had commanded your immediate dispatch, you would not have escaped, and Vortigern would still be King of Cambria instead of dethroned, uncrowned, and in flight."

"If I had made you Captain of the Guard, those wrongs would have soon been righted."

"At least, Ambrose—for I believe not a word of the gibberish Merdin feeds you—you are no fool."

"I am by no means certain. Now you will have your necklace, not of amber, but of hemp of the same color, and instead of the King's picture hanging from it, you will hang."

"Bah, you South Cambrians are a windy lot. Couldn't you say it short and in plain words? I have failed twice, and must pay the price of failure, but it won't be long before you follow me. That too is foretold by a truer prophet than the Singer of Camlon."

I thought to make the price higher, and see and hear him perish in a wicker cage raised and lowered over a bonfire, but I thought upon his courage, honored it despite my fury, and was content to have him hanged.

He threw me a knowing smile as he was being led forth.

3

Six of the seven days that measured a phase of the changing Moon, Gerald drilled my army in arduous Roman fashion. He marched the men over hill and dale, strengthened their wind by running and rough games, taught them how to bivouac, staying dry and warm in the roughest weather, let no grease gather on their hard bodies, and never let them blunt, but always sharpen, their aptitude with arms. Although his quartermaster provided them with plain, good food in abundance, they learned to tramp ten leagues on empty bellies, then not glut themselves, to drink from running brooks instead of stagnant ponds, to attend their persons so as to look clean and feel proud, to take care of the cuts and skinnings got in swordplay, to give scrupulous and loving care to their weapons, which were their best friends in battle, and all else to make them the best fighting force of its size in all Britain.

On the day that the Moon changed, four of the twenty-eight days in her round, the long well-ordered ranks were reviewed at dawn by no less than the King himself, then were dismissed for every man to spend a day as he pleased, whether fishing, hunting in the forest, gaming, visiting with kinfolk, courting, or loafing. This program had barely started, only twice had I inspected the lately augmented legion, and the great Battle of the Vale was only fifteen days agone, when I marked a brisk betterment in soldierliness, especially among Vortigern's former fellows who had rallied to my banner. And on the same early morning, chill and gray, I was given full cause to wish the improvement twice as great, and the burnished shields and glimmering swords twice as many.

I had noticed a small man, with a well-knit body and a sharp face, watching the review. At once I recognized him as Glyn, the head of the band of hunters whom I had sent forth to track the royal runaways. When I had beckoned to him, he followed me into the building we used as an armory, and there Gerald joined us.

"Well, did you get trace of the quarry?" I demanded, for Glyn's dark, calm face told me nothing.

"Aye, 'Ee Majesty, though we spent a wicked time afore we found her horse-tracks," he answered in a Cornish dialect. "We followed her for four days across monstrous great plains beyond the Severn, looking out sharp for bailiffs, and mainly her rid nor'east, and finally we seen where her went."

I could hardly bear to ask him, for I had already guessed, and I dreaded hearing aloud what was rocking my brain in silence, but I must, and I did.

"Where?"

"To the town on the Soar River the country folk call Lester, and 'em Romans called Ratae, where the King of Midland has her court."

"Did Vortigern lodge in the King's palace?" I asked with no show in my face that my guess was dismally true.

"I reckon her did, for Modred, her had rid on ahead to 'nounce Vortigern's coming, and the King herself, with a monstrous great train, met her outside the wall."

"You have done well. You will be rewarded. Now you may go."

Gerald smoothed the black bar of his eyebrows, as always when he was thoughtful. I waited in enforced patience.

"My liege, I had expected just that, and no doubt you did also."

"Not until Glyn said that Vortigern and the princes had ridden northeast."

"King Malcolm of Midland wedded Enid's cousin. His realm extends from the Severn eastward to Monmouth, and from the Trent southward almost to the Thames, because the princes of Bedford and Warwick are his liegemen. He has more sheep and cattle than any king in Britain, good cornland too, and there's iron-ore and a few who still know how to melt out the metal and hammer it into swords. But he hasn't much of an army, from what I have heard; he's not needed it, since he has no coasts to guard and the Picts are away to the north."

"How soon can we march?"

"At least not until your own realm is secure, the Prince of Monmouth humbled, and Cador of Cornwall and South Devon under your sway."

"You say 'at least.' One month after I wed Wander and get her with child I'll command that we march."

"With some other general than me. I would rather fall on my sword than lead your army, trained by and trusting in me, to certain defeat. That is the way of the Roman."

"But the Song of Camlon——" Then I must stop and stammer, for well I remembered that I had not yet heard it all.

"Bide your time, my liege. Rome was not built in a day."

I returned to my royal chores, and every day liked them less, and when I got to the bottom of liking, every day I would hate them more. My hams had easy rest on the feather-cushion, but my head became lame and aching. The truth dawned on me slowly that I did not shine, as my helmet had shone in battle, at solving problems of state or even settling little matters in dispute. Taxation was an especially vexing issue, for every time I lowered one tax I had to raise another, and if I pleased the merchants and the owners of great manors, I oppressed the folk, without whose support in the long run my throne could not stand. Moreover, Merdin was no great help in these affairs, for although he could do wondrous figuring on a slate, and calculate beforehand in what house he would find a particular star, he combed his whiskers in vain over whether to levy an extra farthing per string of eels, or to forgive a penny per sack of carded wool.

One day when we were gnawing away on legs of mutton, he hurled his bare bone with great force against the wall.

"I have it," he cried. "By Heaven, send for Llewelan!"

"What good would it do?" I asked, a question I had got used to asking.

"If he were your Minister of the Treasury, you could devote yourself to War, and I myself to due service to the Gods, to Law, to Astrology, and to Divination, and to other Arts in which I surpass. Firstly, he can read and write Latin, and Latin words inscribed on a scroll say what they are meant to say, and their meaning can not be twisted by a knavish magistrate. Secondly, he is hard-schooled in ruling, for his vast earldom in North Cambria was truly a principality, his tribute and obeisance to the King being empty show. Thirdly, in *absento*—that, Artay, is a Latin word—he also ruled the Mendip Hills, which he owned through his mother's line, appointing a wise governor, and visiting them four times a year—and do not forget his archers in the Battle of the Vale, and that his summons, not yours, brought them to your banner."

"That last, at least, I know," I answered, the words almost sticking in my crop.

"Fourthly, he is the most trusted and widely beloved nobleman in all Cambria."

Since Merdin said "nobleman," I could let this pass, I being as far above a nobleman as Mount Snowdon above the plain, but I would not forget; and the old man would smart for it in due course, although with no great severity because of his white hairs.

"How did it happen, then, that so illustrious a prince should come to wear a shabby cloak and must finally flee for his life?"

"Because he had no bent for war. Neither had Vortigern's sire, but when Vortigern came to the throne, he cast Llewelan down."

"Then a rustic from the Taff cast Vortigern down—and although he plans to rise again, it will be in a wicker basket over a fire, to be well-toasted before Caliburn carves him for the crows. Merdin, I'll send for Llewelan, and bid him bring his daughter."

"That he'll not do, because he promised his noble wife, on her death-bed, that he would never bring Elain to a heathen court. And she herself vowed she would never go, by the token holy to Christians."

"Perhaps she meant it, but I could have her brought here. He would not leave her at Swan Lake unless I put guards over her, and these could have secret orders; and when these are enforced I doubt if she'll complain."

"And I, Merdin, doubt if my King has wide knowledge of the Lily Maid Elain. Also, I am certain that the King should not play tricks on Llewelan of the Lake, if he seeks his great service to the throne."

So I was forced to abandon my fine scheme, and my anger that the King should ever give ground did not change the fact. Little could be gained by Elain coming to the court until I had attended my business with the King of Cornwall and the Prince of Monmouth, on which I meant to launch forth in about a fortnight. On our southward march I could visit her at Swan Lake.

I was wondering whom to appoint to carry my message to Llewelan and to remain there to guard Elain. Certainly I would not send one of my tall young captains, for in this weather the two would spend too many hours together before the fire. And as luck would have it, or as the Great Gods had ordained, I was going out my palace door when in walked Pillicock.

"My liege, I am no use to any one on the drill field," he told me when he had knelt.

"Now why is that?"

"I cannot keep step with the others on my short legs. Truly I make a show of myself, and spoil the parade, when I go trotting after them. Have I your leave to return to the house of the fairy-child until you march that way to war?"

"You have my leave, and you may carry a message to Llewelan. Since it will bring him here, I'll appoint you to the post of guarding the fairy-child from harm, until I pass that way and again until I return. Are you equal to it?"

"No harm will come to her while I live, and if I may take with me the great beast Cavell, she and I will both live long."

I could not doubt his ringing words and what I saw in his coarse but manly face. And my heart that had been cold with scheming and torn by jealous doubt could not help but glow.

4

Pillicock's short legs made quick work of his journey to Swan Lake, Cavell no doubt ranging out and far to warn him of danger and to bring him hares to eat. Llewelan, attended by one churl, arrived in a little over a week after the dwarf's departure, and at once put on the robe and honors of my Minister of the Treasury. Within a week thereafter he had begun to clean what Gerald called our Augean

Stables, this last being one of those high-sounding terms that he had no doubt learned from his Roman grandsire, although our old-fashioned pigsty suited me well enough.

At the close of that week, our lines formed for our southward march. The weather was most foul. The wind through the hawthorn was as sharp as Elain had told in song. There was fog and rain in the valleys, snow on the hilltops, frozen mud in the roads. The gray days were drearily short, and the nights ungodly long. And now I saw the sense of Gerald's refusing to begin our great campaign—to make me Emperor of Britain—until warm weather. Along with Caliburn, and the ear of Droit, and other benefits heaped upon me by the Great Gods, truly among their noblest gifts was the hard head and the true heart and the stubborn spirit of my great General.

Despite the drizzling rain, my army was in wondrous fettle. Gerald hoped that both Cornwall and Monmouth would yield without a fight, I being inclined to hope otherwise against my common sense. In any case, the men would be shed for a while of their mucky drill field, and bleak barracks, and could forage heartily on the King's corn and on country wenches. Nor did the glowering skies discourage our camp-followers, some of them being farm-girls of the Wye Valley properly married to various soldiers, some were hardy hoydens competing for a penny and no few wantons whom very Hercules could not calm down.

Vivain belonged with none of these groups, yet Gerald thought it unseemly for her to walk in my train, and her heart was set on the adventure. The best I could do was provide her with a nag, which she rode behind the soldiers but in front of the slatterns, which, oddly enough, they appeared to resent. Churls with a drove of baggage-laden donkeys brought up the rear.

On the fourth day of the march, Heaven stopped her plagued frowning and gave us a great smile. The clouds were sucked into the Sun; he came forth beaming, and the cold Earth steamed away frost. It may be that Merdin had conjured in the beautiful bright day, for I had seen him doing hocus-pocus the night before. I chose to believe that the High Gods had granted me the favor on the day of my reunion with Elain, even though they had forbade that she become my Queen. As the men pitched their camp on favorable ground half a mile from

Swan Lake, Vivain came up on her horse, swung down with curlew-like grace, kneeled, and spoke to me.

"You are very happy, my liege, and greatly blessed."

"Truly."

"I ask a boon. It is only to lay eyes again on your true love, Elain, and perhaps talk to her a little while, that I may see for myself that she deserves the keeping of your troth, unbroken since we lay under the linden tree."

"You said 'again.' I did not know you had ever seen her except in a dream."

"I lied to you before—I do not know why, for in truth I saw her plain on Beltane Eve. I had crept out of the forest to catch sight of you, for your coming had been foretold. Perhaps I would not have noticed her—despite her hawthorn beauty—if you had not chosen her to frolic with beside a bonfire, and there I saw you give her a long kiss."

"There's no harm in your seeing and talking with her, if she is alone when I visit her after the midday meal."

Vivain took my hand and kissed it, and then lightly remounted, and rode away in the direction of the lake. Only then, when I could see only her dark tresses, did my eyes speak to my mind of the sheen I had seen on her eyes, and the foxy sharpness of her face, and of her ill-hidden excitement. Still, it was hardly thinkable that she would attempt to harm my favorite, and if I did think of it, unable to cry it down, still Pillicock would stand a close watch, and Vivain had no longer a knife to plunge in a frenzy of jealousy. I hoped that the sunny glimmer on the water, as though this were April instead of late December, would not decoy the two girls into Llewelan's boat. How could I be sure that the witch-child would not give her a sudden thrust overside and watch her drown?

Presently I dismissed the foolish notion as I chewed meat. After-wards I saw that the men's pavilions were well-raised, rather than having to be run up in a sudden rainstorm, for I had little trust in the unseasonable fair sky. With this, and a discussion with Gerald as to the morrow's march, and a brief talk with Merdin, the third hour after noon was well-broached before I left the camp for Llewelan's landing. It happened that I caught a glimpse of Vivain leading her horse through heavy thickets, but she did not glance in my direction. She walked like an angry cat.

Waiting for me in the boat sat Elain, and the sight of her took my breath, for I had not been able to keep undimmed in these nigh three months apart the pictures of her painted on the inside of my skull. They numbered at least a hundred, more like a thousand, showing her angry, spiteful, tender, touched by music, awake and asleep, eating, stroking Pillicock's rough hair, and flushed from amorous play. Her eyes were gray-green as mistletoe, her hair a paler gold than goldenrod, and now a red rose bloomed in each taut cheek, and unless I missed my guess, her temper was high.

How could I doubt but that Vivain had boasted of our love-making in Radnor Forest? I might have to throttle her, I thought, before I was done.

"Will Your Majesty honor my poor house?" Elain asked, taking the oars.

"The honor is mine," I answered handsomely.

"Have you hired a noble Roman to teach you manners?" And her white arms, far stronger than they looked, took a big pull at the oars.

"Have you ever found fault with them?"

"More times than I found pleasure. But we'll not speak of that. I could expect no better from a King raised on the heaths of Taff."

"What ails you, Elain? Did not you relish the visit of Vivain?"

"No, I did not. And I petition Your Majesty that she not come here again."

"Did she tell of my transgressions? I bid you to remember that you refused——"

"I'll not repeat her words to any one. I wish to forget them. I'll remember she is not all-woman but half-witch, and she spent a whole year on an island off the Monan coast—its name I disremember— inhabited by witches. No doubt she cast a spell on you—so you knew not a ha'penny from a haycock—but that too I'll forget."

"Then will you remember what was sweet between you and me, and forget what was sour?"

"Your sword lay between us—not Caliburn, which you now wear, put in your hands by Morgan the Fairy, but another. Yes, and you were faithful to your vow—but that was before you became King."

"No sword parts us now. And, Elain, this should be a day of feasting and revelry, not of quarreling. This is the day that the Sun turns back from his journey southward, the beginning of New Year, and from hence forth the Sun will strengthen, and the days lengthen, and the Black Sow of night waste slowly away. It has been celebrated by all men since the beginning of the world."

"How celebrated? With drinking until they fall down with a wench in a dark corner. Only the Christians do it honor—four days from hence—with fasting and prayer. That day they call Christmas."

"If you pine for their foul sect, leave me on shore."

"No, you are the King. My noble father's life, not to speak of my own, lies in your hands. And it be true that you beat my father's enemy, Vortigern, and put him in flight. For that I will pour you mead, and kiss the cup."

"Then, I pray you, do so with good will. I have great need of your smile, and your love if you will give it, because Vortigern still lives, and plots against my throne; and who but the Gods knows if I will fall in battle?"

"Do not fall, my liege. You are a harsh ruler, and any troth you give a maiden is a weak reed, still whom may we look to but you? Forgive my spiteful tongue a while ago. I was deeply vexed and shamed by a witch."

We came up to the island landing, and Pillicock met us there, and kneeled to me. And then Elain said an auspicious thing.

"Dear Gnome! Will you take your line and hook, and some wild-duck guts, and catch the King a mess of eels? I wish to fry them for his supper. And aye, you may take the gammer with you, for she's lucky at fishing, being old and bent like a hook."

"Aye, my lady."

He called the ancient serving-wench and they went off happily together. Elain led me into the stone house, where she fed the half-dead fire, causing a dense smoke that escaped through holes in a tiled roof. The chill of the room passed off. The last coolness of the chill Elain had put on me likewise sped away. Yet for a space I was content to sit beside her, alive to her perfumed nearness, and watch the bright blaze.

"Tell me of the battle," Elain said. "Did you escape without a wound?"

"I took one deep cut on my thigh from a stalwart fellow's sword. It is nearly healed, but if you will see the scar——"

"There's no harm in that. You took it in my defense."

But before I could loose my breeches and show it to her, she chanced to reach far to stir the fire, and her drawn-up sleeve revealed a fresh cut in the soft of her elbow.

"It is only a scratch," she told me quickly, "given me by a stray cat whom I rashly welcomed here."

I had seen no cat about. Cats do not like swimming, and how had she crossed the waters? Besides, a cat's claws would not have caused six little punctures of her skin, three even with and below the other three. What could I believe but that Vivain had bit her in jealous fury?

"This too was only a scratch, missing the great veins," I said, showing her the pink line where the cut had healed.

"No, it was a grievous wound. The Gods defended you, or you might have bled to death. And, Artay, I believe your skin is as white as mine."

"No, yours is like swan-down. But let us compare them and make certain."

We did so, and I kissed the part she showed, at the curve of her breast. Then we fell to making other comparisons, such as the thickness of my big arm-muscle with hers, much smaller. Yet when both were flexed they seemed equally hard, and I knew now why she could row so swiftly and well. Perhaps the shoe was on the other foot, and rowing had made her strong of arm and big of hand, for she had lived on and about lakes all her life. To compare the smallness of her waist with mine, we must both shed some of our clothes, but no fault could be found with that in such a warm house.

The slimness and roundness of her thighs had no resemblance to my big hams knotted with muscle. Their firmness too was pleasing, but when I hunted a softness nearby, she caught my wrist.

"Wait, Artay," she whispered, her gray-green eyes appearing almost black, and her face beautiful with longing. "My maidenhood cannot stand much more."

"Then let it perish, as it was meant to do."

"But would its perishing today be good or evil? We are not wedded by Christian vows, or by heathen rites, nor will we ever be, and we do not have even the carnival of Beltane to excuse us before the Gods. Now it is true that the crowned King may take any unwedded maiden for his pleasure."

"Full true, and rightly so."

"That last, I doubt. At least it would be more rightful if we lay in your royal bed at Woodwick, instead of on a sheepskin coverlet."

"The King is the King wherever he sets foot."

"It is said that Lucillius, who commanded the garrison at Caerleon, not only feasted here on the waterfowl he snared and the fish he caught, but also he made free with the maidens hereabouts, some of them of good name."

"And he was only a Roman officer, not the King."

"And truly this is the first day of the New Year, an auspicious day, and what happens today brings happiness or sorrow to the year's end. If I yield to you, and bear you a son, it stands to reason he would be blessed, and a daughter would be beautiful and graced. Also, because you are the King, his name and fame will be great. Still, I must ask a boon, perhaps not too great compared to the gift of my virginity, so long guarded."

"Ask it, and if its giving will not harm my throne and kingdom, I will grant it."

"It comes to me to ask for two boons. I have heard, Artay, that you are merciless in hanging those who have wronged you. If I yield to you my treasure, will you spare the life of the next three wretches whom you would otherwise hang, and exile them forever from your realm?"

"Not three but five."

"Now that will be no small goodness that I have done through what may be wicked longing. Remember I have heard Christian preaching. The Christians set much store on mercy to one's enemies. And five lives that might be saved, perhaps to be redeemed of evil, is no small price for a maidenhead lost."

"I would count it only fair."

"Will you remember me always, in joy and pride, and never scorn me, even if we never meet again?"

"I will love you always, no matter who lies at my side."

"That too is a boon, so it was not two that I must ask, but three. It may be, that if I yield to you, you will be less loath to turn away Vivain. It cannot be that you will not take greater pleasure in me than in a half-witch, for my mouth that you will kiss has never spoken spells, and my arms enfolding you have never wielded a knife to take men's lives, and my passion will be greater than hers, because she is but half-woman, and the perfume of my body is that of water-lilies, not the smell of the wild, rank forest. What does her gift weigh, compared to mine? She boasts that you lust for her with a mighty lust, yet I cannot ask you to banish her from your court."

The thought came to me that Vivain's boast was not wholly if even largely true, otherwise what labor of courts, and preparation for war, would have made me banish her from my bed for nearly three months?

"No, do not ask that, Elain, because her witchy visions have served me well, for it may be she is a truer prophet than very Merdin."

"Do you think that my giving to you will reduce your taking from her?"

"By the Great Gods, I do, without quite knowing why, unless when all is said and done, you are my true love."

"I believe that I am—not Wander of Cornwall, not Vivain of the Hill, but Elain of the Lake. Your Majesty, you may do what you please with me."

As I slowly removed her few remaining garments and my own, Elain asked me to be gentle with her, which was not what Vivain had asked, and truly this moved me more deeply than the other. Truly I was gentle, and I took time to save her pain. And for this I was wondrously rewarded, a reward I had hardly earned, since it was of no cost to me and truly my desire. Her mouth was sweet to mine, and her perfume sweet as her song, and I found exquisite happiness in the tightening clasp of her arms. When at last we were fully interbound and Nature would suffer no more delay, she did not cry out, but whispered to me of love, a sweeter whispering than any the Earth Mother had ever made to Lud, God of the Sun.

Then I lay on my side, the fire crackling softly, she cuddled against my back, and both of us floated into slumber, not to waken until we heard Pillicock's great shout as he rowed slowly to the land.

It might be my fate to live but briefly, but short or long, in darkness or in sunlight, Elain was my true love.

Chapter Ten
The Circle of Stones

A cold wind sprang up in the north at sundown, so it came about that my chamberlain made my bed close to the side of my pavilion, away from the gusts through the flapping curtain at the door. I had heard that a Roman gladiator courted death at every combat. One of my ministers had seen with his own eyes a samphire-gatherer on Dover Cliffs, where a hand's slip, or a clumsy foot, could change him to a bag of broken bones on the rocks below. I myself had watched a snake-charmer fondle a venomous viper. But I had never dreamed that a King of Cambria could be dispatched to Elysium by getting out of a draft.

I had slept only a few minutes when Pillicock's big voice wakened me.

"My liege, let me in to deliver a message from Merdin," he said when I had called his name.

It must be of trifling note, I thought, since we were not yet in enemy country, and Merdin's head must be getting maggoty from old age. But I heaved myself out of bed, and one glance into Pillicock's face shook me wide awake.

"There's a young woman prowling about in the brushwood, and I think she means mischief," he told me in an undertone.

"Who is it? Do you think it's Vivain?" For the Moon was young, and perchance a linden tree stood nigh, and perhaps she still hoped to score over Elain.

"No, she's too tall."

"Could it be Elain?"

"My liege, the fairy-child would not hang about a bivouac of soldiery, were you Adonis the Beautiful. This woman is as tall as Elain, but of heavier build. I think I have seen her among the camp-followers."

"What does she intend? Perhaps some of the soldiers have invited her, and she is waiting their call."

"Let us see what she intends. Have I your leave to roll up one of your sheepskin robes? When I am gone, will you lay it against the tent wall where your body has just lain? Sit quietly in the dark, my liege, for not more than a third part of an hour, and I think I'll get hand on her. And call to me from the doorway to make haste with your answer to Merdin's message."

"As you wish."

Pillicock busied himself with one of the robes. Giving him mal-formed legs, the Gods must have atoned for the affliction by making his hands wondrous deft. When with a few, swift movements he had readied the mannikin, I could hardly believe how closely it imitated the shape of a man lying on his side. I spoke to him from the door and he vanished from sight in some nearby thickets. Making a great show of grunting sleepily, I put the decoy on my bed and pretended to snore. Soon I rolled it against the tent wall.

I waited unseen and silent in the dark for not more than a sixth part of an hour. The watch was not weary, for I had never known Pillicock to follow a wrong lead, and truly I was alert as though I myself were stealing up on a beast of the forest with my bow ready to draw. The only light was a pale glimmer from behind my shield, where my night candle burned. Then it came to me there was some one just beyond my pavilion wall. I could even vision her kneeling down close to the bulge in the cloth. Since I did not hear or smell her, it must be that a King appointed by the Gods has a sixth wit. Would that appointment cause me to waken and defend myself if the rolled sheepskin were really I, and I sound asleep? Truly I could not believe it, and could only hope that the Gods did not divine my lack of faith.

Only a moment later I heard a soft sound, and I swear before Heaven I felt a sharp pain in my left side below the arch of the ribs. A few seconds passed, a human throat uttered a deep gasp, and then came Pillicock's voice, very low, under his breath almost, yet aring with his intent. If I were his hearer I would never doubt its tidings.

"Make one sound, and you'll never breathe again."

I heard the footsteps of two persons making for the doorway. As though Pillicock were King, and I Pillicock, I remained where I was, in quiet, waiting his instructions.

"Will you light the candles, Artay?" he asked as if I were his brother.

I took up my night candle, tall and thick with a small wick to last all night, and quickly brought fire to my other candles. Then through the door came my guardian-monster, with his hand strong as a chain clutching the wrist of a fair-haired woman of about twenty. At sight of me, tall and alive, she gasped as though in irremediable heartbreak, her eyes popping from her head and like dead eyes in the candlelight. Then she stood half-dead.

One good glance told me she was a heavy-featured, raw-boned slattern, far from comely, flat-chested and with not much womanliness in her appearance, whom I too had seen among our camp-followers. She had attracted my attention by being the most strident in her scurrilous jeering at Vivain, astride her horse in the wenches' van, and had egged on the others. Then I went to see what she had been up to, although I could readily guess. When I took hold of the mannikin, it did not move readily, for good reason. Pinioning it to the pavilion wall was the blade of a long knife, its hilt outside the cloth, and it must have been plunged with ferocious vim, for it had stabbed through half a dozen folds of tough sheepskin.

"Why did you do it, foul slut?" I demanded.

"No matter why I did it," she answered, speaking as though in a horrid dream. "I'll be hanged just the same, or burned to death, and what do I care? I promised I'd kill you, and I failed."

"It may be that you'll be neither wholly hanged nor burned for a good while yet, that time being spent in various ways to make you wag your tongue."

"Only hang me as soon as you can affix the rope, and I'll show you why I did it." And I had never seen threat of torture open a mouth as quickly.

She groped in her raiment and brought forth a golden coin, of which there were not twenty in all Cambria except in unfound treasure-troves, and this was the largest I had yet seen. Stamped on it was the head, seen in profile, of one of the Caesars, and this too had been scratched to suggest his wearing of a crown and mustache, and these scratches had been lately made, for they were of brighter color than the rest. Suddenly I almost dropped it, thinking that the head was intended to resemble mine. If I owned such coins, each worth forty-eight cows, this was one I might hang on the neck of some greatly trusted liegeman, appointed to some mighty office. Even so, I would have had the mustache pictured somewhat larger.

"Who gave you this?" I asked. "Your lover?"

"Alas, I have none. It was given me by a tall man who whistled me into the dark. He did not tell me his name and I did not see his face."

"Then what did you mean when you said you did not care if you were hanged or burned? That hints of some great love you now have lost."

"The hint is true, but the love is of a different kind than Your Majesty knows. In my whole life I had touched but a few silver coins, never one of gold. With this as my dower, I could marry a land-holder in my own Valley of the Dee."

I put the coin in my purse, and was about to call some soldiers to see to the hoyden's hanging, when Pillicock, his brow wrinkled with thought, brought his lips as near as possible to my ear and spoke quietly.

"My liege, the wench was dazzled by promise of sudden riches. Better folk than she have been so."

"I'll not——"

"Wait, my King, I pray. Once before you set free a prisoner who had sought your life, and profited thereby. Will you believe me when I tell you it is best to set this woman free, bidding her leave the camp at once, and if her face is seen again, its flesh will be burned from its bone in slow fire? It may be that your foeman, thinking you dead, will betray himself when you appear suddenly before your army. I will be watching and perchance discover him."

"You can't watch a thousand. Although it would give me pleasure to have him sweat——" I stopped my tongue's wagging because of a great jump of thought in my mind. To back it, I remembered Pillicock's good counsel until now, and his close watch over me always, and how he had warned me against leaving our lines to make love under a linden tree.

"Pillicock, take her forth, get her knife from where it sticks through the cloth, lead her to the cart-road, cut a cross on her cheek that will bleed well and leave a scar, and send her on her way. It may be a foul Christian will think she is one of their own, and wed her dowerless. At least it may benefit her beauty, for it could not be made less."

"Aye, my liege."

When the two had gone, I drove myself to examine once more,

and with great care, the thought that had struck me so hard as to rattle my skull. It was that the drab had been hired not by a tall man but a small woman. Could Vivain in her fury of jealousy over my choosing Elain instead of herself have gone to such lengths? If so, she was the one who needed a hanging! I dwelt a moment on giving her one, only to know it was beyond my power of will. For what man, even a king, had ever been more greatly loved by a human tempest?

2

It came about that in the mists of dawn as the men broke camp, I had a good look at Vivain through the crack of my door-curtain. She kept glancing in my direction, with no fear or fury evident in her face, and instead a child-like eagerness. Almost regretfully I forsook the notion, or at least smothered it in doubt, that the pretty witch-spawn would rather see my bleeding corpse than see me in Elain's arms. As for being half-sorry, what man, or even king, can account for the quirks and contrariness of his own heart and mind? Although it would be pleasant to tantalize her, watch her boil and steam, and once in a long time, perhaps, when Elain was many leagues beyond my reach, to sooth her itching, surely the countless others who would murder me for this or that needed no addition to their number by a small half-witch. I decided that the knife-wielder's story was in all probability true. An ugly woman lacking a lover might easily take a life for money to buy one.

Presently I spied a boat, rowed by Pillicock, and carrying a passenger whose hair glimmered in the dawn-light. Quite certain that my sudden appearance before the dressed ranks would startle no man into self-betrayal of a mighty crime, and hoping that Vivain would see me and fly into another fit or fury, and hoping too for a greater satisfaction to my heart than to my spiteful spleen, I walked openly down to meet the visitors, and to give my hand to my true love. Then we stood at the edge of the forest, I holding both her hands, with my heart stopped at sight of her still beauty and the mist of tears in her radiant gray-green eyes.

"What if your seed takes root?" she asked.

"Send me word, and the best midwives in Cambria will attend you, and a cohort of my best soldiers guard you and the babe."

"I will send a sign that only you may read. In three moons, when again the day and night are of equal span, I will know for certain, for sometimes the eating of sticky honey, or a sharp frost that stills the rivulets, causes a sign like to that of well-rooted seed, once, twice, or even three times in succession. Yet I will wait still another moon, until the barley-corns planted in the fields by churls begin to take root. If you have kindled me, I will send you a good corn, with a tiny shoot of green showing life. If the time was not auspicious, and your seed died, I will send a corn that has been frost-bitten, and is blackened and dead."

"May the Gods ordain that the seed live! If it be a man-child that you bear me, he shall bear the name Marcus, in memory of the stout Roman who guarded the swords and shields stored in Pillicock Hill. If it be a girl, she shall be named Anna, for the woman of silence who gave me suck."

Then Elain kissed me with great tenderness and sweetness, a kiss the like of which no other wenches or witches with whom I had frolicked could fashion with their mouths or have born in their hearts, although sometimes the inkling came to me, more dim than a tree's shape in the smothering fog of the moors, that long ago I had been kissed in this fashion, perhaps by my mother, Queen Ina, in the little while I had lain on her breast before I had been cast forth by my father for beasts to eat. Yet I had dreamed of many such kisses, a dream that made no sense, for no other woman than Anna had given me her teat, and surely she could not have borne a foster-child the love that this denoted. Indeed, she must have resented the giving of her milk that the Earth Mother had put in her breast to feed her own babe. After this I parted with the Lily Maid and we resumed our march to the Usk.

My scouts knew of a low pass through the mountains eastward and a little north of Caerleon. We took it, forded two rivers on the plain below, crossed to the lordly Usk, and followed him upstream to the village of Usk, where the Prince of Monmouth had his court. Truly I was hard put to it not to laugh when I saw his piddling palace with little more than half the spaciousness of mine, and his palace guard, about fifty fellows of all sizes with every kind of weapon, scrambling to get in line now that my great army had been sighted. Gerald ordered camp pitched a stone's throw from the palace door, and my own pavilion raised, for I was of no mind to sleep in the barn-like building and hear the Prince snore. I kept him waiting a good hour, as I ate a hearty supper, then opened his door with a big thrust of my shoulder and, unattended except by Merdin, made entry.

He was sitting on what he called his throne, not much more than a bench with a straight back and without armrests, the whole covered by red cloth. On his head was some sort of crown, of yellow metal that I took to be copper, and my emptier of chamber-pots wore a richer robe. All this, and his pale face, I saw in a passing glance, for my attention had fixed on Garth, called Earl of the Usk, whom I had captured at the Battle of the Vale, and to whom I had given raiment to wear home.

"Garth, I see you have changed your robe," I remarked, "since I saw you last."

"Your Majesty, you did not bid me wear it after I had returned to my liege-lord," he replied. "Until then, I obeyed you strictly, as His Highness the Prince will attest."

"Then you are spared a hanging until you break the troth to me that you will pledge second to the Prince." Then, turning to the fellow squirming in the chair, "Have you caught a lameness in your legs from the fogs of Usk?"

"Why, no, Your Majesty——"

"I take it that you have, or you would have come to my royal palace well before now, to kneel before my throne. But perhaps I have medicine for your affliction. It is made of hemp, and can be tied in a noose, which, if fastened around your neck, will pass its limberness to you. Need I send for it, or will its mere mention effect your instant cure?"

"Your Majesty, your kingdom is greater than mine," the Prince babbled, meanwhile hopping up. "Still, mine is of great age, I descend from a long line of kings, and I hoped you would treat me as a brother, not as a subject."

"If you are wise, you'll not ask for the treatment my brothers Modred and Vortimer will receive. If you prove a loyal subject, paying a fair tribute, you will outlive them both. Now try your knees on the earthen floor and see if they are supple."

He did so briskly, and I let him take my hands in token of fealty.

"My liege, what do you call a fair tribute?" he asked when I had bade him rise. "My treasury is almost empty——"

"Your palace guards will make it leaner, by their eating. Of the fifty I will take forty, as a favor to you, leaving you ten for show. Of the corn in your grainery, I will take only what my donkeys can carry; and Garth, at least, will rejoice to see them well-loaded and gone, because if they stayed here, one of the old, grizzled beasts might die, to furnish him a robe. The rest will be only six casks of ale, two of mead, the loss of which will save you many an aching head, half a ton of smoked fish, a whole ton of salt-meat, and all the woolen cloth you have in store. Then you may continue to wear your coronet, call yourself Prince of Monmouth, and attend my crowning as Emperor of Britain."

3

Marching northeastward, in one day we had gained the west bank of the Mon. On the following day my scouts collected all the fishing-smacks wintering at the river-mouth, and these ferried across my whole army and its goods before high Sun. In a couple of days they could have landed us across the great estuary of the Severn, but we would have found ourselves fronting the vast marshes along its left bank, while marching an equal time would bring us to Gloster, where wintered many craft, including ferries. Besides, I was burning to get to Stonehenge and hear the rest of the Song of Camlon before I confronted King Cador of Cornwall and his well-famed army. And I take it that the truant heart of man decides far more great issues than his steady head.

From Gloster, which the Romans had called Glevum, we followed the Roman road to Corinium, and then marched almost straight south, a distance of seventy or more miles into the vast uplands of the Plain of Sarum. On the night of the fourth day's unhastened march, we encamped only ten miles from the most hallowed spot in all Britain and I reckoned in the wide world, the Temple of the

True Gods, which Merdin had seen but once, Gerald never, and I in dreams alone. The main of my army was told to spend the day in foraging, although to take no more than half of any cotter's flocks and herds and none of his stored corn. Soon after noon·Merdin and I, and a guard of fifty Mendip archers, planned to set forth for the shrine.

As I was licking the juices of a wooden platter that had served up my hearty midday meal, Vivain begged audience, knelt, and once more asked a boon.

"You may ask it, and if it is in reason, I'll grant it."

"My liege, it is to go with you and the old wizard to Stonehenge."

"What good will you do there?"

"I know ways of invoking a Great God who will cherish you as long as you live."

"Is his name Modo? I recall you have already asked him to attend me. I have never heard his name except from your lips. True, I have not asked Merdin——"

"I pray you, do not speak to Merdin of the God Modo," she broke in. "Because he has never revealed himself unto Merdin, the old man will be more jealous of me than he is already, and perhaps he will try to balk Modo's favor unto you."

"Vivain, the Great Circle was raised to Lud and to other Gods whose powers I know, and when you hear the name of them you spread the fingers of your left hand in a sign I had never seen made by any other. You made it just now."

"It is a most potent sign. It slakes the wrath that Lud and Tyr store against my mother, Calypso the Witch, and a veil is taken from my eyes, and I can see visions of things to come, of which I can warn you, or give you good news. Tonight I will ask a vision of Wander of Cornwall."

"You may do so—in your bed by the watchfire of this camp. Tonight I seek the favor of the Gods I know, and Merdin and I will enter the temple alone."

In three hours we came in sight of the great edifice, surpassing in wonder any tower, wall, and temple that the Romans had built. From the southwest ran a straight road, half a mile long, with a bank and a ditch at either side. At its end a ditch took off to the left in a half-circle, and enclosed by this stood a circle of thirty upright stones, huge, high as a house, with flat inward surfaces, and other stones laid atop them, exactly meeting one another and forming a circular, unbroken band. An opening on the northeast revealed another circle of about forty upright stones, without tops, and within this, an egg-shaped ring of about a score. In the very heart of the temple loomed five gigantic stones, which only a God could lift, four times taller than a tall man, and near them lay a flat stone that made quivers run down my spine, for Merdin whispered it was the Stone of Sacrifice. There was no quarry nearby from which the stones had been hewn, and it was said that they had been transported by sorcery all the way from Cambria.

The Sun was already low, this bleak late-winter day, and the shadows cast were long and black and cold. Still, Merdin would not let me approach the Circles now. Night must fall, he said, and the Moon rise, ere the Gods would come down and speak through his mouth as he sang the Song of Camlon.

The Mendip archers camped a distance off and I saw not one of them glance toward the Holy Circles. The Sun dripped blood into a low-hanging bank of cloud, then the waning Moon glimmered through it, topped it, and cast a ghastly glimmer over the plain.

"It is time to go," Merdin told me, taking up his harp, and his voice shaking.

I had gone into battle in the Vale with not half the tremors of heart. The shadows of the stones were no longer sharp, being gray and obscure, and the stones themselves had lost their different tints, and were terrible to see. In a moment they were towering far above my head. Merdin bid me mount the great slab and lie on my back, and I turned icy cold from crown to heel, because the awful thought had struck me that he was about to sacrifice me to the Gods, perhaps to save me from some worse fate, and if so, I could not raise a finger in my own defense.

"Have no fear," he told me, "except of the song I am about to sing. Your lying there betokens you would be a willing sacrifice, if the Gods ask it, and your guts spilled on the stone would prophesy all that will ever happen on the Earth, but the Gods will not ask it because the sooth they have said has only partly come to pass."

He stood by the tallest of the stones and began to pluck his harp. He played the same refrain I had heard before, then began to sing:

"The bridal song is sung in the palace of the King, and the meats are cold.
And the King lies by the White One he has taken to wife.
But her womb has not opened unto him and she does not swell with child.
He reigns, and the Land of Cambria is at peace, and the corn is more and the forests less.
But away to the eastward his enemy waxes in strength,
And the Moon changes in season, and the leaves green, and the crops ripen.
And the rivers flow and the Sea raves;
Then a dark cloud spreads through the sky, and Thor beats his drums, and flings his great bolts,
And now the Singer blanches and his voice fails,
Such shapes he dimly sees—flitting and fading,
Or solid in the sunlight or pale in mist,
And the Singer must rest the throbbing strings and wet his lips with mead."

Merdin's voice had dropped low and now it ceased, and his hands lay still. I thought this silence must be deeper than the grave's, and graves gaped everywhere in my wild imaginings, swallowing all. Only these gigantic growing rocks stood changeless and immortal. I lay trembling, my strength drained away until once more Merdin sang:

"What is this great, gray land where two kings wander?
It is gray as Death, but it is not Death, for in summer it greens;
And who is this messenger who has searched them out in their hiding-place?
What are the alarms, and then the clash of swords, the thunders of the fray,
And who are the mighty foe with two-edged swords, and who leads the host?
Behold! The blade of Caliburn flashes in the sun,
Behold! The hound Cavell utters his great bay,

And the spear Ron hisses in the air ere it plunges deep,
And Fortune flits from friend to foe and back again,
And at last the King lays down his sword, but does not yield it,
And the long war ends in silence. Yet the Gods move,
And a spot on distant waters becomes a barge,
And three tall queens stretch forth their hands unto bloody hands,
And the barge withdraws into night and silence.
How may he pass away and yet remain?
How then may his fame spread to all lands, throughout all time?
He is no kin to the hook-nosed conqueror from the Seven Hills.
How may he match in glory, he of the fluffed hair and the tilted head?
Although the forests shrink, and the beasts are less and the men more.
And so ends the Song of Camlon,
Sung by Gwydion of the Magic Harp,
And the Singer speaks one more truth, whispered by the Gods,
That the Song is mightier than the Sword,
Mightier than Caliburn, Sword of the King,
And the meaning of that truth the Singer does not know,
And what man can ever know?"

The song ended. I sat on the rock and looked into the gray face of the singer.

"Merdin, I do not know what it means," I told him. "But what the Gods do not give me I will seize with my own hands."

"I think that is what the Song means."

Chapter Eleven
Good Fishing

From the Plain of Sarum, our army marched westward to Ilchester, where we struck a well-preserved road laid by the Romans running to their old fortress at Moridunum. From this place westward we moved through lands claimed by King Cador of Cornwall and the Exe as part of his realm, but not even his scouts were to be seen as yet. The sparse dwellers of the region gaped at us in wonder although with neither animosity nor friendship, and no enemy force existed west of the Stour River or east of Dartmoor.

From thence we made our way to within ten miles of the old Roman town of Isca Dumnoniorum, the city of the Dumnonii, whom we called Cornish, for the same dark-skinned, small-statured folk dwelt hereabouts as on the western moors. Its ruins lay near the mouth of the Exe, the whole valley of which Cador had taken under his sway. The great river was still too far from his capital at Tavistock for him to make his stand, although by arraying on the western bank he could have made us trouble. As it happened, the lower river was dotted with fishing villages and many boats, and a quick dash by fifty fleet-footed men took by surprise the so-called Master of the Fleet, captured him with his wife and children, and fetched the lot of them to my pavilion.

"You and your loved ones will take no harm if you assemble all the fishercraft on this side Exe, and ferry us across," I told him, not beating about the bush.

"And if I don't?"

"You will all hang in a row, the longest of you at one end, the shortest at the other, on the nearest tree-bough that will hold you."

" 'Tis a horrid picture. First will 'ee answer me fair a question, so I can 'bey 'ee orders wi' gladder heart?"

"Aye, I will."

"Are 'ee the same King Artay what furbished a monstrous great army in one day wi' iron swords and shields?"

"Aye, I am he."

"And the same what took a monstrous great sword wi' a jeweled hilt from the hand of the fairy Morgan of the Mere?"

"You see it at my side."

"Then 'ee must be the same what made the lord of the Usk wear a donkey skin."

224

"How did you hear about it?" I asked, warming to the fellow.

"Why, our villages be the cross-road of the world, and we hear all the news quick as a wink."

"Well, quick as a wink you'll hang, if you don't get down to business."

"Why, I'll do what 'ee say. I'll blow a monstrous great horn, and 'semble all the boats, and we'll put 'ee across fast as we're able. And 'em boys will be glad to help 'ee, for King Cador taxes us for ary little mullet in our nets, and her a Roman nohow, not a Britain."

So it was settled featly, and on the second night thereafter we encamped on the west bank, with an open road to Tavistock, to King Cador's court, and to Wander.

Our march could not be hidden on the wide moors, and scared shepherds on shaggy ponies precoursed us with the news. By the same token, we had nothing to fear from ambush. The men marched well on their ration of dried fish, mutton, and corn, and Gerald said that day for day we beat the Romans.

As we came nigh the King's palace we saw his force drawn up in good position in the angle between a big brook and the Tamar River. Gerald and I and the Mendip archers went up to look at it from a distance of a hundred paces. I had been somewhat troubled by reports I had heard of Cador's power, but now, if I were not King, I would have tossed my helmet in the air in exuberance. What he called his army was as large as ours. Although more than a mob of armed men with bronze swords and axes and wooden shields braced with metal, still their undressed ranks and their officers all shouting at once, and the way the dark men stood and stared showed their unacquaintance with good drill, let alone battle.

The fact remained that if we engaged them, we would surely lose a hundred or more of our followers before we put them to flight. So when Gerald had set spies to watch them, we left them to sweat and returned to our main force.

While the troops took their ease before Cador's palace, Gerald, Merdin, and I, and about fifty stout fellows sauntered toward its door. The edifice was fully as large as mine, perhaps somewhat larger, and the cluster of ministers waiting for us wore finer robes than did mine, perhaps because their tin and wool had a ready market in

Gaul. They kneeled to me, somewhat stiffly in the joints, and their chief told me that King Cador would receive me before his throne.

I winked at Gerald, he returned the signal, and we tramped into the palace, managing for the hilts of our swords to clank against our shields. There the King sat, grand-looking on a fine throne, a heavy and handsome crown of gold on his brows, a crimson robe draped over his shoulders and bulging out at his belly, his pale-faced Queen beside him. Instantly I perceived her resemblance to Enid, Vortigern's paramour, later his Queen, who had conspired with him to feed me to wild beasts. They were full sisters, I recalled, and the fact raised my spirits higher than before, and strengthened my thews against any gentle dealing with her lord and herself. Still, it was not likely that the news I would impart to him would provoke him to battle. Although not royal-looking, his face was not that of a fool.

I looked into it once more before I spoke. It had the Roman darkness I saw in Gerald's face, and his eyebrows formed a black bar over dark eyes. I recalled that, like Gerald, he was half-Roman, and that Wander, his niece, was three-fourths Roman, the other quarter being half-Cornish and half-Cambrian. None of these ties with Imperial Rome would affect King Cador's answer to my demands unless I missed my guess. One thing that the Romans could do neatly, so Gerald had taught me, was to hold ground when they could, give it if they must, for their strong point was common sense.

Still it must be that I hated Rome in my deepest heart, and all Romans except Gerald and Marcus, who had guarded the Emperor's stores until I needed them. While I meant to save a modicum of King Cador's pride before his courtiers, my resolve to make him squirm within his royal robes and his own skin was forged stronger than before.

"I am King Artay of Cambria and Monmouth," I told him.

"You are welcome here, great King, if you come in peace," he replied, still seated on his hams.

"I have come on various affairs of state, one of them being to seek the hand of your niece Wander in marriage."

"Why, we have no aversion to that. Truly we see many advantages to the match, to bind our two kingdoms in the bonds of everlasting friendship. We would deplore her departure far to the north. But if thereby the King of Cornwall and the Exe and the King of Cambria establish brotherhood, each honoring the other as his peer, and help guard each other's coasts against the Men of Eire—I will call them men, but truly they are demons in men's guise—and against the raiding Saxons, both kingdoms would be well-served. We rejoice that you see it is no time for us two kings to quarrel, with danger threatening us from the west, the south, and in time, perhaps from the east."

"Where is the damosel? I don't see her."

"She is in call. And when you do see her, King Artay, I pledge you a precious jewel you will avow you have never seen such beauty in mortal maid, and your eyes will gladden, and you will not wish to delay the marriage a single night."

"But there are a few minor matters to discuss first. One of them is of such great moment that I may only whisper it in your royal ear."

He leaned forward so I could speak to him privately without mounting the platform. Instead I gained it in one step.

"It is said we South Cambrians are a windy lot," I whispered, "and I take it we caught it from the Cornish."

"Your Majesty, I don't follow you."

"You will, shortly. Is there glue on your breeches?"

"I am sure that you jest with us."

"Will you get off that throne before I yank it out from under you?"

"By the Gods——"

"Take no oath you cannot keep. Cador, you are hog-fat, and I fear you'd hit the floor with a great thump. The hands that pick you up may not be gentle, and perhaps raise you higher than you wish. But if you pledge allegiance and pay tribute, you shall have the title of Prince Cador of the Moors, a liegeman to no other than myself, and sit your throne when I am out of it."

He looked pale and shaken. Maybe he had dreamed of this in the night, perhaps a worse dream than this, but in the bright morning he had mustered arguments, including the lying heavy on his stomach of his last night's feast, that it was only a dream. He thought upon his army that had looked so fine and steadfast until he had seen my own. He wished he had put less trust in his fine Roman Gods and more in rugged British Gods, calling them by their true names, Lud and

Tyr, instead of Jupiter and Mars. Most of all he wished he had bestirred himself, instead of getting fat and lying long abed with his voluptuous Queen.

He gazed to the right and to the left, up and down, and again into my face.

"Those are harsh terms, King Artay," he whispered in reply.

"They will become harsher, the longer you keep me waiting."

"May I still wear my crown?"

"What do I want of it? My Cambrian crown will be the crown of Britain."

"What portion of my revenues may I still enjoy?"

"They will be my revenues, but you may keep and enjoy a third."

"May I tell my court that I am stepping down of my own free will?"

"In as fine language as you can spout."

"May I hang my General Brutus, who swore to me by all the Gods of Rome that my army could whip any in Britain?"

"No, for I owe him no hate for his vain boasting, but you can reduce him to Captain of your Palace Guard."

"Then I accept. What other choice do I have? And you shall have Wander if I have to lash her to your bed, for then I will be your uncle, entitled to favor."

"I take it she'll not need the whip to become the bride of Artay, King of Britain." Still, an errant question rose in mind why he had said such a foolish thing. No doubt it was only spleen.

"My lord," the Queen broke in, looking at him in alarm, "you are not yourself. Consider well before you speak."

"Woman, I will speak my royal will," he answered fiercely. Then so slowly that I could almost believe his bottom was glued to the chair, peeling off some of his skin as he broke the bond, he rose up. I stood beside him, almost a foot taller.

Yet he spoke with no little grandeur, bearing out the stories I had heard of Romans behaving grandly, even when being fed to lions.

"Liegemen of the King! It comes to me this is a great day in Cornwall, to be long remembered, for this day I renounce the name of King and by the leave of that great conqueror, King of Britain and Cambria, assume the title of Prince of the Moors, and will rule here under the King. My liege, I wish to be the first of the Cornish to pledge my fealty."

I sat on his throne; he kneeled on the dais, and I gave him both my hands. The Queen followed fast, with a sideways glance under lowered lashes, for she was a deal younger then her lord, and when I bid her rise, addressing her as Princess of the Moors, she called me Caesar. Still, I had best not drink a cup of mead that she might offer me, unless I had seen it poured from a new-broached cask. I was collecting many glories—so I thought with mingled pleasure and fright—but also I was amassing many enemies.

The ministers of the court likewise made obeisance. I was still seated on the throne when I bade the Princess summon Wander. To my amazement, the door in the rear led not to an outbuilding, but to another room under this same roof! While I had seen inner walls in the ruins of Roman houses I did not dream of such a thing in our British palaces. Before the Gods, I would have a room built on to Woodwick as soon as I returned there with my spoil.

2

Wander meant white in the old Cambrian tongue. The same name in modern Cambrian was Gwynever. Still, I had had the notion she would be dark as most people half or more Roman, and that her naming had referred to her purity or had some other poetical significance. Actually she was almost as white as snow.

Her hair had a pale gold tint, still it was fairer than flax. Her eyes almost matched it, such a light, bright brown that they looked like gold, of the kind that had been found in Cambria, not red like Roman gold. Her skin was almost too white, I thought, to look quite human; perhaps she was more beautiful than human, resembling the Roman Goddess Venus of the White Arms. In form she was like Venus, very tall and shapely. Doubtless the Gods had shaped and painted her to be queen of no kingdom less than all Britain. I could picture her on a silver throne studded with jewels, and wearing a bejeweled crown of massy gold. Where I could not picture her as yet, it somehow being beyond my imagination, was beside me in my bed.

In all truth, I was deeply shaken by her, without wholly knowing why, and rejoiced I need only sit quietly on my throne until she paid her addresses to me. This she did in royal fashion, dropping on one knee, the full gaze of her beauteous eyes on mine.

"Your servant, King Artay of Cambria, Monmouth, and Cornwall and the Exe, soon Emperor of Britain."

While I had relished being addressed by the latter god-like title, and had occasionally called myself so, still as yet it was only a hint from the Gods, not my solid winning. As I gave Wander my hand to help her up, it struck me that she must be an unusually truthful person, and no flatterer. Doubtless, seated beside me on the dais of my great palace, she would be a good wifely counselor and a source of strength. Being of ancient Roman lineage, she would help rally to my throne all the people who boasted Roman blood. And I thought how fine she would look standing beside me on the May Day and such like ceremonies; and what a royal-looking couple we would make. Still I could not vision her lying down, my thoughts skipping over it for some unknown reason. Perhaps the sudden and vast enlargement of my domains had mazed me somewhat, and reduced my natural heat.

"Wander, I have asked your uncle for your hand in marriage, and he consented," I told her, my voice a little tremulous.

"My liege, you pay me too great honor."

"I will be honored also if you too consent."

"It would give me intense pleasure, but it is no small thing for a maiden, kinswoman of many kings but daughter of none, to become Empress of Britain, and I would not have you find fault with me too late, and put me aside."

"How could I find fault with a maiden beautiful as a Goddess?"

"My liege, I have one frailty of body and what may be a fault of mind, neither of which can I help. I cannot remain well, and a fit mate for a king, if I dwell amid hills or on hilly ground. When I passed a summer in the far-off Cotswold, I wasted away almost to death. My mother climbed a hill in the fourth month of my kindling, and became so short of breath that I was well-nigh miscarried, and any air blowing down from hills is to me rank poison."

"That stands to reason," I answered, although seeing no remedy as yet, since Cambria was a hilly country. Even so, my heart did not fall as steeply as I could expect. When I had wedded her, I might build a palace on the Isle of Mona, as flat as a board, keeping her there, and visit her when I could spare the time from affairs of state and war.

"But it comes to me, that when you have conquered the Hecanas and foes beyond you may move your court to the Valley of the Dee or even of the Severn, to be more midway of your realm."

"Why, that's a good notion. In due time it will stand in the Valley of the Thames."

"The fault that may lodge in my mind came to pass from my birth-sign being the Archer. Also the full Moon, who in the Roman faith is Diana and likewise an archer, looked through a wall-port into my face before the cord was cut, and waked me from a sleep that was like death. The wizards read it that I would have her favor always, and remain as chaste as she save for the love of my lord. But in due to her, four nights in every Moon, on the night of her change, I must be wholly chaste, and lie alone, unattended except by my old serving-maid Helena, who cut the cord. These nights I must pass in a dark house in a nearby copse or forest, unguarded except by a ring of thirty-three soldiers, for I was born on the eleventh month, and three times eleven is thirty-three. The wizards said further that they must come no closer to my bower than three arrow-casts. If I do this—so spake the wizards—I may bear a son to my Lord the King, and bring to his banner all the Romans left in Britain, and he will reign long and rule wisely."

"It is no great thing to ask," I said. "Think you that a stay of two months in Cambria would bring on the sickness? It will take that long for a suitable palace to be raised on the Wye or the Severn."

"My liege, I think I would die before then, but if you take me in marriage, we may pass the night here, in feasting and in wedded bliss, and when you depart tomorrow you may leave me here, until you return from the wars and from palace-building, and send a boat for me. And doubtless, since the crescent Moon has all but wasted away, rising just before your Lord the Sun, and cannot grow littler, but only larger, tomorrow night bringing the New Moon, tonight I will conceive by your royal seed, and when you send for me I will have a son, truly a prince, a-suckle at my dug."

I did not think the latter outcome very likely. Too well I remembered the Song of Camlon, that my Queen would not grow round of belly for a good while yet. Even so, I became warmed and some of my unwonted bashfulness passed off.

"In that case, Wander, I will make you my Queen."

"Now those are good tidings," Cador broke in. "I myself will give you her hand."

It appeared that no great preparations need be made for our joining. The ministers had donned their best robes at news of my coming, and Wander's women-in-waiting had washed her face, hands, and feet, and dressed her pale hair. Merdin told me to bring forth a ring that had been taken from Enid's finger, red gold from a Roman coin set with a handsome pearl, and I brought from my chest a circle of gold that I had made for the occasion, by the smelting and pounding in a smithery of a dozen small gold coins, which I had found in Vortigern's treasury. Wander stood beside me on the dais, and I was astonished at her height, considering that most Romans were of middle height. Still I would not confess that her beauty surpassed Elain's, even if more taking to every eye but mine. I would stop thinking about Elain, at least until Wander and I parted. Although the marriage was one of state, which did not preclude my having favorites in the way of kings, and I was more in love with Caliburn than my soon bride, still she would have her due.

Merdin stood below the dais, and directed the ceremony. First I was told to put the ring on her left thumb. It would hang only on the tip, having been fashioned to fit Enid's fourth finger, still Wander remained serene as the wives of the Caesars whom Gerald had praised, causing me to doubt that she fully grasped her high appointment by the Gods. I could almost believe that her thoughts flew elsewhere.

"Wander's thumb stands for the Great God Lud," Merdin intoned. "To him is her first allegiance." And that was right, of course, Lud being over all.

When at Merdin's directions I put the ring on the first finger of my bride, she took a good look at it, perhaps admiring its fine pearl or even reckoning its worth. I remembered she was almost pure Roman, and hence she lacked the sentiment of our Cambrian wenches.

"The first finger is the pointer," Merdin went on in his rich voice.

"In this ceremony it stands for the Law of the Druids, which points the way to serve and please the Gods, and thus bring blessings on the King's realm. The ring encircling it pledges her obedience to that law, where it prevails over all other, being in matters of religion, quarrels between his subjects, divination, the keeping of records, and such like."

I did not relish this part of the service, and it came to me that Wander was of like opinion. Could she be yearning for Roman law? Whatever her yearnings, I would teach her to obey the King's law.

Merdin had me put the ring on her middle finger, and I thought surely it would signify her troth to me, it being the longest finger and I so tall a king. Instead it meant that she would stand in the middle between the King and his ministers, persuading him against any course of rashness that boded ill to the realm, and stand with them with all her wifely strength when they counseled wisely. I wondered if Merdin had made it up on the spur of the moment, lest I become a tyrant. Only when I had changed the ring to her third finger did the ceremony run to suit me.

"There the ring shall remain from this moment until you lie on your bier," he told her. "Three is a sacred number, referring to the sky, the air, and the land; to life in the womb, life in the flesh, and life beyond the grave; and most of all to the father, the mother, and the child. Wander, it is your office to bear the King sons and daughters, the first to be princes in Britain, the second to wed the kings of lands beyond the sea to enlarge his realm. You must cleave to him alone. And do you swear, by Diana your Goddess, that if you are ever false to him in word or deed, you will give your living body to be burned?"

She hesitated briefly, her beautiful eyes not quite steady in their sockets. Only the plagued awe in which we Britains held everything Roman kept down my temper.

"Great wizard, I cannot swear by Diana, because she is chaste and has no care for the service of marriage. But I will swear by Lud, who I have heard is the Roman Jove, that I will be true to my lord, and if I am false I will give my body to be burned."

233

"Then, my liege, you may untie the knot of her girdle, signifying the loosening of her virgin knot."

It was a delicate way to put it, but I could scarcely look ahead to its more gross performance, because of the eyes of my mind turning back to the banks of Usk, when Elain had exacted a promise from me ere we set out for Pillicock Hill. When Wander's sash hung free, I beckoned to some sort of chamberlain in whose care I had entrusted the gold head-ring. He put it in my hand.

"Kneel," I said in low tones to Wander.

"My liege, I have knelt once already," she answered barely above a whisper. "How many kneelings do you Cambrian conquerors require? I descend from Maximus, Guarder of the Wall."

"You'll descend to the floor from my fist on your jawbone, if you don't hasten."

For the first time, it seemed, she gave me a glance of quickened interest. A second later she was on her knees with her head bowed. I affixed the circuit of gold over her snow-white brow.

3

Ministers and stewards bustled about preparing the wedding feast. Cador himself approached me with great joviality, and bade me be patient, control my youthful ardor, and not let my haste for a dish fit for the Gods make me slack a number of others fit for the bellies of kings. I hardly listened to him, perhaps because I was in no particular haste for the later banquet and was wondering why, perhaps from wishing that Merdin were enough of a magician to change Wander into Elain. Then the late King, now reduced to Prince, remarked what made me thoughtful. I had noticed again the black bar of his eyebrows and recalled the Roman aptitude for plots and stratagems.

"I am one who does not forget the earnings and deservings of the humbler sort," he told me. "Your great army has had a long march, they will rejoice in your rejoicing, they are your right arm in defending your realm, of which Cornwall and the Exe are now a part, so by your leave, they too shall make merry."

"By what means?" I asked.

"Why, with good ale from the pantries which were once mine."

"How much would you reckon to give them, since you are a generous prince?"

"As much as they can drink. Why not? This is the wedding-day of their King."

I thought of a good reason why not, and that was Cador's army, its numbers as great as mine, still armed and assembled only a mile distant. They were being closely watched by my swift-footed spies, but if they attacked an enemy befuddled and reeling with drink, Cador might turn the tables in neat fashion.

"Prince, I would not dream of my soldiers washing their gullets while those who have served you go dry. While my force remains in array, you may bring up yours in double file and have them lay down their arms in my General's care. Then all may revel together."

At that moment, I believed he resigned himself to being Prince of the Moors. For how long? Until I stumbled, and another King loomed larger. And when that happened, how many others who followed me would reverse the direction of their sword-points? Many, no doubt, but thank the Gods not all.

I bade my own steward supply every dish that Gerald and I would taste, and my own cook prepare it. Pillicock would serve it on his short, stout legs. When Wander herself kissed a cup of mead I had not seen poured, I feigned testing it, then poured it under the table to mingle with dogs' piddle. I drank only enough of Pillicock's servings to heat my blood a little, so that I could see Wander as a woman, not a Roman Goddess visiting Earth. And it seemed I had succeeded when at last I took her by the hand, and amid cheers and yells and bawdy jests, led her from the table.

The royal bed stood in the great throne-room, so I took Wander to the room in the rear I had seen and marveled over, where her serving-wench Helena waited to attend us. The chamber was not large; its rear door had a strong bronze bolt, and this and the front door would be guarded by my own sentries standing without. The bed stood high and wide, second only to the royal bed, and beneath it set the most elegant chamber-pot I had ever seen, with gilt decoration and an inscription in Latin which Wander told me was from the great Roman poet Ovid. As she disrobed, she gave me tantalizing glimpses of various regions of her snowy skin. For some reason I was bashful, nothing like the impetuous lover I would wish.

"My lord, you have marched far today, dealt with great matters of state, feasted royally, and drunk deep," Wander told me when the old woman had gone out the front door and we lay side by side. "I can see weariness in your face, which is not good in the face of a bridegroom, particularly if he is the King. A royal prince conceived when his sire is not in his full vigor would likely grow up puny of body and weak of mind."

"Why, I didn't know it."

"It was well-known to the physicians of Rome, the wisest in the world. In their searchings they discovered that the weak Caesars, Commodus, Gallienus, Constantine, Valens, and in the days of our own grandsires, Romulus Augustulus—to name but a few—had been conceived when the vigor of their sires had been reduced by feasting, frolicking, battle, and games."

A few, Wander had said. I had never heard the names of any of these Caesars except the last, whose memory Gerald had cursed, and wise Merdin was no doubt in the same boat. Truly I had wedded the most learned Princess this side of the Seven Hills.

"I have no feeling of weariness," I answered. "Still, I'll rest a few minutes longer, listening to your voice, which is music in my ears, and heeding your instruction."

"*Appetitus rationi pareat*," she said solemnly. "That, my lord, is Latin, meaning to control the appetite until a reasonable time to give it way. I will speak another Latin saying that you could well adopt for your motto. *A cuspide corona*. A crown won by force of arms. You need rest, my lord, and thereafter you may feast."

"Why, I will learn both of those wise sayings, and many more if you'll teach 'em to me."

"Gladly, when you are free of matters of state and home from the wars."

"I am home now, in my own palace, won by the force of my arms. Although I have heard enough Latin for one night, I am now re-freshed, and my bride shall spend the night in my arms, whispering not the wisdom of Rome but of love in the way of our Cambrian maids." And I put my hand on her glimmering white thigh.

"Wait, my lord. I must tell you that my virginity is not as other maids'. When I was in the Cotswold, and was climbing a steep hill, the demons who live in the rocks and who once had nigh ended my life before I was delivered, struck most evilly again, and I suffered a hard fall. Thereby they hoped that on my bridal night my husband would set me aside as one who had played the wanton. You, of course, know better. Through your eyes you see by your own vision and by the guidance of the Great Gods, and these would not have suffered me to become your Queen, as told in the Song of Camlon, were I not worthy. Still, I say again, *Appetitus rationi pareat*. The hot humors of your blood have hidden your weariness from your own knowledge, and I wish—I would demand it, as a Roman matron, if you were Caesar on the Seven Hills—that you spend this night in sleep, so that the crown prince that I bear you will in good time be worthy of your crown."

I had never heard more beautiful language employed on any subject. We Cambrians loved elegant as well as delicate speech, as used by some of our poets who ranked as earls. Also we revered learning with a great reverence, as shown by the honors paid to our mighty Druids since time out of mind. Although we had never fully yielded to Roman rule, resisting it in our high hills and deep fastnesses, and we were the first of all the English kingdoms south of Hadrian's Wall to cast it forth, doubtless we would have never let the first Roman legion through our passes save for our befuddlement at their wisdom and skills. We had never seen or dreamed of catapults, armor and arms of precious iron, tents of rainproof cloth, and tools of which we had not known the use. Most of all we had been flabbergasted at what they called reports, scrolls covered with little marks, which kept informed every officer of what he need know.

Now I, Artay, born and bred on the Taff, was myself wedded to a great Roman lady, the descendant of Maximus, who had come close to seizing the royal purple of Rome itself. Surely I could not act the churl to such a one. Even so, my veneration of Wander was beginning to be mixed with a slight rancor, of which I was ashamed.

"Still, I'll not wait any longer," I told her.

"My lord, I too am wearied," she replied. "All day, and yesterday too, we have known of your march upon us, and how was I to know that a Cambrian conqueror from the wilds of the Taff could be so gentle and courtly? I was in sore distress, slept not at all, and at my sudden marriage to Your Majesty I came nigh to falling in a swound."

"I am not so gentle and courtly as to delay the making of a son and heir at the first possible moment."

"Why, my lord! Did you think that a king and his bride must do as common folk, that she may present him with an heir to his throne? Perhaps petty kings and queens must do so, but when the very Gods decree a dynasty, conception has been known to occur when the pair danced at the wedding feast, let alone when they lay side by side through the long night. In the morning, when we are both rested, and the Gods know that the auspices are good, the royal seed will be planted in queenly ground, no matter if we both are fast asleep."

I looked into her pale-gold brilliant eyes, which to me were not as beautiful as Elain's, yet were as different from Cambrian eyes as a Roman temple from a circle of stones. Suddenly my feelings took a great turn. All she had told me had fitted into a fine pattern, such as might be seen woven in the silken gown of a Roman matron; all at once it fitted also into another pattern not so fine. I was a Cambrian savage, or so I had been called. I would stick to Cambrian ways, Cambrian thinking, Cambrian savagery, if that was what it was. I took a big roll out of bed and got to my feet.

"Where are you going, my lord?"

"Out."

"Have I displeased you?"

"Everything Roman displeases me, except my General Gerald, and Roman roads for my stinking Cambrian feet. I'll conquer very Rome, if need be, to be King of Britain, but I'll not make bond with Rome."

"You've already done it. Whether or not I see you again, I'm the Queen of Cambria, Monmouth, Cornwall and the Exe, and all else you attain."

"In that case, when you sleep in the Woods of Diana—or wherever you sleep—in the hills or on the plain—be sure you have no bed-fellow. As a man, I care not. As the King, I'd give you empty air to stand on instead of a dais, and your lover would die in the fire, where he would feel some heat worthy of the name."

Meanwhile I was putting on my garments. Then I belted Caliburn on my side, put my shield on my arm, and clapped my crown on my head. I thought to snatch the softest coverlet from off Wander's body, then perceived a better gain. The door slammed like a clap of thunder behind me.

I went out of the palace to where my army feasted and reveled about their bonfires, and the late forces of Cador, now disarmed, drowned their humiliation the best they could manage. All turned and stared at me, and a few who had washed their gullets too well clambered unsteadily to their feet. All supposed I had been flying on wings of bliss with the most beautiful woman in Britain, and they could scarcely believe their eyes to see me armed and harnessed. You would have thought I would feel ashamed. Instead I tingled with pride, as though having won a great victory.

Gerald hurried toward me; Merdin, with a cup too many in his lean gizzard, weaved tardily behind him. Both touched their knees to the ground, and I feared the old man would topple over, but he balanced himself well.

"What is it, my liege?" Gerald asked.

"Send for my old sheepskin robe which I used on campaigns."

It was speedily brought, and I had it stretched on the ground—for the night was fair, with no sign of rain—in the very middle of the assembly.

"Give the men a half-emptying of a water-glass to drain their horns and be in their beds," I instructed Gerald, "for tomorrow we march."

The assembly place was now so still that many of my old army heard the announcement and gave forth a great shout. No few of Cador's old force looked at them enviously. I had hardly removed my wooden shoes and my sword before many of my followers began hurrying about, getting their own bedding, and laying it in a thick circle around me, although at a respectful distance. That my guard would be secure during the night, I need not doubt.

As I was settling down for a good night's sleep, I was aroused by an inward jolt. If my guess was right and Wander had a lover, I had calmly assumed it was some pretty fellow about the court, likely an earl's son "who mouthed Latin and played quoits," as Modred had expressed it at our first meeting, a milksop I would not deign to strike save with the flat of my sword. It had been a fair enough guess. Such sweet-smelling dandies, bathing every month or two, were known to breach maidenheads which shrank from a true man. But suddenly, to save my soul, I could not put away the notion that the breaker might be no other than Modred himself.

True, he was supposed to be at the court of the King of Midland, two hundred miles to the northeast. That was about ten days' journey on foot, five days on horseback with a spare mount. And what if he had been visiting King Uther of Stour and the Avon at the old Roman town of Durnovaria, where the King kept a force behind Maiden Castle, a fortification built on earth, or at Wynham, his capital, on the west bank of the Itchen? One lay within fifty miles of Tavistock, the other eighty miles, two days by horse. Modred would very likely come to see this King, one of the richest and greatest in all Britain, to league with him for putting down the upstart King of Cambria.

What would be two days' ride to that limber, resolute man? Four days' march on his feet like a red-deer stag's would not turn one hair of his red mane, if the prize were worth it. There were a score of retreats, within a league or so of Cador's palace, where he could bivouac a day or two, hunt, fish, and run about at night. And what could suit him better, next to taking my life and kingdom, than beating me to the bride promised me in the Song of Camlon? Why, you could light a fire from the mirthful sparkle of his eyes!

I forced myself to sleep, as I knew how, only to waken an hour before the first gleam of light. A story Merdin had told me had been weaving through my dreams and instantly made seizure of my thoughts. It concerned the Roman Goddess Venus, her lover Mars, and her husband, Vulcan, a lame and ugly fellow, whom we knew as the God of smiths and called Wellan. I wondered if it could be re-enacted these thousands of miles from Mount Olympus, and thousands of years after its real happening, in the time and realm of Artay, a King of Britain?

4

When I rose there was business of state to attend to, before going about my pleasures, and to this I gave careful and urgent attention.

First of all, I offered Cador's soldiers the chance to pledge allegiance to my crown, and although I did not tell them that the alternate was a hanging, they guessed as much, and not a fellow faltered. Then, before I restored them their weapons, I had Gerald tell off a hundred, most of them married, to remain at Cador's capital with two hundred of my troops. This force of three hundred I put under the command of a loyal and able Centurion who had been with me on my first campaign. In Gerald's absence he was to report to Earl Bedwyr of Glamorgan, who had come under my banner in South Cambria, a sturdy old man whose loyalty of heart, firmness of will, and power of mind fitted him to be viceroy of my new domains. Then I appointed twenty rough, keen fellows who liked a rough life, to watch the fords of the Otter River and the roads from Wynham, and to run or ride with news of any enemy force on the march to make me trouble.

This done, I went happily on with my plan for turning the tables on Wander and her lover, whom the morning freshness in my brain told me was Modred more clearly than had the fancy-working mysteries of night. Patently the loop in Wander's guard was her old serving-wench Helena, she who had slid the bronze bolt of the outer door of Wander's chamber and had stood guard outside the inner door. At first I was at a loss how to get at her without alarming the quarry, then it was as though the Gods had put her in my hand.

I had hardly started to question Bryan, a Cornishman in my service whom I had dispatched two months before to spy on Cador, and who had wiggled his way into the royal forces, when he told me that his fellow in arms, called Fergus, was Helena's son!

It was a simple matter for Gerald, and a natural-seeming move, to order all the Cornish soldiery, new under my banner, to line up, hold their arms aloft, and be searched for secret weapons or other articles giving evidence of treasonable design. Others of my old army would help in the ransack, but Gerald alone, by my strict command, must examine Fergus. And into his hand I slid what I wanted found in his pocket or rucksack—the copper coin bearing the crude likeness of King Vortigern that I had taken off the torn throat of Riis, who had tried to ax me at Fish Fair at Collen, seven months before.

"I don't like the look of it, my liege," Gerald said quietly.

"Why not?"

"Because of the honor of a Roman I inherited from my grandsire Janus."

"Is your honor more important than mine? It is my own honor, that of the King, that must be avenged. And to comfort you, Fergus will take no harm other than a little healthy fright."

With a little more grumbling, Gerald undertook the business. Meanwhile I summoned a faithful follower from Caer Dyv, who was the leader of a two score or more fishermen with me from the first. First I asked him about the tools of their trade, some of which they had brought with them to the Long Burrow on the moor, and which they had loaded on donkeys to use when my army needed fresh fish. His reply proved of great satisfaction to my heart beginning to burn. Then I asked him which one of his band was the most skilled with the kind of tackle I had in mind.

"Your Majesty, there be a lubber from Crab Bay, his name being Mog, what can throw 'at thing true as an arry from a bow."

"He's the man for me. Can he throw it through an open door?"

"Iffen he stand close by. 'Ee see, King, it spread out in the air. 'Tis the nature of it."

"Is six feet about the right distance?"

"Six to twelve feet, it make no difference to Mog."

"We'll bivouac awhile behind Black Tor. When we get there, send him to me."

One other errand needed to be run before we could march. It was to send a trusted man to speak in secret to Helena, tell her that her son Fergus was in grave trouble, and if she hoped to save his neck from the hempen stretcher, to come in secret, hard behind my army, to a grove of oaks at the foot of Black Tor, which I had noticed while scanning the scenery on our eastward march.

No doubt Wander saw us tramp away, our shields clanking, and her beauteous eyes shone like stars. Well out of sight of the town—and I had passed the word that any followers would be arraigned as spies—we made across the moors to Black Tor. In a little while an odd assortment of folk met in the grove. Besides the King, there were Helena and her son Fergus, both white in the face, a wind-tanned fisherman called Mog, and six of my soldiers swift of foot and level of head. Merdin and Gerald were both absent by my provision, lest they throw cold water on my enterprise.

Happily the old woman needed no more scaring than she had

already, to tell me all I needed to know and to pledge, before the Earth Goddess, the Goddess of seeding and harvest, to obey my commands. These last were simple enough—to lay one stone on another stone by an outbuilding of the palace as a sign for my spy, and to feign sliding the inner bolt of the outside door of Wander's chamber. Only one small candle would be burning—this was always her mistress's command—and the cheat would not likely be discovered by a pair of inmates so enthralled and in such haste. As I had guessed from Wander's cackle about Diana, the lovers would meet not tonight but the following night, when my Lady the Moon hung fresh and new over the western moors.

My army took the next day off to bath their bodies and wash their garments in two pools behind the Tor. In the evening I passed the word to Merdin, Gerald, all my captains, and a few in the rank who were the sons of earls to be ready to follow me to see a fine sight. My first notion had been to invite the whole force, for every man-jack would have gladly marched the whole distance and return, then I bethought myself of its effect upon them, how in spite of everything Wander was my wedded wife and nominally their Queen, and I did not wish to open myself to a charge of coarseness and indelicate feeling to the stuck-up Romans to whom the report would surely come. My well-chosen party moved close to Cador's palace under cover of darkness. My spy reported one of the two stones set upon the other. Bidding the others wait in silence and apart, Fergus with his tackle, half a dozen of my fellows stoutly armed, and I came close to Wander's chamber. The palest ghost of candlelight shone in the crack of the door. I asked Fergus if his draw-string would hold under powerful tugging. He said the whole rig was made of almost unbreakable linen cord to hold lunkers weighing a hundred pounds.

He made ready his equipment, gathering it in a certain way into his hands. I flung open the back door, seeing nothing but the glimmering white bed, with no upright posts to cause us trouble, and its two milk-white occupants. Fergus threw his net like the tried fisherman he was.

It was a form of purse-seine, round, with leaden weights around its edge which could be contracted with the draw-rope. Seeing that he had made a perfect cast, he yanked on the rope, and at the same instant some of my armed fellows helped shove the weighted edge under the upward-leaping bodies of my two white birds. They did not leap far, truly they did little more than heave, a different kind of heaving than before we came, ere the closing net had them helpless to move. All had happened so quickly that my hen-bird uttered only one cry, and my cock-bird made no sound.

I had seen in a Roman ruin a damaged piece of statuary, a copy of a Grecian work, Gerald had thought, showing an old man and two boys intertwined by serpents. Gerald had said that the former was named Laocoön, a priest of Apollo who had profaned the temple. I wished that the stone-carver were here to make another statue, because the two lovers were in even a tighter fix. Naked legs and arms ran every which way, above or below one another, and they could not move them an inch for lack of leverage, so tightly pressed the net. They could only stare at us with round eyes.

At once I flung open the inner door. "We've caught a couple of strange fish," I shouted to Cador and his dame, and to courtiers on sheepskins about the wall. "Come in and name 'em for us."

Meanwhile one of my captains opened the rear door and summoned the sight-seers. I made haste to light the other candles in the chamber so all could have a good look. I reckoned it would be the finest look that my guests would ever have at the Queen of Cambria, Monmouth, Cornwall and the Exe in her entanglements with Prince Modred, until lately heir to a throne.

The first to enter was fat Cador, who threw me one bewildered look, gazed at the bed, then broke into cackling laughter not as hearty as I had sometimes heard.

"'Tis a jolly jest," he told me. "I know not when I've seen its equal. King Artay, you are a sly one, I do confess. But I swear to you by the Gods I had no knowledge of the scandal within my own palace, or I'd have put my foot down."

"Now's no time for windy speeches," I answered. "'Tis the time to laugh."

By now my sight-seers were crowding through the door and they laughed enough for us all. They bayed and held their sides, and some of them pointed at a choice contortion, looking howling at the others. The roof well-nigh rose from the noisy mirth, and I reckoned I had paid Wander off for the whopping lies she had told me as well as her betrayal of my person and throne; and she would no longer think of me as a barbarian from the Taff. On the night Modred had freed me from my prison-bonds, we had declared we were even, and shook hands on it. Now I had countered handsomely for his arrogant trespass since then.

Cador, his queen, and their former official did not laugh as heartily as my followers, and then I happened to note that Gerald kept a straight face.

"What ails you, Gerald?" I demanded. And the others' laughter ceased to hear his reply.

"My liege, I would still trade places with Prince Modred," my great General answered.

"And that," said one of my captains, a high-born fellow who knew Latin, "was essentially the remark of the God Mercury when Venus's husband, Vulcan, had her and Mars in the same fix."

If I had known this ending to the story, I would have never played my fine trick. I was thinking that I would never get shed of Romans and their cursed getting ahead of us in everything.

5

At my command, all the spectators left the room, one of my officers taking Modred's sword. Other of my fellows were told to stand guard outside both doors. Then with the knife that Gerald had lent me on May Night, which he had since given me as a souvenir of the hangman's sudden leave-taking, I cut the net around the sweat-wet bodies of my two captives, careful not to prick their princely skins. With great serenity Wander got out of bed, and without a glance at me began to dress. Meanwhile Modred reposed with his hands clasped under his head.

"What is your command, my lord?" she asked when she was again her regal self. "Is it that I hang?"

"No, I want you to live on, not as Wander the White but as Wander the Whiting. I will be famed as the Cuckold King, but I won't be the first to bear the title, and I was the laugher, not the one to be laughed at behind my back."

"There's meat to that, and good wit," Modred broke in quietly. "Still, Artay, you must learn not to care what people say of you, or how much they laugh behind your back. It is only the furtive expression of frustration and jealousy. Care only for what they say and do in your presence, the tribute to your power or the lack of it. I am no Roman, let alone a Greek, but I assure you that's the only civilized attitude for a man of parts to take."

"I'll remain an oaf from the Taff," I said grumpily.

"On second thought, that would be best. Thereby you'll have a better chance of conquering all Britain."

"My lord," came Wander's queenly voice, "have I your leave to go while your royalties confer?"

"Yes, and I may see you a year from now, when I'll know the upshot of your night's sport."

She dropped on one knee—actually it seemed no mockery but true obeisance—and I let her through the inner door. Before I spoke again to Modred, I looked about me. The coverlets on the bed were much finer than I had seen during my brief occupancy. On a bench beside it was a pitcher of some liquor—I guessed it the finest mead—two silver cups, and a tray of dainties. A little vial that I sniffed contained some delicate perfume unknown to me. Not one bug crawled the sheet.

"I told you, Artay, that I lived for pleasure," Modred said, sitting up. I had sat down on another bench against the wall.

"Yes, Prince, you did." Meanwhile I was admiring his smooth body, and taking in the lively cock of his head, the red thatch of his hair, and his thrice-lively eyes.

"I thought it would pleasure me greatly to have first turn at your betrothed and now your Queen. You see, I heard that my vision of you sneaking into camp *sans* clothes had had no substance, and you turned the awkward situation into a triumph. It stung me a good deal, I confess. The difference between us is, what promises me to be triumphs turns into awkward situations. King Artay, shall I dress?"

"As you please."

"Then I'll wait a bit, until I can make myself clear. Truly I had no great yearning for Wander, of herself, although she may well be the most beautiful woman in all Britain. It is said that her mother conceived while gazing at a statue of Venus in a ruined temple at the old Roman camp at Moridunum."

"Modred, do you think we can leave out the Romans?"

"Gladly. I get a little sick of them myself. Do you know, Artay, that you are truly my brother?"

"You mean your half-brother."

"Yes. I thought you might doubt it, for the story is quite strange. I don't know that old Merdin told you the true story; anyway, I will not, short of torture. Of course that was never important in royal families; infanticide is among the most common of kingly crimes. But you and I have a strong bond. You have what I lack to be a conqueror; I have what you lack to be happy; we should be one person. Yet we are close enough that it will shake the Gods in their high seats when one of us kills the other."

"Do you think that the time for that has come?"

"I considered the notion, then rejected it. You are not a hedonist, like me—pardon that fine Greek word—still, you're not a spoil-sport. That is, I hope you are not one."

"No, and I'm going to let you go—with a warning. If any harm ever comes to Elain through you, I won't fight you at the last, but hang you like a felon."

"My brother Artay, I will never harm Elain or let any harm come to her that I can prevent. Although I once told you I never swear, this I swear by the God Bacchus, the Roman God of pleasure and of wine. There, I have failed to honor your request to leave out Rome. And that leads me to advise you not to put Wander away—I mean to let her be Queen in name at least—if you wish to realize your ambitions. It would be well to have children by her, if you can bring yourself to do it. Or to acknowledge as your own any child I might have by her."

"By the Gods, do you think I would leave my crown to my enemy's bastard?"

"Why not? This demand of common men that their own sons succeed them is ridiculous. If a babe she might bear is a bouncer, fit to follow you, in three years you would forget whether you or I was its father. The patrician class of the most logical people I know

247

of—I won't mention their name—widely practiced adoption of infants, to get good heirs. Still, do what you think best."

"Modred, I admire you greatly, but you are a most discomforting companion."

"By the Gods, you are beginning to talk like a—gentleman. I have seen a few but am not one myself. Still, I am willing that we swear off playing scurvy tricks on each other, if you are. If so, I will dress, go my way—you will go yours—we will meet from time to time until our last meeting, the awful outcome of which we will both face like men."

"Modred, do you believe in fate?"

"A fate that even the Gods cannot change. They too are bound hand and foot by Fate. In my opinion, it is the only belief that a civilized man—I am fractionally civilized—can live with. Any other is not respectful to the Gods. We must assume they are not to blame for the hell raised on earth."

"Hell is a Christian word."

"No, it comes out of the Far North, beyond Caledonia, even more uncivilized than Britain."

"Well, I will drink a cup of mead with you, if you warrant it unpoisoned."

"I've had three cups without ill effect. Not that Wander wouldn't poison both of us, if she took the notion."

So I filled the cups with my own hand and handed one of them to my brother.

"If you will, you may speak the pledge."

"Gladly." Modred picked up his cup, I mine. "Artay, I pledge you, on my honor as a prince, that I will do my utmost to check your designs, and to balk you in every way I can, short of letting others bring you to your death. That I reserve for myself. The final Battle of the Giants will go down to future ages in song and story."

"I make you the same pledge."

"May you escape our father's knavish tricks. May you have Elain for your own. May you discover the strange truth of Vivain, and some strange event, which I know not, that brought it into being. May you weather the great storms that will beset you, according to the prophecies of the Song of Camlon. May we honor each other always, each his deserving. May we each remain the other's most feared and respected foe."

"I wish its equivalent to you. Now let us drink, then I'll pass you out the door you came in, and we'll meet in the wars."

So we touched our cups and drank, and the mead sparkled in my veins, and I loved in some dark way this bright-faced Prince, and I greatly loved my Fate, whatever its dealing.

Chapter Twelve
Stout Foemen

Our troops were in mighty fine fettle, Gerald told me. And hearing the story of Modred's invasion of the King's bed and of its outcome, they had roared and slapped one another's backs. Instead of despising me for a cuckold, they honored me for playing such a good joke on the royal lovers. All of them greatly admired Modred as a prince, but were irked by the airs put on by the Romans, and thought that both had got a handsome due for their frolicking. On the whole they were pleased, I thought, after netting the two very fine fish I had let them go without loss of their noddles. Perhaps they perceived that if every adulterer were beheaded, the great army of which they were so proud would be decimated, as in battle bloody beyond description, and a great many of their married men would suddenly lack wives. I had noticed that men speak in public a great deal differently than they think in private. They suppose that certain utterances and postures are required of them, but in their own heart of hearts they are hard to fool.

My quick exit from Wander's bed had made me the more eager to enter Elain's. Hence I had intended that we return to Woodwick the way we had come, except for our side-trip to Stonehenge, and the men could rest a solid week at Swan Lake, where I would take delicious rest. So when Gerald proposed a different route, I could hardly force myself to listen in good part, and instead scowled and cursed at him, for which he cared not a rap.

The reason he cared not was that wisdom stood staunchly at his side. Instead of merely getting home, we could combine the march thither with a victorious campaign. He said that all he had intended at first was to cross the Severn at Gloster and in little more than a day's march northeast subdue the stubborn prince who called himself Ross of the Wye.

"That's what the King of the Midlands would expect us to do," Gerald said. "Instead I want to raid the Valley of the Severn from its confluence with the Avon northward and then westward into our Plynlymon moors."

"Why should we raid my own kingdom?" It was all I could think of to say.

"Some of North Wales is your kingdom in name only. The sight of your army, and of a few gallows-trees for traitors, will be good for some of the earls raised by Vortigern, and will save us trouble later. That will be merely aftermath. Our main object is to overthrow and uncrown the King of the Hecanas. He'll be a menace to us every way we turn until you hold his realm in an iron grasp. Mark you, he's only a liegeman of Malcolm, King of the Midlands, but he protects his western flank, and if we reduce him by this much, from the Midland Gap to your own border, and north to the Mersey, you'll annex a realm as large as all Cambria. The risk is great, but I think it's outweighed by good hope of success. Then Lester, Malcolm's capital, would lie open to our attack. If he stays there, we'll take him; if he flees north he's balked by the vast forests beyond Trent; eastward lie the prodigious marshes around Wash; if he comes south he's in trouble with the kings of Thames."

As Gerald spoke in his quiet way, I had been watching his black eyes. They had slowly brightened until they appeared to glow. Hard put to it not to let my own eyes catch fire from his, I thought to speak in an offhand manner.

"Before then I am to humble Ross of the Wye?"

"The other campaign will outflank him. He'll make haste to join your banner."

"You told me before you would undertake no great campaigns until warm weather."

"Artay, a good officer is never remiss in changing his mind if conditions change. It is the stubborn, inflexible mind that loses battles—like that of Vertas, who kept on following Herminious into a death-trap. Our fortunes have been phenomenally good. You have an army of two thousand—for Cador's whole force will follow you in joy. The Cornish have ancient ties with us Cambrians. It happens that they hate the whole tribe of Hecanas, who are overbearing fellows who come down the Severn clean to Sabrina and beat them at trade and making love. Nor could they ambush and murder them, because 'twas against Cador's command—he lived in peril of their warrior-king. Finally you have taken their fancy with the trick you played on Wander and Modred. Nothing pleases an army as much as a prodigious joke; they march on their bellies, 'tis said, but they push on when the going's hard on their funny bones."

"Will they find good belly-timber in the Severn Valley?" I asked.

"Crops were good last year; we'll find plenty of corn as well as beef and mutton. Some of the Cornish will begin pining for home and attempt to desert; all deserters must be caught, regardless of the trouble, and straightway hanged. Cador is so subdued by last night's events that you needn't leave the strong force you planned— unless, that is, you intend to prevent the Queen from entertaining visitors, in which case you'll need to post your whole army as palace guards."

I did not especially like the joke, but saw no way I could fittingly take offense.

"Finally, my liege, this will be no picnic-supper under the trees. The Hecanas have always been war-like, and would scarcely yield to Rome. They are well-armed with home-smelted iron. The country is heavily forested. If we possibly can, we must take them by surprise. Still, the gamble is a good one, and the conquest of all Britain was never a small chore."

When the new-conquered army heard we would straightway march to war, the roar of joy that went up shook Lud's sky; and only the sections tolled off to stand guard in Cornwall looked glum. Our camp-followers danced and frolicked on the grass. They had heard that gold and silver ornaments were thicker than wood-ticks in the Severn Valley. I caught a glimpse of Vivain in the company of a tall, brawny peasant girl whom for a moment I mistook for the slattern who had tried to stab me. She gave me one of her witchy smiles and waved her hand.

I was nothing loath to sacking Cador's treasury of its gold and silver and jewels, a process that required heavy shakings, upside down, for some of his minions. However, I left him abundant corn, beasts for slaughter, mead and ale to supply his greatly diminished court until another harvest. Then, with my viceroy properly gowned and maced, our great army began its march. Somewhat to my relief, I did not get sight of Wander, although I doubted not that she gazed at me from some retreat, and what she was thinking, and what luck she wished me, I could hardly imagine. Still, I could hardly believe she would put a bad mouth on me in the hearing of the Gods. Who else than I could make her Queen of Britain?

We crossed at Gloster as before, and for sixty miles saw nothing of the fierce Hecanas, only peaceful cotters, shepherds, and hog-and cattle-drovers. By sending scouts ahead of us, traveling at night, we safeguarded as far as possible against runners bringing the news of our raid to the Hecanas' King. During this part of the journey the men foraged only enough for their daily needs, and to capture a good number of cattle and sheep, which the hoydens were allowed to drive before them, milk or butcher as the case might be, and earn their rations. The forests we saw kindly grew on the opposite bank, until we were a day's march beyond Avonmouth, then for reasons unknown except to the Gods they took the notion to spring up on our side of the river, so deep and wide that we could not ford to the open land across. Happily, it seemed, the river ran low and did not fill its bed or flood its banks, and we were able to advance four abreast between the flow and the dark and dismal woods.

Then, without the slightest warning, we blundered into ambush. Where our walking-way was narrow, there burst from the woods about five hundred Hecana tribesmen, who had been waiting on a wide front and who attacked us from the side when enough of us had marched into their reach. Howling, they cleaved with long-swords at our astounded ranks before our men could shed their rucksacks, let alone get hand on their shields, which they had slung on their backs for comfort. Luckily my own South Cambrians, whom Gerald had strictly trained, led our files, and these were the men who bore the brunt, and they were not men to lose their heads and throw down their weapons and die like sheep. Howbeit, those who did die, and we lost sixty in thrice-sixty seconds, would be more sorely missed than thrice their number of late-caught Cornish.

The latter ran to their new comrades' help, which augured well for their fighting-spirit and future constancy. These, and the doughty defense of my yokels, many of them fighting with loaded backs and shieldless arms, soon drove the ambushers back into the forest, where they appeared to melt away, as far as our eyes or ears could tell. Gerald yelled for no man to follow them, lest he fall into a trap. Nothing remained for us but to array ourselves, facing the silent woods, wait for what happened next, glance not at our dead and hear not the groans of our wounded, count the measly twenty we had killed, and bitterly take stock.

"Why didn't our scouts discover the lyers-in-wait?" I asked Gerald when with a flushed face and sunken eyes he came up to me.

"My liege, I cannot answer, but—there's a small band coming toward us, and I think we may know in a trice."

I too heard them, making more noise than the fox-footed foe. And it was truly a small band, only ten of the forty scouts we had sent forth, led by grim-faced Glyn.

"Where are the rest?" Gerald asked.

"General, they be cut down," Glyn answered, panting. "Not one cry out of 'em, and I never missed 'em till we 'sembled at the brook. Such woods I never seed for being thick and dark."

And I had supposed no forest could compare with Cambria's Black Forest! So I was thinking in an otherwise empty head, waiting for Glyn to finish his report.

"'Ee can't see thirty steps beyond 'ee peepers," he went on. "We was following deer-trails, trying to keep up wi' 'ee, and never seed hide or hair of ary one. 'Ee ought to hang me, for 'em good men dead."

"'Twas my fault," Gerald said quickly. "Only today I mentioned to Your Majesty the name of Varus—he who led our most eastward army into ambush at Teutoburg Forest. My liege, our march has been told the King, by his spies or by a traitor among us. Now we must give up hope of a fast march and easy victory. Supplies will be a great problem. Those cursed Roman maps showed forest only on the eastward bank, and I'm in the habit of believing everything Roman. I offer it not as an excuse for my derelictions. If you have any one who can replace me, I'll resign my command. If you turn down your thumb, I'll fall on my sword."

"Don't ever leave me, Gerald."

I spoke impulsively, not as a king should. I did not know why Gerald's eyes filled with tears.

2

So began our war with the Hecanas, of whom I had never heard when I was a boy on the Taff, although now foremost in my thoughts and evil dreams.

They set traps for us in the day and raided our lines at night. Thank the Gods they did not know the craft of the bow-and-arrow, or they could have turned us back; as it was, many a man fell with a skull broken by a stone hurled by a sling. Instead of thirty scouts we sent forth three hundred, fanning out almost in hand's reach of one another on our exposed flank, and every day we lost several, usually stoned, but sometimes hacked to death by a well-hidden swordsman who fought fiend-like until he fell. If we advanced five miles between sunrise and sunset we counted it good. Often, when fallen trees formed a labyrinth, or the dwarf beach and hazel caused well-nigh impenetrable thickets, we gained hardly a mile.

Again our Mendip archers stood us in good stead by hunting red deer, the tallest and fattest I had ever seen, and as thick in the woods as sheep on the Cotswold downs. No man with slow, dim eyes can man bow-and-arrow, and creeping up and down the deer-trails, they discovered many a lyer in wait, and skewered him with a well-aimed shaft before he could hurl a stone. Never did they fetch in less than five of their edible quarry, sometimes as many as twelve, which served every man and hoyden in our host with nearly half a pound to a whole pound of succulent venison before he slept. Gerald had once told me, "Live tonight!" The good supper waiting them was no small factor in causing my soldiers to resolve to live today; and they scanned the thickets with shrewd care, and even the earls attended to their needs in full view of the wenches, rather than enter the edge of the woods.

As the meat sustained their spirits, so did their growing skill at defense and attack. More than once those woodcock were caught in their own deadfalls. The dismal fact remained that no day passed without our losing a score or more good men, and our crawling pace gave time to the enemy King to fix us a hot supper, not to our taste, when the lay of the land would suit him.

When and where? Merdin star-gazed with his trinket, and wrote figures on his slate, and pored over the guts of every Hecana corpse he could get hand on. Still he could tell me nothing better than that the star Mercury was in the House of the Crab, hence we must move slow and sideways, or of the Scorpion, hence we must expect his barbed tail to sting us a good while yet. What the spilled guts told him he did not tell me. He could only comb his white beard and mutter.

On a night of heavy rain I did not stop the men from raising pavilions, although I slept rolled in a sheepskin beside a watchfire. I had hoped that the thick weather would blind the two-legged wolves as they blinded us, only to have them raid at both ends of our line. Our loss was heavy, and it would increase before the storm passed, to judge by the ominous, long-hanging clouds, and a dismal drizzle of a kind that generally lasted half a week. My mind greatly burdened and jobs waiting my hand, I had Gerald assemble a great number of our soldiers to watch Merdin sacrifice a spotted bull. It was an especially fine animal, caught by a forager on the lower river, and the old man had been saving him for a time of severe need, and that time had come. He scarcely glanced at the guts and told us no auguries that he perceived, only murmuring that the will of the Gods be done. Then eight stalwart soldiers heaved the carcass on a great fire.

His fat had barely begun to sizzle when the Sun broke wanly through the heavy rack. As his vapors went up, the wind began to veer, the mantle tore at its folds and joinings, the blue sky showed through, and the rain trailed off to a sprinkle and stopped. How could any sane man doubt that the Gods, angry with us lately over some slight, or carousing somewhere and forgetful of us, had been pleased with the offering and had granted us a boon? What I could not understand was their plain preference for spotted bulls over any other kind. Their burning flesh smelled just the same to my big, keen nose.

Gerald and I went to our business, which was doleful. We had made it our firm policy to recover as many as possible of the bodies of our dead and bury them with military honors. The ceremony slowed our advance at times, but this loss was recouped ten-fold by the heightened spirits of the men—they perceived that we counted them as men, not feed for the dogs of war. This morning there were twelve stoned or hacked to death, a round dozen, a fearful lot when seen laid in a row. My cold comfort that there were not thirteen, a villainous number, was abruptly dissipated.

A captain beckoned to Gerald to look at something just within the edge of the woods, not far from where I had slept. In an open place lay the body of a young woman with a knife-hilt thrusting from her bosom; but my first assumption that she had gone there to meet a lover, only to be slain by the Hecanas, proved untenable. The sharp-eyed captain pointed out that she was wearing leather shoes with pointed toes, and that no other footprints showed in the rain-soaked ground.

If this was suicide, and I could hardly doubt it, it was the first in the history of our campaign, and the news of it was certain to cast a pall over the spirits of our host.

"Perhaps another of the wenches wore the same kind of shoes, and knifed her in a quarrel," I proposed.

"My liege, it does not stand to reason," the captain told me. "Do you remember the little fair we passed the second day's march from the Tor? I saw these very shoes in the Greek huckster's booth, the only leathern shoes for sale this side of Ludton—so the fellow told me—and I remember their great cost, five silver shillings. Besides, two hoydens would not go out into a rainstorm with butchering tribesmen about. This woman crept away from the fires to die by her own hand."

I looked at her plain face and rather burly form and some vagary of mind caused me to remember the hoyden with the gold piece who had tried to murder me in my bed. Meanwhile I was groping for a vague recollection of having noticed, perhaps a fortnight before, the woman who lay dead at my feet, and seeing her happy and animated. I let it go as Gerald withdrew the knife and looked at it. The blade was of well-smelted and hardened iron, the hilt decorated with agate, and altogether a more costly dagger than would be commonly carried by a camp-follower.

"How will we bury her, my liege?" Gerald asked.

"In the same grave with the soldiers, and with the same honors," I answered. "She was one of our host."

Both Gerald and the captain seemed pleased with this reply, although I did not quite know why. It would have seemed the kingly part to have her tossed in a shallow grave with a stake through her breast to keep her ghost from wandering and making trouble.

To march heavily laden in damp clothes was known to cause

stuffed-up noses, if not chills and fever, so after the funeral Gerald let the men loaf in the sunlight while our scouts sallied forth in search of enemy sign. Merdin was pluming himself on the sudden change of weather, and combing his beard with pride; and his working such a wonder sped my thoughts to my other magician, if this she could be called—at least she had proved a seer of no mean power. Having neglected her lately, at which she had pouted, and hoping she might have visioned the next ambush the Hecanas had laid, I sent for her, and spoke to her out of hearing of the men.

"It's a pity you didn't warn me of the attack last night," I said.

"I did not know of it," she answered. "It was not foretold me. And I have confessed to you, my liege, that the visions sent to me are few and often false. So many have been false, perhaps the workings of that evil witch my mother, Calypso, whose love is Vortigern, that I have not dared speak of them to you, lest you heed them to your harm."

"Still I want to hear them. What have you visioned of today's march? Will it go peacefully, or will we be ambushed?"

"I think it will go peacefully."

"What about tomorrow?"

"Tonight I may dream of tomorrow. Now my eyes are empty."

"Except for their shining. They are bright as jet. Vivain, did you know the poor wench who knifed herself?"

"I know all the camp-followers, and knew her better than most. If my liege will recall such a trivial thing, she was at my side the last time you deigned me a glance."

"Why, I remember now. I was mindful of having noticed her, but could not think where or when. She must have had a heavy purse, to buy those leathern slippers."

"My liege, it was I who bought them, from a Greek huckster at a little fair some forty miles this side of Tavistock. He asked five shillings, but accepted three."

"Still, that is the worth of three cows. Your purse must be heavier than I knew."

"My liege, many soldiers come to me to explain their dreams or to tell their fortunes. I charge them a penny, twelve pennies make a shilling, and I sold to a gypsy a precious jewel that Queen Enid had given me, when I promised her I would not yield to Vortigern, which promise I kept, as you know full well."

"Aye, I know it well. And why did you buy the leathern shoes and then give them away?"

"You probe deeply, my liege. The shoon were the finest I had ever seen, and I had never worn any on my shell-hard feet. They were too large tor me, but I thought I could fill the void with grass. One of the scouts slain three days ago was Linnett's lover. She grieved so weefully over his death that, as though I were a princess instead of a witch-child, I gave them to her."

"I am glad that you did. She was buried in them and can wear them proudly beyond the sea-mists. And where did she get her costly dagger?"

And where did I myself get this time to waste on such trivial matters?

"My liege, I did not know she had it, or I would have guarded her more closely against self-harm."

This care for a homely hoyden pleased me, for gentleness is seemly to womankind, and did especial credit to this wild, brown half-witch. And how bravely she had followed me through three great campaigns, in summer's heat and winter's cold, herself hot with wrath or chilled by my rebuffs, yet with no complaint, and doing her witchy best to help me! Her clothes were nearly as ragged as when I had seen her first, and her face as dirty. At a distance of six feet I could detect a smell as wild as a ferret's. My eyes rejoiced in her small, sharp face and roamed greedily over her form.

I found myself wishing I had a good reason for a side-trip of some kind, perhaps to some circle of stones nearby, to make sacrifice to the Great Gods and some lesser God who had power over this particular region. In which case I could take Vivain with me, and being not then on a campaign of war, and instead paying my due to the Deities, including the Earth Goddess, enjoy her without the shame of breaking my vow. But the remembrance of twelve cold corpses lying in a row drove forth the notion quickly. Gerald had received reports from our scouts and was assembling the troops.

"Vivain, have you had any vision of the enemy striking in full force? He must do so sooner or later."

"No, my liege." But her voice wavered and I knew she had visioned something.

"I bid you speak what you have seen, good or evil."

"King Artay, only last night I dreamed a dim, confused dream. Great numbers of men were working in great haste to prepare their defense against you. Some of them carried logs, some delved in the ground."

"Do you think they were building a great fort which we must take by siege?"

"My liege, I have told you my dream—all I saw or remember. Whether it told of a true thing, or whether it was the witchcraft of my mother to lead you to misfortune, before the God Modo I do not know."

"I'll ask one more question. You speak of the men working in great haste. Would not that mean that they feared we would fall upon them before they could complete their undertaking?"

"It is for you to read meanings, my liege, not for me."

For a moment I was inclined to order a fast march, regardless of how many of my men's lives would be lost to lyers-in-wait. The inclination faded quickly as I perceived the solemn truth that Gerald was the General of my forces, and my best and only hope of victory lay foremostly in him, not in the visions of witches. Even so, she had set my brain to work along a new line.

I gave Vivain leave to go, then donned my helmet, buckled on my sword and shield, and took my place with Gerald at my right hand.

3

"Why can't we divide our army, and send half to fetch a long circle and catch the Hecanas in the rear?" I asked Gerald. "Then we'd have 'em like a nut between a cracker."

"We can, if some problems that would tax Hannibal could be overcome," my General replied. "I've been wrestling with them ever since the war of attrition began."

"Who was Hannibal? I don't remember your mentioning him."

"In truth, we Romans do not speak of him more often than

necessary. He crossed the Alps, which we thought an impossible feat, fell upon us on the Apulian Plain, and destroyed one of the greatest armies we had ever put into the field. We defeated him at last, but only the Gods know at what cost. My liege, Hannibal would send five hundred of our best swimmers across the river in the dark of night, ferrying on logs their shields and swords, and would attempt the feat that you describe. But how would we explain their absence to the rest of our men? No one but you and I and a few captains must know the plan, because we have traitors in our midst, a fact that by now is almost as patent as yon Sun in the sky."

"Could I tell them that the Saxons are raiding our coasts, burning our towns, raping their wives, and we've sent a force to balk them?"

"Yes, but don't mention their wives. Many would take what we used to call Greek leave. I thought of an invasion by the Picts, but the Saxons are better. Now consider this. Our encircling force could make only a forced march without supplies. We have to be almost on the enemy before we'd dare risk it. That means we must know what place on the river they've chosen to make their stand. To that end I've questioned three loyal fellows who were born and raised up here, and drifted across to Cambria. I think I know what they'll do. If their General is able, but not great, I'd be almost sure. I mean if he's just short of great, he'd see all the advantages of the place I mean, and not perceive that an excellent enemy general would expect him to seize upon them. But I suppose that's a Roman subtlety that you won't care for."

"Still, we are able to get it through our thick head." And at that the dark face reddened.

"I only meant, my liege, that in Roman warfare the deep and detailed study of one's antagonist is regarded as essential. Of course it's impossible in this wilderness of Britain."

"Is the place far or near, and what is it?"

"The north bank of a tributary out of the North Malvern Hills that we must cross. The nearest ford is about two miles up from the juncture, and the north bank is steep and sandy, and could be made almost unclimbable with a little digging, and still look natural. Above are thick woods to make an excellent ambush."

"Why, I doubt not that they're working on it even now—men moving dirt and logs for a barricade!"

"It could well be so. But no matter their advantage, a surprise attack from the rear would cook their goose. My liege, have I your leave to risk five hundred men—the Gods know how many more if we attack without support—on the chance this guess is right?"

"Would you try to hasten the march, to arrive there before their fortifications are completed?"

"No, if we gain two miles a day for the next ten days I'll be satisfied. Just now we have bright weather and rather open woods because of the light soil, but this afternoon and from thence on we must creep. Otherwise we'd lose so many men that the men's spirits would drop into their wooden shoon."

"You're in command," I told him, gulping.

"Between now and then I'll be picking the men for the flying flank. Good swimmers, good woodsmen, fellows who can leave ale and women alone until the job's done. I'll have Glyn guide them, if that suits you."

"It suits me well."

Even before noon one man was killed and another knocked silly by flung stones. Then the forest darkened like the sky before a cloudburst, and every rod of its edge a hundred paces inward had to be combed before we dared advance. Our best friends were innumerable red deer and wild hogs. The former belled and the latter squealed at sight of Hecanas, and often warned us of their ambush. Even so we lost, on the average, a man an hour, the greater part from our valiant scouts, and a disheartening thing to our whole force.

I reckoned we would lose from eighty to a hundred in the next ten days.

Those days were the longest in my yet life, Sun rising and Sun sinking in dreary monotony, with our force weakening despite the care we took; at last the tributary that Gerald called our Rubicon, known to the natives as White Water because of its sandy bottom, lay five miles northward of our encampment. All day no stone had been thrown, no hair or hide of Hecanas had been seen, and jollity pervaded the campground, and it was a wondrous thing to see the gaunt, wind-burned men toasting their meat, gnawing, talking, and laughing, about the high fires.

Ten at a time my raiders crept away, unburdened except for their swords, shields, and a day's ration. They were assembling about a half-mile down-river, where driftwood lay in heaps, this to help them ferry their weapons for their long, cold crossing. By the time the fires burned down, all twenty-five score had taken off, proud to be chosen, athrill over the coming exploit.

To command them was Erskine, from North Cambria, the second-best officer in my army, with Glyn to guide them. The rough plan was for them to swim the river tonight, make their way two or more miles inland, and under cover of darkness wheel back to a landmark their guides knew, cross the river again, and come into their position. One of a hundred things going wrong could foil the whole enterprise. In that case no great shift of fortune from bad to worse—no high wrath of some unknown God, merely his scowl—could fling our whole force on the horns of death. With one leg of our nutcracker broken and impotent, Gerald would probably pronounce our position untenable, in which case we must strike westward into Cambria, losing men like sheep torn out of a flock when ringed by wolves.

Still, I slept well, and was half-elated, half-depressed to waken in a dark, foggy dawn. My men would be cast down, fearing a succession of deadly ambushes on their day's march, and the lie I must tell them of nearly a third of our force leaving in the night to fight the Saxons would deal them a bitter blow. The fact remained that our flanking force became much less open to discovery and their chance of success greatly increased.

The light had hardly cleared when every man-jack in our main army perceived their diminished number and were gathering in troubled clusters or searching for friends they could not find. Evil rumor poisons the fighting heart—such was Gerald's saying. Good soldiers could iron themselves against great hazard but blanched and lost their vim when thrown against the ominous and the unseen. Gerald thought to wait till they had broken fast before assembling them for the announcement, thinking that with filled bellies they would take it in better part. For once I overruled him. It had come to me that this matter was not greatly concerned with military tactics and strategy, but more with human nature of a downright sort, and I too was a man before I was a king.

I was brought the biggest birchbark horn and roared into it full-voiced.

"Five hundred of your comrades are on the way to Cambria," I began, which I hoped was true in the long run. "They left in the night at your King's and your General's orders because of a threat to my throne, to our Motherland, and to your wives and children." To my strange relief, this also was true in the larger sense. "The rest of our great army will continue our northward march to overwhelm the brave and stubborn foe. We will penetrate the ambushes where they lie and put the lyers-in-wait to the sword. When at last they make their great stand, all who do not join my banner will go to their Gods, and a full half of the loot of the King's palace shall go into your pokes. Our force is reduced in numbers, but your glory of victory will be thus increased. I, Artay the King, pledge you my troth in return for your own. Now stand for royal inspection."

This last command I gave on the spur of the moment, and to judge from the way he stood, and his flushed face, Gerald was pleased with it. I thought that some stones might be hurled from the forest as the lines straightened and steadied, as an assembly of troubled men changed to an army, staunch and calm, of one mind bent on victory. As I walked down the lines, straightening shoulders, punching bellies, and examining sword and shield for rust or dirt, praising or chiding as Gerald had taught me, I felt one with them in a curious way, and they stood and looked as though they knew its truth.

We began our march; and it was a good sign, I thought, that the woods were free of ambushers as far as we could tell, as though a good general, not quite great, wished to encourage us to go boldly and fall into his great ambush. Just at high Sun we came where White Water entered the Severn on our side of the flood. We rested the troops, although in good position to meet sudden attack, and then a mere fifty, with a sharp-eyed captain leading, went up the tributary as though looking for a good ford. If Gerald had made the wrong guess, they might be stoned. If it were right, the foe would lie quiet as a wolf beside a deer-trail. Within the hour the band returned, all calmly as they had left except for their captain. His eyes glittered like naked iron in sunlight.

In a moment he, my other captains, Gerald, and I had drawn apart as in casual-seeming talk. The captain of scouts spoke almost under his breath.

"I didn't see hide nor hair, but I'll pledge my life to the Gods that the whole blood-thirsty tribe is there, just where the General said."

"What are the signs?" Gerald asked.

"There's a good deal of down-timber, but some of the logs have been moved to form a rough barricade. I wouldn't have seen that if I hadn't been looking for it, as you told me. The bank has been steepened with shovels—the sand's mottled-looking, some of it weathered more than the rest. The whole bank along the shallows is still as a grave, from men holding their breath."

"How long are the shallows?" And tension crept into Gerald's voice.

"A good three hundred paces."

"That's all right. We've over twelve hundred fighters and we'll march in a column of eights. My liege, by your consent I'll have the camp-followers and the donkey-train stay here, and start cooking a midday meal. If we're being spied upon, which I don't doubt, 'twill look as though we mean to move the baggage after the troops have occupied the ground across. My reason is, there may be traitors among 'em, trying to play tricks. And I'll post twenty of the Mendip archers to stand guard, with orders to stop any man or woman who starts wandering about, one warning, and then an arrow through the gizzard. When they hear our ruckus the archers can come on the run."

I agreed, and Gerald gave orders to the captains. We formed our lines, and when we came to the shallows, marched their whole length on the bank, then halted and faced the waters.

Gerald bawled his orders for friend and foe alike to hear plainly.

"Rucksacks off, sword in hand, shield on arm. If we haven't scared 'em out, there may be some lyers-in-wait in yonder down-timber. Cross in four waves, each of two lines ten feet in depth, the waves fifty feet apart. Keep your lines straight. First two lines, advance!"

He signaled to the trumpeter at his side. A shrill blast broke forth, and it was a splendid thing to see the men's set faces and ready bodies, for well they knew this call was never blown for engaging in petty skirmish, only for attack in main and bloody battle. With that realization they heard the hum of arrows arched high over their heads. The thirty Mendip archers behind our last line were launching their shafts as fast as they could let fly, to dart down at a steep pitch behind the log barricades. I wished to the High Gods I had three hundred such, and cursed human limitation whereby the art of making and mastering such perfect weapons took half a lifetime.

Howls of pain and groans of dying men rose from under the hail, although the hidden army did not show itself, hoping that we did not yet guess its number and would go on with the crossing and not retreat until it could fall upon us according to plan. My place was midway of the front line, where all could see my burnished helmet and moon-bright sword, and now we reached the steep bank, the second line of our wave close behind us, and we tried to mount up on the run. This we could not do in such deep sand, but we forged on, howling, and suddenly the battle was joined; the most terrible and ferocious joining I had ever known.

The flight of arrows ceased because the archers could not pick foe from friend in the dim forest-edge. As we sought to clear the crest, the tribesmen hacked at us with their long-swords, and they stood thicker than blackbirds in a pea-patch, and that was the single advantage our belabored and desperate front ranks possessed, for again the enemy got in one another's way. Even so, we would have been decimated or obliterated except for the second wave already surging up the wicked steep, and soon a stout fellow had taken the place of every stout fellow who lay still in the bloody sand. And all the rest were seeking openings for their swift swords.

A giant of a man who topped all the rest, richly arrayed, with a gold crown held to his head by a strap under the chin, stood on a fallen log just behind the press of foemen, looking hawk-like right and left until my helmet caught his eye; then he leaped down and went for me, and at his great cry, *"Hecana!"* his men made room for him. My soldiers too knew the plentiful room my long arms needed, they gave me that room, and it came to pass that we two kings fought each other as though alone and apart. The noise of battle about us, the clatter and crash of iron and the wolfish howling of the foe and the crying out upon Lud and Bran of our Cambrian rustics and the high-pitched yells of the Cornish became of no more mind to us than would crashing thunder and flaming lightning and wind-driven rain, had we fought on an unpeopled moor. I knew my opponent for a master swordsman, and he the like. If not the equal of Gerald or Modred, he did not miss it far. How he compared to me must be written in blood.

One sound I still listened for, in some cool corner of my brain, and the interval was unwordly long and immeasurably short before I heard it cut through the blast like a sword-edge through soft flesh. It was the trumpet calling in our outlyers, and between dodging one stroke of my foeman's sword and he parrying one of mine, I prayed in one falcon-swift upward swoop of prayer to the High Gods that they had not failed the rendezvous and could be wolf-swift in attack. For otherwise—as I had known beforehand—I would lose half my army, if not the battle.

The din loudened and the shapes of men surged and flitted at the corners of my eyes, and I knew Gerald's great nut-cracker had begun its deadly closing. Over the edge of the bank poured the moiling fronts, and its noise changed because an ever-greater number fought on its steep slope and in the shallow waters at its foot, and it came up to us kings as the noise of a hurricane on a raging ocean ascends to the Gods. He and I fought on, sometimes on open ground, and often amidst the fallen logs of the barricade.

I know not how many times I was atop a log, with my foeman hacking upward with high-raised shield, or when the tables turned. Once in dodging a stroke I fell backward, only to spring up before he could jump the log and finish me. Once he toppled forward almost on me, and I hacked him a great gash in the side, without slowing his deadly onslaught. But perhaps he knew the wound was mortal, because he began to fight not with cold and studied power but in a frenzy of haste, as though his hope of victory had died, and all hope left was that our souls would wing forth together.

So swift and terrible his strokes that I was forced back, and nearly toppled down the bank. But I caught my footing and the mighty hack intended to cleave my helm slashed half the sleeve from my tunic. In the trice ere he struck again, I lacked time to raise up Caliburn, and I swung him sideways with a jerk of my forearm, as though heaving an ax, and the blade caught my enemy squarely in the neck. The edge was whetted to cut a hair, and the massive corded column that upheld the royal head cut like tallow, and as I gazed his head toppled, crown and all, and his blood gushed up, and for what seemed a long instant he stood headless, so short when a second ago he had stood so tall; then he dropped to his knees, and then prone. When the kingly head had stopped rolling I looked down at it, now so little use to him or any one, the eyes wide but unseeing, yellow mustache and beard turned fiery-red; and I slipped the strap from under his chin and looped it to my belt. Meanwhile I could not believe the silence that had set in. No man of all that roaring multitude gave voice above a whimper, and the ripple of the shallows, and now and then a loud or a soft splash came clear to my startled ears.

I stood on the crest of the bank and looked down. A few bodies of friend and foe still stuck on the steep slope, but the most who had died there had slid down, and at the foot where it began to level lay what looked like a hedgerow of dead men, washed in blood and lining the full length of the battleground. Now and then, pressed upon by shifting bodies on slightly higher ground, one of them rolled or slid slowly into the water. And glancing up and down the clear shadows, I saw many a dark shape under or almost afloat on the flood, and these were being briskly swept down-river, sometimes wheeling, sometimes lying straight and still as on their biers.

I was the King, and I could not withhold from making a rough guess at their numbers, roughly verified by the numbers of men still standing, motionless except for panting. Of the great host assailing us, uniformly clad in gray from the woolen cloth of the Cotswold, not one man stood tall, and not one lived except for a spare scattering of wounded. Of my divided army of seventeen hundred, not more than fourteen hundred had united, the others piled with the enemy in the long red heap or swallowed by the flood. Counting the Hecana tribesmen at a thousand, fully half of the men engaged in this great battle of the ford had taken off, the Gods knew where, leaving only clay to turn cold and rot. The thought struck me that the crown of Britain was being bought at no small price, even by Artay, the choice of the Gods to succeed Caesar.

Then glory swept my being, body and brain, and the hilt of Caliburn thrilled in my strong grasp, and my shield rang a little, as though it had been lightly struck. And the pang of remorse faded, and the glory increased, as the soldiers struck their shields with the hilts of their swords, and raised both with a great cry. The Sun broke through the clouds and glimmered on the burnished irons. When I raised Caliburn, and brandished him three times in remembrance of his giver into my hands from the waters of Witch Lake, the soldiers' shout was louder than before, and it reached the ears of the Gods in their golden thrones, and I feared no Gods!

4

My great antagonist, the King of the Hecanas, would be buried in his royal robe, his shield on his arm, his sword at his side. I was half-inclined to restore his crown to his brow, until Merdin told me it would be unwise, for if his former subjects smarted under my rule and heard the tale of him lying crowned in his mossy grave, they might take it as a sign that he would rise up and return to them in some guise to lead them in rebellion against me. Besides, the crown was more massy than my own, weighing a full pound, worth nearly a thousand cattle.

When the men had rested, emptying horns of ale which the camp-followers and baggage-tenders brought them, Gerald set them to digging a long grave for their fallen comrades. Not so much to save great labor, which would take a full day in which yokels might form bands to impede our passage, and which the King's ministers might use thriftily to sack his treasury and make off with his stores, but rather so that his dead warriors could join their comrades already afloat on its waters, I ordered them heaved into the river.

As Gerald and I were making for the mouth of White Water, where tonight we would bivouac, I told him of Vivain's vision of seeing men at work with timbers and moving earth, pointing out that it had come true, and how my faith in her troth, as well as her witchcraft, was greater than before.

"Had she told me of that vision, and I had believed it, we might not have won the victory and instead met dire defeat," he answered, a rasp in his voice.

"I don't read your riddle, Gerald."

"Her description would have meant to me the building of a fortification to defend the palace, which they were in great haste to complete before we could attack, and so I would have ordered a quick march at whatever cost of men ambushed along the way, and then I would have fallen into the great ambush. Happily, you read into it another meaning."

"I can't say that I did, at first. I too thought the vision was of a great fortification. Only when we came to a trap——"

I fell silent. So he did not interrupt me when he said quietly:

"She didn't waste her breath telling me. She knew I'd not believe her. If you cast back over everything she's said, you will find it can be taken two ways. To speak bluntly, it was mainly because of Vivain and certain other camp-followers under her thumb that I appointed twenty of our precious Mendip archers to watch their band."

"By the Great Gods, do you think that she serves Vortigern?"

"Not any more, if ever. She serves her own loves and hates. She's no more a half-witch than Pillicock is a gnome—although perhaps more of a monster."

"By the Gods, I don't know what you mean!"

"I withdraw the charge, my liege. I have no evidence on which to base it, only wild surmise. I pray your pardon. It is rightful that as General of the Army I should act on my suspicions, performing my duty as I see it, but it is not my place to make insinuations against a favorite of my King."

"You'll not be beheaded, Gerald, old friend, especially on the day you've won me a great victory. Except for you, I would not have won four crowns—Cambria, Monmouth—that one was guilded copper—Cornwall and the Exe, and now the crown of the Severn."

"My liege, I command men who follow you, as I do. It might be that, save for me, you would not have won those crowns; save for you, my sword would have rusted in its sheath. Since I have troubled your ears until now, now I will seek to please them. I think that your fears of further trouble with ambushers is groundless. The power of the Hecanas is broken beyond repair. Pray give thought to whom you will appoint regent in this vast new kingdom you have won. And, my liege—have you ever in your days seen such brave, stubborn, last-ditch fighters as those two-legged wolves? When our victory became certain I hoped to take prisoners, but no mother's son of 'em would submit except to dire death. Tonight, if you will, let the men feast. And if you wish to please them mightily, in your pledging drink to the souls of their brave enemies beyond the sea-mists!"

"Gerald, I have a feeling that you would make a better king than I."

"No, my liege. Not a better or a worse. I can only act in your name."

We were both a little drunk on the strong wine of victory, and now our voices were getting husky with emotion, to which we Cambrians, even half-Romans who breathe our air, are too much given. So I changed the subject to common things.

In two days' march we came to the Hecana palace at the junction of the Severn and the Tern. All the underlings had fled, and only the King's ministers huddled at the door to greet me, half-trusting that I would let them keep some remnants of their honors, half-afraid to run lest I should have them pursued, caught, and hanged. We stayed here nearly a fortnight, installing a viceroy, hearing entreaties, reaffirming in office some of the old King's servants and supplanting some of them with our own pick, and conducting such like affairs of state. I did not feel inclined to hang any one, perhaps from admiration of the tribesmen's valiant stand against us and from thinking how close we had come to defeat. Actually I had stretched only two necks—one of a great minister who was caught sending an appeal to Malcolm, King of Midland, the second belonging to a steward who served me a cup of poisoned wine.

Only one incident of our stay was out of the ordinary. My spies reported that every day for about a week a fellow dressed in rags visited a certain tree within a nearby copse, and appeared to be looking carefully at the ground. I had them lay for him, catch and pinion him, at which he squealed like a pig and shrieked like a woman, or so they told me, and when I went to look at him, I recognized him instantly as a kind of clerk attached to the King's treasury, who had worn a robe somewhat finer than his office. I too looked carefully at the ground, and it did not take me long to see where it had been freshly dug.

One of my fellows delved also, and brought me up a richer treasure in gold coins than I had thought existed in all Britain, except ancient treasures guarded by gnomes of the rock or by fairies in deep water. Mainly they were half-ounce pieces, and bore the heads of various Caesars, and their total weight was about four pounds, riches beyond avarice to any one less than a king, and the worth of a great earldom. When I had locked them in an iron-bound chest lined with iron plate, I took thought of what punishment to give the clerk. It would be easy to hang him, yet Merdin protested this simple and natural act, on the ground that ministers and other officials of the court were no doubt party to the plot, and the fellow would betray them before the noose tightened, and I would have a batch of hangings on my hands.

"Many of these you have sustained in office," Merdin told me. "They are as well-suited men as any you can find, for no man can be blamed for one try at withholding gold from a conqueror who may soon reduce him to beggary, and with his eyes bedazzled by the yellow stuff. Why not pretend to believe the clerk's story that he had hid it to save it for you, his mother being a Cambrian, even though a child of six summers would gag on it? All the plotters will shudder at their narrow escape—they've been pale and couldn't eat since his arrest—and I trow they'll mind their duty from this time forward."

Having won the great realm and the gold too, I was in the notion to hear and heed.

Many weeks went by before I slept in the royal bed at Woodwick. We had no touch of trouble with the semi-independent princes below and above the big market town of Salop, athwart the river and numerous roads, but received a big load of it when it came to pacifying North Cambria. A miller who lived on the Dee had gained great influence and indeed power with all the yokels in those parts, mainly because of a wondrous mill, the like of which we had never seen, the grinders being turned by a water-wheel instead of with yokes of oxen, and whose charge for grinding corn was only one bag in ten; and also by his independent and proud spirit, which by nature we Cambrians admire. I did not feel free to hang him. He was regarded as a magician as well as a great public benefactor, and it might have started a small, stubborn rebellion. Also the Princes of Mona and of the River Clwyd and the Conway, only nominally subject to Vortigern, were loath to get it through their heads that they must pay tribute and give levies.

A fat old man of Caerhun played both ends against the middle in matters of religion, calling himself a Christian Bishop and an Archdruid, depending on whom he addressed. Although Merdin would have rejoiced to see him hang, I thought to make use of his famed mastery of Latin. So I had him inscribe a document, only two words of which I could make out, these being Rex and Regina, and which was studded with many an "ergo." The sense of it was that since I had crowned Wander with my own hands, she was rightfully Queen of my realm, but since our marriage had not been consummated, she was not my wife, and I could take another if I pleased. I had him make several copies, all on Roman-like scrolls of parchment, to be read by Latin readers to the rustics throughout my kingdom. Below he wrote A. R. Britannica, and I affixed my mark, which was a roughly drawn picture of a Cambrian harp.

May Day had come and gone when I received a token from Swan Lake. I went apart from my followers and courtiers before I broke its seal, and my hands trembled unduly, and my heart tumbled to the bottom of my gizzard when I saw what it contained—a single grain of barley-corn shrunken and frost-bitten instead of a sprouting seed she had promised to send if she were with child. In these long moons since I had parted with Elain, I had all but convinced myself that our wondrous and beautiful passage in the stone house beside the fire on the shortest day of the year had got me a son, and I had intended to make him my heir to the throne of Britain, and thereby I would have good cause to keep her with me, and she would be absolved of her vow never to live at a heathen court. I searched the little cabinet of beechwood with sore care, hoping to find a green shoot that had started and fallen off and withered on the journey, but found no shred of it. Instead there was the dried leaf of a certain kind of willow tree by which Cambrians symbolized mourning.

For half a year thereafter the same courier was continually tramping back and forth to Swan Lake with messages between Elain and me, as I sought to persuade her to give me her white hand in marriage, or to take up lodgings near my capital if not in it, and everything else I could think of, to have her lovely company at my sore need. She replied that Wander had been my first choice for a bride, Vivain for a paramour; that the Christian God and the Gods of Britain had frowned on our love; and besides, that the tale spread through Cambria that I was turning tyrant; and she was nigh half-decided to turn Christian, adjuring heathens like me forever. I rewarded the messenger handsomely, hoping he would bring better news, all to no avail. Perhaps a threat of hanging would have fetched better results, Elain being tender-hearted to everyone but me.

In these months I too was often on the go—here and about everywhere except to South Cambria. A pretender rose like a snake's head in the Valley of the Clwyd and had to be scotched by a force of five hundred; the last of the old dynasty of Mona ensconced himself in a big earthen and timber fort, and nothing would do to dislodge and behead him but three cohorts of a hundred men each tediously ferried across Menai Strait and thrown with no small loss against his barricades. Also I sat up late in talk with Merdin, Gerald and Llewelan. To these I had not told my troubles over Elain, being ashamed to confess myself at such loss, but I harkened well to the counsel of my elders on matters of state.

By now the fact was plain that we could not march this summer to conquer the rest of Britain, because that arrow must not be launched from a half-drawn bow. The petty kings had wet their breeches over the news of my taking Monmouth, Cornwall and the Exe, and finally the whole Valley of the Severn. During our necessary solidifying of my now vast domain, they had seen the need of ceasing their quarrels with one another and leaguing against me. Not all the reports brought by my spies were bad. Happily the fierce and barbarous Brigantes had their hands full turning back the Painted Men swarming over Hadrian's Wall. I myself would overthrow them in due course; at present they were my unwilling and unconscious allies. The Saxons in their horned hats raided the eastern and southern shores from Humbermouth to The Solent, and some had settled in wild Kent, and they eschewed only the coasts running westward of Vectis because of Uther, King of the Avon and the Stour, and his ally Loth, King of the Thames. Also they thought best not to harry Cornwall and Cambria, because of our watch-towers and their fleet guards.

The best news then told me was that Malcolm, King of the Midlands, had forsaken his capital at Ratae, called Lester by the folk, and was building a fortified capital called Warwick on the Avon, where he posed a threat to both great monarchs, Uther and Loth. They would keep one another on close watch, with bristling swords, as cock-grouse menace each other while the falcon swoops unseen. My realm being secure at least till spring weather, I thought to pay a long and fruitful visit to South Cambria.

Winding up a few pressing matters, I had time to grant audience to Vivain, who dwelt in a house I had built for her three arrow-casts from Woodwick. She was helping some women weave a wondrous cloth, long enough to cover half of one wall of my palace, and showing pictures of our great battles of the Vale and of White Water. Kings of Gaul possessed such cloths, she had told me, and these were counted among their richest possessions, and besides, they warmed the edifice on windy nights. However, if any male-creature, man or beast, laid eyes on the great arras before it was completed the gains won in those battles might be lost; hence the weavers worked from dawn to dark without a churl, a jack-dog, a tom-cat, a rooster, or a gander ever strolling in their door, only bitches, tabbies, hens, and geese keeping them company.

"My liege, my eyes rejoice to see your face confronting mine once more, but the tidings that I bring may be of sorrow," she told me, her small, brown, witchy face dirty with what I thought was dried tears, although still entrancing to the sight, and a wakener of tingles in king or clown.

"Still, I'll hear them."

"Pray let me tell you in my own way, lest you cast me forth before you have heard me out. First, I will speak of the ancient custom of Cambrians and many Britains sacrificing their first-born unto the Gods. It is told of old that the Great Ones rejoiced in this deed of love and troth, and the crops were good, and the wolves abjured the folds. Still I pray you not to return to these old ways, since folk are so few and beasts so many, and although the infants go to bliss beyond the sea-mists, still their mothers would weep sorely at the loss. Unless some great war is breaking, where the balance is deadly even, and you direly need the favor of the Gods, let them be content with spotted bulls, and if not spotted, snow-white, and I trow your great strength will prevail."

"It must prevail, or the Song of Camlon will not be fulfilled."

"The latter part of the Song is sung in riddles. It comes to me that it did not promise that an heir of your body shall rule Britain, or even that you will reign long. Now that may be because the Singer was begrogged, or another had taken up the harp, but it may be because demons work against you and against your throne. Such may be balked if you act in time. My heart drives me to tell you of a vision which my mother, Calypso, saw in her boiling cauldron. To make her tell me I conjured her by burning dry leaves of the linden tree under which I was conceived, whereby she took a fit of coughing, wracking her scrawny throat and chest, and which would not cease until she did my will."

"Where did you see your mother? I thought she lived in the Black Forest."

"She went forth, riding I know not what, and came to my bed-side. Her mission was not to serve you, whom she hates, or to give comfort to me, whom she loves, but to taunt me with the telling of part of her vision but not all. It was that in twice-nine years you would be overthrown, and lose your crown and—such were her words between her cackles of evil laughter—your very life."

I could almost hear the witches' mirth in the silence of the night. "What more did she tell you?"

"Nothing more, until I employed the charm against which she is powerless. When it was laid, and her laughter had changed to wracking coughs, I demanded to know your conqueror's name and abode. It turned out that she knew neither, for when she told me so the coughing stopped, and she knew only that he is lately born in Cambria, south of the Wye, and on the day that night and day were equal length. But take thought, my liege, before you act. It could be that Calypso had misread the vision, for not always does her boiling cauldron tell her the truth. My liege, how many male infants do you suppose are born every day in South Cambria?"

"That's easy to reckon. Two hundred turned eighteen in all Cambria between May Day of two years ago and of last year. That's less than one a day on the average, less than one in two days in South Cambria. Taking the day before and after the day so dark in my fate, three days in all to make sure, I doubt if more than one need be sacrificed, at most two or three, and that would be a trifling loss compared to the balking of the will of the Gods by some demon."

"Even so, you had best not tell Merdin or your General Gerald. The old man is failing from old age, the General is a Roman who does not believe in witchcraft, and before you know it the babe which the powers of evil mean to be your murderer and heir will be taken out of your reach. Have you an officer you can trust with the mission?"

"The very one."

"The mother should be proud to give her babe to save your throne, even so you can reward her with a purse of silver."

"Why, she shall have twenty silver pieces, the same whether one or two or three. If she's a churl's wife, it will mean riches; if a slave's, she can buy his freedom. Babes die by the score by flux or fever, or slain by wolves. The Gods will be pleased that their will is not thwarted. You have pleased me by prevailing over your wicked mother, Calypso. My soldiers have slain whole armies who opposed my royal power. I would not be worthy of my crown if I lost it for the sake of a squalling infant not yet a fortnight old."

"I pray you, say no more. Only do what your duty bids."

"I will set about it at once. You have my leave to go."

I gave Vivain a gold pin I had taken off Enid; then I made haste to call my hangman, who was ardent in his office, who lived in deadly fear of witchcraft, and who would carry out the all-important mission without fail. It was the law of the Druids that the hour and date of every birth be written down in numerals, so that the infants' lives could be foretold by the stars, and these records were kept by the tax-collector in every bailiwick. The fellow, whose name was Aran, I charged straitly. Once assured that the babe's nativity fell within the prescribed time, he was not to alarm its dam, but to dispatch it mercifully in one stroke, then pour the silver blood-money into some receptacle with a cheery jingle.

"She'll soon dry her tears, unless she's the wife of a great earl," Aran replied.

"In any case, you must not fail, for it is the will of the Gods that I found a dynasty to reign forever in Britain."

We were standing by the wooden door of the room I had built for Elain, and it opened and closed with no visible hand touching it. Perhaps it had not been well-latched, and a puff of wind had thrust at it, then sucked it back. Even so, Lud was the God of winds, sucked or blown by the Sun, and I, Artay, was King of Cambria, Monmouth, Cornwall and the Exe, and all the Valley of the Severn clean to the watershed of the Trent, and to fulfill my fate I must be King of Britain. How could I doubt I had proven my fitness before the Gods?

2

That night my sleep was broken and my dreams evil. I could not think why, unless all my great winnings of the past thirteen months, and the affairs of state with which I had wrestled, and especially my long continence since my parting with Elain, had taxed me more than I knew. Another two weeks must pass before our spies, sent forth to locate Vortigern and his two sons, could bring their reports; after which I had resolved to visit my true love before the outbreak of war. Meanwhile I thought to essay a great boar and red-deer hunt in Radnor Forest, taking also wild cattle, and the kill should be given to a hundred or more cotters in the region of the Wells whose flocks had greatly suffered from the raids of wolves. So I set forth with a great train, and with hawks and hounds, and Ron thrust his iron beak into many a wild heart, and once more I knew the joy of a winged hornet flying straight as a swooping falcon from my throbbing bow.

But after ten days of royal sport, I was compelled to return to Woodwick, as though I had there an assignation with some one. And although I had planned no such act, it being the impulse of the moment, I was hardly inside the door when I ordered that Aran the Hangman be summoned to speak to me in private.

"My liege, Aran, who went to South Cambria with two armed followers eleven days since, has not returned."

Why, that need not surprise me! He would have to search the records of every bailiff in the region, which could not be done in a day. Quite likely he had found not one babe born in the fateful period, in which case Vivain had merely dreamed the visit of her mother, Calypso, with dire tidings.

"Then send for Vivain," I told the servant, although I had no notion what I wanted of her or of what to say to her.

"My liege, Vivain is not in her house, and has not been since you went forth to hunt, and since she took her bundle, and the wench who went with her lives east of the Trent, the rumor has spread that she has left your kingdom."

"Now that does not stand to reason. The lands east of the Trent are held by my enemies."

"My liege, I can only repeat what I have heard, but this I know. A salt-merchant saw her at Harewood End nearly a week gone, and she was traveling eastward."

And now it seemed that evil dreams besieged my brain even in my wakefulness.

I was soon wakened from those dreams. Merdin came into the palace, looking ten years older than when I had seen him last, his eyes dim and watery, his skin gray as a fresh cadaver's, his beard uncombed.

"Artay, will you come with me to my lodge—at once?"

I led the way there, walking tall as I was able, and we went into the dim room where he did his own cooking and kept his harp, the head of Bran, his great chest, his hour-glass, and his bronze ax.

"Will you sit down, my liege, on yon bench? It is the best my house affords."

"If you too sit down."

"I must. I am too weak to stand. First I will speak of Vivain. And if it were ever jealousy that caused me to question what you thought was her witchcraft, it is not now. I have now established her true descent. Her father, Murray, was a mighty earl on the island of Mona. His wife was named Enid, of royal descent, and the sister of the Queen of Cornwall and the Exe, now deposed by you. Their daughter was Vivain."

"She told me——" But what I was going to say stuck in my throat.

"She told you many things. It was given out that her father, the earl, died of eating the death-apple. Actually he was poisoned, in all likelihood by Enid's own hand, so she could wed Vortigern. His unnatural daughter did not avenge the death of her sire. Worse than that, she became Enid's creature, and has been ever since, in every way but one, and of that I will speak later or not speak at all."

"Merdin, have you forgotten how she warned us of the ax-throwers lying in wait—in the very copse she had seen in a dream?" And my voice was too flurried for the proper voice of a king.

"That was her bait—for you. They lay in a place impossible to surprise, and all escaped except the officer who had caught his foot. Do you remember that he offered to buy his life with information of value to you? But Vivain shut his lips with her dagger before he could give it. She was very quick—her own pretty neck lay under Gerald's sword, and he would have gladly sullied it with her blood, and your command would not have stopped him, had the officer lived long enough to tell his secret. And I trow you have at last surmised what the secret was."

"Go on, old man, but make it as short as you can."

"She would not lie with you in your pavilion. You must untie her virgin knot under a linden tree, with heart-shaped leaves—the same kind of tree, she told you, under which she was conceived. Aye, she was a virgin. Of that too I will speak later or not at all. That linden tree was the only one in the camp environs. As you were pleasuring her—or thought you were—she uttered a great cry which you took for an outburst of passion. Instead it brought the King's men who were lying in wait. You were captured, and so was Pillicock, and by some miracle I know not even now, you both escaped."

"Vivain was captured also," I said, stubborn die-hard that I was.

"If it were part of the plot, what of the man in their party that she knifed?"

"What did a churl's death count in comparison with your death by torture before the multitude at Vortigern's palace? Mark you, Vivain is not only greatly skilled in histrionics of all sorts. Her head is wondrous long—and she was not sure your army would not rescue you before Enid's and Vortigern's purpose was fulfilled, and she wished to retain your child's faith in her."

"Don't be windy, I pray you, Merdin. Get to the point."

"All in good time. Remember also that when one of your captors, Morys of the Glen, sought the office of Captain of your Palace Guard, it was his whole intent to send you to the Gods. Vivain passed the signal for you to appoint him. I motioned for you to pass him by. Happily, you identified him by his voice. Otherwise I wonder if you would have believed Merdin or the demi-witch—as she called herself—Vivain."

"Merdin, I would have heeded you, as I almost always did."

"In that, I rejoice. Artay, I do not believe that a tall soldier called forth the big, coarse slattern and gave her a gold piece to stab you through the wall of your pavilion. I would take oath before the Gods it was Vivain who sent her on the murderous mission, with gold from Enid's hoard."

"I wish I had hanged Enid."

"Another needs it as much or more. And, Artay, when we found the body of the hoyden who Gerald thought had died by her own hand, you ventured that she might have been murdered by some one leaving footprints exactly like her own. Now I am persuaded that you were right. I think that Vivain bought two identical pairs of leathern shoon. The huckster had shown one pair to the captain who spoke to you, and told him he had no other, but it is the way of hucksters, especially Greeks, to have at least two of every article or garment, so if the purchase of one incites the envy of some one at the fair, he can supply its like. I believe that Vivain had bribed the slattern with one pair, then perceived that she was wavering, and went with her, wearing identical shoon, with no intention other than killing her, the crime to be deemed suicide, and this whether or not her creature kept her bargain and sent you to your Gods."

"Why should Vivain hate me with such venomous hate?"

"I do not call it hate. I know not what to call it. True, you stood in the way of Enid, her mother, and hence in her own way. Still, there is something more, terrible and monstrous, that I do not understand."

"Will you guess at it, old man, for my comfort's sake?"

"Not now. And there is no comfort for you, Artay, in all that I must speak, and the worst is yet to come. True, you did not act on her vision, as she called it, of men building a fortification of timber and earth, and therefore your army did not perish at White Water. Yet you believed her augury when she sought audience with you eleven days ago."

"Yes, I did."

"Now she and your hangman Aran have fled the court and, I think, the country. Another has gone hence, resigning his high post—Llewelan of the Lake, and no doubt he has gone home. Now the time has come for me to ask a straight question, and I charge you, give me a true answer. On the shortest day of the year, when the year turned back, you visited Elain at Swan Lake. Did you put her with child?"

"I had hoped to do so, but I received a token from her that the seed died."

"What was the token?"

"A shrunken grain of barley-corn. If it had sprouted, it would be a sign that she had teemed."

"Was the seal of the packet broken?"

"No, it was not, and what in the devil do you mean?"

"Have you had any communication from her since?"

"A messenger went back and forth. You know him—Egan."

"He too is a creature of Enid. Artay, I won't keep you waiting any longer and will tell you the dire and dreadful news. Elain bore you a babe on the day equal in length with the night. That babe has been slain by Aran's sword."

It did not matter if I blanched or showed any sign of weakness. Merdin knew me to be more deeply stricken than any sign could show. The heavens I had once wished to fall had done so, but the Gods had not broken their necks, and instead my heart, which I had so little heeded in my dizzy ascent, had cracked from top to bottom, and it bled within my bosom, and the blood choked me, and I thought that this moment would be my last, and I need never again glance into a glass, or know myself for a living thing to face what I had done. Instead I lived on. I was too greatly alive to die except with a sword-stroke through my helm to the arch of my ribs. I thought of taking the Roman way, and falling upon my sword. I thought of climbing the great cliffs of Snowdon, and of leaping with all my might, and of being shattered into a skin bag of broken bones, unworthy of burial, on the rocks below. But I could launch upon neither of these dark roads until I knew the answer to one last question. Until then I could never find respite beyond the sea-mists and my soul must wander forever in the fog and rain, blown by the wind.

"Why? Merdin, I ask you why. I am Artay, King of Cambria, Monmouth, Cornwall and the Exe, and the Valley of the Severn. In the name of your allegiance, I charge you to answer."

"Then I will utter all that my mind can reach. This much I know: between the ages of fifteen and eighteen, Vivain dwelt on an island off the coast of Mona with eight other beautiful maidens of high birth. The tale was told that when a fisherman touched their strand, he was chased and caught, and his mates visioned him living among them ever after, dining and drinking like a prince, the nine comely neophites in witchcraft serving his every need. So widely spread the story that often young men would desert their vessels, to swim to the island. Artay, none were ever seen again. Mark you, when an old faith falters, as did the Druidic faith, and as law fades, as faded Roman law, many outlandish cults come into being, and the most evil of all is the cult of the God Modo."

"Modo! He is Vivain's God. She wished me his ever attendance."

"If you had told me of that curse, which you took for a blessing, I would have seen the light much sooner than I did, blind fool that I am. Modo is the God of murder. I do not know what horrid rites those female fiends practiced on their captives ere these were slain, but I have heard rumors of like worship all over the known world, almost always by virgins of ancient lineage and great beauty, wherever

Rome called back her eagles and the vultures flew in their stead. I doubt not that they tortured their prisoners in ways unspeakable, those unnatural hags, who would still flourish on their accursed isle had the Sea not risen in his wrath and swept half of it away. I believe that Vivain felt passion for you, although of a loathsome and abysmal sort, whose only gratification would be your death directly or indirectly at her hand. How did it begin, you may well ask? Artay, I know not, for her sire was a nobleman, of nature gentle in a son of this dark age. How did she fall in love with murder, for there is no other term? Is it because murder is a final and complete exercise of vanity and power? It may be that neither of us will live to know the answer."

"Was she jealous of Elain because I chose her, choosing life instead of death? What does it matter, now that I have lost her? Gods! Gods!"

"You have lost her forever. And if that is all your punishment, the Gods are merciful. In your swollen pride you have slain the babe of your own begetting—such evil that the Song itself would not pronounce in words or sound in notes. Yet in that self-same song redemption is hinted. Mourn, atone if in your power, but do not despair."

"Redemption is far distant, if I ever find it." I rose, took off my crown, and set it atop Merdin's chest. I removed the golden chain from about my neck, and the golden rings from my fingers, and put these with the crown. Lastly I unclasped the golden broaches of my ermine robe and laid these and the robe too with the rest. A mangy coat of sheepskins that Merdin wore in rough weather was hanging on a nail, and it fitted me well enough.

"In the name of the Great Gods, what do you do?" he cried. "You are still Vortigern's son and the rightful King."

"I go to Swan Lake. Then I go on a long journey, where perhaps my heart will mend, or cease its wracking beat. As still the rightful King, I appoint Gerald regent of my realm, and you his chief minister. If it is the will of the Gods, I will return. Farewell."

"Go, but return, lest not you but the wolves rule Cambria, and the last light fails."

And that was the last human speech I heard as I went forth into the drizzling rain and blowing mists that the Gods had sent since I had come hence, the sign that they had turned their bright faces from me, and I was accursed. The palace doors and the doors of my minions were closed, loiterers had fled from the wet, and no gaze followed me as I headed southward.

3

It was possible to tramp from Woodwick to Swan Lake without passing a single village or coming in sight of more than a few far-scattered cottages. I took this lonely way, veering from it only once to visit briefly a fair at the junction of the Wye and the Garth rivers. I concealed my sword and my shield in a copse of dwarf ash while I visited the settlement, and since I did not walk as tall as before, no one dreamed that I was once, and still so in name, the King of one of the greatest realms in Britain.

I had silver in my purse, and I bought angles and small leaden weights for fishing, lines for setting snares, and a small store of dried fish and wheat-cakes. I did not yet know my destination after I would leave Swan Lake. I knew only it would be some lonely region of wide horizons, visited only by the Gods of wind, rain, mist, and snow, where I must live by my own hands.

In three days' march I had gained the shores of the lake which so often I visited in dreams. There I hallooed, hoping that Elain would send Pillicock to get me in her boat; and if she did not, I meant to swim to the island by my soul's great need. Neither thing came to pass. Elain and Pillicock both came out of the stone house, and the dwarf hauled sturdily on the oars, and Elain sat in the bow with her back to me. Not one glow of hope warmed my heart that she had come to meet me. The explanation of her action was all too plain— she did not intend I should ever again enter her door.

When the boat touched the landing she took Pillicock's hand and stepped ashore. And then I knew the truth of Merdin's words, that she was the most beautiful being in Britain, warm with human warmth, while Wander was the flawless image of a Goddess. The mist had been wiped from my eyes too late, I thought. If I had sought this great prize with the same ardor I had sought my crown, I might have had her to keep always.

"Artay, you come in humble guise, although still armed for battle," she told me quietly.

"Elain, I carried arms before I was a king, although otherwise I came and went in humble guise. Although I have put aside my crown, I am still a man of arms, so this is my true self."

"Will you use your Sword to kill the new-born? That is a strange role for a soldier."

"Elain, I beg your leave to speak. That is the only mercy that I ask, the only boon. I cannot undo my monstrous crime against the Gods, you, and my own body and soul, but it may be I can answer questions which must have risen in your mind, whereby what seems an unnatural act may seem more natural in one who was demon-driven, and your hate of me will be reduced in some slight measure."

She considered awhile, looking out across the lake. Pillicock strolled into the woods.

"Yes, Artay, you may speak. I hope you can tell me what will make your dreadful stroke against me come within the scope of human wickedness, not of inhuman evil. My first thought was that you had had a son, born after mine, by the creature Vivain, and you wanted him to inherit your throne, and mine would be in its way. But Pillicock told me this could not be true, and so did my sire, Llewelan, that you were not another Vortigern, that you had never turned against your own, and looking into your face worn and white, that much I can believe."

I could only bow my head and wait.

"Will you sit, Artay? The grass is green and soft, and will receive you still, for it bears no malice for blood shed far and wide upon its innocent growth. You are shaken by some great storm and my hate is mingled with pity. I too will sit, and hear what you have to tell me, then we will part forever."

"Elain, the packet I received, which I supposed you had sent me, contained a barley-corn shrunken and dead."

"That bears out what Pillicock told me. But the one I sent you had a living shoot."

"The false was substituted for the true. And the messenger I sent to you, beseeching you to come to me, brought back surly answers."

"Artay, I expected a message from you, after sending the packet.

289

Every day I watched for your messenger to appear on the shore, and if you had bid me go to Woodwick and dwell close to you, where you could see and love your son—and see and love me—I would have done so. But no messenger ever came. Those I saw on the shore were drovers of cattle and swine, or men filling water-casks. I took it you were too full of your great plans to conquer Britain to think of your babe taking shape in my womb, and even that I forgave you, knowing your vaulting ambition. But I was no Marcus Cassius, to stand watch in life and in death. I was no Roman, only Elain of the Lake, and finally I was ashamed to run ever to the casement, and I hung a looking-glass that I had found in a cranny, once belonging to Lucillius, who built the house of stone. It showed the strand where our boat lands, and into this I could look as I wove a wondrous cloth, fit for a queen. And after the babe's birth, and Pillicock delivered him with his strong hands, and I saw three men in fine raiment on the shore, I took it you were home from the wars, and your thoughts had at last flown to Elain and to your first-born, and I sent Pillicock in a boat to bring them to my house, and I could hardly forbear from going with him, such was my happiness, and refrained only because the day was rainy and dark and I feared I might take fever, and the babe would suck it into his body with my milk. Two of the three came; the third would not come. I know now the reason, because the Earth Mother had touched his heart with pity."

She told me all this with dry eyes and in quiet tones.

"Will you answer one question about the babe?" I asked. "I must know the full measure of my evil-doing, or I can never atone."

"A Christian priest would tell you that atonement is in your power. That is almost beyond my credence. But I want you to know the full measure. Ask the question."

"Was my son well-formed and without blemish? Was he strong and well?"

"He was well-formed and without blemish. He sucked with great force and much noise. I named him Lear after his great ancestor, who was mighty even when uncrowned, driven forth on the wild moor, and mad."

"I have little else to say, except that I too went mad when a voice of evil foretold that a babe born in South Cambria on the last day of summer would inherit my throne and crown. Now I will go."

"Artay, I have something else to say. I want you to hear it, so if again you believe you are a God and not a mortal man, at least the darling of the Gods, you will check the pride that again will turn malignant and destroy you as you destroyed your first-born. You are not wholly to blame for your terrible puffing-up. Merdin must bear part of it, for his deceits, to one of which I was party, although I rue it now. The Song of Camlon is ancient, and some of it was of no doubt inspired by the Gods, but Merdin made cunning use of it, to persuade not only the people but you yourself, that you alone, of all men, was their choice to be King of Britain."

"What else could I believe, Elain, when one prophecy after another came true? If you tell me that this too was a cheat——"

"Artay, I think you are descended from Lear, and are Vortigern's eldest son," she broke in, in deep solemnity. "How it came about, I know not, but this much I had from my sire, Llewelan, plighting his troth. Perhaps your mother was a bawd, perhaps a favorite, but I do not believe it was Queen Ina, as Merdin told you; there is no evidence that she ever bore a son before she was slain to make room for Enid. And it comes to me that when you know the truth, it will be more terrible than in your darkest dreams. If Llewelan knows— and I think he does—he would not tell me. Out of Vortigern's conceiving you was born his hate of you, that much my sire let fall, and that hate is most real, and can never end until one of you two dies. But I do not believe that he exposed you in the forest for beasts to eat. That part was Merdin's lie, or so I think, because in the Song of Camlon it is told that the King of Britain who would arise was found in a wild boar's burrow."

"Elain, you have yourself seen and touched the holes front and back in my shoulders made by the teeth of Droit."

"Made by two little cones of bone which Merdin thrust into your baby shoulders, a little deeper every day, dipped in vinegar, which is the soured juice of the apple, the fruit of life, and hence purifying a wound against putrefaction. Llewelan found the two pieces in a tiny wooden casket which Merdin once forgot to replace in his chest. The boar you call Droit was a big boar, famed for his fierceness, that

291

dwelt in the forest eastward of Collen Village. A churl was hired to draw him forth with repeated baits of corn, and Merdin kept him there until he was ready, for no hog, wild or tame, will roam far from rich feasting. It was not enough for Merdin that he be old and fierce; also he must eat men, to make the people believe he was indeed Droit of the Song, and so your heart would be hot against him. Who better for him to eat than the King's man Ian, companion of Riis, who sought to kill you with his ax at the Fish Fair, and whom Cavell killed? It was not Droit who made away with Ian, but very Merdin. And who better for you to find lying dead, his side gashed, than Griffith, the drunken slave who years before had profaned Merdin's harp, and whose life had been spared awhile for this very need? Yet the fight you fought with the great beast under the canyon walls was full fair— it was one of the tests Merdin put to you, to find out if you were fit to rule Cambria and, so his dreams sped, all Britain. Merdin would cheat the people, but never himself, and he was the last of the great Druids, and he loved his homeland with a deathless love, and when it came to achieving his great design, his heart was as hard as—yours."

She need not have said this last to remind me where that same design had fetched me. I had listened to her exposure of the monstrous stratagem worked upon me—I could not say against me—without beads of sweat bursting from my pores, so sick was my heart as I gazed into her face and perceived what I had lost.

"Behind every great conqueror there stands a wise old man, or perhaps a wondrous woman, or so Llewelan told me," Elain went on. "Behind Alexander there were both, his mother and a Greek magician whose name my father gave as Aristotle. Behind the first and greatest Caesar there were both, his mother, who was sometimes called Cornelia, and the great soldier Marius. Behind Attila, of our grandsire's time, there was at least a woman of great power over him, his affianced wife, whose name I have forgotten. Behind you stands terrible Merdin."

"Will you tell me the other cheats put on me, so I may measure what truth is left?" I asked.

"From whose hand did you take Caliburn? Not from the hands of a fairy, dwelling in the bottom of the mere, but from mine. He was a sword once worn by a Cambrian king. Merdin told my sire it was

Hugh the Mighty, but that Llewelan doubted. Artay, I have lived on or about waters all my days. I can swim as far as I can walk. Do you remember the two swans whose taking puzzled you when we were at Pillicock Hill? They were laving in a pool, and Pillicock and I swam under water, caught them by the feet, and drowned them. Do you remember a heavy patch of floating weed only a short way from where I brandished the Sword? I had only to swim back to it to get my breath, and forth again. I wore a cow's-bladder filled with air on the small of my back, to offset the weight of the Sword. Merdin asked my sire, Llewelan, that I practice the deceit, so you would have no doubt of your choosing by the Gods, and he agreed, and I was easy to persuade, for I loved you even then. Now I wish that I had not loved you, and not played the trick. In a sense that self-same Sword, the Sword of the King, cut off my babe's life."

"You know by now that Vivain came to me with the prophecy that an infant born on the last day of summer——"

"Yes," she broke in quickly, wiping away the first tears I had seen her shed, "although at first I did not believe it, or any mitigation of your awful deed. My father had it from the follower of Aran, your executioner, the one who did not come to the island, and the only one of the three who is still alive."

"How did they die? Did the Gods strike them down?"

"No, Pillicock swam under their boat, upset it, and pulled them down. Afterward he brought up their bodies and buried them in a secret place."

"Then he has the right to kill me, too, and bury me in the same place. I would not raise a hand against him."

"He will not harm you. He knows, as I do, that you had broken with humanity in your great pride of place, and when you had seen a thousand young men die to win you that place, what mattered to you the lives of one, or two, or three new-born babes, if thereby you could retain it? It is a madness that afflicts all kings. Murder spawns like maggots in carrion about a throne, and that is why I would never sit one, even if a just king, not a slayer of babes, would set the crown on my head. Now both of us have said all that can be said. It comes to me we will never meet again. Now return to your palace and your throne and to the great wars you must yet wage to be King of Britain, and if under your rule the people wax and the beasts wane, and you are not a tyrant, and you serve Britain before your own wickedness, then the Gods' wrath will be assuaged, even as is hinted in the Song of Camlon. But never dream that the innocent blood you shed must not exact from you some awful price. And it must be that not all my love for you has turned to hate, as usually it seems, for now I tremble for you in my inmost heart."

"It is a great boon. And not now will I return to my throne and put on my crown. I have appointed Gerald to rule in my place, and I go on a long journey."

"Will you tell me where? I cannot help but ask. The hope of a whole people lies in you, despite the evil you have done."

"Why, I'll go to a lonely moor, where the only shape of man that I may see will be my own image in its black pools. I will live with the wind and the mist and the rain. Do you remember the song you sung to me? *Gone are white blossoms and little bird's fife*. When they return it may be I will also, but I do not know. It lies in the hands of the Gods."

"*White was my blossom, my perfume sweet*. Truly it was, for you alone. *Now I pass him unknown, he is deaf, he is blind*. Yet I ask a boon, my liege. Take Pillicock with you."

"No, I want him to stay with you."

"I do not need him now. What is there to harm me? The snake has bitten me, and crawled away. But Vortigern and Modred bide their time. An enemy lies in wait, wherever you turn. Grant my boon, Artay, for the sake of what is lost. You wish to see no man's shape, but Pillicock's shape is that of a dwarf, despite his manliness within. I ask you again—take him with you."

I looked into her eyes and answered.

"Then I will."

She called him and he came out of the thickets, tears streaming down his coarse face, as on that day she had sung to me on Pillicock Hill. He kneeled beside her and she stroked his rough hair.

"There, there, dear Gnome," she told him. "I told you you could stay with me all my life, except when you served Artay in war, and this war that he wages now is with the Powers of Darkness. Go with him into the moor, and when the war is over, bring him back safely to the folk who need him. I charge you, Gnome. I am Elain of the Lake."

"And I am Pillicock the Monster and I will go with the King."

4

Pillicock and I made our lonely way to the most desolate moor in all Cambria. He brought his sling, an ax for fuel-cutting, and the clothes on his back; I had Caliburn and my shield and a Mendip bow and quiver of arrows which a chieftain had given Llewelan, and which Elain had given me at our parting to help us sustain our lives. Also we had our small foodbag, and the fishing and snaring tackle I had brought on my southward journey.

At the wind-sheltered foot of a Tor we cut sod and built a rude hut, with a roof of bushes that would emit smoke and shed rain. For fuel we cut wood in the low forest on the flank of the Tor or used dried turf from marshy spots, which burned smokily yet giving forth grateful heat. There was never a question of our getting enough to eat. Pillicock was adept at snaring hares and heath-hens; when we wanted fish we found them in any pond; the arrows that I launched and carefully reclaimed supplied our larder with wild ducks and geese, but I never shot swans, thinking of them floating on Swan Lake and a swan-white damosel who dwelt there.

I cannot say that I wrestled with evil spirits. Indeed, there were none that I knew of in or about this whole expanse of lonely moor, and the strange thought struck me that if they existed at all, they were somehow a projection, perhaps only a kind of shadow, of human beings. I bade Pillicock tell me a detailed story of the birth and the murder of my son Lear, which he did manfully, knowing my sick soul's need ere again it might be whole. Meanwhile I had stood Caliburn in a corner and hung my shield on a peg thrust in the wall, and both might have rusted in this damp climate had not Pillicock kept them shimmering-bright.

Mainly my occupation was to watch birds and beasts. I had never perceived before, at least with clarity and a thrilling heart, how beautifully they were made and colored, and how wondrously they performed the functions which Nature expected of them, each in his own realm, whether ground, water, tree-top, or air. The white herons wheeled and dipped like the angels of which Elain had sometimes spoken. Often I saw them stop mid-flight to look at something, then speed effortlessly on. Wild ducks winged southward in countless flocks, and no few rested or bathed or fed on our moor ponds, and the pochards were the swiftest, uncatchable by any hawk except a ger-falcon, and the mallards the most vivid to the sight by token of the young-wheat green of the drakes' heads and the startling blue of their wings, and the wigeons the most swift in taking off, and the teal the most quick to scatter and disappear.

I noticed the conduct of different kinds of beasts and birds with their own kind and with one another. Except for the meat-eaters, feathered or furred, who must kill to live, on the whole they lived at peace, courteously one might say, and no one kind denied another's right to live; and although the strongest or the most clever got their fill first, none were dogs-in-the-manger. A drake swan beat with his wings and drove away a mink who menaced the cygnets. A bitch-fox fought like a fiend a polecat who stalked her kits, and how he could have eaten such rank meat I could not guess, unless his own rankness blanketed its smell. Each beast had his own burrow, in the defense of which he would die, and I reckoned that the burrow of the king was his whole realm, and he must fight to his last breath against invaders, and I would do the same with a high heart, if again I donned my crown. As for taking the realms of other kings, I had only fierce, rapacious eagles to set me an example. No wonder the Romans had carried bronze eagles on a stick, and it might be I would have one painted on my banner.

The pleasant autumn slowly succumbed to the assault of winter. Wildly the wind blew, and when it rested, the sky-blue waters of the shallow pools turned into gray ice. Most of the waterfowl took off in clamoring flocks, and the fish would not bite our bait, and Pillicock and I would have been hard put to it to fill our bellies except for the catch of his snares and a magnificent red-deer stag that I shot in the wood. It was no comfort to go abroad on these bitter days, yet I did so, tramping far and wide with no aim that I knew, and Pillicock strode manfully beside me.

The winter fought a delaying action against blithe spring, but could not balk her long, and one morning she was ensconced in the whole land, the gray grass suddenly green, the ponds sky-blue, waterfowl returning from their refuge in the South, small birds chirping in great joy, fish swirling in the runnels, animals in new fur, flowers bursting to bloom, and the marsh-hawks shrieking in ecstasy over rich feeding now in store, and the marsh-donkeys braying all night. It came to me then that resuscitation was the gift of the Great Gods, that sickness came and either killed or passed away, and no disaster this side of death was irremediable, and perhaps after death there was some kind of waking on its other side. And on May Day, Pillicock and I saw what looked like two moving upright sticks a long way off. We watched them climb a Tor, stand and gaze, descend, then make their way toward our hut.

One of them proved to be my chief scout, Glyn; the other was a captain I knew as Alan, one of my best. They kneeled to me, and at my bidding took off their clothes drenched from wading, and hung them by my smoky fire. Then they covered their loins in respect to me, and Glyn, who knew me better than the other although his rank was lower, spoke to me first.

" 'Ee General, who 'ee call Gerald, bid me seek 'ee out."

"How did you know where to find me?"

"The wench Elain told me 'ee would come to this moor, because the dwarf tell her 'fore her left wi' 'ee, her would bring 'ee here."

I thought I had made the decision myself. "Speak on."

"By 'ee leave, Alan will tell 'ee what Gerald say."

"Not only what he said, but what's common knowledge," said the tall captain. "My liege, first I must catch you up on what seems ancient history now, although it has all happened since my General was made regent. Late last fall Malcolm, King of Midland, died, whether from sickness or poison no one seems to know, nor does it matter. As you would expect, Vortigern took his crown."

"Yes, I would have expected that of my father. He's a purposeful man."

"After your conquest of the Severn Valley both of their royalties had quit Lester to establish their capital at Warwick on the Avon. This happened before the regency, as you know. There Vortigern fell foul of Uther, King of the Avon and the Stour, and Loth, King of the Thames. We could hardly bring ourselves to believe that in six weeks Uther and Loth both were overthrown, one beheaded, the other sent into exile, and Vortigern had proclaimed himself King of Eastern Britain."

"I can hardly believe it now," I said, my sweat starting and my voice thick.

"It is only too true, but you have not heard the worst. At Vortigern's first court, he put aside Enid, and wedded Rowena, the daughter of the great Saxon chieftain Hengist, whose name you know only too well. And straightway Vortigern opened his ports to the Saxons, and they are swarming in like bees to honeysuckle."

"Are you mad?" I demanded. "Even Vortigern would not sell out his native land to the horned-hat pirates."

"Alas, I am not mad. My liege, I am telling you the truth, which Glyn will attest. Vortigern has made a pact with Hengist, which kings call a treaty, and the meat of it is if Hengist helps him recapture your realm and the Midland Plain and permits him to hold all lands west of the Test, the Upper Thames and the Upper Trent and to the summit of the Pennine Chain, the pirate chieftain can have all the rest for a province of Saxony. It is my duty to tell you Hengist has already seized Kent and Thanet. The Britains who lived there are dead or are chained thralls. It seems fairly certain that when his power is great enough, he'll turn on Vortigern and take all."

"How great are the combined forces of Vortigern and Hengist?" I asked quietly. Not that this mattered just now.

"Over three thousand, and increasing every day."

"Have you any personal message for me from my General?"

"Only this. I will quote him word for word. *Come back, King Artay, if you yet live. I can lead an army but I cannot rally and unite the people. Only you can save Britain.*"

Vaguely mindful of a prophecy, I rose from my seat, took up Caliburn and my shield, put one on my arm, and belted the other at my side.

"Is the Sword in good edge, and the shield aglint?" I asked Pillicock. "I can hardly see in this dark hole."

"As fair as when you fought Vortigern in the Vale," he answered.

"In that case, assemble our gear quickly. Captain, have you and Glyn eaten dinner? We have good meat and honey-mead."

"We ate on the top of yon Tor."

"Then dress, for we march at once."

I had held my voice down, so as not to appear boastful in the hearing of the Gods or my followers. Still, the room seemed a little brighter, I knew not why, unless it was from the shining of three faces. And perhaps my face shone a little too, for the thought struck me that if the Gods had heard—and who can say they did not lean down to hear my answer to Gerald's message?—it had done more to modify their wrath than the sacrifice of a hundred spotted bulls.

Chapter Fourteen

Trial by Battle

In the two-day march of us four travelers to rejoin our army on the east bank of the Exe, we passed within two hours' journey of Swan Lake. I had nothing to say to Elain to help my cause, I had only a mighty longing to lay eyes on her, but since in the southeast Saxons were swarming ashore every hour of the day, we did not turn aside. We came to the west bank of the river shortly after nightfall. There, at the rendezvous Alan and Gerald had arranged, we found fifty of my men, sent across to erect a pavilion for me and guard me through the night. My great General wished me to present myself before the main force in the bright of morning.

Here, too, Merdin and Gerald were waiting, but neither showed his face until I had entered the pavilion and I had put on my ermine cloak, my rings, broaches, and necklace of gold, and seated myself on a bench with my crown on my head. Then Merdin came in, his old eyes burning, and kneeled to me.

I gave him my hand and raised him to his feet. "I come not as a conqueror, but as the vanquished," I said. "Why have you received me with this ceremony?"

"Your worst self vanquished your better self," the Archdruid answered. "Great evil has been done against the Gods, but now the tables will be turned, the true King will again prevail, and by victories with the Sword you will assuage their wrath."

"Some of it, but not all. Yet I will fight the Saxons until I am victorious or overwhelmed. Have you news for me?"

"All the news is evil, concerning the waxing of Vortigern's power and that of the alien Hengist, who flies his banners in the holy air of Britain. Also, another disaster has befallen us since Alan's departure. It will be my task to seek to retrieve the loss before I die—I ask no more than that, and to see you crowned King of Britain. The head of Bran, who went before us in the battle, has been stolen from my lodge."

"His spirit will go before us yet."

"That I believe, but the soldiers need him in their plain sight, to bolster their spirit for the great war soon to break."

"If you hope to recover him, it must be that you believe he was not burned or drowned in deep water, but hidden, or delivered to the enemy."

"The jar of precious oil in which he reposed was also stolen. I believe he has been buried in some secret grave, until the stealers, traitors to your throne, can recover him for the uses of the enemy. I did not guard him with enough vigilance. And that is why, when my faltering course has run, I will come to a cruel death, as was foretold by an Archdruid at my nativity. Now I go from you, that you may receive Gerald, who will speak of things of far greater moment than the wailings and the prayers of an old Druid."

"Except for you, great Merdin, the good things that have happened would have not happened; and if I had perceived your greatness in its full, which was made known to me at last by Elain, the evil things that have happened would have not happened likewise; and I would have conquered Vortigern before he betrayed Britain."

"Elain also told you of my tricks and stratagems. This she has revealed to me. I did them that Vortigern's hated son might become King of Britain, and the evil that he did against the Gods be avenged by your own hand, the rightful hand. Will you tell me in full truth that you harbor no hate against me in your heart, even for the wounds that I put upon a helpless babe? If you cannot tell me that, my course is already run, and I know not what I will do to hasten the savage death awaiting me, but I will do something."

"Who am I to harbor hate in my heart for trickery, and for trifling wounds you gave me in my infancy, I who have dealt my own heart and the heart of my true love a grievous wound that can never wholly heal? In your score of years of service to me, you believed you were serving the blessed land you love, and it may be that your belief will yet be proven truth. Even so, I ask a boon. You speak again of my being son to Vortigern, descendant of great Lear. Others have told me so who would not knowingly tell me a lie, but sometimes in the middle of the night on the lorn moor I doubted this also. Has the time come to tell the secret of my nativity? If so, I entreat that you do so, for good or evil, and it will not diminish the fury of my war against the invader."

"Artay, it is most evil, yet as I stand before the Gods, you are indeed the son of Vortigern, descendant of great Lear. More I cannot say, for my lips are closed by a vow unto Lud, Tyr, the Earth Mother, the head of Bran, witnessed by flowing water at my feet, by massive oaks spreading their branches above my head, by the sky arching over me, by the invisible wind, by the ground on which I stood that gives forth corn that the folk may live. Howbeit, if you live to conquer the invader of our Britain, I will tell you where to go, where lies buried in silence the dread secret of your nativity, and it may be you can bring it forth, and take the toll owed to us both."

"I love you, Merdin, and I wish that your blood also flowed in my veins, along with great Lear's. Now you have my leave to go."

2

Gerald, entering and kneeling, was his compact, calm self, the stress of his regency in my absence unapparent in his dark face. He kissed my hand, and then he told me why he had had me stay tonight on this side of the river instead of crossing over to the main body of my followers. Much rumor had been whispered of my disappearance. Some believed I had been slain, others that I lay in enchanted sleep. Even my fifty guardsmen only half-believed as yet in my return; the glimpses of me that they had had, unrobed and uncrowned, had not persuaded them I was really Artay the King. Gerald wished me to appear before my army suddenly, in full regalia, in bright morning.

He spoke first of the princes and people of the lands I had conquered—Monmouth, Cornwall and the Exe, and the Valley of the Severn. There had not been the slightest wavering of their allegiance. The Gods knew it was not in love of me, in Cador's case, or in others whose power had been reduced, but in plain terror of the Saxons. Great folk believed it better to bow before me, a rustic from the Taff, than to be butchered by Saxon axes; and churls who had no land to lose at least had a measure of freedom which they did not wish to change for a dog's stake and rope of slavery. Only those who were slaves already cared naught for the coming war; they alone could sleep dreamlessly as swine.

The thought came to me that if I conquered, I would free all slaves born in Britain, and no longer permit rich merchants to buy up debtors, and prisoners taken in wars between petty kingdoms, and have them shipped away and sold in Rome.

The Saxons well-earned their terrible fame, Gerald told me. Before attacking they threw their iron-headed javelins, then rushed in a close press, and because they fought with short weapons, hatchets and double-edged daggers a foot and a half long, they did not fall foul of one another. Thus they wrought great carnage. Their weakness lay in their shields, of beechwood bossed with iron to protect the hand. To take advantage of it, our soldiers must keep their heads in the uproar of battle, thinking coolly, waiting their chance for a shrewd thrust. The mere appearance of the enemy aroused terror, from their being uniformly tall, and savagely bearded. Many wore helmets of wild-boar hide, from which protruded horns or tushes. Often they went into a frenzy of fury, which they called the Berserker's Way, and at all times they made a hideous din by calling on their War God, Woden. Rarely would they retreat or yield if the leader of their company had been killed, for unless they conquered they would follow him into dark death.

"Our soldiers can parry the hurled spears with their iron shields," I said.

"Yes, they can, in the main."

"I doubt if any thrown weapon is of much use to an army, since mastery of it takes too long to learn. Hurling axes is an old sport in Cambria, yet how many of our yokels can throw straight enough to make the bronze ax useful in battle? Only a few score. It seems to me the Saxons would do better to use their javelins as thrusting-spears."

"I have thought so, and thank our Gods that Hengist has not thought so."

"Both of us know where five hundred thrusting-spears, made by the Romans, lie waiting for soldiers' hands to pick them up."

"I have considered them, lying neglected in the chalk chamber of Pillicock Hill, but the time is short, our trained soldiers none too many, and I thought best for them to keep the arms that they know well."

Then with a prickling skin, I asked what seemed a casual question.

"Have the invaders brought horses, for courtiers to ride, for transport, and for swift communication in battle?"

"No, there was no room in their crowded boats for horses. Hengist's and Vortigern's aim was to land as many soldiers as possible to outnumber greatly the armies that opposed them, to win a quick and crushing victory. They use horses they have foraged here for the purpose you name."

"Gerald, could our present forces do a holding action against the armies of Hengist and Vortigern for about three months, without greatly depleting our strength?"

"Yes, my liege, I think we could, if we choose good stands, such as hilltops, fords, roads through the forests, passes through the marshes. But mark, their losses would be replaced by new arrivals from Saxony, whose women must farrow like sows to make the multitude of fair-haired howlers; and who would take the place of those we lose?"

"Would it be possible to enlist five hundred yokels in Cambria, Monmouth, and Cornwall, provided we could arm them well, and promise them a noble part not in the worrying skirmishes but in one, great, final battle, where we could risk all?"

"My King, I believe that we could. Women and old men and younkers under sixteen would till the fields and tend the flocks and herds if they would hold fair hope of your turning back the Saxons and crushing Vortigern, the traitor-king. If we would enlist men as old as thirty-five, I am sure we could."

"The Mendip archers are nearer forty. I want settled men for the chore I have in mind, for it demands no great endurance, and they would be steadier, and more patient."

"I still cannot surmise what the chore might be. The terrain permitted our great stratagem at White Water, but in the open lands——"

"Gerald, could we also take up five hundred horses from all the lands that we dare enter, on the excuse of preventing their seizure by the enemy, and have made five hundred saddles that need be no more than flatboards on top, wide enough for lean Cambrian bottoms, flaring sideboards for skirts, and strong leather cinches?"

"Perhaps so, my liege, but what would be the use? All horses plunge at the smell of blood, and our rustics could not sit such saddles, or even better ones."

"I think they could sit them if we would hang a loop of leather on each side, for the support of the rider's feet. Once when I rode our old mare Llamrei up a steep hillside to chase a wounded stag, I fixed ropes to the sides of the saddle, and they proved a boon. Our recruiters could take two months to collect the men and horses, while old men, handy with knives, would shape saddles. Then for one month the recruits would be trained on a lonely moor—for a single charge on horseback, each with a spear in his free hand, which he could thrust with fair aim, attacking the enemy's flank or rear. Gerald, my old friend, might it not tip the balance in a close contest? If we were losing, might it not turn the tide? I ask for your fair opinion."

"My liege, I think that it would. The Goths fought on horseback, and they had not merely loops of leather in which to brace the feet, but a flat rest of wood or metal, never seen before, hung on a strap, and they enveloped and crushed many a Roman legion. Britain was conquered by foot-soldiers—and other ways of making war have been forgotten here. By the Great Gods! There is no time to train armed horsemen for maneuver, but one ferocious charge with spears—why not?"

"And who could school the riders and lead the charge?" I asked bluntly.

"My liege, it is too soon for me to propose any one, but the thought strikes me that you have considered this also. By the choice of an able leader, the venture is half-won, or at least its aspect changes from shadow to substance."

"Why not Alan, who came with Glyn to summon me from the moor? He is one of your best captains. His voice has a ring that lifts men's hearts. His mother was a wild woman of the River Boyne, and he spent his later boyhood on an Irish horse-farm, and served a season as a charioteer under the King of Kildare."

Gerald replied with only a half-nod, and plainly did not wish to discuss the matter any more tonight. He wanted to go to bed and think. Long-assured of the steady power of his thinking, I let it drop.

In the dawn ten big trawlers assembled on our side of the river, and just before sunrise our party started across. The oars had hardly dipped when we heard shouting on the other bank, and before we were half-way over the whole army had massed there, and the yelling loudened as we came nigh, I standing in the bow of the foremost boat, wearing my bronze horse-tailed helmet, my shield on my arm, Caliburn in my hand. Oddly enough, the uproar died away as we touched land. The throng parted to make an aisle through which I could pass, and now that the rising Sun showed them clearly that their eyes had not deceived them, the men stood with almost the same expression on every face, of wonder that they could not express in words, sudden and fierce hope, and something more that I had never seen before, except on the day that Merdin had first held up the head of Bran. They remembered that they had never lost a major battle under my banner, and it must be that they had talked across many a watchfire about those heart-stirring times, and in my absence the fame of them had turned to wondrous legend. Suddenly a tall yokel gave a great shout.

"Art-Tyr!"

Now the prefix meant God in the old tongue of Cambria, and as Art-Tay meant the God Mercury, Art-Tyr meant the God of War. The Great Gods knew I was no God, or no kin to one unless Lear had descended from the Gods, as story told, and I would never again half-yield to the illusion, but I was full-willing that the men should believe I was Tyr's avatar, now that they must face, under my banner, the greatest threat to Britain since the landing here of the first Caesar.

"Not Artay, but Artyr," another shouted, slurring the hyphenated name to make it sound more human, removing some of its grandeur, but better suiting the ears of the throng. And so I was dubbed, for far and wide the men were shouting it, and then they fell into chorus, and a great rhythmic roar went up to that very God, as he sat at his table above the dome of the sky, his sword girded, his shield on his arm, his battle-ax at hand, his war-dog crouching at his side, his war-horse waiting at his door, his grisly feast spread before him, his drinking-cup of Gargantua's skull in his hand, his brain plotting battles more bloody than ever fought before.

Artyr! Artyr! Artyr! Artyr!

The name was not far removed from Arthur, not an uncommon Cambrian name. So I was thinking as I stood with my shield and my Sword raised, and I would take it for my own if I could win the war and if, somehow, at long last, win Elain. And I would win both if life remained that long in my body, and strength in my big hands, and ardor in my heart, and the light of my great cause in my soul.

3

Whether Gerald called this a withdrawal in strength, or a holding action, it remained bloody and dire war.

When we engaged the army under Vortigern's banner, who were mainly men of the Midland Plain, and those who had followed Loth and Uther, always we held our own and frequently advanced. The hearts of these sons of Britain were downcast and ashamed that they were fighting their own countrymen in the service of a sea-rover from Jutland, who knew not our Gods, and they shrank from our swift steel. But when the Saxons led the attack in numbers greater than ours, often we must give way to prevent our slaughter, and then our troops thanked Heaven for their long and tedious drilling, because their orderly retreat never turned into a rout. Where the ground was favorable, they established new lines, from whence their iron fangs could slash again and send many of the fair-haired heathen to their false Gods.

Often we ambushed and killed their scouts, and again and again our swift runners fetched a circle and smote them on the flank, and eleven times in the waning and waxing of three moons, our whole force was engaged against Hengist's and Vortigern's whole force in battle hot, fierce, and savage beyond telling, yet not decisive. It was little comfort to Gerald and me that their losses were far greater than ours, for their numberless dead were replaced by new arrivals from Jutland, and ours would bleed our army white if we did not conquer soon.

We had fought clean across the Plain of Sarum, from Avon of the South to the Avon of the West before we came to the Hill of Badon, where Gerald had planned to make our great stand. The word passed among our soldiers that tomorrow we would conquer, and rid the land of the brutish invader, or at least pinion him in Kent and Thanet, where he had strongly settled; and if we did not conquer we must yield him all of Britain except dear Cambria, guarded by its hills, and there would be no peace in Britain in our lifetimes or the lifetimes of our sons. Veterans, they saw for themselves that the place of our great trial was well-chosen. We occupied high ground that could not be outflanked, and the foe must first fight his way across a bold, wide stream before he could begin his ascent, and our men vowed that this ascent would be unto his heathen heaven.

One hour before sundown an officer stood forth from the enemy host holding a white flag, and this invitation to parley we accepted by showing a white flag. The officer came forward, meeting one of our officers, and they spoke but briefly ere our delegate returned with strange word. It was that Modred, elder son of Vortigern, wished speech with Artyr, King of West Britain, in view of both hosts, and that Hengist would plight his troth not to move a man against us, during that intercourse, if Gerald, Artyr's General, would make the same pledge.

I suppose I should have been astonished at this invitation. I had not seen hide or hair of my antagonist throughout the campaign, and took it he had become Vortigern's ambassador to the King of the Brigantes, or perhaps to Gaul, or even to very Rome. For that matter, I had not laid eyes on Vortigern, whose great affairs kept him out of the front ranks, although we had all seen Hengist and his brother Horsa in the thick of the fray, shouting unto Woden. The truth was, nothing that Modred could do on earth would surprise me very greatly, except his being false to himself.

I accepted gladly, and at once we two tall men were walking toward each other in the clear sunlight of late afternoon, and his sword and shield looked mirror-bright, and mine likewise glimmered, and his face was bright as though with happiness at our reunion; and mine had flushed, to judge by its pleasing warmth. I stopped at our side of the stream, because I was the higher in rank; he nodded in acknowledgement of this and waded staunchly across. Then we seated ourselves on the pleasant grass, he less awkwardly than I, for he was a more supple man.

"I trust you are well, Artyr, and fairly whole," he told me, his head cocked and his eyes shining in their wont.

"I have three trifling wounds, healing well," I answered, "which are more than you can show."

"My wound is in the heart. I have no part in these evil doings of our sire. I mean, of course, his deal with Hengist—as for fighting you, he has every right, or at least abundant motive, considering what's between you. Like some famous fellow whose name your Roman

General would know, I have sulked in my tent. Now I must do what I promised Hengist, in order to get his permission to parley with you. I am to make certain statements, the truth of which seems rather apparent—although now and then you have made appearances a liar. Then I am to offer you certain terms."

"Why bother with the statements? They are that I am outnumbered, my strength is waning while his is waxing, that ultimate defeat and death are certain unless I yield. Now get to the terms, so we can clack our tongues on more pleasant matters."

"Your surmise is wonderfully accurate. The terms are more generous than you would expect. Hengist is not happy over his losses, as no one knows better than you. Also he puts no more trust in Vortigern, our royal sire, than do you or I. Despite my father's wrath, he promises you all Cambria to you and your heirs forever. He swore it with his hand on his talisman, and in the name of Woden, and he would die before he breaks his oath. Our father is to have the whole Valley of the Severn, eastward to the Trent, and northward to the Mersey and the Don. Hengist will take the lion's share, all South Britain, including Cornwall, all Eastern Britain, and most of Central Britain. Mark that he puts our father between himself and you, which is a compliment to your prowess as a conqueror. At the same time he outflanks your southern border, and he could make quick work of crossing Sabrina, for the fellow knows ships and walks like a duck."

"I guessed some of what you had to say. Now guess what I have to say."

"Firstly, that you'll not yield an acre of Britain, except Kent and Thanet, which are already lost through settlement there of Angles, Saxons, and Jutes. Secondly, that you'll yield to our father only enough land for the gallows to hang him, which is more than the traitorous dog deserves. Thirdly—but I reckon there's no thirdly, since you seem to have rid yourself of South Cambrian wind."

"My brother Modred, you have hit the mark."

"What rid you of that wind, my brother Artyr? And what brought that expression in your eyes, as though you had died and were journeying back from death. Wait! The journey may be short. I failed to tell you Hengist's pledge if you refused his terms. He will himself take Cambria and settle it with Saxons and wipe out the Cambrian race, man, woman, and child, since its wild heart is so hard to tame. It's a sound notion, Artyr—and I'll call you Arthur, if you don't mind, since you're no more of a God than I am, than Rufus is a gnome, than Vivain a half-witch, than Merdin a magician instead of a king-maker, than you are Queen Ina's son. A sound notion, I tell you—for thus he will bottle up Vortigern and soon dispose of him, and all Britain can become a province of Saxony. I think Hengist hopes that you will refuse his terms."

"I've already done so."

"This doesn't change it? Very well. I was hoping it would not, and tomorrow comes the great battle, with Horsa, the greatest warrior on the Continent, meaning to engage you yourself, and slay you. I fear that he will do so. I fear you are fated for dire defeat, your whole army destroyed, and the Angles, Saxons, and Jutes will take our beautiful Britain, and the bards will sing no more, and the mistletoe will die on our great oaks, and the harp will be silenced, and the poets who now rank as earls will eat scraps from the kitchens of earls. I told you that I live for pleasure. I cannot live pleasurably if Britain dies, and I will pray to my God Bacchus that you will win tomorrow's battle. And a cup of mead in my hand, I will ask that you live on, so that when the moment of destiny overtakes us both, we may engage one another at full prowess, and one of us will be slain, and the other become King. And what dreadful destiny it is, since we are not only brothers of the loins, but also brothers of the spirit!"

"Modred, my head is thick and I still do not understand."

"You will, when you drink from the Well of Silence, which is also your destiny. Now I go from you, and I think we will not meet again until that awful hour. And it may be that the King, my father, will be slain by then—so was told by Hengist's spaewoman, but that will not rid me of my obligation, for you will still be his living shame, and I must cut off and uproot you, ere his soul can find peace."

"I cannot doubt you. I see the truth in your eyes, from which the merriment has died. Nor can I protest, for I am Arthur, King of Cambria, Monmouth, Cornwall and the Exe, and the Vale of the Severn, and you are only Modred, elder son of a traitor-king. As soon as the war is over, I will seek to draw water from the Well of Silence of which you speak, and drink of it deeply. Now will you carry a message to Horsa, the great warrior who is Hengist's brother, that I will be in the front line of our forces, about in the middle, and to bid none of Hengist's followers have at me, lest the fellow's spear or ax or dagger deprive him of the glory he seeks; and if he finds me quickly, I will not seek any other adversary."

"I will give Hengist your answer, and give Horsa your challenge. And may both be backed by your great deeds, and the power of the Saxon be broken for as long as I live, that we both may live until the appointed hour for one of us to fall."

We both rose, he dropped on one knee before me, and when I gave him my hand he took it with quick, strong grasp, and by that token our fates were bound, and I need not fear Horsa, and the High Gods would not let me fall, nor could they cause me to fall, until he and I had kept our rendezvous.

4

Quick to perceive our strong position, Hengist had arrayed his veteran troops to lead the attack. Indeed, his whole front body was made up of Saxons, and again I was astonished how they laughed and made sport with one another, as might our own fellows, and I little doubted that their jokes were no more or less gross than those our rustics cracked, since the rank and file of both armies could not understand a delicate one, any more than would I. Well they knew that this was the last mirth of no small part of their number, and the mouths that roared would have dust and grass to eat in the death-struggle.

Vortigern's army was deployed behind the Saxon body, and no doubt had been ordered to fall to when the Saxons had pierced our front and driven us to frantic rout.

A trumpeter blew on a great cow-horn, at which all laughter ceased, and the men stood calm and ready. At its second sounding they began their advance, and at the bank of the stream the first and second ranks hurled spears, which most men parried by their agile shields. Yet slight miscalculations of speed and distance by a few of our fellows let the shafts plunge home. Then came the charge, which we did not wade midstream to meet. Instead, standing in shallow water, my soldiers smote the foemen laboring up from the deeps, and before we knew it, as by an evil miracle, its clear waters ran red, and dashed against the rocks which they stained red.

My followers killed so many of Hengist's front rank that we had room and time to draw back to the first table of the hillside before the second rank could kick free of the floating or sinking dead. It was on this flat that Horsa found me, and it was here that we engaged, while friend and foe pressed forward or back, and now the tide of battle was rising like a tidal bore in the funnel of the Severn when driven by strong winds on the Sea of Eire. It seemed that a wind beginning as an eerie whistle was rising to a gale and that distant, low rumbles of thunder swelled to a continuous ear-blasting roar.

At this stage in the battle my whole business was with Horsa, and I thought of nothing else, leaving it to my great General, standing on an eminence, to note where we were holding our own, or where we were beaten back, and to dispatch orders by trumpet or by runners. Never before had I fought a true master of the Saxon weapons of hatchet and dagger, and my first strategy was to hack to pieces his light linden shield; but this availed me little in the long run, for soon he dropped the iron boss and both his great hands were free to wield his close-range weapons. Leaping away from my great hacks, he would come at me like a wolf. Sometimes I parried his swift dagger or plunging ax on my trusty shield, but sometimes I must give ground, ere again I could swing Caliburn in his star-bright wheel.

Horsa gave no ground, still he was being tried to the utmost of his strength and terrible skill; and he shouted unto Woden as he aimed his death-stroke. I knew full well that in the next instant I might feel the deep-plunged iron or bronze through flesh or bone or skull. He had a like awareness of Death standing at our very sides, starting to point his finger at one of us, only to see Fortune shift again, for truly Death's hungry eyes could not keep track of the blazing action, and great Spectre though he was, he must have felt a fool.

Then a deep voice shouted in my ear from close to my side.

"Slash his left arm, my liege!"

I recognized it as the voice of Pillicock even before I grasped the words. With ease he could have felled Horsa with a stone from his sling, save that this was an appointed duel between his King and the greatest warrior in the enemy host; and I would have been shamed, and would have no choice but to put my savior to the sword. And now I saw what Pillicock had seen, that Horsa's left arm was weakening, although not from any visible wound, and its strokes were mis-aimed or fell short. Since Horsa did not understand our British speech, he was not put on guard.

As he aimed his next hatchet-blow I fell back a pace, and as his arm came fully extended I hacked down at it, a short, quartering stroke of great power. It caught him on the wrist, severing it cleanly, and hand and hatchet began their fall together. Before they hit the ground Horsa had pointed the stub at me, so that its fierce jets of blood would strike me in the face and blind me, meanwhile pouncing at me with his drawn-back dagger. I was all but taken off guard, not knowing this was commonly the last resort of the Jutish sea-rovers when a hand was cut cleanly off in battle. They called it the Red Spout, comparing it to the spouting of a whale, and often thus they turned defeat into a standoff, the two souls taking wing in the same instant and hence companions in all their wanderings amid the stars.

Just in time I dodged the red fountain and the white iron, and my next stroke cleaved Horsa's helm, skull, teeth, and neck, so that the two sides fell asunder with a horrid neatness, like a split melon still fastened to the vine. He toppled backward, and after a brief catch of my breath, I gazed over his body to the moiling troops.

Our front still held, but had been forced back to the very crown of the hill, and the lines were thinning fast; the Saxons were shouting a high shaking shout that usually presaged victory. A glance to the field showed Vortigern's army advancing at double quick to break our last resistance and share the carnage. And then, that instant, I saw something from the corner of my eye. As I stared the wondrous truth blazed in my brain. A body of horsemen of at least five hundred led by Alan belted down the almost unclimbable steep of the hill, and no horse or rider tumbled, and swiftly they cut across the hillside until they enveloped the enemy lines, and attacked him on the flank.

The Gods must have shouted in their high seats to see the great charge, the down-slanted spear-points thrusting into the enemy bosom, and few of them missed their aim, and if so the target was knocked down and trampled by the maddened horses. My footmen surged down the hillside they had lately yielded to fall upon the remnants of

315

the line, and the slaughter grew gigantic, souls taking off in companies until I thought I heard the whistle of their swift dispatch, and the sky must have filled with them as when great flocks of waterfowl take wing at once from the Severn marshes. Then I too stopped shouting in exultation to look for Vortigern's army. If he struck with fierceness now he might yet save enough of the foe so that they could retreat, rebuild, and remain a menace to Britain.

Vortigern did not strike with fierceness. He did not strike at all. What was once his army, now a mob, hustled on his heels as he made off on his horse. He was heading for a nearby forest, whose heavy growth would shield its retreat, but I knew it would never again be a power in Britain.

All I could think of was Modred's face, dark with shame. I looked for him in the press, and he was not on horseback with his brother Vortimer, and I saw no tall runner that might be he, and anyway, I could not picture Modred running like a scared sheep. And now I must decide whether or not to cry havoc, which cry I was strangely reluctant to give, although I knew not why. And then I perceived there was no need, for although Hengist and a handful of followers had been surrounded and captured, their preservation likely promised by my long-headed General, the remaining Saxons who yet lived fought savagely on, to kill a few more of us before they joined their comrades in dread death, and these were being annihilated. As I watched and listened, their numbers swiftly dwindled, and their cries to Woden became far apart and faint and soon ceased altogether, and an awesome silence closed over the blood-soaked field.

5

Before I could come up to Gerald and he to me, both of us walking swiftly toward each other, I rejoiced that Hengist was not among the fallen. His oath, if he would give it, to keep a treaty of peace was worth a thousand times more to Britain than his red corpse.

The business was done briskly—indeed, with almost unbelievable dispatch, considering its great moment. We spoke together through one of my spies who knew the Saxon tongue. I did not mention the rope, let alone torture; I did not put upon him the slightest humiliation, for the direness of his defeat spoke silently in his ear with more eloquence than any windy South Cambrian could employ. He took oath before Woden that in his own lifetime and that of his sons, he would reign over his own folk settled in Kent, Thanet, and on the South Downs, and not stir out of these dominions, and their coast would be closed to his countrymen in their bright-sailed ships, and their numbers would grow only by natural increase.

A fellow who could write Latin set this down on two pieces of parchment, and Hengist and I fixed our mark to each, and he took one and I the other, and before I knew it, he and his handful had departed and grew small on the empty plain; and I wished I had a mirror into which to gaze, for gazing back at me in wonder I would behold the King of Britain.

On the body of Hengist's treasurer, we found a small sack of gold coins, and these I had smelted to make the crown of Cambria stand higher and more massive. In it the goldsmith set a handful of jewels, taken from the fingers and neck-plates of some of his great earls who lay dead on the field.

I did not go to Ludton to be crowned, as did some kings of old, partly because the once great city had dwindled to a dismal village, and partly because it was too far to march my army without great cost to the war-torn countryside, and I meant for the men to see the ceremony at any cost.

It was performed on an open plain in view of the ruined baths of Aquae Sulis, and took only a minute. Merdin carried the splendid crown on a fine pillow; Gerald took it and handed it to me; I set it on my head. When both had knelt to me I restored it to Merdin's care, then donned my helmet with its horse-tail plume, and reviewed the troops. It was again a business of straightening shoulders, punching bellies, chiding, and praising, a business as familiar now as tending their cooking-pots, but they were pleased with it, and when I was done they shouted Artyr to the high skies.

Then I called for a birchbark horn, and after one shouting cohort after another had caught sight of it and fallen silent, I roared through it loud enough to wake the ghosts of pot-bellied Roman officials taking ghostly baths.

"Soldiers of the King! Ere you wet your throats with ale, I bid you shout again. I led you to battle and was crowned as Artyr, but now the land is at peace, and I was never the God of War, and instead a rustic from the Taff, and here and now I take the good Cambrian name of Arthur. Sound it before the Gods!"

Chapter Fifteen
The Great Druid

After sounding the name forth with great vehemence, the shouters feasted. I reflected in solemn wonder that they could drink themselves into a stupor, if they so chose, without risk of an enemy army falling upon them in their helplessness; for my scouts had reported Vortigern's rabble breaking up into motley bands, each seeking its own path of flight, as though to escape by any means the plague of disaster that had fallen upon their recent King. The only other armed force south of Hadrian's Wall was the Brigantes, and they were busier than beavers trying to turn back the innumerable horde of Painted Caledonians who swarmed across its ruin.

Even so, with a few exceptions my troops drank with moderation. Perhaps they could not yet believe that a parcel of blood-thirsty Hecanas would not at any moment burst from the woods, or that a force of Saxons, escaping the count of my spies, would not suddenly appear over the hill, shouting to Woden, and bent on massacre. It set me to thinking of Gerald's problem of the defense of my realm in the future, the maintenance of a trained army not so great as to impoverish the land, yet adequate to defend a thousand miles of zigzag coast against the wild-eyed Men of Eire and sea-rovers not under Hengist's sway. And what would I, the King, do next? I hoped to reign in peace, with Elain at my side. But how could a peaceful reign win me the world-wide fame, to be perpetuated in song and story to folk unborn, that had been half-promised me in the Song of Camlon? And what had I done or won since my parting with Elain that had brought me one step nearer to my winning her?

Perceiving the deep fatigue of battle upon all my troops, I had suffered them to eat and drink before burying our dead. What to do with the countless Saxon dead I did not know, except to leave them to the Birds of Death, whom they had held sacred to Woden, and to whom they would gladly serve a great feast in trade for Woden's favor in their hereafter. Meanwhile a hundred picked men with some knowledge of poulticing and bandaging, and of chopping off limbs and cauterizing the stumps, cared the best they could for our wounded. Also a hundred yokels from the Mersey River, dour, slow-speaking fellows notable for their honesty, collected the weapons, purses, and gold and silver ornaments from the fallen Saxons. When the revelers had rested, these two detachments took their turn at feasting, and through the late afternoon and long evening the sobered men toiled stolidly in their last office to their fallen comrades.

All of the following day the mournful work went on, while I conferred with Gerald, Merdin, and others of my leaders and good counselors as to the appointment of governors, and the establishment of the King's law in those regions lately overrun by the enemy. About the third hour after noon, a churl of our baggage train came up to Merdin, as the old man was drinking from the unsullied stream above the battlefield, and spoke to him privily. At once they went off together, and I thought no more of it until suppertime.

I had never known my great bulwark, Merdin, to be late for his vittles, let alone forgo them. When he did not appear, my anxiety became so great that I sent men to search the ruins of Aquae Sulis, thinking he had gone thence to see and muse upon some wonder of old. Others of my couriers scanned all the campground, while still others questioned the donkey-drovers, to try to find the churl who had summoned him from our parley. All but this last search was barren of result, and soon I wished to Heaven that it were likewise.

A Cornish churl came back with my messengers, without fear or guilt on his homely face. I was so frightened by now that I took great pains not to frighten him, lest it would stop him from telling a straight-forward story.

"What is your name, friend?" I asked.

"King, it be Gowan."

"What did you want of the old wizard, Merdin?"

"Why, I wanted naught o' her but to tell her what the wench gi' me a siller sixpence to tell her, and a penny would have done me well, and her was so comely and sweet, I'd ha' done it free."

"What was it that you told him?"

"'Twas only that her knew where King Vortigern's thieves had hid the head o' Bran, in a bottle o' oil it were, and they'd stuck it in a bush when they was flying from 'ee after the wondrous great battle, and if old man get her 'ee pardon for the lies her told, and 'ee pass to leave 'ee domain, her'd take old man there, and her could have the head."

"The lies she told," I muttered to myself, as in a dream. Then speaking out, but still holding my voice down, "How did the wench look? Had you ever seen her before?"

"Why, King, I'd seen her a hundred times, up until 'ee went off into the moor, and so had 'ee. Her be small and brown, wi' black eyebrows what flare up like a she-gobblin's. Her name—why, her name—it be Vivain!"

I bade the bugler blow the call to summon my troop of scouts, led by Glyn. I would have summoned my whole army save that their blundering through the forest would have mazed all footprints. Gerald looked into my face, then laid his hand on my shoulder.

"Be of good heart, my liege. Why should Vivain do harm to Merdin?"

"You shame your great office, General, when you ask that. You know the answer all too well. He has come upon the cruel death that he foresaw. Not only my heart but my realm have taken a grievous wound."

2

It hardly seemed possible that I would know Merdin's fate tonight, unless his ghost came to my waiting-place and told me. The prospect increased when the churl Gowan was able to lead Glyn to a point on the flank of the forest where he had seen Vivain waiting after she had sent him on his errand, and in which direction the old man had headed to speak to her. Glyn and his band searched the damp ground with trained and eager eyes, and in only a minute or two one of them raised a cry. He had found where the two had met and taken down a well-worn deer-trail into the dim woods.

"The wench is walking afore, the old man behind," the finder announced.

With utmost care, despite the pitching Sun that would soon end the hunt, Glyn and another fellow followed the tracks, Pillicock and I close behind them, and the remainder of the band fanning out and flanking our advance. We had gone not more than two hundred paces when Glyn glanced back at me, a dreadful darkness on his face, and shook his head. Then he stopped, pointed, called to his men to form a circle, their arms ready, around the spot he indicated, and I went forward alone.

Immediately I came upon a lately sprung deadfall which a woodsman had set in the path, no doubt to kill a red deer making for his feeding-grounds in the falling dusk. I did not even glance at its mechanics, whereby the cleanly sawed trunk of a dead, topless tree had been made to crash down across the path when a walker tripped a trigger no doubt concealed in a thorny bush. I gazed only at its catch.

Apparently Merdin had tried to leap forward as the trunk toppled, had caught his foot in the thorns, and had fallen on his side, for the mighty cudgel lay across his loins. I stooped and touched his face, expecting to find it chilled by the chill of death. But a little life was in him yet even though his thighs and pelvis had been smashed almost flat, and his broken bones thrust through the flesh.

My hand on his face arrested his swift drift into death, and he opened his eyes. I saw recognition of me come into them, and then a wonder such as I had never known, blank lineaments turning again into Merdin's face as I had seen it a thousand times, thoughtful, wise, the uncracked mirror of his mind and being, and he gave me a dim smile.

"King Arthur, the foretelling of my end, which I had told you, has come true," he said. "Not wholly, though. How often the prophecies of the Gods hit and miss in the same outcome, perhaps because of imperfect passage between them and us groping mortals! It is not a cruel death, after all. I feel not the slightest pain. My body is dead below my waist, and ere that part mortifies, my upper part will catch its chill, and it too will swiftly die, but I draw my breath with ease. And abating even further the cruelty I expected, you have found me before the wolves that prowl this forest have smelled my ruin, and gathered here to feast."

His voice, manly and resonant, was the same as when at night we two had strolled forth under the stars, and he had spoken to me of their vast designs.

"Wait in silence, Merdin, until my followers can heave off the crushing weight, and we will bear you to your tent." And I half-rose to call them.

"I pray you, Arthur, do not let them touch it, lest I die screaming in infinite pain, instead of at peace. Can you not see that my thighs are shattered into fragments, my back broken, and my loins crushed? I wish never to be moved one inch from where I lie, in life and death. The Gods have given me breath to speak with you, in my last hour, of matters momentous to your realm and to your fate, and which, coward-like, I have concealed almost too long."

"Then I will have them build a fire that I may see your face, and leave us to final parley, a last council-of-state between the King and his great maker and foremost minister."

"My liege, there is one most urgent matter demanding first attention. Only a few feet further on, the head of Bran, in his jar, sits upon a stump. Vivain pointed to him, and I saw him through a rift in the thickets, and in my haste to reach him I looked neither right nor left, and so did not see the deadfall into which she was enticing me. It may be that she made away with him, but perhaps not, in her haste to fly, and in that case, rescue him, and give him utmost care and reverence, and keep him in your treasury to leave to your heirs, for thus his great ghost will safeguard your realm forever."

So I straightway summoned Glyn to search for Bran. It had come to pass he had already found him, unstolen or even desecrated by the fleeing harpy, and at my direction Glyn set him in plain sight of Merdin's eyes and in reach of his hand, so that the first Archdruid could keep company with the last Archdruid, at this passing. Then I thought of a matter hardly less urgent, or at least as close to my heart. So I ordered that six good trackers be sent to follow the tracks of Vivain, as long as the lingering light or firebrands would reveal them, and if pursuit tonight proved hopeless, to mark the direction of her flight, so I might surmise its most likely destination.

"And the rest of you may return to camp, while Merdin confers with the King."

"My liege, I'll 'point the men for the duty, rest 'ee mind o' that, but the rest of us will not return to camp while 'ee stay here in the wood. 'Ee and the gaffer can talk till her last breath, and we'll not listen, but leave 'ee we will not."

"Your duty is to obey the King."

"My duty is to guard the King when witches range these woods, and 'ee can kill me wi' 'ee wondrous Sword, but 'ee can't make me leave 'ee."

"My mind is dazed, but do your duty as you see it."

At once Merdin's deep voice rang forth again.

"You will wonder, Arthur, that I fell into her trap, when I knew her strangeness. I can only say that since the loss of Bran, I have grieved greatly, bewailing my lapse of care; and I feared he would take dread vengeance on me and perhaps on you; and in that disorder of my faculties I clutched at a straw. And how could I dream that the hate that is her element, while of most damosels the element is love, would cause her to seek my life? True, she believed that I had balked her from becoming your Sibyl, a post by which she and her mother, Enid, hoped to obtain their goals. No little of her great flood of hate broke harmlessly against me. Stooping to look at her, as I might an imp in a bottle, I did not half grasp her dedication unto evil and perceive her histrionic powers, which in the end tricked me to my death. And in the end the very Gods employed her to make their prophecy come true."

His voice, though low, remained resonant, and I could not forbear, myself, from clutching at a straw.

"Merdin, if the tree-trunk were raised gently from your body, is it not possible that you could live, be borne in a litter, and counsel me still?"

"No, for even now my time grows brief. Henceforth I must not waste breath, and hoard it for matters of most dreadful moment. I bid you dwell briefly on the prophecies of the Song of Camlon. A stanza that you never heard foretold you would be King of Britain: this I withheld lest you reduce your great endeavors. Also it hinted that your name would go down to people yet unborn, in song and story, and your fame would equal that of the first Caesar and the great Macedonian who conquered the Ancient World. Forge your will as iron, so that this too may come to pass!"

"How may it come to pass? I have won only three battles of note. I am King of an island at the edge of the known world; beyond lies Ultimate Thule, of which Gerald spoke. Merdin, if I wage other and greater wars—in Eire, in Caledonia, in Gaul, perhaps at the gates of Rome—I will wreak havoc on our young manhood, and how then could the greatest of all the prophecies come true, that by my reign the folk will become more, and the beasts less? I pray you, even if you thus spend your last breath, tell me the answer."

"The Song is mightier than the Sword."

"I know not what you mean."

"Nor I. It is only the vision of a vision dim within my soul. Arthur, my mind wanders, and I have few moments left to speak what I must speak. Take up my harp and keep it by your hand, and let little children touch it if they will, and poor folk who love its wild sweet music, but never let it be profaned by the hand of the scornful. The hour will come when you will need its song and solace. For it comes to me that before your greatest conquest, not of kingdoms but of men's minds, you must again pass through the fire. That much is hinted in the Song of Camlon, but the language is not plain, and I speak from an inward inkling, and by the same inkling I dream that you will emerge greater than ever, and achieve immortal fame. Of that I will say no more. And this last office that I ask you to perform may of itself be like unto fire, in the way of inflicting pain."

"I accept the office before you name it."

"It is concerned with your request, which you have made thrice, that I tell you of your nativity. That I cannot do, without breaking my sealed oath, but I can tell you where you may yourself go, to know the truth you seek."

"Where? Speak quickly."

"To a mean house in the hills and woods of Taff, and there you must dip your cup in the Well of Silence, and drink it even though it be more bitter than wormwood."

"To our own house? Is that what you mean? Then the Well of Silence must be the woman Anna. She has uttered no word in my whole life."

"Nor in mine in twenty years, save once, when she was in the delirium of fever. Yet you must somehow, without harming her, persuade her to open her long-locked lips, for I cannot open mine. Even were I free from my vow, I could not tell you now. I am fading into the dark mists of death, and my mind shuns all troublesome things, and will not grasp at them, and these too fade away, along with happy things that I have known. Arthur, King of Britain,

I now depart from you. I go beyond those mists, I think to the sweet Elysian vales where heroes dwell. Have I not made you King of Britain? My liege, will you take my hand in yours?"

"It is a weak hand, Merdin, compared to yours."

"Nay I feel its strength and its living pulse. My strength departs and my pulse falters. Most strange! My last vision is of the world to come, a thousand and more years hence, changed beyond credence from the world you know, and even there your name is known, resounding still in song and story, Arthur the King!"

"Farewell, great Merdin, last of the Archdruids!"

"Farewell, my liege. And now my last vision fades, because I fade. A boon, great King! Grant me a boon."

"Aye."

"Give me your leave to go."

I bent and kissed his tear-wet cheek. His hand pressed mine, then the pressure slowly weakened, and his soul was cast from him, and I saw it winging upward through the firelit tree-tops, and far away the thunder rumbled as Lud smote his gongs of bronze, and one great flash of lightning filled all the sky, and I saw the shape of the Gods leaning down with extended hands.

Chapter Sixteen
The Well of Silence

As the night lowered, I remained sitting at the side of my dead. Often my thoughts, which ranged back through the spacious times and scenes I had spent with Merdin, caught as though in thorns, and I must confront again a matter that perplexed me to my core, which was the disposition of the mighty corpse. I thought to have made a casket of silver, studded with jewels, and have it borne in solemn march before my armies, and be interred in some historic spot in Britain, perhaps on the crest of the Hill of Badon, where we had crushed the invader and routed his traitorous ally; and there a worker in marble, brought from Rome, would erect a gigantic image, showing him with his harp under one arm, and a pole with a bronze crook, which is the sign of a Druid, in his other hand; although truly, for my part, I would rather have him portrayed combing his white beard with his fingers. And always my noble intentions, rising like a wave rushing toward shore, smote against the rock of the declaration of his own desire.

He had told me solemnly, in his perfect mind, that he did not wish to be moved one inch from where he lay in life or in death. And suddenly I knew that settled it, beyond any wish of mine to do glory to him, and hard upon that realization came another of equal clarity and force, that it was my wish also because it had been his, and the greatest glory I could do him was to obey it. So I gazed once more into his serene face, dimly revealed by the bonfire. Then taking the head of Bran under my arm, I ordered our departure.

And before that night had passed, a tale was told, the birth of a legend that might live a thousand years, and who first whispered I know not. Yet in the gray of morning, when Gerald reviewed the troops, there was not one bosom that did not harbor it, or one that was untouched by its wonder.

It was that Merdin was not dead, and instead lay in enchanted sleep where the witch Vivain had cast him, and that an invisible wall had been built around him by the same spell, so that he could never waken and escape until world's end; and no man could enter the magic prison where he lay. You would think that Glyn and the other scouts would refute the story, but the firm faith of the multitude overpowered the witness of their own eyes, and soon they too, so easy the seduction of men's minds, believed in it as steadfastly as the rest.

No one went to hammer on the Invisible Wall. I took it that before long this whole region of the forest would become a forbidden region to the foot of man, a place accursed, and only wolves and deer, and innocent birds, and other denizens of its dim depths would pace or fly through the Wall in the course of their natural affairs, never dreaming it was standing there in the minds of their brother, man. And when the great tree-trunk that lay athwart a skeleton had rotted away, and the bones too had moldered or been carried off, the exact whereabouts of the ruin would become unknown; and folk who came after us would say it lay in this or that direction, as their grandsires had told them when they were toddlers. And thus the tale would live on till the forest itself had given way to plowed land.

Deep in the night the six scouts sent to trail Vivain returned to the campground, and I had left orders for their leader to come to my pavilion. There he told of how the tracks had led northward for about a league, and then they had been drowned in a shallow swamp, and the trackers had entered it for a depth of a mile, guided by torchlight, and ahead of them had heard a piercing scream. Guided by their recollection of the sound, they had come upon a bed of quicksand still bubbling and hissing as though it had just swallowed some one. It was the firm belief of the scout and his fellows that Vivain had fallen into it and had been sucked down, for it was well-known that witches frequently met this end to their lives on earth, quicksand being witch-traps set by the Earth Goddess, who hated them. Even so, the creatures did not die, according to the folk, but lived on in some sort of under world, where they made hideous revel; and sometimes they rose up near enough to earth to seize the feet of hapless travelers who had blundered into the traps and drag them down to their halls and devour them; and hence it was never any use to probe the sand in search of their bodies.

"And if the Earth Mother couldn't kill her for what she done to the old wizard, at least she's paid her off, and the witch won't do no more devilment, this side," the scout told me, big-eyed.

I was by no means certain of this last. On Lorn Moor I had come to believe that no supernatural creatures, from demons to dragons, were as perilous to man as man himself, with his strange urgings, his unaccountable malignance, and his implacable will.

Vivain was heading eastward, the scout told me, when the hunters lost track of her. Perhaps Thanet or the North Downs was her goal, although possibly she meant to double back to Fosse Way, the great Roman road that led to York and to the land of the Brigantes in North Britain. It did not seem likely she, or Vortigern either, could achieve much in that realm beset and harried by the Painted Picts, although possibly she flourished best in sorely troubled kingdoms.

She would be a needle with a venomed point in the haystacks northward. My best hope of catching her and of crushing her Adam's apple in my hand was to post spies about Vortigern and Enid, wherever they might be. Another seemingly needless precaution I took before sunrise. It was to dispatch ten picked men to Swan Lake, as a guard for Elain. Then I made quick plans for my journey to the Taff.

So quiet would lie the land after word of my victory, all traitors in flight or in hiding, that Pillicock and I could safely go unattended. Yet I yielded to Gerald's insistence that our way be precoursed and guarded by some fifty of my veterans. To take Pillicock with me was more important than his wish and mine. The monster knew strange arts, and it might be he could help me draw water from the Well of Silence.

So he and I went forth, both of us on horseback. He had his sling and I carried my Sword and shield but no mark of a king except a little dragon of silver, to be worn over the heart along with the ear of Droit, and a mark of the overlordship of all Britain which Hengist had handed me, with a great rough burst of Jutish laughter, when he had marked the treaty. My guards halted all traffic on the road until we two travelers had passed, and we rode across what seemed a land forsaken, and a little smoke from the roofs of distant huts seemed to enlarge its solitude.

The distance was perhaps ninety minutes' flight for a purposeful crow, half an hour for a pochard duck. Because the great marshes of the Severn blocked our straight road, and wide Sabrina itself, we must go by way of Gloster, three days' ride. In late afternoon we came in sight of our homestead, and my heart leaped, and then was all overcome by wonder, to consider what had happened since I had seen it last. One of our churls herding sheep on the down saw me and recognized me, and despite his fright of Pillicock he forced himself to run to meet me, and when I had dismounted, he dropped on both knees and wept. We went on to the house and saw Anna's white sow near the door, no fatter than when I had seen her last, and I knew that the Woman of Silence was somewhere nigh.

2

Anna came up from the byres, glanced once at me, and I thought that her eyes widened, then she hurried in. I followed her, bidding Pillicock wait, and motioned for her to sit on the bench, while I, moving slowly and cautiously, took off my Sword and shield and sat down beside her. She moved to the end of the slab, fearing I would touch her, but did not get up.

And I noted again what a beautiful woman she was, delicately fashioned. Seated on a throne in an ermine robe, she would be more queenly than Enid.

"The gaffer is dead," I told her quietly.

She drew a long breath, let it pass, and said naught.

"He bade me come to you, and have you tell me the truth of my nativity," I went on.

She only made a little motion with her hand.

"Will you tell me, Anna? Will you try? I am King of Britain. It is needful that I know, to establish my true descent, and also to reward those who have done rightly by me, and to take vengeance on those who have done me ill. Merdin swore with his dying words that I was Vortigern's son. Is it true?"

Her head dropped a little in a half-nod.

"Was Queen Ina my mother, as Merdin once told me?"

Her head moved a little sideways, in a half-shake, and then what looked like terror blanched her dark face and she started to spring up.

"Wait, Anna. Do not leave me." And I held out my hand to hers. She would not let me touch it, crouching back. Still she did not rise.

She opened her mouth, and kept it open a few seconds, and a terrible strain came into her face, but no sound came forth.

"Wait here," I said. "I go to speak to my follower, Pillicock." For I had decided to try to breach her silence in a way dangerous to her wits and perhaps to her life.

"Pillicock, if you saw again the kind of toadstools that you ate on Pillicock Hill, so that you could sleep and Marcus Cassius could speak through your lips, would you recognize them?"

"Surely, my liege. They have yellow tops with strange markings."

"They did not grow on the moor. But toadstools of many kinds grow on the mucky side of the hill above the pool, and I bid you go there and look, and if you find any, pluck two and bring them to me."

He hurried away. In his absence the light dwindled, and the first stars showed themselves, and the dusk thickened. One of the churls brought wood to feed the half-dead fire, and when he had done so, I bade him wait at the sheep-fold with his companion, telling him I had seen wolves nearby, and I would call them when supper was ready. I had seen no wolves but I had seen ghosts. They appeared to haunt the shadows of the hut as they had haunted the great ring of Stonehenge. Then Pillicock returned, and in his hand were two toadstools with yellow tops, which looked to me the same kind as he had eaten.

"They look the same, but grow taller than on my hill, so I cannot take oath that they are the same," he told me.

"Have they the same markings?"

"Yes, the same strange white spots."

I took them, and bade him sit quietly against the wall, so if Anna ate them and spoke, he could bear witness.

"Will you eat them, Anna?" I asked. "I think they are medicine that will unlock your lips."

She gazed into my eyes, more steadfastly than I could remember, then slowly put one of the poisonous-looking plants to her mouth. My heart quailed, yet I did nothing to stop her from eating both of them. In the growing firelight her blue eyes looked intensely dark. Then an icy thrill coursed my backbone, for suddenly she began to speak.

"Vortigern, give me the key and let me go."

And then the strange blackness left her eyes and they were wildly bright.

"What key?" I murmured. "Where were you when this happened? Try to tell me."

"You brought me here by trickery and have locked the door," she said as though fighting inutterable terror. "Do not harm me, your sister. What have I done to harm you? I have only set free the hawk that you tortured because she would not hunt for you. I will buy you another hawk. See, I have silver that our father, the King, gave me. Oh, you are only plaguing me for the sport! Is it not true?"

There was such longing in her voice as she said this last that the entreaty wracked my heart. I glanced at my Sword that I had unbelted, and I wished to the High Gods that I had had it in my hand at that very place and time; and the sport of Vortigern would have ended quickly. What place and time? It came to me with an awful inkling that the place might have been a keep or outbuilding of the winter abode of old King Lot, Vortigern's father, on the Isle of Mona, and that the time was before my birth.

"Aye, only your half-sister, that is true, but what difference does that make? You are the King's son by his first wife, Ellen, and I his daughter by his second wife, Gladys, the sister of Merdin. But he loves me, and he would be wroth if he knew you have played this base trick to frighten me. If you let me go, I'll not tell him of it. But if you don't . . ." And Anna's words died away.

"Speak on, speak on," I cried. She did not seem to hear. A long silence followed, then her voice came forth again, half-choked with weeping, although now her burning eyes remained dry.

"No, no. It's an evil thing; the very Gods cry out against it. Vortigern, do not shame yourself with such ineffable shame, and despoil me forever. You are the son of great Lot, descended from mighty Lear. You are heir to the throne of Cambria, the foremost kingdom in all Britain, and I take oath before Lud and the Earth Goddess, I take oath by the Sky and the Stars and flowing waters and the Great Deep, that if you pursue your most horrible intent, they will take implacable and awful vengeance. Do not strike me! You have made me bleed already, but even that I will forgive, and never speak a word of this to any one, if only you let me go."

She fell silent again, but I could not cry "Speak on! Speak on!" My tongue dried in my dry mouth, and a great horror was on my heart, and I would close her lips save that the very Gods had opened them at last, moving through my hand, and it was my remorseless fate to hear all.

"Open your hand! Do not strike me with your fist. No, I will not yield to evil unspeakable, and I beg you, if you will not spare me that, thrust your dagger through my heart. See, the barred window darkens as the clouds roll up the sky. It is a sign, Vortigern, of the terrible wrath of Lud, and of Gods forgotten who made Lud. See, the lightning flashes and thunder roars and the rain beats on the roof. Vortigern, a vision passes before my eyes, and in it I am silent, in a little house, and the only one I know is my Uncle Merdin, but one is there whom I can dimly see, he is like the ghost of the dead, but I think him the ghost of the unborn, and he tells me that unless you relent, you will be driven forth from your palaces, and harried through the land, and he will seize you, and your might will avail nothing against his might, and he will rend from your bosom your still beating heart and feed it to his dog."

"King Arthur!" Pillicock cried in an anguished voice. "Bid her be silent."

"That, I cannot," I answered, for now I knew that the awful visitation of speech to her long-locked lips must continue to its end.

But the end came quickly. A scream of pain rose from the lips twisted in agony, and when her breath failed, it rose again as though she were being dealt repeated blows, and still again, then it fell away to a moaning like that of strong men wounded unto death, and who knew not that they made a sound, or that they yet lived. It went on and on, and the Gods shut their ears, or else they looked down through our mean roof, their terrible eyes on mine. Then it sank to a little whimper and died away.

Anna sat on her bench with both hands pressed to her breasts. She tried to draw her hands away only to press them down again, but it appeared that she kept trying to uncover them for some great purpose, and that at last she succeeded, and her breasts seemed to bulge forth under her smock, and a dim and tender smile curled her tortured mouth. And then I knew who she was, no longer a dread surmise in my resistant brain, and then I knew who I was; and as she remained silent, the same silence that I had briefly broken and which would never again be breached, I rejoiced that I, no other, was the one who had come into this heritage.

Then up spoke Pillicock, and his manly voice rang in the silent room.

"A boon, my liege, a boon!"

"Ask it."

"I ask that I, not you, deal the dread stroke that must be dealt King Vortigern. It is not to pay the debt of my hundred stripes, got when I would not become his clown; the vengeance I now abjure. But unwittingly you have slain your son, and it is written in the stars that you must slay your brother or be slain by him, and the very ground shudders at patricide, and the sweet grass shrinks down."

"Speak on, Pillicock," I cried.

"If your own hand commits it, it may wither, while I am a monster already, whom the Gods themselves misshaped from no sin of mine. They are too just to afflict me further, even though I strike at your command and in your name. I pray you, let me be your hand in that last darkling moment and forever haunted spot where you two must meet, and Anna's prophecy come true. I ask it in the name of Elain, my angel-child whom I love, and who loves you. Now I charge you to let Anna speak to me through your lips."

I looked into his dark and yearning eyes, and knew Anna's answer.

"Pillicock, my liegeman, I appoint you as my right hand to make my mother's prophecy come true."

3

My troops had marched northward while Pillicock and I were performing my mission, and I met them at the junction of Severn and Avon. Here Gerald told me of his plans, and I listened to them as in a dream, the same dream that had weaved endlessly in my mind ever since I had left the homestead, sometimes dimming and sometimes brightening, as does the world when the full Moon races through clouds. These were important plans. I kept telling myself so, because my great kingdom must be well-ruled and stoutly guarded against dangers within and without, and the breachless evil of my begetting had naught to do with this, and must not shadow it.

So Gerald related his intention to quarter the army here for a month or more, in ready communication with the West Central Britain and Central Britain, and with east access to South Britain. He would send forth detachments to any troubled spot in my whole realm. He said that North England above the Mersey was as busy with Picts as a dog with fleas, and its King would not bite me now; and that the lands of the North Folk and the South Folk and the region of the Wash north to Humbermouth were plagued by raids of Angles, Saxons, and Jutes, to the slaughter of whom he would attend as soon as my realm was secure.

Nothing would add as much to the security of my realm, and increase the prosperity of its people, as the slaughter of four-legged wolves that pulled down half the sheep of Britain, a good fourth of our calves, and no few children and grown folk, whom the gray devils knew to be defenseless against their glistening fangs. I thought how joyfully I would undertake the task if I were free. Leaving Gerald to conduct affairs of state, I would organize bands of hunters, and also see to the smelting of iron to make good knives and javelins, and the training of hounds to track them to their lairs. Nay, they were not gray devils. They were only beasts who killed as their dams had taught them, and the horrid hunger in their bellies had been set there by the Gods. Still, to think of them stretching their legs and dying gave me a great pleasure, obscuring for awhile all thought of my business with Vortigern, not to be delayed much longer.

But I had to come to it, when Gerald gave me the latest news of Vortigern's shattered army. His men had been seen flying in all directions, his younger son, Vortimer, had fled to the South Downs, seeking refuge among the Saxons settled there, and rumor had it that Modred had been seen in Cornwall. Vortigern himself had disappeared as though the Earth had swallowed him, and I wished he would remain so for awhile, until I could rally my inward forces. But soon from Vivain came a parchment, written in fine Latin, delivered by a salt-merchant who had met her on the flank of the Chiltern Hills, and soon translated into Cambrian by a good Latin scholar. It was addressed to Artorius, Rex Britannica, and thus it read:

If you, great King, have business with Vortigern, you will find him in hiding in an ancient fortress of stone in the Roman town of Venonae, north of the Avon. Move quickly, if the business is urgent, for he intends to make for Lindum, and from thence to Eburacum, in the kingdom of the Brigantes, as soon as he dares venture out and can replace his mare, who has broken her leg. Pray accept my most humble obeisance.

Vivain, daughter of Calypso the Witch

"The whole thing is a mockery!" I burst out when I had heard the reading, and felt the parchment, and looked at its writing.

"It may be so," Gerald replied with no great vehemence.

"In the first place, she could not have written it. She doesn't know Latin."

"I think, my liege, she does. She is adept at many arts and crafts, and if she had been in command of the enemy, as was Boadicea in the Northern War against the Romans, and she were Vortigern, the Hecana King, and Hengist rolled into one, we would have had it hotter than we did."

"Well, if she thinks I will walk into her trap, she is only a fool."

"A fool would not have signed herself daughter of Calypso the Witch. She knows you have laid bare that lie, and I think it was a taunt to you for ever believing it. Hate is her element, as Merdin told you, and she is most strangely driven by dark powers we cannot see, and she has been set on that darkling road by some happening we do not know; still, she can tell the truth when it profits her."

"By the Gods, would you have me take this bait?"

"What did she have to win by offering it? She had something, be sure of that, but she knew that if you took it, you would march with a strong force, and there is none to oppose you in all this part of Britain. Mark you, King Arthur, you are not done with her yet. She moves and feeds her malice with implacable purpose. And I think she was feeding it when she wrote you this letter."

"With what food?"

"I asked you what might she win by offering the bait? You forget that she is the daughter of Enid, and feels for her the nearest to natural love that her strange heart can know, and Vortigern put away

Enid to marry Rowena, daughter of Hengist. She would as leave have an enemy split Vortigern's breast-bone as one of her own party. She cares naught who wields the sword, the knife, or slips in the poison, as long as the hated one is well-dispatched, and his shade must wander forever—or so believe the worshippers of Modo—blown by the winds, pelted by the snow, chilled by the rain, in search of revenge he may never have. It is in my mind that if you move swiftly, you will find Vortigern where she told you."

"And I tell you again, Gerald, that if you are right you, not I, should be King of Britain."

"For that little piece of insight? Still, if you should die without heirs, I would seek the crown in lieu of a greater contender. You were once my scholar, and I have become yours."

"If I should pass beyond the sea-mists without heirs, I bid you, here and now, seize the crown, with the power of our army of veterans, overthrowing any other contender, and that is the inviolate command of Arthur, King of Britain."

"My liege, I was half-jesting. Mark you, no royal blood flows in my veins. My grandsire was a Roman, a mere Centurion, who wedded a hill-woman. I am no poor soldier, that I grant, although of a rough-and-ready sort. The Gods would laugh to see my lean hams on the throne of Britain."

"I doubt if they would laugh long, or unduly loud. Maximus himself had no royal blood. If this came to pass, would you wed Wander, whom I have duly made Queen, even though she was never made my wife? I recall you envied Modred, with her under the net."

"Yes, I would wed her, and lock her door of nights; and take her with me on my wars, and post guards about her when I turned my back. But reconsider the command you have just given me, I entreat you."

"Would you, if you were King, seek not to conquer Gaul, or even Eire or Caledonia, and rule justly, as the Gods give you to see, and cause the beasts to be less, and the folk more?"

"All that I pledge to my King. And I see in your face that you meant what you said. Affirm it once more, before these witnesses, because my heart faints and my head reels. Remember what you called me, long ago. A drover of cattle to the byres, and sheep to the pasture."

"I was not much more, in those days. Aye, I reaffirm my command. Disobey it at your bitter shame and deadly peril."

Tears in his eyes, Gerald dropped on both knees and kissed my hand.

"Great King, my liege, for whom I pray to both Lud and Mithras, before the Gods I will obey your command."

"That matter settled," I said lightly, for my own eyes smarted, and the witnesses, a number of my captains, were weeping openly, "I will start at once for Venonae, to settle a matter with my father, Vortigern."

And although I had no thought of dying until my full time, and no intimation of it such as the jumping of my eye or a tingle in my hand, still I felt as relieved by Gerald's oath as I was exultant to be setting forth in search of Vortigern. In all truth I exulted over both, without clearly knowing why.

4

To dodge the heavy forest between Severn and Avon, my followers and I took up the left bank of the latter, setting our course to intercept the great Roman road, Fosse Way. By this somewhat indirect route, Venonae was a hard march of two days, an easy one of three. With me went five able officers and about three hundred troops, for I would have been ashamed to take more in this peaceful region. Ahead of me fanned out thirty scouts, led by Glyn, to protect me against ambush. We saw sheep- and cattle-herders, who knelt as I passed, and a few smoking cots, and in a hole in the road five miles from the town we found the well-picked bones of a war-horse, and scraps of skin told me it was Vortigern's mare. Nearby a gleaming in the grass caught one of my fellow's eye, and there he found a gold locket, engraved with the Roman letters V.R., which no doubt stood for Vortigern, Rex. Inside was a lock of hair too pale to be Enid's, and I took it to be that of the Saxon lady, Rowena. I pictured Vortigern hurling it away with savage force.

So far Vivain's letter and Gerald's reading of it appeared to be valid; and I could vision the former King walking the rest of the way to Venonae, cursing every step. Soon after this I sent scouts forward to the ruined town, to pick the most likely building for him to huddle in, but on no account to show themselves. At such tasks they were adept, and in a short while Glyn and a few others returned, while the rest stood unseen guard against the fugitive's escape. Glyn told me that only one building in all the ghostly city still had unbreached walls and a strong gate, and a little smoke was seen rising from a vent in its roof. I no longer doubted that we had trapped our fox.

My whole force broke from a copse in a jog-trot and swiftly surrounded what was now a prison. To break down the door, we would have had to make a ram, but because he knew that an hour's delay would serve him not at all, and only make me more difficult to deal with, and putting his last trust in his cunning to save him somehow yet, he opened the door to me, and knelt at the threshold.

I entered with Pillicock and one squad of men, these to search the building for ambushers and traps. It proved to be one large room, perhaps once an armory, with solid stone walls, and Vortigern was its only occupant larger than a rat, one of which scurried across the floor and dived into a cranny. Two stone benches stood near a low fire on a stone hearth under a kind of hood of stone, through the top of which smoke escaped through a vent. Over it Vortigern had been roasting, on a spit, a piece of meat that I thought had been cut from his dead mare, and that he had brought this whole distance from the place of the animal's fall, which was ill fare for a king.

All my followers except Pillicock I had bade go forth, and wait for me at the entry. I sat on one of the benches, Pillicock on the floor close to the hearth, and I signaled Vortigern to seat himself on the other bench. As he did so, I began to perceive how slight was my acquaintance with him, really. Only once before had I seen him at close range, which was when he had handed me a cup of mead after my victory over Modred at the May Day games at Woodwick, two years or more gone. He was nearly as tall as I, but now the kingliness had gone out of him, there was very little to be marked in his face and form, and scores of men in the army, arrayed as kings, would have shown more grand. There was a kind of commonplaceness in his face. At present it was ghostly-white and his eyes rolled.

"Well, what have you to say to me?" I asked when I had looked my fill.

"Only that you find me, King Arthur, no longer Fortune's favorite, but Fortune's dog. Let it be a lesson to all men, even you, how the favors of this world are temporal, one moment given, the next snatched away, and the favorite cast naked to the wind. Why, it would stir to pity a king with a heart of stone."

"It stirs me, I do confess."

"All I can do is entreat from you a few crumbs of favor, lest you some day fall in the same pit of calamity, and ask it of some other. Yet I will give something in return. If you let me go in peace, a king granting a brother's boon unto one who was once a king, I will promise before the Gods never to employ against you such sway as I yet possess over some former subjects, and to live meanly in some foreign kingdom, such as the Brigantes', and take no part in its affairs, until I come to penurious old age, and the Gods see fit to end my melancholy days, and bear my spirit beyond the sea-mists."

He was a North Cambrian by birth, I was thinking, yet he was more windy than we South Cambrians.

"I do not mean to kill you, if that's what you are thinking."

"Why, I would have wagered that you would not, for you are famed for mercy unto those who have opposed you fairly, in causes they thought just. Still, I thank you from the bottom of my heart, and thank the Gods that watch over you, and guide your actions."

"How could any King kill his sire who gave him birth?" I asked. "Out upon such wickedness! For you are my father, not my brother, as you just spoke."

"I meant that we were once brother-kings. Their respect and magnanimity to each other, even from conqueror to conquered, is well-known. But the father-son relationship is deeper still. Truly I am your sire, and I got you of Queen Ina, my first Queen, and my best, and I rue the day I parted with her, over a trifle, for otherwise you would have been my heir, instead of Modred, and this sad day would have never come to pass."

"It does not seem sad to me. It seems most fair and jolly. And where is Modred, now that you speak of him?"

"He is my son no more. In my affliction he deserted me, speaking unfilial words. I care not if you impale him on your triumphant Sword, for the Gods know of no sin greater than the desertion of a father by his son. And truly, I know not where he has gone, although he set his steps toward Cornwall. And I would follow him swiftly, if I were you, for he's bent on mischief."

"Vortigern, you wear a little leathern sack under your cloak, fixed to your belt. What is it?"

"Why, 'tis a gift for you, if you'll accept it, and as you promised, suffer me to go my way in peace."

"I did not promise that. I promised only that I would not kill you. Unlatch the bag and toss it on the floor."

He did so, and I heard the clear ring and clatter of gold coins.

"Will you give me half its contents, to ease my way a little on my journey?"

"On your journey you'll not need it, nor in the days to come. What else do you bear about you? I see no weapon."

"I have none except my sword, and this I unbelted when I saw you making toward my door. I have stood it in a corner, for you to add to your trophies."

"Still, I'd best make sure that you've not forgotten some trifling belonging, such as a knife. Take off your clothes."

"My son Arthur, great King, it is a sin against the Gods for a son to gaze upon the nakedness of his sire. That is a law so old that I know not its source."

"Still, I'll commit it. Make haste, my father Vortigern. I like not the smell of the half-cooked horsemeat and am in haste to complete our business and go."

He disrobed, one of the few times in all his day that he had done so without help of a serving-wench. It turned out he had a dagger in his left arm-pit, and this he tossed on the floor with his gold. Then I turned to Pillicock.

"My liegeman, do you remember this great King?"

"Full well." And the dwarf's eyes glowed darkly.

"Perhaps he does not remember you?"

"Can it be Rufus the Dwarf?" Vortigern asked. "I believe it is."

"He would not have made a good clown, Vortigern my sire. It is well that your efforts failed, for how could a clown perform the office I have appointed him? Pillicock, will you likewise remove your clothes?"

"My liege, I am a monster, hateful to the sight. Do not ask me to lay bare my misgrown legs."

"Your brawny arms more than make up for them. Also your back has been wondrously marked. Let my father see the scars and guess at their source."

"My liege, I will obey your command, but I pray you not to play with Vortigern as cat with mouse. If you will suffer me to say so, it would please the Gods better if you complete your business and be gone."

"Who can please the Gods? If we spend our days trying to please the Gods, when we know not their temper or their appetites, we had as well join a monastery in Gaul. When you are naked, as is our host, show him your back, a fine sight for his eyes, then sit quietly and do not run and romp and make sport, for I think he is cured of the inclination to have you do so."

Vortigern was already fish-belly-white, but at sight of Pillicock's back with its hundred welts, he turned gray as ashes in the wondrous fireplace.

"Still I think my servant counseled well," I told my royal sire, "and we should hasten our business and be gone. Vortigern, it was once my fixed intention to behead you with Caliburn, and perhaps I swore to do just that, but I have repented it, and as I told you, I will not take your life."

"Now that's a wondrous mercy."

"It may be so, but I doubt it. I have appointed Pillicock—you call him Rufus—to kill you in my place."

"That monster? A dwarf take the life of Vortigern, once King of Cambria, and then of South Avon and the Ouse? It is a good jest, Arthur, but I am saddened by my late loss, and I cannot laugh."

"It is no laughing matter, and to that I take oath."

"If I must die—and I still think you will relent—slay me as the king I once was, once your great enemy, with one lusty stroke, but do not send me naked and ashamed unto the Gods. I would rather die in the clutch of a serpent than those terrible arms. You too are a monster, Arthur, if you suffer it."

"What do you expect of your offspring, out of Anna's womb? Now I will go forth and leave you and him together. I doubt not you will do some shrieking before he is done, but that will recall some that you heard in a moment of great sport, ere I was conceived. See, I will pick up the knife and the sack of gold and keep them as heirlooms. Pillicock, seize him firmly in your arms, so I will know the tussle is well-begun, and you may call me when it is near its end, and I will bring you this knife so that Anna's prophecy, which Vortigern has well-nigh forgotten, may come true. For if I leave it here, he may snatch at it in a final agony, and do you or himself harm. Come forward, Monster. At last you will please the king who so greatly admired your agility on your short legs, and no doubt the strength of your long ape-like arms. Seize him around the waist, or his neck if you can reach so high, where Enid and, after her, flaxenhaired Rowena were wont to clutch him in their fierce passion. Fall to!"

"Wait!" Vortigern cried in such a kingly voice that it made me jump.

"A brief moment, if you like."

"I may as well die for a wolf instead of a sheep. You cannot give me a death I would dread more than this. Arthur—Artay—Ambrose—rustic of the Taff, whatever you were and are, you are the child not only of rape but of incest. If Merdin hasn't told you of it, I tell you now. I hated her from the moment I was done with her, and hated you, its fruit, with a most loathsome hate, and my soul has been curdled from it, but all I have done of evil will be expatiated by the loathsome death you give me. And you must live with it yet, your most base borning, and this deed will not give you peace, and you will rouse up from your dreams in horror on many a night, and the crown that you got by such horrid legacy will cause cankers on your brow, and you will never find comfort or forgetfulness in this world or the next. Now set on your monstrous executioner! I was once the King!"

Pillicock moved slowly toward him, his coarse lips twitching, his malshaped limbs agleam with sweat. Then Vortigern gave one wild glance into his face and toppled to the floor. For a moment he writhed in agony, his hands clutching his chest, and he uttered a shapeless sound, and his mouth gaped as he fought for breath. Then his twisted body eased, his limbs relaxed and lay quiet; and, black in the face, he died.

Had the Gods, angered by my too long sport, smote him the death-blow, or had they snatched him from the grasp of my executioner, in last respect to their once viceroy, their descendant, for all I knew, and to balk me, an upstart king, base-born? I only knew, gazing down at him, that my crown lay heavy on my brow, and I felt a smarting under its rim, as though it were causing canker. Aye, and I knew too that my own evil deed against the Gods was not yet absolved, and that absolution would be hard to come by, and a great wave was rising that must soon crash against the rock, and a mighty storm was brewing that must soon break, harrying land and sea, and great oaks would topple, and unimaginable change ensue.

It seemed that I looked all through the world, in one glance lightning-swift and far, and the only vision given me, perhaps no more than an errant fancy of a disordered brain, was Merdin's harp. I wished I could draw my hand across its magic strings. I could play it better, now, than I had played the Roman lyre for Elain to sing. When the wave had struck and the storm had broken and both had drawn back from the desolation they had wrought, could I not play it as well as Merdin while she sang angel-sweet?

Then I remembered that I was Arthur, King of Britain. So I went out of the grim room where Roman soldiers had kept their weapons, impotent at last, and I ordered that fallen logs be brought and a great fire laid for a funeral pyre for Vortigern, my sire and once the King. I myself dressed the corpse in its mud-stained yet royal robes, and brought it forth and gave it to the flames, and these leaped fiercely ere it was consumed, and I knew not what Lud and Sun God said to me in their crackle and roar, knowing only that these were tidings of no small account; yet deep in my heart I found not dark premonition of despair, but star-bright hope.

Chapter Seventeen
Elain and Vivain

The ashes of the funeral pyre had scarcely cooled when my veteran band again marched, their lean legs seeming tireless, making our return to the campground of my army at the junction of Severn and Avon. Here most of the men who had followed me to Aquae Sulis resumed their places in the ranks, but Pillicock and I must journey on. Neither he nor I had seen Elain face to face since I had departed for the moor.

Llewelan had returned to his duty at Woodwick when the ten guards I had sent to Swan Lake began their rounds, and now I brought ten more, trusty South Cambrian yokels, to relieve the first ten, because such a small number grows lax not in intent but in discipline when there is no bugle, no drill, no rigid inspection, and little time-tried routine of military life under a strict officer, to keep them toeing the mark. Such detachments must be frequently replaced.

The fellows I had sent were stout fellows enough, and the shores of the lake were easy to patrol. As elsewhere throughout my realm, no armed bands of marauders dared sally forth. Still, I could not rest until I had seen with my own eyes that all was well, if all could ever be well again, with Elain and me apart.

We crossed the Severn at Gloster, as before, and struck the old Roman road that touched Caerleon and from thence ran westward to Cardiff at Taffmouth. It so chanced the darkness fell with us still two leagues from Swan Lake, and instead of making camp, I ordered that we push on, for I was back on my native heath, knowing its hills and dales, and I took no thought of ambush. As we came nigh the lake we saw one high fire and one low one, and heard sounds of jollity.

In a moment more, I had given the guards a healthy start by my sudden appearance among them, and no little abashment too, for they had little semblance to a military party, their present occupation being the roasting on a spit of a ham of venison, and emptying horns of ale.

"And who are those four long-faced loons about the little fire?" I demanded, although their long robes and staffs revealed them as Christian pilgrims, most likely making for Patrick's birthplace at Banwen in Glamorgan.

"Why, Your Majesty, they're naught but almsmen, who begged leave of us to pass the night here. And 'twas 'em who gave us the meat and ale, which the master of Collen Village gave unto them, in payment for a prayer that the river clear of mud to make fishing better, and which they couldn't use 'emselves, being sworn to take no vittles richer than bread and water."

"While you're eating and drinking, who is patrolling the lake shore?" For all ten of the hearties stood openmouthed about the fire.

"King, we can see every foot of the shore, the Moon being so bright. Likewise, we can't ford the brook that feeds the lake, her being so high, and the men must walk half-around and then walk back. And it happened both sentries come by here just as the meat got done, and they thought to eat supper. The brook's out of its banks 'cause of that same heavy rain that muddied the Taff."

Then my voice harshened still more, because I looked for something on the shore and did not see it, another sign, so I thought, of the laxity of their guard.

"Where is the barge I bid you build, to keep guarded every minute, so that the boat of Elain of the Lake can be kept at the island?"

"Why, there she is, Your Majesty! Can't ye see the stern of her sticking out of yon bed of rushes?"

"Yes, I see her now. Has she been there ever since sundown?"

"Every blessed minute since Leod took her to cut wood, 'fore the noon. And more'n at, she's chained with a wondrous great lock, and I keep the key."

I heaved a big sigh of held-in wind, now that I had assured myself that some semblance of proper guard had been kept. Moreover, in the moonlight even brighter than had shown me Caliburn brandished above the waters of Witch Lake, I could see Elain's boat on its stake on the shore of the island.

"How long since you have seen Elain of the Lake?" I asked, more mellowly now.

"No earlier than the fourth hour, when she and the granny went out to fish in her boat, and they stayed till close to sundown, and went back."

It came to me that both were sound asleep by now, and I should wait till morning before visiting the island, so that Elain could mark my approach through the casement or reflected in the Roman looking-glass hanging on the wall; and thus I would not take her by surprise, and she could take second thought, and perhaps better thought to my own thinking, before she spoke to me. Still, you could as well ask me to sleep the night under the sword that hung over some Greek fellow of long ago as he sat at meat, a tale that Gerald had told me. My eyes had not yet seen Elain's beautiful self, tall and well, and they could not close in slumber until they did so.

I had the sergeant free the boat chain, and Pillicock and I rowed swiftly across to the island. As we came nigh, I saw a water-jar lying on its side, and then we both beheld a sight that alarmed us greatly. On the bank lay the old serving-wench Helena, wearing naught but her smock, and when we hurried to her side we found her heaving troubled breaths, as the old do when they have a seizure. I could not doubt that since Elain had gone to bed—at most two candles burned in her chamber, glimmering faintly in the cracks of the wooden shutter of her casement—the granny had remembered her empty water-jar and had gotten up to fill it, then as she leaned down, the blood had rushed to her head, and she had fallen in a fit.

I bade Pillicock take her by the feet while I put my arm about her withered chest. We lifted her slight weight of no more than eight stone to carry her to the entry, under a dark stone arch which was often seen on Roman edifices. And there, though we dreamed it not, an evil fate was waiting Pillicock and me.

There we were both struck down by unseen foes. Unable to rise and resist, stunned and sick, yet I was not knocked insensible, and I retained remembrance of my own identity and a faint power to question what had happened, and why, and most of all, how. Here was a mystery that somehow I must solve, despite my pain and weakness, because it pertained to something greater in my mind than I myself. And my brain worked at the implacable command of my will, and visions came to me as pale lightning flashes in a dark room, and suddenly I perceived that those who had felled Pillicock and me could not have known I would touch Swan Lake tonight and we had merely interrupted their affairs. Then my intermittent gleams of wit joined in a faint but steady beam, and I knew that after striking down Helena, our assailants had seen our approach across the moonlit lake, and that Elain, not I, was the object of their visit here and the victim of their design.

2

Pillicock had tumbled to the floor with me, both of us felled by cudgels of some sort, and the blows had been intended to crush our skulls. What had spared us for the nonce was the stout bronze of my helmet and a cap of boar's hide, stuffed with leather, that Pillicock habitually wore to make him look taller. And the terror and shock of my realization that this attack was incidental to this night's affair revived me further. Instead of sinking deeper into trance I thrust upward against the lowering pall, and my soul rose out of it as a bird wings forth into open sky above low-hung fog, and dim and strange I heard one of our attackers speak to the other.

"There be life in 'em yet, I reckon. Shall I bash their brains out and be done wi' 'em?"

"Not here. Have ye no foresight, Duglas? Them brains, and the blood too, will be hard to wash up, when we've done what we come for, and the guards'll see it, and will hunt us hot, and will look under the robes of our pardners on the bank, and slaughter 'em all. We've got to drop 'em in deep water, and stow their boat so she too 'll sink, and the guards will reckon she's beached behind the island. This we can do when they're grogged with ale, and 'twill be morn afore they take alarm. 'Twill give us time to raise our own boat, which even the sharp eyes of the monster didn't note. Then we can go back the way we came through the flooded brook into Witch Lake, and get a long head start. And if we cut off the wench's tongue as well as blind her, she'll not tell how we look, and 'em gold pieces what the witch gave us will be ours to spend, not taken off us afore we swing over a fire."

"Before Modo hisself, Melvas, ye have a long head!" the other cried. "But what will we do wi' 'em for now? Both are sweet-asleep, but they might rouse up——"

"What of 'em two straps you had left over, after binding the wench?

353

Put one about the legs o' one, and t'other about t'other, and fast 'em tight wi' the knot ye know, and we'll drag 'em into the chamber, where we can watch 'em. Then if either of 'em wiggles, give 'em another rap that'll put 'em back to sleep."

So Pillicock and I were dragged into the room of sweet remembrance, and neither of us twitched a muscle or an eyelid, although I knew he was as widely awake as I. And now that room was one of dreadful aspect, its sweet airs turned into a mist of evil to beslime every stone of its walls and floor forever. In an ancient chair with a straight narrow back sat my beloved Elain, her hands lashed behind it, her ankles strapped together, another thong encircling her waist, a fourth her throat and a fifth her forehead, so she could not move an inch, and a cloth had been fixed in her mouth. A fire burned low on the fire-bricks in the center of the room, and by it lay a thing used in the ritual of some horrid cult. It was an iron mask, belike some adorer's concept of the God Modo, lean in the cheeks, its human appearance transformed by a dreamy smile of its thick but finely molded lips. It was lined with what I thought was clay, and its eyes were holes through this and the metal itself, because I saw light through them.

Then, watching from under my eyelids, I noted a ghastly thing. Elain did not once close or blink her eyes. Then I perceived that their upper lids had been fastened somehow to the upper socket, perhaps by nothing more than glue put under the eyebrows. With all the strength I could apply I thrust against the strap that bound my ankles, and could not move them a single inch. Except to crawl, which would hasten my death and end all hope of helping Elain, I was as helpless as that first time in my blundering life I had fallen into the hands of a cunning foe; and tonight there was no arch-enemy, who strangely loved me, to set me free.

The two men called Duglas and Melvas, ordinary-looking fellows whom I had never seen before, their faces in no way signaling fiendishness or even brutality, took two thin yellowish sticks, perhaps a foot long and half an inch in diameter, and lighted their ends in the fire. They burned slowly, with yellow smoke but no visible flame, and with an intense brightness and I thought extreme heat. These they thrust through the back of the mask into its eyeholes, which now gave forth a vivid light. And as Melvas held the mask in his hands, Duglas spoke to Elain in a strangely respectful tone.

"Damosel, I was told to remind ye how once ye said our mistress had the Evil Eye, which ye told the Druid, and he balked her plans, so tonight ye'll truly see the Evil Eye looking into yours, and then be through wi' seeing forever more. Melvas, bring the Mask of Modo close to the wench's eyes."

"Aye, for so I am bound, but I could almost wish I was in my grave."

He did as he was bidden, holding the horrid mask a bare three inches from the beauteous eyes of Elain, fixed open and wildly staring; and the narrow beam of intense light bored straight into them. This lasted no more than a minute, Melvas slowly thrusting forward the incandescent sticks, while I strained with the frantic utmost of my strength at my bond. And I was starting to make the fatal move of crawling forward, in the desperate, hopeless hope of seizing him before he saw me, when Elain bit through her gag and uttered a piercing scream.

In that instant I heard a little popping sound, and I knew that Pillicock had burst the strap that confined his misshapen legs, and in the next instant he was on his feet, and hurling himself forward, at last the monster that he was named, a monster of revenge.

Melvas saw him and hurled at him the iron mask. It missed, and Pillicock caught Melvas's arm, and I heard the bone break like a stick. Then he seized him by the head in his two terrible hands, oblivious of his struggles, and twisted the head until it faced backward, shattering its bones and rending its cords. The man dropped dead from his grasp and Pillicock dived at the legs of Duglas, under the blow that the terror-stricken man had tried to deal with a piece of firewood. The fellow fell, and his scream of pain was cut short and his own eyes were darkened by swift death, as Pillicock crushed his Adam's apple with a chopping motion of his hand. Then Pillicock ran on his short legs to a chest, threw it open, and quickly brought forth a knife. Running behind the narrow, high-backed chair, he cut the straps fastening Elain's neck, forehead, waist, and wrists, and took the cloth from her mouth, and lastly the thong binding her ankles.

355

Only now did his gigantic strength wilt in his malformed body, and he dropped on both knees, weeping, at her feet.

"There, there, dear Gnome," she said to him, stroking his rough black hair with her still numbed hand. "I love you, Gnome. And the coarseness has gone from your face and it is beautiful."

"That could not be," he answered, choking, "unless your eyes are dimmed."

"Aye, they are dimmed, but I feel no pain."

He rose then, and got warm, half-melted tallow, and with this he anointed the upper part of her eyesockets, until the stuck skin and lashes came free. When this was done, he ran to me, and slashed the strap that the King's strength could not break. Then he went out the door, and I, in my bewilderment of mind, did not know his mission, until he re-entered, bearing old Helena in his arms. Her he laid on a cot by the wall, and I knew by the look of her that life was in her yet, and her breathing was no longer in troubled gasps, but peaceful, as though she slept.

And then I too went to the chair where Elain sat, and dropped on both knees before her, I, Arthur, King of Britain.

"Has my face changed also in your sight, Elain of the Lake?" I asked.

"My liege, it blurs before my wounded eyes, but I can see your shape, and it is still the shape of the King."

"Will you take me back and become my Queen?"

"Arthur, I cannot become your Queen, now or ever. How could a half-blind queen tell one great lord from another? I would mar the majesty of your court. But the hate in my heart is gone, and there is nothing to forbid your entry there, in due time and season, if indeed you were ever wholly gone from there."

"Then will you grant me a boon?"

"Aye, if it is in my power to give."

"My heart is deeply wounded at your wounding, and it cries for some redress that only you can give. On the wall hangs the lyre that you found on Pillicock Hill and brought hence. If I play the tune of the wind through the hawthorn, have you breath and spirit to sing the ancient song? Thereafter Pillicock will carry you to your bed, and you may sleep, knowing the nightmare of your wakefulness has passed."

"Arthur, I cannot plainly see your face, and never can again, but I hear your voice, and it is changed, and it has no more its haughty, cruel ring of implacable resolve and imperious pride. Yes, I will sing the song if you will play the melody, for my throat has taken no harm, and truly it feels stronger than before, and thereafter I will sleep till the morning breaks."

So I took down the lyre, and steadied my trembling hands, and plucked at the strings to see if these were in tune, and then I played through the melody. And at its second playing, the notes soaring up from my loving hand, Elain sang with ineffable loveliness:

> *Still through the hawthorn blows the cold wind,*
> *And the lowering clouds are gray,*
> *I will search the lorn moor, but who will I find*
> *To take my forlornness away?*
> *Wild are the winds that blow through a life,*
> *Till heart, hope, and happiness chill,*
> *But the wind through the hawthorn cuts like a knife,*
> *And gone are white blossoms, and little bird's fife,*
> *And in death and decay lies all that was blithe,*
> *And the deep frost violets kill.*
> *Once the hawthorn and I, our hearts could meet,*
> *White was my blossom, my perfume sweet,*
> *He gave me his shadow, I slept at his feet,*
> *And I would that I slept there still.*
>
> *Still through the hawthorn blows the cold wind,*
> *I pass him unknown, he is deaf, he is blind,*
> *Bed, I will come to thee; sleep I shall find.*
> *Blow rain, blow snow, blow soft, blow shrill,*
> *While I drift with the mists where I will."*

And after a long hush, almost as deep as that in which lay Melvas and Duglas, Pillicock's deep voice came forth, and its beauty was akin to Elain's in a different way and timbre, and of another meaning.

"My Lady of the Lake, may I carry you now to your bed?"

"Aye, dear Gnome, Pillicock the Monster."

"Sleep you shall find, peaceful sleep, and when you wake, the cold wind of the moor will have died down, and the hawthorn's heart and your heart can meet again, and no more will he pass you unknown, for his ears are open, as are his eyes, and it may come to pass that before long you may sleep not at his feet but in his arms."

3

While Elain and Helena slept, Pillicock and I searched the garments worn by the two he had slain. Although we found the pieces of gold that their mistress had promised they could keep when the light she hated had been darkened, we found nothing to give absolute proof that this mistress was Vivain and not Enid, although both the dwarf and I knew perfectly well it was she. And in a corner we found two pilgrims' robes and staffs, proof beyond dispute that the four seeming-almsmen were masqueraders in concert with Melvas and Duglas, their part to distract and befuddle the guards while the blinders' boat crept to the island out of the flooded brook flowing from Witch Lake.

Neither he nor I would dream of giving their corpses to the sweet waters where Elain had laved, and on which floated majestic swans, so we dug a pit on the island, and interred them both, and left them to the mercy or the vengeance of the Gods. And with an ax which old Helena wielded to cut fuel, Pillicock chopped to fragments the Mask of the Evil Eye, and I thought that Modo, God of murder, crouching in his dark lair, shuddered at the ring of every crashing blow. Then it came to me that his retreat was not an ambush in the dim forest, but a tower standing on an illimitable moor, and it was the Dark Tower known in Cambrian folk-tale, and it was there that Childe Rowland came.

Pillicock and I hurled the fragments into deep water, where they would sink harmlessly into the sand of the bottom; and I thought that Modo in the Dark Tower felt himself sinking, and half-smothering; and his power, although still great, was a little less, and in time to come it might be greatly less.

When Elain and Helena wakened we bore to the boat their most prized possessions, including the beautiful lyre, and then we carried them to the boat also, and began to row toward the shore. We saw our guards come to the margin and gaze at us, and the four whose pilgrimage to evil had been balked rose from their solemn crouching and huddled together, gazing. I could picture their wide eyes and their darting, frighted thoughts. And when two hundred paces from my followers, I raised a great shout.

"Catch those four knaves, and bind them!"

But their bivouac was at the edge of the forest some distance from my party. Frantically the masqueraders hurled off the mockery of their robes, and scuttled like hares. Because I feared some of my followers would be ambushed, and I craved their full strength in Elain's defense until I found her an impregnable citadel, I shouted to them not to follow on. Whereby all four miscreants escaped into the wood, and all sight and sound of them was lost.

I had already reckoned where I could keep Elain safe while I attended to one great matter, an affair of state as well as of my heart, but beyond that, the future was shrouded in mist.

When we gained the shore I set the men to making for old Helena a litter which four of them could bear. And I would have ordered the same for Elain, if she had let me; but she told me that she would walk with Pillicock and me to our immediate destination, and that she did not need even our guiding hands, for although her whole visual world had dimmed, it was still beautiful in its softened colors. She could see well enough to avoid obstructions and never stumble. Very strangely she could distinguish a smile from a frown on the face of a passer-by as far as five paces.

And from the way she walked beside me, stalwartly and steadily, and from the undiminished beauty of her eyes, I could have never known the light that entered them had dimmed.

When we gained the junction of the Severn and Avon, where lay my great army, I built in its very midst a great pavilion of sheepskin robes, where she and Helena could abide in full safety, unless the Gods themselves should smite them. Meanwhile I sought far and wide for news of Vivain, and before long received a reliable report that she had been seen on the slopes of the Beacons, traveling north, a likely enough place if she had awaited somewhere near Swan Lake for news from Melvas and Duglas. If so, she had lingered there in vain too long for her own safety.

At once I dispatched Glyn with his whole troop of scouts, with

359

orders to track her and stay on her track until they could surround and pin her down in some last retreat, but to lay no hand on her unless she tried to break through the ring, and then only to capture and hold her for my coming.

Then I bade Gerald tell off five cohorts of our Cambrians to be marched at leisure to a point east of Drygarn Fawr, the Birthplace of Rivers, from whence they could strike quickly any reach of the coast on Cardigan Bay southward to Land's End, or, if need be, to Carmarthen Bay. Both regions were being raided by wild-eyed marauders from Eire, who had supposed that my army encamped east of the Cambrian Mountains gave them opportunity to slaughter and burn. And I would accompany this force, and keep in touch with Glyn; but not for Elain's added safety, only because I could not let her out of my frequent sight, I had her go with us, as well as her old serving-woman, now greatly mended.

We had spent but one night in our new camp when Glyn came to my pavilion, his eyes glittering.

"We've caged 'ee bird," he told me, too excited to pay me formal address.

"Well, where is she?"

"Where 'eed never guess. Do 'ee remember the village, up a bit from the road, where 'ee capturer took 'ee on a horse, after they'd caught 'ee under the linden tree wi' Vivain? They was a smithy there, where 'ee guards made merry while 'ee got loose and took off. 'Twas there where her went to hide when her knew we was all about her in the wood, and 'twas there we fenced her in, and her's there now."

"Have any of you laid eyes on her?"

"What need, Your Majesty? We knew 'em footprints by then, little bigger than a fox's, and how her walked, and how her wiggled under logs and wormed through thickets, from dawn till dark on the go, in rain or shine, and 'twas the best we could do to keep pace wi' her, once we found track o' her. And we found this pin 'ee had given her, which she had cast off like King Vortigern threw away his trinket with his letters on it. Perhaps because her hate of 'ee bubbled up in her and drove her well nigh witless, but more likely it stuck her sharp when she fastened it, most like in the neck. Maybe she took it for a sign 'ee great Sword would be quick to follow. Twice in the night her sought to break through our line, and we need only whistle to one another to make her turn back. And now she cooks her meat in the forge, rabbits mostly what her can sneak up and catch like a lynx, and once her fire gave off yellow smoke and a sharp smell, and we thought she was doing witchcraft, but we never knowed what kind."

"We will start in an hour."

4

I had thought not to tell Elain of my errand, the full purpose of which I did not yet know, and to explain my absence from her today and tomorrow I told her I meant to survey a site for a summer palace.

"I wish you would not lie to me, Arthur, on matters that concern me deeply, because it ill becomes a king. I caught sight of Glyn, and I know what business he was on, which was to find Vivain. My liege, I entreat that I go with you. The matter concerns me hardly less than you, for while she gave Merdin to cruel death, and struck twice directly at your royal person, and many times more perhaps that we do not know, yet at me, who had never harmed her except to warn Merdin against her, she struck to maim me alive, an act of abysmal hate, or of malice immeasurable. Hence I wish to look into her face before she dies."

"You know, then, that her death is certain."

"She must be killed as a viper in a gate, who bites children. Your realm is not secure as long as she lives, and the sweet ground on which she walks is fouled, and cries to the Gods that her footprints be washed out by the fragrant rains, until they can be found no more from here to the world's end."

"How can you look at her, with your dimmed eyes, and what do you hope to see?"

"If I stand close to her, and strain hard, I may see her lineaments, and I hope to see that despite the tale of her being born of woman, begotten by man, she is yet some creature of Weird, perhaps a changeling put in Enid's bed, and truly the spawn of an evil witch, got by a goblin, or perhaps the daughter of a succuba or a banshee, or the foal of a bitch were-wolf. If so, I can wash my hands and go my way. But if she is humankind, fashioned by the Gods, how can I bow to the Earth Mother and to Lud, knowing they too are evil or they could not make evil?"

"That last I cannot answer, nor could have Merdin, or any Wise One of Old whose fame comes down to us, but you have my leave to go with me, to look upon and speak to Vivain ere she dies, and I ask only that you wear a dagger at your side, ready to your hand, and that you wear the little cross of silver at your throat, which the Christians believe is some sort of talisman against the Powers of Darkness."

"It is not permitted that I wear both, I know not why, so I will wear the dagger."

We started forth, and with Glyn to lead us, and the scouts fanning out in search of ambush, we soon entered the dark wood. There we followed the paths of deer, wild cattle, and wild swine, and I thought upon how little I had done to make men more and beasts less, and truly it seemed to me that the forest had spread wider, and the plowed land had receded, since I had come to the throne. Howbeit, with the maintenance of just law, and the onset of peace, the tide of savagery might turn back, and the great boon be given by man himself, unto himself, out of his own nature. And shortly before noon we came in sight of the abandoned village, and then the smithery, and then some one sitting just inside the door, and I knew her for Vivain.

She rose just before we entered, and took her stand in a corner behind the forge, and in her hand was a little glass cup that she held with care, as though it brimmed with a potion of some sort.

"I was expecting you today, my liege, and my Lady Elain," she told us, "and I beg to be excused from kneeling, lest I spill what I have here, a medicine for all my ills."

"What ills?"

"They are too many to recount. And I pray you, forgive my not offering you a horn of mead, because, first, I have none, and second, you would not taste it if I did. And I pray too that you not come closer to me, ere our courteous talk is done, for the cup contains a subtle poison, and if I fear you will lay rough hands on me, I will swallow it straightway, and such is its power that I will drop straightway dead; and the question in your eyes, Elain, will never be answered, no matter how you peer; and the furrowed brow of the King, as he contemplates me in horror and dark wonder, will never be smoothed."

362

"Vivain, will you answer one question, before your God Modo?" Elain asked.

"Aye, beautiful Elain, I will answer it, in all truth, for all my games are done, and my pouch empty. But Modo is no longer my God, for he is only a concept of imagination of the wicked, to give a little sanction to their pursuit of the bents of their hearts."

"Are you of man begotten and of woman born?"

Vivain laughed softly and musically, and the laughter rang a little against the anvil that no forester dared touch, because once it had sung a god-like song under the hammer-blows of the smith, and on it had been shaped the wondrous iron of husbandry and war.

"Look at me well, Elain, out of your weakened eyes that I thought to darken forever, and see for yourself."

"I cannot tell, Vivain, at this distance, for your face is blurred in my sight."

"Then ask the King what he sees."

"I see the shape of woman, small, delicate, and lovely," I said in all truth. "I see a face brown, elfin-like I think, most pleasing to the sight, and only the shape of the eyebrows is strange, and I doubt not that many pretty faces bear the like."

"Elain, I am of woman born and of man begotten, the same as the King and yourself. Only my heart is different from either."

"And why is that?" I asked.

"How can I answer? It may be that every human soul on earth must choose between two paths, and most take the weak and easy way, but a few take the hard and strong, the path I took. I fell in love with evil when I was eight years old. Eels were frying in a pan for my father's supper, and Enid, my mother, bade me drop in a poison she had got from a Greek dealer in medicine. She herself could not do it, because my father, Earl Murray, was on guard against her, suspecting that she had visited the bed of King Vortigern, and wished to be rid of her husband so she might wed the King and become his Queen. So although it was her stratagem, it was I, Vivain, who emptied into the pan the little vial. And knowing well what I had done, yet I talked to my sire of childish things as he ate his great meal, and often he laughed in pleasure of me, or roughed my hair, and once he kissed me. And then I sat with him awhile as he emptied his wine-cup, and

I saw his eyes grow wide, and the sweat bead his face, and then he cried out in extremity of pain, and soon pitched to the floor, and I watched his death-struggle, and I knew my power."

"The power has failed you at last," I told her.

"Aye, as all power fails at last. But while it endured, mighty within me, I grew to great beauty of a strange sort, and although small, I had great agility and strength, and think how many I have overwhelmed, whose heads towered over me! King Arthur, it was I who sent word to the King of the Hecanas that you were making a stolen march, and no less than ten score of your tall yokels fell in the ambushes that he laid, twenty times as many as you have ever felled with your great Sword Caliburn, I who am hardly your Sword's length. And it was I who persuaded Vortigern to league with Hengist, although I had never dreamed he would take Rowena and put away my mother Enid, one of two whom I greatly loved, and for that I brought him death. And it was I, no other, who lay low the great magician, truly he who made you King. Only by plaguing mischance, no fault of my planning, do you stand before me now, instead of long since having been eaten by the Birds of Death, or rotting in your grave. I was no witch, but real witches hid from me when I walked the forest, knowing their powers were puny compared to mine. Now you know all. What death do you give me? Unless it be quick and easy, I will drain this cup, and only Vivain will have conquered Vivain, and you will live and die unavenged for all my deeds against you and my many slain."

"Vivain, you shall hang as soon as Glyn can fetch a rope."

"Why, that is an easy passing! My neck is slender, and will break when first the rope tightens. And will you grant a boon? The light is dim, now that the fire dies, and the day murky, and I wish to look well into your face, as Elain looked into mine, to seek an answer to a question. If you fear I have a knife about me, stand beyond the forge out of my reach."

I drew within five feet of her, Caliburn in my hand, and she gazed at me searchingly, her eyes wildly bright.

"Why, great King, you look like a great king, and that is most strange."

"Nay, I look like a yokel from the Taff."

"Now that too may be, but you do not look as your heredity would indicate unto my reason. You were not begotten in lawful bed, but in a dismal room where Vortigern had tricked Anna, and locked the door and pocketed the key, and where he beat her into insensibility ere he achieved his purpose. Great King, you are a son of incest, horrible even to Tyr, the God of War, yet you did not grow thwart and disnatured, as great Lear wished for the child of Regan, when she had cast him forth. Instead of a horrid visage, from which women, and men too, must turn their faces lest they puke, you are tall and fair. But now I shall atone for this lapse of the Gods, and you will look as you should look, the last villainy of great Vivain, and then I shall become the Queen of the Under World."

She said this last so quietly and calmly that I thought her wits had turned, and Elain's yell of warning came too late. With a quick movement of her wrist she dashed the contents of her cup into my face.

It must be that I stood taller than she reckoned, for the oily liquid missed my eyes, and instead it splashed and spread and ran down a little below my eyes, and wherever it touched I knew pain almost beyond bearing. No red-hot iron could sear more quickly and more deep. My only thought this side of madness was to guard Elain from some other secret stroke. But she needed no guarding, now, for she had bared her dagger; and Vivain cowered and ran, and her yells of terror were so piercing that they stabbed through my agonized cries. She fled to a corner of the room, but there Elain came on her, and again and again the iron blade plunged deep, until at last her shrieking ceased, and she slid down the wall onto the floor. Then Elain slashed at her bloody skirt, cutting off a part, and with this she ran to me and wiped my face, and the warm blood seemed to be an antidote for the liquid fire, for the worst of my pain passed off. But the truth was, as I was soon to know, that its power to consume had been exhausted, now that it had eaten through my skin and flesh almost to the bone.

Not far from the forge stood a wooden tub half-filled with water, its bottom black from soot, and I knelt beside it and looked at my reflection, and it gave me back my visage almost as clearly as a Roman looking-glass. And a visage it truly was, for its lower half was burned well-nigh black; and when scars replaced the seared flesh, it would still

365

be unfit for human sight. And the next I knew I was standing beside Elain, and she was stroking my hair.

"Poor King, poor Arthur," she told me, weeping, and then I saw, in utter wonder, that she looked full into my face without turning away her gaze. "I love you, Arthur."

"How can you bear to look at me?" I asked.

"I need only refrain from straining my dim eyes, and then I see not the ruin, and my mind calls back the face of my true love, and that is what I see, and will always see."

"Do not say so in pity," I begged. "I have paid the price that the Gods exacted for my awful deed, but pity I cannot bear, even from my true love, because once I was King of Britain."

"To the King of Britain I would have never become Queen. But there is nothing to part us now, and we shall go forth together, into the World of Man, more beautiful than any court, and you shall wear a cloth to spare men's eyes, and it comes to me that if you will play Merdin's harp and I will sing, we will charm their ears and delight their hearts, and we will have no names but the Singer and the Harper, and together we will make such songs as will never die."

Chapter Eighteen

Arthur the Great

Elain fixed a cloth that she cut from her own shift to fasten over my face below the eyes. This I wore when we went out of the smithery, from whence Vivain's strange soul had sped and where mine had been reforged. Then from one of the pale scouts Elain produced an ungent; and in the very house where I had lain a prisoner until Modred had released me, she gently anointed the burned flesh; and her white hand shrank from it no more than her lovely gaze.

Meanwhile wide-eyed Glyn had stopped a gypsy on the ancient road, and bought his horse for me to ride back to our campground; also a harnesser made a sunshade for Elain's eyes. One of the scouts told his fellow that it was his guess that in slaying the witch Vivain, I had had to slay her in nine shapes before she would stay dead, the first being a long-beaked bird, the second a giant spider, the third a viper, the fourth a bat, and such like guise from the fifth form to the eighth, which was a dragon whose tail the scout thought he had seen sticking out the door. The ninth manifestation was a tiger, a most awful beast whom all had heard of, but no one, as far as I knew, had ever seen; and she had clawed half my face away before I had slit her heart with Caliburn. And as she died she had resumed the common shape of Vivain, whose body lay in a corner, looking wondrous small, and bathed in blood.

The hearer of this account told it to another, this time as known fact. Before the night had passed, every man in our company had heard the tale, and it became a solid part of what could be called a legend, growing up about the person of King Arthur, and which might continue to grow or to die away if better legends took its place. And on that factor hung the success or failure of a vast adventure to which, by now, I had committed my heart and soul, a greater adventure than to slay the Giant Ritho of Mount Snowdon, in a way of speaking, and surely of greater happiness to me and my true love.

On the following night, when we had gained the encampment of the troops east of Drygarn Fawr, and the tale of Vivain's death was winging swallow-fast about the cooking-fires, I had Pillicock come to my pavilion and, he being of strong eyes, removed my cloth and let him see my face. He did not shrink, he only looked quickly away, his dark face paling.

"Do you see why King Arthur must go to the sweet vales of Elysia, to heal his grievous wound?"

"Aye, my liege. If you sat your throne, you could not long hide your face from your people; and the image they hold of you, thrilling their hearts, would be destroyed. Yet they must have a dream or they cannot live."

Replacing the cloth, I told him the secret destination of Elain and me, no palace, no enchanted island, but the beauteous wide world of the folk, who were greater than any God of War and Thunder. And then I asked Pillicock if he would go with us.

"You need not ask, my liege," he told me. "I am forsworn."

"Then I will lay upon you a particular task. When we go by Taff-mouth can you get a net for catching running salmon, of strong cord, say twenty feet long and four feet deep, and can you carry it on your back with your heavy rucksack, its total burden being about twenty pounds, counting its leaden weights as ten pounds?"

"You need not ask, my liege. You know the strong back that the Gods gave to me, to solace me a little for my malformed legs."

"It comes to me that often you have seen disks of lead, passed long ago as coins each worth a penny, perforated and used in place of egg-shaped weights more commonly used."

"Aye, my liege, I have often seen them."

"Pillicock, in Cambria the folk give the best food that their huts afford to wandering bards, but in some regions, across the waters and even sometimes in Britain, they are given scraps from the plates. I am King Arthur. With me will be Elain of the Lake and Pillicock of Pillicock Hill. We cannot eat leavings, nor sleep in beds where all night we are louse- and flea-bitten, without our strengths wasting. The day may come we may need such strength as we have now to serve some need of Britain so bitter that the men would follow a six-horned goblin if he would lead them to victory. For that sake, and for our well-being and our pride, you are to remove the leaden weights from the net you buy, and replace them with coins of gold, taken from my treasury, and blacked with lampblack, so that they look like such leaden disks as are commonly seen. When the need arises, or when we yearn for a great feast of precious viands to recall the days when I was King, you will remove one of the gold pieces, scour away

369

its disguise, and take it to a money-changer, for it is well-known that dwarfs are often guardians of treasure. Since the changers are mainly Jews, who themselves dwell at hazard and must often fly from greedy earls and even poor folk incited against them, they will pay you a reasonable worth of the gold in white money and red, and tell no one of the dealing, lest their own hoards of gold become known. And when the folk who hear us sing are so bitter-poor they can give us nothing but a crust, their faces red with shame, we will tell them that Elain is no mortal, but a fairy or a good-angel taking human form, and if, when we are gone, they will look in a certain nook, they will find her gift to them, and by that giving will our gold be most blessed. Now tell me, truly, Pillicock, if this jar will hold water. I have been through fire, as Merdin foretold, and it may be I must yet meet my great foe, my brother Modred, the outcome of which meeting I know not. I charge you tell me if there is some great fault with the plan that I do not see. Would you say that by going forth unto the folk richer than any earl, we both run with the hare and hunt with the hounds, and we will be only making-believers in our great adventure?"

"A purse-mouthed carpist might say so, King, not I. For there is one thing that carpists cannot abide, and that silences them featly, and that is common sense."

"Then tomorrow we march, and between here and the Taff, confer much with Elain, as to a fitting and long-remembered leave-taking between King Arthur and his subjects; for if we stole away, a hundred tales would be told, to trouble them greatly, and to trouble the reign of King Gerald, who will follow me. And if my brother Modred does not challenge me to meet him ere Arthur, with his true love and their follower Pillicock, vanish in the haze of distance where he cannot find me, he may go his way in peace, as I go mine."

"This too I will do, and fear not that your passing will not be as long remembered as your coming, for Elain is rich in wit, and took great joy in her device to put in your hands the Sword Caliburn, and will take even greater joy in this."

He departed, and on the morrow we marched, and throughout the second day, and the third, and that night we camped in the lower valley of Taff, only a league from our homestead, and from the camp-ground I made a pilgrimage to the little house I loved. There I did not remove my face-cloth, explaining to the churls and to my mother, Anna—although she did not appear to hear—that I had suffered a grievous wound in battle, but it would soon heal. And also I spoke lightly of Vortigern having died, at which her busy hands stayed still for a brief space, then went on with her tasks.

But when I came to leave, one of my bodyguards brought up a messenger who had approached their lines, and we spoke briefly in the twilight. Only a few messages ever delivered to me had greater import, or longer stopped my heart.

"I come from Modred, Prince of Cambria," he told me when he had knelt. "He bade me tell Arthur the King, to meet him, if he will, tomorrow on the Cliffs of Dun, you alone and he alone, that the long account between you may be settled to the satisfaction of you both, and of the Gods."

The Cliffs of Dun were rough, gray crag often mantled in mist, lonely and forsaken as a wilderness in a dream. They overhung Sabrina about ten miles from our homestead. Since a last meeting with Modred was part and parcel of my fate, I could not think of a more fitting place.

"Tell your master Modred, His Highness the Prince, that the King accepts the appointment."

And when I had returned to my pavilion I bade Pillicock polish Caliburn until he gleamed like a bolt of lightning in a dark sky, and whet his edge, and wash with vinegar the jewels set in his hilt, and to make my shield match him in shimmering brightness. Then I went to my bed, and dreamed wildly.

2

At sunrise a heavy mist lay in the valleys, and welled up the hillsides, and an army could move unseen to the foot of the Cliffs of Dun. These were all but unclimbable from the narrow white beach of Sabrina, too steep to start with and today slippery with clammy fog; but I mounted the great down behind and came on them easily. And since their tops rose above the smother, I emerged into bright sunlight under a shimmering blue sky, and there stood Modred, tall, his

371

accouterments agleam, and his eyes big and brilliant with pleasure at my coming.

He dropped on one knee before me and I bade him rise.

"My liege, when I invited you here I hoped to show you a fine view, but instead we stand on an island, in a dismal sea of mist, and although there are slight movements in its depths, and almost imperceptible pulsations on its surface, it suggests death instead of violent life, as does the true sea; but perhaps that is more fitting, when two great foemen keep their last rendezvous."

"Since we are great foemen, Modred, not liege and liegeman, did you not hail me wrongly?" I asked.

"Aye, I did. A liegeman may not seek or accept battle with his liege. Then I will hail you as King Arthur, or better yet, if I have your leave, as my brother Arthur, and then we can speak more freely, with more enjoyment than if the difference in our ranks stood between us."

"Modred, you have my leave to say what you will, in any way you will, and I will do the like. And you have my leave to sit on this crag that seems carved by the Gods as a seat for giants to overlook the world, and also we can enjoy the cordial sunlight for a space, until it darkens for one or both of us."

"Then we will." And when we were both seated, "Arthur, as one schooled in good manners by my mother, Enid—at least her concept of them, a dim remembrance from her Roman forebears, which she herself observed only on rare occasions, when she was not mixing poison with some one's mead—I should not mention your face-cloth. Yet as a windy Cambrian I cannot refrain, since it bears out a story running like wild-fire through dry forest, that at last you overtook the damosel Vivain, and she proved a witch indeed, having nine lives, all with terrible and different bodies; and before you ended the ninth with the great Sword Caliburn, she dealt you a grievous wound."

"Truly she did, and is that all the news you know?"

"Aye, since hearing the news of the death of our sire, and of great Merdin."

"Modred, you will be pleased to know I have found a bard, whose talents may not equal his zeal, who will presently go forth to sing of Arthur the King, and magnify his fame throughout Britain, and extend it into alien lands; and perhaps cause it to live and grow through generations to come; and thus the prophecy of the Song of Camlon may be fulfilled."

"Now that is a good notion. What is any king without an excellent bard to lie about him? Take the countless Caesars whose names neither of us knows. They were hailed as Gods, no dog durst bark when they spoke, the whole civilized world was their dish and toy. One of them boasted of breaking two dozen maidenheads in a single night, yet even his name I know not, because he lacked a good bard. But do not let the singer tell the truth about you. Truth-tellers in song and story are loathsome bastards, who should be hanged as enemies of the people. And let him not tell of the dread violence of our dark age, of murder, rape, and incest, and men burned alive, torture, and the poisoned cup, for our folk see little of it in their innocent fields, and like not to hear of it. In future, brighter ages people may not believe it. Still it comes to me that for century beyond century our earth will remain uninhabitable, and life intolerable without kind lies. What figures the very Gods would cut if we told the truth of how they conduct the affairs of earth! That man is an unmitigated liar, to all others and to himself as well, is his greatest merit."

"The singer shall lie vastly, fear not."

"Will I have a place in his song?"

"You shall be the great adversary, the embodiment of evil, instead of its real protagonist, a small brown maiden who could melt a heart of stone."

"That suits me well enough. I would rather be vilified than ignored. But what of Wander? The singer must not sing of the joke you played on her and me. It was too close to earth."

"She will be untrue to me, frolicking with my kinsman Modred, but all Arthur will do is chide her gently, and she will seek sanctuary in a nunnery but sleep with her window unlocked."

"Arthur, if you are wise, you will have the King a Christian, convert of a disciple of Patrick."

"Nay, he will pay due to the true Gods. The Christians are a foul sect, soon to disappear."

"Who are the true Gods? They change with every tide of history. And this foul sect you speak of has already swept southern Europe and in time will prevail in Britain. Their Redeemer, so they call him, was at least human, being born of woman and suffering death. More, he taught the only loveliness by which man does not grow fangs and turn beast—to do as he would be done by, and be kind to little children, and tell them lies. You had better make your hero a Christian, if he is to outlast the great oaks, let alone live ever in song and story."

"Bah! Have we met here to blow Cambrian wind at each other? What do you want of me, Modred?"

"To kill you, or be killed by you. You are my father's living shame, and now you are his slayer. I rejoice his traitorous, incestuous life is done, yet he remains my begetter, and besides, you wrested away his crown that I would have worn. What choice do I have, in honor?"

"Modred, do you challenge me to battle to the death?"

"No, but pray you challenge me, as the greater to the lesser, and how may I then refuse?"

"How can I? You have given me no offense since you lay with Wander, and for that you were paid in full."

"Arthur, I have lain with her since, and got her with child. Belike he will become the King of Britain instead of your own descendants out of Elain. Truly, I dread the outcome as much as you, one or both of us slain, and our pleasant intercourse and joyous understanding ended forever."

"Then I will remove my helmet, for your head is bare, and we will fall to."

"And let us do battle at the very edge of the cliff, where a misstep by one of us will hurl him to his death."

So I bared my head, and bared Caliburn, and fixed my shield on my arm, and he drew forth his own swift sword wielded by great Lear, or so legend had it. We bowed our heads to each other and engaged. And we fought at the cliff-brink, over the sea of mist, and the Gods who had set us upon each other had a fine sight. Truly, no two swordsmen could be better matched, both of us tall, within a few days of the same age, of equal reach and agility, and it seemed of equal mastery of the sword. The iron clattered and rang. A sea-bird who flew nigh, on some business of her own, expecting to find the cliff deserted in its want, shrieked and hustled away. Deep down below the mist we heard the surf breaking on the beach, with a low roar, and not far we heard it burst against rocks. And truly I found great joy in springing back or aside from his mighty strokes, and a mighty pride in my prowess, as so far I parried or dodged them all, and a mighty pride in him, my brother Modred and companion of my soul, for his dodging or parrying mine.

We had fought a full half-hour, and our breath was being spent, and ever the likelihood increased that one of us would stumble and pitch over the brink, when under my cold thoughts of battle I recalled the last time I had intercourse with Modred, while he lay in Wander's bed with his hands under his head, and we had pledged each other. And then I thought of the rainy night he had come where I lay in a mean house, awaiting death at my captors' hands and how Modred had cut my bonds. And, too, I thought how Elain would sing of him, in the days I had hoped would come, and how different the fellow was than our listening rustics could believe, and how different I, the hero of the Song, was from her picturing. And then a loose stone rolled from the top of the crag, toppling in silence, till at last I heard it strike the base of the cliff and shatter. And then once more the sea-bird ventured nigh, and the Sun was as bright on her white wings as on our deadly iron, and she gave a cry of surprise, as well she might, for what fools we were to be leaping about at the edge of death. Why, Death would not take perhaps for a whole year, in which again she could mate, and lay, and hatch fledglings under her warm breast, and gather food for them! And then suddenly my soul rose in great rebellion against the Gods.

"Modred!" I called as I leaped back from his hack.

"Arthur, my brother!"

"If I ground my point when I count three will you do the same?"

"Aye."

So I counted, neither fast nor slow, and the Gods did not let a blow go home in that measured time, and then I grounded my point, and he did the like.

"I am the greater in rank," I told him.

"Aye."

"So I may speak when you may not. Is it not true?"

"Aye."

"Only fifty steps below us on the down, under a blue rock, I have put by a flask of mead that I meant to drink if I won the battle. Will you fetch it, that together we may wet our throats?"

"Gladly."

He went down on his springy tread, like a stag's on turf, and at once returned with the flask. I removed its wooden stopper, and handed it to him, and he drank deep. And then I drank, marveling at its delectable taste, and set the flask aside.

"Modred," I said, my voice trembling, "let us abjure the war between us, make peace, and go our ways."

"You, the King, could say it, while I ached in vain to do so, but I can tell you that it is my whole heart's desire. Still, is it not the will of the Gods that we fight to the death, and will we not waken their wrath?"

"If so, let them go and sit and bite their own thumbs."

"Then sheath your sword, great King, and I will do the like," he cried with a joyous cry that rang against the rocks. "And by your leave, we will swig again at the flask, and then I will defy the anger of the Gods, that my honor be upheld and my defiance of death proved forever. It was I, not you, who set the challenge, while you would have gone your way in peace, so I, not you, must prove it was not vain-glory, since I have accepted your first offer of peace between us. So I will descend the cliff, braving its slippery crags, and if I topple and die I will know their wrath even as I hurtle down, but if I live to gain the beach, I will know we have both done well. And in that case I will board the boat I have moored not far off, and make my way to Caer Dyv, and from thence to Rome, and there I will gaze on the remnants of its beauties that will delight my eyes, and there I will find companions of my soul. Shall I open the flask, my liege? Shall we drink deep?"

"I shall drink deep, Modred, for if I sleep in the Sun awhile no harm is done, but I pray you, sip lightly, that your head may not be dizzied lest you pitch from the rock."

"It is my King's command, and I will obey, and truly my hope of a safe descent has greatly risen, partly because my head will remain clear, but mainly because of your brotherly concern."

"We will drink, and then I will lift my face-cloth, so you can behold my ruin."

I did so, and he cried, "Gods! Gods!" yet he did not avert his staring eyes, and I replaced the cloth.

"I know now the name of the great bard who will go forth and sing the fancied glories of Arthur the King," he told me.

"Aye."

"But I know his true glories, without which the song would die in the swan throat of Elain. Now I depart. And if I live to gain the beach, I will call."

"Live, Modred, for the sake of all who love bravery and mirth."

He went over the cliffside, groping his way, and almost at once he was swallowed in the sea of mist. A dread silence closed down, and I thought he had toppled, to fall in the wet sand with a soft, squashy sound which the fog would smother. And then when I was turning to go the way I came, intending to strike the beach at the nearest point, and seek what was left of him, and give him solemn burial, I heard a call rising clear as the falling song of a skylark.

"Arthur the King!"

"Aye!"

"I am safely down, and now I go my way."

"Farewell, my brother."

"In the song of Arthur paint me black as Modo if you like, but do not leave me out."

"No, I'll not."

"Then I'll meet you in song and story a thousand years hence. Hail and farewell."

3

Within the fortnight, Gerald had assembled our total force on a headlong jutting out into Sabrina eastward of the mouth of Wye. Before mid-afternoon of the day of the full Moon all my lean veterans had either paled or flushed with a kind of fever no apothecary could treat, for it was born of a secret sense of some great event impending, an inkling not born of what they had yet heard or seen, and instead risen from their heart of hearts, and that boded great change.

Their evening meal was solid, although not a feast. No casks of ale were opened, no mead-horns emptied, and after supper they stood in friendly groups, gazing down-river. The immense Moon heaved up over the southern Cotswold as the twilight lingered on, and she brightened as it faded, and climbing staunchly, was two hands above the horizon when the last westward glimmer faded away, and no light was left but hers, wondrously silver, and the gleam of great stars, and the red glow of watchfires burning low. This hour of transition I had spent with Gerald in my pavilion, and there we plighted certain troth, and spoke back and forth of the great battles we had fought, but more of our days together in the Valley of the Taff, of the common affairs of the homestead, and of dreaming we knew not what, and of winter fires when we lay in a close ring, and of our sheepdog and the white sow that loved Anna. At the last we wept, and then I put on him the crown of Britain and dropped on one knee before him, where I remained until, in a choked voice, he bade me rise.

And then not a shout, or anything like it, yet a human utterance of awe and wonder, rose from the throng lining the shore. So we stood at the pavilion door, and we saw the distant flare of torches and little points of candle-flame rising from a dark shape still distant, and the shape came nearer, and it was a big barge, with men rowing against the slowly rising tide. It drew nigh amid a breathless silence, and now we could see what appeared to be three tall queens, clad in shimmering white gowns, all wearing golden crowns. And one, the most beautiful, I recognized by the way she stood, and soon by her lovely lineaments, and she was not truly a queen, but my true love. And one had dark tresses, like many Cornish, and a black forelock hung athwart her brow, and so the men could not doubt that she was Morgan the Fairy, who had come up from her sea-caves for some great advent. The third crowned damosel likewise I did not know by sight, and she might have been an earl's daughter, but as likely had sprung up in the wheat field of a churl, for beauty is cast far and wide in Cambria, found in the huts of poor folk as readily as in the palaces of the rich, and truly she looked queenly.

I came forth from my pavilion wearing my face-cloth, with my shield on my arm, Caliburn at my side, and my bronze helmet on my head, but without my ermine cloak. At my side walked Gerald, and behind me came Pillicock, bearing his rucksack and a fish net strapped to his back. The men made an aisle through which we passed, and the three queens dropped on one knee as I went aboard the barge, Pillicock hard behind me, Gerald halting on the shore. And when I had bade the queens arise, one of them spoke to the oarsmen, and they pushed out perhaps ten boat lengths from the shore, and there they held the barge motionless with gentle silent dippings of their oars.

"Soldiers of Britain!" I shouted, and now they were so closely massed that every one heard me plain.

"Arthur the King," they shouted in reply.

"Nay, I have put aside my crown, and Gerald will wear it, and reign in my stead, while I journey to Elysia beyond the sea-mists, and there I will abide, and be healed of my wound, and it may be I will linger there for many a year, and it may be you will not see my face again. But if the storm of war once more breaks over our fair land, and the folk have need of me, I will return, although it may be in some guise you will not recognize, of different name and lineaments, and I will overthrow the foe. Meanwhile guard the land well, and I too shall keep close watch of it, from the Elysian hills, and if I return it will be with an army of your brave comrades fallen in the deadly battles that we fought and won; and although their forms may be invisible, you will know that they fight beside you. And it will come to pass that our Britain will wax strong in the years and centuries to come, and ancient wrongs will be righted, and the folk will be ever more and more, and the beasts less. Farewell, my great companions. I will hold you in my heart, and pray hold me in yours, and we will keep faith with one another to the end of Time. Farewell, sons of Britain, farewell, farewell!"

"Farewell, Arthur the King!" rose their great shout in reply.

Then I clanged the hilt of Caliburn against my shield, and every man did likewise with the hilt of his own sword, and the great sound of ringing iron reverberated over the land and across the waters, and echoed and re-echoed to the seats of the Gods amid the stars. Then the rowers dipped their oars deep, and hauled strongly; and with the lifting tide behind her, the barge began to glide swiftly seaward.

Silent the throng stood to behold our departure, to be renowned, centuries without end, as the Passing of Arthur. And the tallest of the three queens and the most beautiful, Elain, who was my true love, stood with her hand in mine to see the scene recede, the mighty host massed but at warlike carriage, on every left arm a shimmering shield, in every right hand an upraised sword, in austere salute, unshakable hardihood, and deathless troth. My banners fluttered, fading. The big stars waxed in brilliance as the watchfires dimmed. The Moon, that would not forget, cast her sheen on the breathless sea. The Watchman of the Ages sounded his great bell.